THIRTY-THREE
SWOONS

Also by Martha Cooley

THE ARCHIVIST

THIRTY-THREE
SWOONS

A Novel

MARTHA COOLEY

LITTLE, BROWN AND COMPANY

New York • Boston

Little, Brown and Company
Time Warner Book Group
1271 Avenue of the Americas, New York, NY 10020
Visit our Web site at www.twbookmark.com

First Edition: May 2005

The characters and events in this book are fictitious. Any similarity to real persons, living or dead, is coincidental and not
intended by the author.

Library of Congress Cataloging-in-Publication Data
Cooley, Martha.
Thirty-three swoons / Martha Cooley — 1st ed.
p. cm.
ISBN 0-316-15901-8
1. Greenwich Village (New York, N.Y.) — Fiction.   2. Loss
(Psychology)—Fiction.   3. Divorced women — Fiction.
4. Birthfathers — Fiction.   5. Cousins — Fiction.   6. Theater — Fiction.   7. Dreams — Fiction.   I. Title.
PS3553.O5646T47 2005
813'.54 — dc22   2004013317

10 9 8 7 6 5 4 3 2 1

Q-MB

Text design by Meryl Sussman Levavi

Printed in the United States of America

For my parents

Time passes or stretches out, time surrounds, and things are lost in it, continuously, without fail . . . How we go through it, what we do during the only real time granted to us, the present, that confluence of what is no more and what is not yet, is the play's story.

RICHARD GILMAN, *Chekhov's Plays*

THIRTY-THREE
SWOONS

PROLOGUE (December 1999)

THINK OF me as real. Whether or not I am is unimportant, an idle theoretical question.

Same goes for truth. Consider it irrelevant! There's no such thing as a true story, only credible or questionable ones: those we believe, and those we don't. As to this story, think of it as not just one but several, nested inside each other. Like a Russian *matryoshka*, one of those rotund wooden dolls with a horizontal seam around its middle. You pop open the doll and inside is a slightly smaller version, which you also open, which contains another, smaller one—and so on, till you reach the tiniest, most enwombed of all.

Russians use *matryoshkas* to teach their children the mathematical concepts of volume and proportion. But these nested dolls are also useful for communicating a fact about history and, more broadly, about time: any event, human or natural, is simultaneously prefiguration and echo, forerunner and follow-up. Knowing this, people may find it easier to conduct the business of living with some appreciation for absurdity, some tolerance for paradox; even, from time to time—though this is less common—with some glee.

Seva was capable of that: of gleefulness. Which is why I so enjoyed our collaboration.

IN MOSCOW, a while back—during the early decades of the twentieth century (which in a few weeks we'll be calling "the last century," the one we just fled, whose teeth marks are still visible)—in Moscow lived a theater director and set designer named Vsevolod Meyerhold.

Seva had luminous dark-brown eyes, a pronouncedly curved nose, and mobile, almost twitchy features. His hair was perpetually tousled, as if it had never occurred to him to comb it. A true maverick, Seva believed that all the usual, tired rules of stage performance existed merely to be broken. Curtainless stages and exposed wings, revolves and ramps and multilevel sets, montages and freezes and action amidst the audience—all these were Meyerholdian innovations. He knew what he wanted: an overthrow of expectations, a revolution! Russia's theater had never seen anyone remotely like him before. And neither Russia nor the rest of the world would see anyone quite like him again.

Seva was thick-skinned. He loved it when spectators were outraged by his productions—the more jeers, the better. Mostly, though, his audiences were exhilarated, like children in a fun house full of distorting mirrors. "Mystery and the desire to solve it," he wrote, "are what draw so many people to the theater." In the theater, if not in life, people thrill to bewilderment.

SEVA LOVED Paris almost as much as he loved plays. Though he visited it only a few times, the French capital was a site to which he returned frequently in his reveries.

He could readily summon to memory the city's views and sounds, and when he was feeling low, the smell of French tobacco renewed him—as did a certain fragrance his wife liked to wear, which she'd obtained in Paris. For Seva, whose nose was nearly as sensitive as a perfume maker's, simply remembering the odors of Paris was profoundly comforting. Not unlike daydreaming, to which he often had recourse, especially while in prison . . .

I'll get to all that. But before I go any further, I ought to explain what I'm doing here, why this story's being told by me and not by somebody else. In theory anyone could tell it (anyone, that is, willing to lay claim to a certain kind of omniscience, as storytellers must), but in practice I'm it—there's no one better suited.

I'M HERE for the simple reason that I was Seva Meyerhold's doppelganger, his double. Everybody has one, of course. You can't go through a lifetime without one, acknowledged or not. A doppelganger is simply an alternate self, invoked as needed, active as required: the ego's private retainer. Loyal, yes, but also reliably independent. When necessary, an *agent provocateur.*

Perhaps as a child you played with a friend termed imaginary by your parents? When you recount a personal experience, are you tempted to pretend it happened to somebody else? Ever worn a costume and felt that powerful elation which results from having become, for a few intensely satisfying hours, an utterly different *I?* Then I'm sure you know what I mean. There's nothing at all unusual in this: having an incorporeal double is one of life's inevitabilities. It's of a piece with having a shadow for your body, an echo for your voice, a reflection for your face as you peer in the mirror and wonder (aloud or silently, unnerved or excited), *Just who* am *I now?*

As for what doppelgangers actually do, the possibilities are limitless! We're prompters; we get balls rolling. In some circumstances we furnish the so-called voice of reason; at other times, a sublime hint of eros, a refreshing shower of humor, a jolt of fear, a flash of fury: whatever's useful at the moment. There are no straightforward guidelines, only improvisation.

SEVA SIGNED me on because he was starting to encounter impediments. He sensed what was coming: his government was locking up its artists, and colleagues were turning one another in. Seva understood that in life as onstage, a double is good protection, a safety net for the self. The only question in his mind was what exactly to *do* with our partnership.

Here I let him take the lead, and eventually things got dicey. Just as transactions between people are sometimes botched, so too a person's relationship with his or her double can founder. Under extreme circumstances, it can even be sundered altogether. Though I should've been more insistent, Seva had me lulled into a false feeling of security . . .

In the early days of 1940, he died in prison, and I sidelined myself.

What can I say? My stint in Butyrka, waiting with Seva in his dank cell, nearly did me in. My sense of failure was profound. And although I hoped for a new partner to show up quickly (someone beguiling, to help me get over Seva), the right candidate simply didn't appear.

I WAS not, however, entirely unemployed. For reasons and in ways I'll explain before long, I infiltrated various individuals' dreams.

I did this under Seva's auspices, in the guise of the director himself. And each person on whose nocturnal stage I performed was connected in some way with theater—hence amenable to my appearances, however unexpected they may have been.

All dreams, I think, are essentially rehearsals. The dreamer tries out speeches and gestures, not for an audience but to see where improvisation might lead. To "mysterious allusions, deception and transformation," as Seva once said, and thence, if the dreamer is lucky, into the clear.

My most recent oneiric intervention involved a woman named Camilla Archer, a fifty-year-old American residing in New York City. I was drawn to her partly because she loved theater, which meant she knew a fair bit about Seva's career and accomplishments. Plus, someone else linked us: her father, Jordan Archer. Seva had met him many years earlier, in Paris. About Jordan, more anon—but first a few words on his daughter, before I let her speak for herself.

CAMILLA WAS in considerable distress when I first encountered her.

In a nutshell: her cousin, Eve Pell, had just died unexpectedly, and the deceased's sole offspring—a young woman—had begun asking questions about Eve's past. These inquiries made Camilla quite uneasy, which I found curious. Wouldn't a daughter naturally want to learn as much as possible about her dead mother? Camilla's resistance to her young relation's inquiries reminded me of a bear doing its best to prolong hibernation, even though in some recess of its mind, it knows the season for sleep is over.

What's causing this woman to stonewall? I wondered. My question soon gave rise to an idea. I could mastermind a series of nocturnal vignettes for Camilla that would have the effect of rousing her, not swiftly (as if the bedsheets, so to speak, were being yanked off) but ineluctably—as though a feather were tickling her mind while she slept and the only way to get the tickling to stop would be to wake up . . .

Yet why, one may ask, would I bother to intercede in such a situation? What, in short, did it have to do with me?

Remorse, for starters. I was swimming in it.

As Seva's partner I'd urged denial upon him (*Just look the other way!*), and history had pounced, tearing him to bits. After his passing, I had but one aim: to perpetuate the remarkable mental energies that had been generated by our collaboration. Like two sticks rubbing together, a human being and his or her double always give off mental heat. Sometimes it's mild, sometimes strong, sometimes—as with Seva—nearly incandescent. This was, after all, a man of rare talent. And when such a human being dies, the heat that's been created is dispersed, like flying sparks, in other minds. Which it then warms. Or ignites!

Ergo my draw to Camilla, who struck me as fine tinder for Seva's sparks.

IN THE first of Camilla's dreams, I took a recent event, a shooting spree at an American high school, and mingled it with one from the distant past: an outdoor theatrical spectacle. I had in mind the sort of thing that used to take place on Russian streets during the Revolution—lively, ribald, didactic. Into these entwined events I introduced Vsevolod Meyerhold.

In addition, I gave Camilla's father a key part in that first dream. Jordan Archer's presence on her nighttime stage got his daughter's attention immediately. Thereafter it was easy to proceed with additional episodes and keep the pressure mounting. By the time her final dream rolled around, in a few months, my collaborator would feel deeply rattled, and just as deeply invigorated.

I CONFESS that by urging this woman to dream in a certain direction, I was also satisfying my own desire to revisit days past. If only Seva and I could have teamed up in a different era!

Silly longing; I should know better. The Russian poet Aleksandr Kushner said it straight out: "Nothing on this earth is cruder than to beg for time or blame the hour." Seva's mise-en-scène wasn't a pretty one. The utopia he (and so many others!) tried to conjure was nothing but a catastrophe in the making. All that midcentury savagery—see what's come of it? First that series of outlandish spy games between Russia and America; and now, as the century draws to its close, the entire house of cards is collapsing. Russia's old thugs have been reanointed as its new oligarchs.

As for the West, it's in a nasty muddle of its own. Warring in the Balkans yet again! And peeking anxiously eastward toward the next outbreak, another likely bloodbath, this time in a hot, sandy place . . . One needn't, however, look to the latest battlefield to see what's wrong. One has merely to visit any shopping mall, wander its halls, finger its goods, play the video games, watch the rapt faces of the children as the fireballs descend and the villains cackle maniacally till the good guys arrive to blow their faces off.

Ah, I long for a new kind of drama to spook us, embolden us! As Chekhov put it, in *The Seagull*: "One must portray life not as it is, and not as it ought to be, but as it appears in our dreams." Well, we can only wish. I can safely assert, though, that my American's nighttime dream-labor was worth the disruption it entailed. To her came a peek behind appearances, the best thing a dream can offer.

TIME TO take off! I could make a few additional remarks, but I don't wish to prejudice you. Seva felt strongly about this. The audience, he insisted, should always be *de*familiarized.

ON THAT note, the curtain. New York City, May 1999. Enter CAMILLA.

ONE

A BITTER medicinal smell, something like iodine. Then a sudden clearing, blankness in my nostrils. And then jasmine, gorgeously subtle at first but soon heavy, pungent, fetid: as if jasmine blossoms were rotting, as if rottenness itself underlay the fragrance, lending a brown tinge to the blossoms.

And now a murky iron odor, reminding me of something. I can't find the name for it. Images flicker across my closed eyelids. A city, not American, someplace in Eastern Europe. Sarajevo? No, this city is grander, imperial, with massive buildings—St. Petersburg, it must be St. Petersburg. Yes, the Winter Palace. I smell wet wool and sweat and excitement. There's a crowd in the palace square, I'm in the midst of thousands of people. We're participants in one of those vast spectacles Russians used to stage on the streets during the Revolution: reenactments of battles, with ordinary citizens playing the roles of Bolsheviks and Czarists, and soldiers playing themselves.

I hear the roar of artillery, rifles, handguns. People are shouting all around me; a great rocket soars upward, its noise deafening. Then a hush. Everyone begins fervently singing the "Internationale" while five-pointed red stars light up above the palace. A red banner appears behind it, fierce yet jolly.

The lights begin to dim. Now I see a man, tall and slender, taking a bow on a platform erected at one end of the square. Captured by a spotlight, he's wearing a black cape; although his eyes are masked, the rest of his face is very pale. A large placard, suspended by ropes, drops down behind him. It appears to be an advertisement for a play. The man in the cape points at it enthusiastically, then calls out to the spectators.

Announcing Columbine's Scarf, *he proclaims. Ladies and gentlemen, my theater troupe performs this marvelous drama so strangely, you won't recognize the original! We've got a real band with a conductor, and action right in the audience—involving you, dear spectator! Come see it!*

A clown emerges from beneath the platform. Clambering onto the stage, his movements jerky and awkward, he joins the caped man. Together they make vulgar gestures and goofy faces, to widespread laughter. Then a vast, all-white curtain falls, concealing the entire platform and square.

A teenaged boy slouches onto the forestage. He is wearing a black trench coat and a mask, and he's joined by another boy, another, another; they run in circles, a blur of trench coats and masks. Above them flaps a large black banner lettered in white. WELCOME TO COLUMBINE, *it reads.*

The caped man reappears, pushing his way through a slit in the white curtain. He's waving frantically, trying to get the boys' attention. Please, don't do it! he cries. No more death!

Then I see my father, directly behind the caped man. Apparently unconcerned with what is happening around him, he produces a large bottle of perfume, opens it, and sprinkles its contents on the curtain. Once again I smell the sharp odor of decaying jasmine.

The caped man inhales deeply, then begins to smile—knowingly, it seems. Something in his expression suggests he's been waiting for this very moment. Moving to one side of the forestage, he turns to face the opposite side, tosses off his cape, raises his arms above his head, and initiates a graceful, swift cartwheel, then another, another, unhesitatingly.

Sorrow! *he exclaims as he travels head over heels across the stage.* Sorrow, sorrow, sorrow! *His rhythms are perfectly synchronized, yet his speech and movements are entirely at odds, which makes the overall effect indefinably compelling—light and urgent at once. Watching, I know I've never witnessed anything like it.*

The man cartwheels off into the wings. Alone now, Jordan pulls a book of matches from his pocket. He strikes one and holds it to the curtain, which bursts into a dense, silvery mist that evaporates—poof!— and is instantly gone, along with everything else. My eyes open.

THE PALM of my left hand was brick red and sticky. I sat up in bed, peering at it.

It seemed I'd reopened the cut bisecting the pad of my thumb, and it had bled during the night. There were spots on my sheets, a delicate trail of them.

I got out of bed, rinsed my hand, put ointment on the cut, and bandaged it tightly. Then I regarded my eyes in the mirror. The taupe-colored skin below them was just a little puffy. Not bad, given how fitfully I'd slept.

I blinked, remembering the iron odor. Yes, the smell of blood: my thumb.

And gunfire, something called Columbine—I must've been dreaming about the shootings at that high school in Colorado. But wasn't this dream taking place somewhere else? A public square, a massive open-air stage. A scent, too. And Jordan, yes—what the hell was he doing there?

I've always been a lively dreamer. Normally my dreams are strung-together nonsense, each episode like a crazy quilt or a spilled set of puzzle pieces. None of the edges fit together right; the composition is semi-coherent at best. But this particular dream was different. It had the feel of a real-life event, and Jordan was in it—a most abnormal occurrence. I hadn't dreamed of my father before. Ever.

AS I was fixing breakfast, the dream temporarily forgotten, my phone rang. I was surprised to hear Danny's voice.

"You up?" she asked.

"Sure," I replied. It wasn't Danny's habit to phone me first thing on a Sunday morning, though that didn't mean she had something important to tell me. She might simply feel like chatting. Or hearing me chat. Talk as blotting paper, something to soak up spills of feeling.

Her mother—my cousin, Eve Pell—had died two months earlier, without warning, after contracting bacterial meningitis. Since then Danny's moods had become difficult to gauge. Some days she'd call me repeatedly, gabbling about trivia, as if she were the most empty-headed twenty-five-year-old alive and her mother's death hadn't affected her in the least. Other days I'd hear nothing from her, leave messages at her office, and get no callback. I'd start worrying, wondering if she was holed up in her apartment in Brooklyn, not eating, refusing all contact. One day she'd shown up at my shop and begun to heave things around. She didn't break anything, and I managed to calm her down, but the episode revealed how shaky her hold was. I wondered how she was able to get through a day on the job without coming unstuck.

"You by any chance going to your shop today?" she asked.

"I am, actually," I said. Normally I don't work on Sundays. But I had things to catch up on, and the weather forecast was dour.

"Leaving soon?"

"I'm having my coffee now. What's up?"

"Just wondering if I might stop by later for a little visit."

"Like when?" Something in Danny's tone was putting me on alert.

"After I leave here. Say, five-thirty." Now I realized she was calling from her workplace, a graphic-design firm on Seventh Avenue. I could hear background chatter, several early-bird colleagues conversing in the hallway.

"Sure," I said. "But you're at work now? Why on a Sunday?"

"Oh, everyone's here. We all had to come in for this big project that's way behind schedule. Total mismanagement. Welcome to the world of design."

"You get paid extra for this?"

"Hah."

"Everything else all right?"

"All right," she echoed neutrally. Not for the first time, I was conscious of how much her voice resembled her mother's. The same pitch, the same rough timbre, just this side of gravelly. Since my cousin's death I'd had a few uncanny experiences of answering my phone and thinking *Eve* before registering the reality of her daughter on the other end.

"Don't be staring at any walls, okay?" I said, aiming for a spot between jokiness and concern.

"I've got tons to do here," Danny responded evenly. "Actually it's been good to be busy with something other than Mom's closets." She paused, then added: "I've packed up the last of her stuff, by the way. All I have to do now is ask Sam if he'll cart some boxes to the Salvation Army. Then the whole thing's behind me."

"Good," I said. "So I'll catch you at the end of the day."

I HUNG up the phone and finished my coffee, contemplating Danny's call.

The whole thing. She'd been referring, of course, to the process of emptying first her mother's gardening store and then Eve's rent-stabilized apartment. The latter task had turned into more of an ordeal than it should have, thanks to Eve's landlord. Though I'd paid him for an extra half month to give Danny more time, he'd been hounding her relentlessly since her mother's death. One evening he'd threatened to toss any remaining possessions out the back window and into the alley.

That focused my own pent-up anger. After staging a fight with him in the building's dingy lobby, I'd used one of Eve's keys to score a series of long gashes across the front door of her apartment. "Art for art's sake," I'd said to Danny, happy to make her laugh.

So the clearing-out job was done, yet the whole thing, as Danny called it, wasn't behind her—couldn't possibly be. It was still unspooling, a chain of improbabilities whose initiating event had been that most ordinary of complaints, a headache. With astonishing swiftness, Eve's symptoms—a pounding head and stiff neck—had been followed by delirium, coma, a spreading purplish rash, and blood poisoning, which was what had ultimately killed her. *Wham,* one doctor at the hospital had said (not realizing I was eavesdropping) to another, a young intern. *Seventy-two hours, man! Never saw anything like it.*

To me Eve's meningitis had arrived as a natural disaster might have—some unannounced tornado stem-winding down an unsuspecting street, everyone looking the other way. And something more was en route, too. I could feel it. Not another death but a shake-up of some sort, necessary and unavoidable, for which no preparation would be possible.

GATHERING MY things for work, I glanced at the Arts section of the paper before shoving it into my bag. Cirque du Soleil, the Canadian circus, would be coming to Madison Square Garden, and tickets were going on sale that week.

Unlike lots of plays, circus acts are always both funny and sad, sweet and grotesque at once. They're an old art form, after all—old, wise, and playful. I ought to go, I thought. It'd do me good. And I should take Danny. She'd love it.

A switch flipped in my memory: *clowns.* A dream (had it been only last night?), involving my father in a circuslike performance, outdoors, in a strange city. Not American, perhaps Central European . . . Jordan had been doing something with perfume. And there'd been another man, wearing a cape, who'd cartwheeled across the stage. A theater director, I was sure of that. I thought I recognized him, yet couldn't think who he might be.

And the scent in the dream—jasmine, yes, definitely jasmine. But not quite right. A bit *off,* somehow?

LATER THAT morning, shortly before noon, Stuart and Sam entered my shop at the same moment. Having nearly collided at the door, they were as taken aback as I; I wasn't expecting either of them. They greeted each other cordially.

Stuart I've known thirty-two years. He's short and thin, with large gray eyes and a minimal gray beard. His body's supple and agile, a perfect mime's body. In college in New England, which is where I met him, Stuart was something of a celebrity. He used to hire himself out as a mime for community events and frat parties, and during those four years he made enough money to cover his massive book bills. His dorm room looked like a very cramped library. Books were stacked everywhere but in one corner where Stuart stored his props: top hats, canes, feathers, face paint, and black patent-leather spats.

He still performs occasionally, for friends—never formally. Sometimes I wonder if he's missed his real calling, but Stuart claims he's happier watching a mime than being one. A mime's work is terribly gloom-inducing, he says. That's how Stuart talks. He strings together words that might seem affected coming out of someone else's mouth, but sound entirely natural emerging from his. When he speaks, his hands talk, too. He's got remarkably flexible wrists and broad palms, each with five long snakes attached: his fingers. I've never met a man with nicer nails.

Stuart and I first encountered each other in our college's theater on a cold Saturday in December. That autumn, having worked hard and happily on two productions, I'd decided I wanted to be the theater's props manager for the rest of the year. Normally this job was rotated between two students, but on that afternoon I cornered the director and began lobbying for a change in policy. She was not easily convinced, and we began sparring.

Stuart happened to be waiting around for an audition to begin. Hearing me press my case, he sidled up to the director and began tipping his head from side to side like a slightly manic cuckoo bird. Both the director and I fell silent, at which point Stuart launched into a spot-on pantomime of our debate. We began chuckling at him, no longer contestants but an audience. Winding up his improvisation with a bow, Stuart said: "Give this girl whatever she wants." His voice, which I was hearing for the first time, was as attractively reedy as his body.

"Who *is* she, anyway?" he added, pointing a sharp forefinger at me while aiming his words at the director. "Camilla Archer?—never heard of her! But I can tell she's good with props. Only a totally obsessive person would hunt you down and harass you right before an *audition!* Has this girl not heard of an *opportune* moment?"

Won over, the director relented. That's Stuart: he performs a bit of magic and things change, often for the better. But he's a jouster, and I'm an easy mark for him. "If we were in a spook house at an amusement park," he asked me once, "and you were really scared, and we were holding hands, would you let go of my hand if I ordered you to?" When I shook my head, he jeered, "Of course you would—to prove how brave you are!" I asked him why, in that case, he'd even bother to order me. "Do you have any idea," he retorted, "how appealing you are when you're unnerved?"

SAM SAID something similar to me—*I like it when you're flustered*—soon after we met. I took this as a good sign, proof of his ability to see behind surfaces.

That was a long time ago. Sam and I met in Eve's gardening store. We lived together for two years, were married for seven, and have been divorced for nine—which means we've been co-orbital, as he puts it, for eighteen years. We both still live in the West Village, and we still co-own my shop, The Fourth Wall, which we opened at the start of our marriage. When that union ended, we saw no reason to shut down our business, which was clearing a small but reliable profit.

The Fourth Wall is an odd little place. It sells performing-arts memorabilia and curiosa of all kinds, including scripts, scores, libretti, posters, photos, small props, and costumes. Opening a specialized store was never a goal of Sam's, but he went along with the idea, and we came up with a division of labor that's still in place. Sam seldom accompanies me on my buying missions and never mans the shop, preferring instead to handle its bookkeeping and taxes.

He's also a successful publishing consultant with a great eye for well-conceived quirkiness. Mostly he packages and publicizes books featuring the work of contemporary photographers, several of which have done quite well. In addition, Sam also owns a lively art gallery in Williamsburg, Brooklyn, a neighborhood he spotted long before it became trendy. The gallery was launched by Lila, his current wife, whose name, Stuart likes to point out, is a shortened version of my own. (*And she's a lot shorter than you, too,* he adds, which she is. Younger and prettier, too.) A couple of artists actually run the space, which operates on a shoestring but shows interesting work. Sam's quietly proud of it.

Then there are the kids. Three-year-old Zeke is Sam's and Lila's son; Abby is a seven-year-old redhead, Lila's from a former marriage, now Sam's adopted daughter. He adores them both. The children are what Sam's always wanted, what he and I didn't manage to—what's the right verb, *conjure, concoct?*—while we were together.

"SO WHAT brings you two here?" I asked. "On a Sunday, no less?"

Stuart gave Sam a deferential, you-go-first nod.

"Just wanted to say hi," Sam said. "Plus I have a favor to ask you."

The favor, I figured, would be a short-term loan from The Fourth Wall's account. Sam's gallery sometimes has minor cash-flow problems.

"Ask away," I said. "Unless . . ." I gestured at Stuart, thinking Sam might want to speak with me in private, but Sam shook his head.

"No, it's okay," he said. "This has to do with Danny, actually. Maybe you'll have some ideas, too, Stuart. I mean, you know her pretty well, don't you?"

"Not very," Stuart replied. "But go ahead."

Sam gave a preliminary shrug. I knew that shoulder roll, as I knew most of Sam's repertoire of gesture. It communicated confusion.

"She called me last night," he said. "Wanted to know if I had room in my cellar to store a few boxes of stuff she'd taken from Eve's apartment, and if I could drive the rest to the Salvation Army. Then she said she'd gone through her mother's papers and found something she wanted to discuss with me. When I asked her what it was, she said she'd rather tell me in person."

He glanced first at me, then at Stuart. "Wonder what's up."

"Taxes, maybe," said Stuart. "Your cousin wasn't too good at that kind of thing, was she?" he asked, turning to me.

"That can't be it," I said. "Danny and I have already been over all the paperwork. I've dealt with the insurance companies, Social Security, the IRS, everybody—there aren't any outstanding bills to pay."

"I figured as much," said Sam.

"She called me, too," I said. "This morning. Wanted to know if she could stop by later and talk with me about something." Within me, a little balloon of unease began slowly expanding. "When are the two of you supposed to get together?"

"Thursday—I'm taking her out for a drink. I guess you and I should check in afterward?"

Stuart gave one of his polite but perceptible frowns. "Maybe Danny doesn't want to talk with both of you about the same thing. Maybe she wants separate responses to separate matters."

Sam shrugged more aggressively this time, then turned to me. "Let's just confer later," he said. Though bland, his words twanged my nerves. Stuart noticed my discomfort.

"Cam, what sort of shape is Danny in, these days?"

I shook my head. "I really can't tell. She's back at work, and she seems to be eating and sleeping all right . . ."

"But has she been talking about Eve with you or anyone else?" Stuart prodded.

"Depends what you mean by talking." I decided to attempt straightforwardness; with Stuart there, Sam might do the same. "The truth is, I think she's suffering. Acutely. But more because she's angry than because she's grieving."

Sam's face was a perfect blank.

"Hmm," said Stuart. "What's it boil down to?"

Stuart is intolerant of lengthy psychological explanations. I produced as short an answer as I could: "Let's just say she never had her mother's undivided attention."

"Love, yes. Attention, no," said Sam. His phrasing surprised me; I hadn't expected him to take Eve's side.

"A distinction without a difference?" asked Stuart.

"No, I don't think so. I mean, a kid knows whether he or she is loved, which is all that matters—"

"Oh please." Stuart's breeziness barely concealed his scorn. "Let's get back to where Danny's at. Of course she's angry—but that's not news, is it? She's been angry at her mother for years! What's new is having to figure out how to be angry at a *dead* mother." He paused. "It'll be a while before she can say anything about what she's actually feeling, I'd bet. So she'll express her inner troubles in some other way. She's not drinking, is she? Pills? That's the kind of thing to watch out for."

"We're aware of that. And a little blunting of pain isn't necessarily a bad idea either." Sam had iced up; he was registering Stuart's dismissiveness. "If Danny needs short-term help from booze or drugs, I say fine. I'm sure she's not abusing anything. That's not her style."

He was right; I nodded in agreement.

It was Stuart's turn to shrug. "For what it's worth," he said, "*I* think the biggest issue for Danny has got to be fear. She's alone now, in a whole new way."

Sam clenched and unclenched his right fist several times, a signal that either the conversation or the mild muscular ache he occasionally suffers in that hand was disturbing him. I was fairly certain which it was, since we were discussing Danny. He glanced at his watch.

"Gotta go—I'll check in with you after Thursday, all right, Cam?" He leaned over and kissed my cheek. "Take care of yourself. Bye, Stuart," he called over his shoulder as he left.

THE DOOR closed. Stuart raised his arms straight up over his head, then released them downward, slowly, his elbows bent and palms turned upward. Dipping his knees, he bobbed both forearms simultaneously, as if handling something spherical and heavy.

"Oof." He exhaled, his hands flopping to his sides as he dropped his imaginary burden. "Beats me how folks do it."

"Do what?"

"Carry so much at once. A wife, two kids, and an ex-kid, plus there's an ex-wife . . ."

"Danny's not an ex-kid," I said. "And for the record, you were kind of rough on Sam. He's as worried about Danny as I am."

Stuart cocked one skeptical eyebrow at me. "Well, you know what? The man didn't say so, but he's actually concerned about *you.*"

"Oh please," I said, mimicking his earlier rebuke of Sam.

Stuart wagged a forefinger in disagreement. "This is a three-way, my dear. Sam knows you're bearing the brunt of this situation. He *could* offer to spend more time with Danny. He's the father figure in this setup, right? The one steady male presence in the girl's life, the only guy who was around from the time she was a kid—am I right? Well, the man feels guilty, which is why he showed up here. To mollify you."

It was fruitless to argue with Stuart about Sam. Although not consistently displayed, Stuart's animus was old enough to elude my attempts at uprooting it. "What exactly is a brunt?" I asked, to divert him.

"Brunt?" Stuart rose to the bait. "It's Middle English, for fire or heat. It means a direct impact or hit. Or, metaphorically, the hardest part."

"Thank you, Webster, I know *that* part. I was hoping you'd tell me the word comes from some medieval cookery book. What brings you here, anyhow? You didn't say."

"Didn't exactly get a chance to stick a word in edgewise, did I? What with all the yakkety ex-husbands around here." He stuck out his tongue and twisted it into a corkscrew.

"Don't be arch."

"Aaaarch," he crooned. "Lovely word." Extending one arm in front of himself and cocking its wrist downward, he spread his thumb and fingers into an upside-down U. With two fingers of the other hand, he mimed a mincing walk-through beneath the arch.

"Time to go, Stu," I began.

"Bye-bye," he sang. "She's evicting me—*there's* a first!"

"Quit it," I said. "I've got a client coming in this afternoon to pick up a purchase I haven't wrapped—"

"Okay, Cammie." Airborne, Stuart's hands wafted downward, two large feathers settling on my head, the warm palms sliding down to embrace my ears. He leaned over and kissed me on the nose. I smelled his aftershave, a clean, subtle citrus, familiar and reassuring.

"I was over on Seventh Avenue running some errands, passed by your shop, and there you were! Actually I was wondering if you wanted to grab lunch, but we can do it another time."

Stuart and I often eat lunch together. It's a pleasant twenty-minute walk from Bedford Street, where I am, over to Washington Square, then up University Place and over to Fourth Avenue, where Stuart's bookstore is located.

"Soon," I said. "Something to look forward to."

He gave me a clipped salute, chest thrust forward. I walked him to the door and watched him march eastward. Halfway up the block, he was still miming a soldier's erect progress. "You look ridiculous," I called after him. Without breaking step or turning around, he raised a hand and lowered all its fingers but the third.

WITH CARL, the man with whom he's lived for half as long as I've known him, Stuart owns Backstage Books. It's dedicated to theater, with the best selection of plays in the city, lots of biographies and critical works, and journals of all kinds. Above the shop is Stuart and Carl's apartment, which is nicely furbished, thanks to Carl.

Carl's a benign presence, consistently easygoing about my friendship with his lover. He doesn't interest me much, though—no more, I suppose, than Sam ever interested Stuart. As for Sam's Lila, she doesn't interest me either. She's thirty-seven, thirteen years younger than I am, and the difference shows: in our bodies, of course, but also in our frames of reference. To her, JFK's the Oliver Stone film, not the memory of a gym class interrupted by a teacher shrieking the news.

Lila doesn't try to undermine Sam's and my ongoing connection. I sense she realizes it won't lead to the demise of her marriage to a man she obviously loves. Whether the feeling's mutual is something I'm unable to evaluate. Sexual heat, compatibility—I have no idea whether any of it's in place for Sam. Maybe none of that matters as much to him as it once did.

I'm ongoingly grateful to Sam for making it possible for me to continue running my own show at The Fourth Wall. I'd be completely at sea in a regular job. In this I'm like my father, who never enjoyed being an employee; other people's professional priorities simply didn't interest him. Jordan was a perfumist, and he spent most of his time in his lab, focused on his central obsession: odors and the architecture of their molecules. He never knew what he might hit upon while he was mixing things up, and he liked it that way.

So do I. Though I'm no artist, I'm a decent sleuth. I cater mainly to bona fide collectors, and I know the kinds of things they're seeking. There's nothing like my shop in New York City, or anywhere else in the country, for that matter. I don't go in for the posters and T-shirts sold by those theater souvenir stores on Broadway. There you won't find a letter written by Giuseppe Verdi to his neighbor in Bussetto, thanking him for several kilos of superior *parmigiano*. Nor could you purchase a snapshot of Maurice Ravel sitting in the back of a New York taxi in 1936, necktie askew and expression dismayed, as if he'd just caught a whiff of his own death, which did arrive, a mere twelve months later. These are the sorts of small treasures I offer.

My job's something like that of a theater coach, except my clients aren't actors. They're designers of private dramas in which props themselves are the stars. The people who come to my shop want to acquire objects other people can't readily find: recalcitrant gems. My role is to pep-talk this variant of desire. *You,* I tell each of my clients, are in pursuit of something most people can't appreciate, *can't even imagine!* How many other people, I ask them, are really capable of understanding what it means to own a conductor's baton custom-made for Arturo Toscanini, with the maestro's initials inscribed on its tip? Or a silver cigarette case owned by Sir Laurence Olivier? Or a little stuffed rabbit that sat backstage at the Helen Hayes Theater throughout the entire run of *Harvey?*

Naturally I know all the serious merchants of memorabilia in the city, and I go to all the best antiques shows and estate sales. But I also scavenge. I've found breathtaking surprises in streetside trash and unkempt attics and cellars. It's not all golden, this line of work. It's a bit like being a private investigator: loads of time goes into following up baseless rumors and barking up wrong trees. Although I've been at it for years, occasionally I wind up in a tricky situation. Once or twice I've had to defend myself against charges of theft. Infrequently but memorably, I meet a genuinely deranged individual—someone who believes he's a famous director, or a world-class cellist, or the man who *really* wrote all of Edward Albee's plays. Such encounters supply their own form of drama, reminding me that although I'm no actress, I can still play my part in the theater of the absurd.

AFTER STUART left I spent a frustrating hour readying one of my client's purchases for pickup. This man, an odd and very rich duck, had recently paid a hefty sum for a pair of wheels from a large wooden wagon that had appeared in the New York premiere of Brecht's *Mother Courage.* As I fumbled with cardboard and packing tape, I distracted myself with a mental inventory of Eve's apartment. What, I wondered, might Danny have been referring to when she spoke with Sam? What had she found while going through papers there?

I pictured the cramped, dimly lit study at the rear of the apartment. This room had usually been a total mess. After Eve's death I'd been gratefully surprised to find all her important personal and financial documents in one obvious place—an ancient metal filing cabinet beside her desk. The desk itself was a nondescript oak worktable with a couple of off-kilter drawers. Instead of a chair, Eve had used one of those miserable backless stools popular in the Seventies, the kind you tuck your legs under. The only other piece of furniture in the room was an old rocker, its cane seat pockmarked with holes into which Eve had inserted bunches of dried flowers.

Eve hadn't been interested in interiors. Her eye had always landed first on gardens, shrubs, trees. The only good furnishings she'd owned were several Stickley armchairs and an unusual Art Nouveau rug. These had come from the family apartment, as Eve used to call it: the place on Ninth Street in the West Village where she and I grew up.

I spent the first eighteen years of my life in that apartment. Dan Pell—Eve's father—and his second wife, Sarah—Eve's stepmother—had agreed to take Jordan and me into their home after Jordan promised to cover the rent. Dan was broke, so Jordan's offer must've seemed too good to refuse, even given that Dan had no idea who he was dealing with. My father and I had materialized more or less out of thin air. About our existence Dan knew nothing until we arrived from Paris, the city where Camilla Archer, née Pell—Dan's sister—had died during childbirth. Mine, that is. I was a few months old when we landed in New York.

DANNY SHOWED up just as I finished tidying my back office.

I can always tell it's her when she enters The Fourth Wall: I can smell her, faintly but distinctly. She favors Guerlain fragrances, which seem made for her. Very few twenty-five-year-olds can get away with wearing Jicky, Champs-Elysées, or the other Guerlain old-timers (which seem made for women over forty, with checkered pasts), but Danny's one of them.

"I'm here," I called. "Come on back!"

All six feet of her appeared. Though she's large-boned and tall like Eve, Danny's never looked anything like her mother. She's got brown eyes; Eve's were dark blue. Danny's long brown hair is streaked with blond highlights; Eve's hair was short, dark, and curly.

She gave me a little wave; I took in the flash of red fingernails and her usual silver rings. "How goes it?" she said, stepping toward me.

"Just fine," I said, hugging her. Her eyes were a little red, but otherwise she looked good, her color restored. The chic, pulled-together Danny, I thought, immediately suspecting this judgment was premature. "You smell super."

"This *is* a good one," she said, giving the underside of her wrist a quick sniff before extending it toward me. "I just started wearing it. It's a Guerlain called Lui. Mom had a bottle of it, but she didn't like it so she gave it to me. Good thing she did—it didn't suit her at all. You have no idea how much perfume was in her bathroom closet, Cam. Like a damn department store. The only one she ever wore was that one of your father's—what was it called, Lune?"

I nodded.

"Well, there's none of that left. I threw out the one remaining bottle, it was nearly empty. All the other stuff must've been gifts from her fuck-mates." Danny's voice thickened with sarcasm. "You'd think Mom would've had to label each bottle. You know, this one is Jim's, this John's, this George's . . . Wouldn't do to get them confused, would it?"

"Cool it," I said.

"Oh come on. She's dead. I can vent to my heart's content!" Her snicker sounded forced.

I leaned in for a close sniff of her scent. It reminded me slightly of Chanel No. 5. Both fragrances have the same bottom notes of iris and vanilla, but a woody, shadowy underlay in the Guerlain distinguishes it from its famous sister. On Danny, I could detect a hint of fern.

I have a decent nose, though I find certain scents hard to recollect. The best perfumes can't easily be called to mind. One of my father's—Lune, my favorite as well as Eve's—was maddeningly elusive. To this day I can summon only its initial notes, not the delicate medley arising hours after its application. Lune was the olfactory equivalent of moonlight dappling the surface of water, apparently serene, yet really not.

"Have a seat," I said, releasing Danny's wrist.

Taking the chair opposite mine, she dropped her leather backpack on the floor and sat in silence, staring downward. When she was in high school, she'd sometimes done the same thing: gaze vacantly at her knees, her hands clasped between them.

"How's work going?" I said.

"Busy. Frustrating. In addition to everything else, today I was asked to design the cover of a new art book. Sam would hate it! Tacky photos of fat old people in casinos. Like bad Weegee." She shook her head. "Still, it's a gig. Work's basically fine," she ended.

"Keeps you out of trouble," I offered.

She frowned a little—whether in response to my platitudinous remark or to something else, I couldn't tell. We sat in further silence.

"Care to tell me why you're here?" I asked at last.

MY DIRECTNESS seemed to rouse her. Training her gaze on me, she said steadily, "I've been thinking about my father. About his relationship with my mother. He wasn't in the picture for very long, was he?"

The question was completely unexpected. As a child Danny had occasionally asked about her father, but her interest in him had never been sustained. During her high school years she'd referred to him as the garden boy, in reference to the fact that Eve had said she met him on a landscaping job. Otherwise Eve had rarely spoken of him. He'd died in a hospital, of a freak infection, when Danny was a toddler.

"No," I said, "he wasn't. In fact, I think you'd just turned three when he—"

"I'm not referring to his dying," she broke in. "I'm talking about how Mom didn't want him around. Do you know why?"

"Nope."

She frowned. Clearly, monosyllabic answers weren't going to cut it. "Your mother didn't normally acquaint me with her reasons for doing things," I added.

Danny nodded, but I could tell she wasn't satisfied. She'd been asking many questions about Eve since her death, seeking, I supposed, to weave my perceptions into her own, and thus render the whole more graspable. I'd been responding to her inquiries as vaguely as possible. It wouldn't be right, I'd decided, to off-load my own messy feelings onto her. I'd kept them to myself while Eve was alive, so why discharge them now? Yet Danny was continuing to press me. Occasionally our dialogue felt like a subtle tug-of-war.

"When your mother became pregnant," I continued, "she hadn't known Billy for more than a few months. She was living upstate. But you know that already."

"Billy Deveare," said Danny. "What kind of a name is Deveare?"

"Got me," I said. "Could be British, could be French . . ."

"She ever describe him to you in any detail?"

"No."

She twisted one of her rings, pried it off her finger, pushed it back on. "What was it about him that made Mom not want to have him around?"

I shrugged. "As I said, she didn't talk about it—not with me, anyway. You're not actually surprised to hear me say that, are you?"

"Mom was like that with everyone," she replied tersely, as though detecting in my question a case of special pleading. "Do you know if Billy wanted her to keep the baby?"

"Eve never said. She wasn't in love with him, though. That's the impression I got, anyway. I don't think she cared what Billy thought."

Danny tugged her ponytail loose from its elastic band, gave it a shake, and re-banded it. I knew these repeated-motion tics. When she was very young, she used to perform them frequently, sometimes as a prelude to a tantrum. I half-expected one now, though her tone remained calm as she asked, "Anything else you remember?"

I THOUGHT for several moments.

"I don't think Eve disliked Billy—she just didn't want to see him after you were born. I guess he went along with that." The birth itself had gone smoothly, according to Eve; within a matter of weeks, she'd found a babysitter and returned to her job as a landscaper.

"When your grandfather got sick, your mother had to move back to the city."

Whatever Eve's plans might have been up to that point, they'd been altered in 1974 by her father's illness. Danny was six months old when Dan was diagnosed with advanced emphysema. Sarah, who'd grown infirm physically and mentally, was completely unable to handle him. My father wasn't around; he'd bought a small house in New Jersey in 1970 and seldom came into Manhattan.

I remembered phoning Eve to relay the information about Dan. She and her parents had barely spoken for a number of years. My news must have surprised her, yet she betrayed nothing of what she was feeling. Within a week she'd shown up in New York and begun making arrangements for her parents' care. I hadn't been prepared for such bustling efficiency. My memories were of a headstrong teenager with a messy bedroom.

During Dan's illness, Eve and Danny stayed with friends in a walk-up in the Bowery. They came to the West Village only when Eve needed to be at the family apartment. Her tousled hair restrained by a bright silk scarf, Eve moved with the easy assurance of a woman who took the swell of her hips for granted. She dressed casually yet fashionably, favoring snug jeans, V-neck shirts, and boots with high heels.

Eve had struck me as an assured yet oddly detached parent. She seemed not to have succumbed to that helpless infatuation most new mothers experience. Right from the start, she was glad to accept my babysitting offers whenever I made them. I was twenty-five and single, with little but work—at an antiques shop—to occupy me. It was fine by me to pick Danny up on a Sunday morning, take her for a stroll or over to my place on Cornelia Street, and return her later in the day. I enjoyed being with her. She was an unfussy baby.

Not until several years later did I realize that Eve had begun collecting, on those days I freed up for her, a set of partners on whom she could rely, men for whom sex had as much weight as a bubble. Sex had always been a kind of remedy for Eve, and if her child had to be made to disappear regularly so she could obtain it, that was a cost she'd pay.

Dan died about eight weeks after Eve's arrival. After his death Sarah was installed in a nursing home. She'd gone willingly, relieved to drop the pretense of family unity now that her husband was gone. At that point I'd expected my cousin to head back upstate, but Eve surprised me by announcing she'd decided to stay in the city for good. She'd found a cheap rental, she said, and was planning on opening a gardening shop in Chelsea. She was coming home.

IT WAS time for me to quit shuffling my deck of memory cards. Danny awaited some sort of statement about Billy Deveare.

"If you want me to tell you what kind of man your father was, I can't," I said. "Honestly, I think he was just some guy who impregnated your mother. Since Billy hadn't meant much to her in the first place, she must've thought it'd be a mistake to give him a role in raising you."

"Apparently." Danny shifted sharply in her seat, recrossing her legs. Her fingers returned to her hair, worrying its elastic band. "But who the hell knows what my mother really wanted?" She redid her ponytail, the movements of her hands practiced and aggressive. "You ever meet anyone—*anyone*—more clueless about herself than Mom was?" The elastic band fell into place with a short, loud snap.

"Well, look," I said. "Eve did know she wanted a kid. She could have terminated her pregnancy, right?"

I'd hit a nerve. "Oh, fuck her *wanting* me," Danny said. Turning her head slightly to indicate that I wasn't to involve myself, she wiped her eyes with the back of one hand. Then she fumbled around in her backpack.

"I've got something for you." She drew forth a Polaroid snapshot. "My parents," she said, handing it to me.

THE SNAPSHOT showed a man and woman standing far enough away from the camera that their full bodies were visible. I turned the picture over, looking for a date. There it was: *October 31, 1973,* written in ballpoint in Eve's strong hand. Next to it were the words *Danny's father.*

"Where'd you find this?" I asked.

"With a bunch of other photos," Danny answered. "In Mom's study. I'd seen the others before, but not this one."

I returned to the picture. Eve was recognizable after a few moments of uncertainty; she was wearing a long, close-fitting skirt, a hip-length blouse (not tucked in but tight enough to reveal her curves), and flat, ballerina-style shoes. The man next to her was of indeterminate age, tall and slender. I noticed his clothing first. He wore a fedora hat that hid his hair. His trousers were a narrow cut, and the wide collar and placket of his pullover flattered his shoulders. Of his face I had little impression, for he was wearing one of those classic black eye-masks.

"Of course," I said to Danny, pointing at the mask. "They must've been going to a Halloween party."

"Yeah," said Danny. "Recognize Billy?"

I peered again at the photograph, then lay it down on my desk. "No. But why would I? I never met him."

Danny reached over and gave my forearm a shake. "Cam—there must have been someone who did. . . . Your father, maybe?"

The question surprised me. Danny rarely alluded to Jordan.

"I doubt it," I said. "Anyway, it doesn't matter if my father did meet him. He's gone." Waiting a beat, I decided to state the obvious, to make her contend with it. "They're all gone, Danny."

WE SWITCHED gears at that point, talking about other things. A client had given me a pair of tickets for the latest Robert Wilson production at the Brooklyn Academy of Music—was Danny free, did she want to go to BAM with me? She did, and seemed to brighten at the idea.

By this time it was nearly seven. I opened my shop's front door while Danny wiggled her arms through the straps of her backpack. We stepped outside. Placing my hands on her shoulders, I rotated her gently so she was facing in the direction of the subway, then gave her a light shove.

"Fix yourself a decent dinner," I said. "Have a bath and go straight to bed, okay?"

She rolled her eyes, blew me a kiss, and took off toward Sixth Avenue. Watching her stride gracefully off, I summoned an image of her with Sam and myself—the three of us holding hands, walking along Bedford Street. Sam and I used to spend a lot of time with Danny when she was young. Even then, she was already tall and wonderfully loose limbed. Distractible, too, the way kids are if they're lucky.

After she'd rounded the corner, I went back inside. On the far wall of my office is a dartboard, which I conceal behind a puppet-theater curtain I found in a flea market in Los Angeles. The curtain is made of black linen; stenciled across its center is the French word *cabotinage,* which refers to theatrical barnstorming but also implies over-the-top self-advertising. It's a funny word—I like it.

I pulled the curtain aside, then went to my desk. In its top drawer I keep a bunch of small photos—head shots—along with a set of brass darts. The darts are beautifully knurled, with glittery silver flights, those feathery bits at the end. I love their midair shimmer and the nice thud they make when they enter the board's cork.

Choosing three photos of Eve, I affixed them to the board, slipping their edges under the wire rims demarcating the board's score zones. Then I stood back, took aim, and threw. After missing the first couple of times, I hit my stride and struck all three targets regularly, including the one nearest the bull's-eye. *Yes,* I hissed after each toss, just as Eve taught me to do when we played darts in the central hallway of the family apartment. *Yesss!*

After a while I took down the photos, replaced them and the darts in their drawer, and drew the curtain across the board. Glancing at my desk before pulling my office door shut, I saw Danny had left the picture of her mother and her man. Slipping it into my bag, I locked up and headed home.

INTERLUDE

ENLIGHTENING THOUGH it is, Camilla's account thus far leaves certain questions unaddressed, and I'm not fond of loose ends. So I'll pause her narration briefly—as I shall from time to time, in the interests of clarification.

Upon first encountering her, I saw that Camilla took the physical particulars of theater seriously. (Her storefront windows, for instance, were dressed with an exceptional pair of burgundy-colored velvet curtains salvaged from a defunct theater in Lucca, Italy.) People who collect memorabilia of any kind covet idiosyncrasy, and Camilla, keenly aware of this fact, offers her patrons all manner of *objets* that are extremely difficult to find or duplicate—items for which a true fan of the stage will pay plenty. Her taste in collectibles runs the gamut from the exquisite to the whimsical, even the grotesque.

My favorite example of the last sits in a corner of The Fourth Wall. It's a prop from a regional theater's production of *Little Shop of Horrors:* a small mahogany griffin, the usual half-lion, half-eagle creature, but with an odd twist. A carved bit of spittle drips from its mouth, as if it had just chomped down on something juicy. If you look closely, you can see a tiny set of toes, apparently human, sticking out at one side of the creature's mouth. Such delightful perversity! It's one of the few objects Camilla refuses to sell.

Observant she definitely was. I noticed this about Camilla right away. She'd have to be, in order to make her living—which is entirely respectable. But this trait hadn't translated, I also saw, into anything close to clear self-perception. She wasn't in the habit of examining the obstacles to her happiness and doing something to dismantle them. Basically, she was bumping into herself coming and going.

I USE the term "happiness" advisedly. Too often it sends people bounding in the wrong direction, like eager dogs with impaired snouts. All sorts of foolish schemes are devised for obtaining happiness, as if it could be procured like an item on a supermarket shelf, when in fact it's merely a subjective climate. It arrives and departs, and the aleatory music of its coming and going is as strange as a loon's cry.

This brings me to a related matter: fearfulness. Few people who utter the words "I know myself" say them with confidence. Like children trying to ascend the slick surface of a playground slide, adult human beings scrabble in vain for a purchase on their identities. They're afraid of contradiction, the crisscrossing vectors of their desires, even the mixedness of their physical bodies, whose genes reflect such turbulent blending. This fearfulness explains why many people can't see past their own noses, and why happiness keeps skipping away from them.

On top of which there's a wild card in the game, love, which tends to subvert whatever humans assume is true about themselves. *I'm this sort of person, I'm not at all like that:* such statements go out the window when love shows up! I'm not speaking solely of romantic love, by the way. Family enmeshments can have similarly deranging effects—as they did with Camilla.

And then there's love of country. Talk about upheaval! Ah, I'm in memory's grip now. I'm revisiting Meyerhold in his prison cell, where he is contemplating his life's work, Russia's future, his own fate . . . Well, I suppose the time has come for a condensed version of his biography.

SEVA DIDN'T start out Russian. His father was a Silesian German whose forebears were in all likelihood Jewish, and his mother was from a German family in Riga, Latvia.

Seva was baptized a Lutheran and given the name Karl-Theodor Kasimir. At twenty-one he renounced his religion and changed his name. He ceased being German-Russian and Lutheran, and he no longer called himself Karl-Theodor Kasimir Meyergold but rather Vsevolod Emilevich Meyerhold. He was thus a man accustomed to changes in mask and costume. Moreover, though he could sometimes play the role of the imperious artist, he was a tolerant human being—much more so than most Russians. And he was drawn to talented outsiders.

Seva's father owned a liquor distillery in Penza, a small Russian city located four hundred or so miles from Moscow, where the Meyergolds lived a comfortably bourgeois life. Although Seva mistrusted everything his father stood for, he loved hanging around the distillery. The place had good sets—bright, noisy workrooms, a big cafeteria where everyone ate lunch—and the action there was always lively. The distillery was known for its own brand of vodka, called Meyergoldovka. It also produced delicious cordials made from fruits—red currants, black currants, strawberries—which were harvested locally and crushed in huge cisterns. All his life Seva could summon to memory the exhilarating odor of those fermenting berries.

THE FIRST time I beheld Seva, he struck me as such an interesting-looking man. Had I been asked, that's how I would've described him. It was only after we began collaborating that he became, in my eyes, so terribly handsome. Ah, that sounds ridiculous! Where's the word, the one right word?

Gorgeous: Seva became gorgeous.

He had a magnificent nose. In caricatures the St. Petersburg press portrayed Seva as a man with a pronouncedly hooked beak, but actually the curve of his nose was quite refined, like a straight line tugged ever so slightly downward at each end. Above his upper lip (that lip with its wanton cleft, the mouth's voluptuous décolletage!), the flesh pitched steeply outward to meet the base of the nose. All the angles of Seva's face aimed powerfully forward, suggesting the man's strength of character. Seen straight on, his finely arched brows and lustrous brown eyes lent his face a warmth that both compelled and cautioned, like that of a banked fire that retains more than enough heat to leap alight and burn hard.

When I first met him, he was tall and slender, but as time passed he put on weight. His despair settled in his belly. He ate too much, and in this he had an accommodating mate. Where food and drink were concerned, his wife, Zina, tended toward excess. She adored her *blini* slathered with *smetana,* and she gradually grew plump as a city pigeon, which made her even more desirable in the eyes of many men.

She wasn't the most faithful of wives, though she did love Seva—more than she liked to admit, in fact. He knew right from the start that she'd be unreliable as a sexual partner but forever *fidele* as an artistic one, and the second loyalty mattered more to him than the first. After all, he could have had other women whenever he wanted, though he wanted few. I'm not alluding here to what's called "sexual preference," one of those Americanisms that dispel any possibility of randiness or complication. The fact is that Seva always liked women and never sought men, though they certainly sought him. After his first marriage ended, he commenced a routine with Zina that continued throughout the course of their relationship. They made love a few times each week, with sufficient exuberance to satisfy him, if not her. Her ego had a prodigious need for stroking, and sometimes she confused one need with another. It's a common enough mistake. Seva could tell when she was being unfaithful, and either humored her or simply ignored her. He knew she'd be back, and she knew he wouldn't leave. It worked for them.

HOW DID Meyerhold and I become partners? Serendipitously.

Actually Seva wasn't consciously seeking a double. It was Vladimir Telyakovsky, his boss at the Imperial Theaters in St. Petersburg, who insisted that Seva find himself a pseudonym under which he could carry out his extracurricular activities.

By this time—the year was 1910—Seva had established a solid name for himself. He wasn't content, however, designing and directing lavish productions of familiar dramas at the state playhouses. It was mostly hackwork, and who had time for *that?* St. Petersburg was ripe for a venue in which experimentation would be celebrated.

Thus was born the Interlude House. Seva overhauled the former Skazka Theater to create a lively cabaret atmosphere, installing old café tables and a set of stairs that connected the low, small stage with the auditorium. When its makeover was complete, the place exuded a shabby unpretentiousness that everybody liked. It was instantly popular.

The opening show, *Columbine's Scarf*, was a pantomime full of strident music and outrageous, clownish costumes. The set evoked nastiness and excitement at the same time, and everyone was impressed, including Telyakovsky. Nonetheless, Seva's boss insisted it was unseemly for Meyerhold to continue his directorial work at the Interlude House unless he could do so under an assumed name.

Telyakovsky had a point. Seva's official job wasn't terribly demanding; he was seldom required to undertake more than two big works in a season. Malicious eyes were on Meyerhold, waiting for him to get into trouble. Telyakovsky didn't want all of St. Petersburg to know that his star director was moonlighting.

WHAT TO do? A writer friend of Seva's suggested that perhaps a certain character in a short story by E.T.A. Hoffmann, the German author of fantasy tales, would provide a good cover for Seva's unofficial activities.

Hearing this, Seva perked up. He was familiar with Hoffmann's popular stories, whose grotesqueries made for memorable late-night reading. He wasn't aware, however, of a tale entitled "Adventure on New Year's Eve." Seva's friend gave him a copy and ordered him to read it, which he did. He was enchanted.

It's a story about a married painter, Herr Spikher, who, while in Italy, temporarily loses his ability to cast a reflection in a mirror. This doesn't happen by accident: it's the nefarious work of a beautiful, enigmatic woman named Giulietta and a strange individual named Dr. Dapertutto. Giulietta convinces Spikher to surrender his reflection in return for her love—not a bad deal, according to Dapertutto (who slyly tells Spikher, "Your wife will have all the rest of you, while Giulietta will have only your shimmering dream-self!"). Spikher finally manages to pull himself together and fend off the evil pair, using the scriptural command for banishing the Tempter.

Who knew what any of it meant? But Seva was taken with the description of Dapertutto, "a tall, thin man with a pointed hawk's nose, sparkling eyes, and a maliciously twisted mouth." Seva didn't mind that this fellow was the embodiment of the tale's most sinister implications; he liked the man's charm and boldness. Here, he decided, was a mask he could use.

"Dapertutto it is, then," he told his friend. "Seems I actually resemble the man, too, except for that twisted mouth of his. He can direct my work at the Interlude House and write a couple of articles I've been meaning to publish. Maybe I'll open an even bigger studio-theater, and he can run it."

Thus, in a fun-loving spirit, was I called forth as the director's double.

THE INTERLUDE House closed after an embarrassing rout in Moscow, to which it traveled. Far too refined for their own good, Seva's Muscovite audiences failed to get the point of farces and pantomimes. He was frustrated by this reaction, but he also realized that the time had come to try something new.

He wasn't prepared to give up being in St. Petersburg—not yet, anyway. Seva loved his adopted city. (It's impossible to dislike a place so decrepitly beautiful! Could one ever hate the ravishing and malodorous Venice? The two locales elicit the same response, a kind of shock: here, love and death have merged seamlessly.) Seva responded strongly to St. Petersburg's contradictions. The city's canals are peaceful, but its river is another matter. The Neva is disturbingly animate. Even in the dead of winter, when the river's surface freezes into a broad swath of white immobility, its waters continue their roiling below. In the springtime they smell of danger, and one fears falling into them. (Moscow's waterways are less compelling, which is one of the reasons Seva liked to visit the capital from time to time. There he could focus on the city's great wide sky, shape-shifting clouds, and magisterial light.)

So St. Petersburg was home—at least for a time. Seva started his days with a cup of tea fortified with a dollop of sweet gooseberry jam, which he bolted down at six in the morning. Most of his daily labor involved directing and set design. But he was a committed teacher, too, and because he sought to communicate his enthusiasms as widely as possible, he decided he needed a new atelier.

Thus was launched Dr. Dapertutto's Studio, Seva's private acting workshop, in 1913. On top of this came a new medium, film. In 1915 Seva oversaw the production of Oscar Wilde's *The Picture of Dorian Gray,* and it was splendid. He'd have made a wonderful filmmaker had he chosen to go that route, but he surrendered the screen to Seryozha Eisenstein—a born film director and a good friend. (It was Eisenstein who hid some of Seva's papers in his own dacha in 1938, after Seva's theater had been liquidated. Seryozha suspected, rightly, that things would start disappearing unless countervailing measures were taken. Of course plenty of things vanished anyway. People, too.)

UNTIL THE civil war got going and Seva went off to Yalta—where he was arrested by the Whites, escaped, and joined the Reds—he worked indefatigably as a director.

He liked artistic puzzles and difficulties. Whenever he was trying to work out a technical or aesthetic problem, I served as his audience. I'd lob into the air a variety of questions, ideas, and options that Seva would then juggle. Had someone entered Dr. Dapertutto's Studio during such sessions, he or she would've found Seva's behavior confusing, to say the least. It would have looked as if the director had drunk too much vodka, when in reality he was undertaking a much-needed refinement of theatrical principles.

How, wondered Seva one afternoon, might he make all the eager actors auditioning for places in his studio understand that he was sick of watching them try to portray merriment or sadness without ever stopping to consider that perhaps *both* emotions ought to be communicated at once? This he found very frustrating. In the large, bright room where his students undertook their physical exercises, he began experimenting with solutions to this pedagogical problem.

"Come on, come on, come on," he intoned to himself, snapping his fingers noisily. "What should I get them to do? Pranks—I need some good pranks . . ."

This was my cue. *Hamlet,* I prompted. *Handsprings.*

Seva grinned, spun around once, and instantly assumed the aspect of the melancholy prince. "To be," he began sonorously, then quickly inverted himself—hands flat on the ground and feet pointing skyward—as he performed the play's famous soliloquy upside down. It amazed me to see how long and easily he could stand on his hands.

Fetal position, I offered next. Seva brought his feet to the floor, went immediately into a crouch, tucked his head, wrapped his arms around his knees, and fell to his side, his entire body clenched into a ball. "A ghost!" he squeaked, the pitch of his Hamlet-voice unnaturally high. "Doesn't anybody else see him?" Breaking into childish laughter, he rolled his body in a tight circle on the floor.

Fencer's pose, I suggested. Seva leapt to his feet, pulled an imaginary mask over his face, and stiffened one outstretched arm as if he were brandishing a foil. He then proceeded to mime Hamlet's death-fight in slow motion, making it look beautifully balletic. "Follow my mother," he commanded his invisible opponent, the stabbed Claudius, at the end. As soon as the words left his mouth, his entire affect changed again; this time he was waddling and quacking like a duckling in pursuit of its mama. A few seconds later the duck became a long-necked swan as Seva's shoulders pulsed and he hissed at an invisible enemy.

A musical instrument, I inserted into his improvisation. Abruptly the swan fell silent, replaced by a sleepy-eyed owl. "For O, for O," Seva murmured, mimicking Hamlet in conversation with Ophelia. Then he began playing an imaginary flute, whistling its music. After a few lively bars, the tune ceased as Seva extended his make-believe flute before him. "Yet you cannot make it speak," he ended quietly in the prince's voice: half accusatory, half elegiac, wholly credible. A wonderful deep silence ensued while Seva bowed. Then he shouted, *Bravo!,* clapping as if at someone else's performance, and the happy noise of his applause filled the studio.

To me such afternoons represented the best of what Seva and I did together—carefree collaboration, playfulness for its own sake. If I could erase those sessions from memory, I would, but I cannot. They persist, inescapable reminders of my derelictions. I ought to have encouraged Seva to take a harder look at his love for his country, which impelled his art; I could have pushed him to question whether there was something profoundly self-annulling in that love. I might have read the early writing on the dark wall . . . But I simply looked the other way, as doubles do.

WITH THE advent of World War I, many of Seva's acting students went off to fight against the Austro-Hungarian forces. The studio was forced to share its quarters with a temporary military hospital that set up beds for convalescing soldiers on the ground floor. Occasionally these men served as an audience for the students' efforts. Seva liked their frank, unpretentious reactions; he considered them ideal spectators.

Civil war was brewing, too. It broke out in St. Petersburg on February 25, 1917, the same day Seva staged the premiere of Lermontov's *Masquerade* at the Alexandrinsky. Not far from the theater, the czar's men were peppering the proletariat with machine-gun spray. One critic, disgusted by the lavish staging and costumes of Seva's production, failed to perceive its underlying grimness. In his review the next day, he wrote scornfully, "What is this, Rome after the Caesars?"—as if Seva were impervious to the calamities unfolding outside the theater.

He wasn't, of course. A few months later, Seva accepted an invitation to a Bolshevik-sponsored conference on reorganizing the arts in Soviet Russia. That was a risky thing to do, as the Bolsheviks weren't yet assuredly in power. Then, after breaking his contract with the State Opera, he staged *Mystery-Bouffe,* a play by Volodya Mayakovsky—Seva's poet-playwright friend, and a real piece of work.

I've never encountered anyone as hugely smart and difficult as that man! *Mystery-Bouffe* gave me my first look at Volodya in high gear. His play had been underwritten by the Commissariat for Enlightenment (nicknamed Narkompros), which clearly wasn't expecting what Mayakovsky offered—an amusing, heady parody of the Noah's Ark story. At one point during the final dress rehearsal, several Narkompros representatives in the audience shifted uneasily in their seats while Volodya (playing three parts himself) actually climbed an iron fire escape behind the proscenium arch, hooked himself onto a rope, and jumped into space while declaiming his lines. Given how big he was, this was like watching Goliath play Tinkerbell. Seva nearly fell over laughing.

TIME FLIES, they say, when fun is being had; and when there's war, and marital discord, and falling in love, and moving from one city to another.

Much changed in Seva's life between the start and end of the civil war. He moved to Moscow in 1920, and he and Olga, his first wife, parted in 1921. That was a year of drought and famine across Russia, and the marriage was another victim, one could say, of the general desiccation. Its demise was necessary for both parties.

Seva married Zina a year later—the same year Stalin took the helm of the Party and Mussolini seized power in Italy; the same year James Joyce published *Ulysses* and T. S. Eliot brought out *The Waste Land;* the same year Cocteau did *Antigone* in Paris and Brecht did *Drums in the Night* in Munich. The same year, too, in which Seva formed the Actors' Theater, got himself appointed artistic director of the newly formed Theater of the Revolution, and took charge of the State Institute of Theatrical Art, itself soon housing a separate Meyerhold Workshop, which actually ran the Actors' Theater. Seva's professional life had become a multi-ring circus.

The Twenties were his most fruitful years; his work deepened, as did his collaborations with other artists. In the performing arts, miraculous things were happening, and Seva stood at the center of them, their lead innovator. Most of the time he was too busy to be distraught about anything more than the difficulties of keeping his facilities in good running order. Money and supplies were tight, and like everyone else, Seva had to make do with very little. Now and then he'd grow discouraged, and his discouragement would swell beyond the particulars into a general dismay, an intuitive foreboding about the political situation.

AT THESE moments I'd step in. The first thing I did, invariably, was to suggest certain behavioral modifications that might relieve his tension. In addition to directing him toward physical outlets, I was also attempting to dislodge certain of Seva's unproductive mental habits.

Usually my preliminary tactic was to get him to dance by himself. He was a graceful man who loved movement of all kinds; rhythm was the key to his method as a stage director. He had a keen sense of the power of pauses or rapid shifts in tempo, of movements that anticipate or lag behind speech. Seva developed his own system of exercises, which he called biomechanics, to help his students discipline their bodies and better appreciate the ways in which actions and words could be harmonized and counterpointed.

I knew right away when he'd begun imagining a new gesture or movement. First his shoulders would soften and his knees would flex lightly. Then, turning his back on anyone who happened to be present, he'd begin performing whatever he was envisioning. Sometimes he'd end up on the floor; at other times he'd work mostly with his upper body, his legs immobile. He had exceedingly expressive hands, and some of his movements were limited entirely to them— manual dances. After he'd played with his ideas for a while, he'd run to find his journal and make notations. In these moments he was more purely content than at any other time. Even the pleasures afforded him by Zina's companionship couldn't compete with the quiet joys he derived from his own explorations of movement.

And so whenever he grew unusually distressed, I'd begin by encouraging him to shut his door and move around a bit. Although this usually worked, there were occasions when it was unavailing, and I'd urge him to listen to music instead. If Mitya Shostakovich was around, a few minutes of his piano playing might be enough to turn the tide. Mitya liked to improvise, and Seva was always fascinated by what came off the tips of his fingers, as it were.

But if no one, not even Zina, was in the theater (which was often the case, as Seva liked to work at odd hours), I'd go so far as to suggest that he engage in a bit of onanistic activity. Sometimes this was just the ticket. Like so many work-obsessed people, Seva could be curiously insensitive to the promptings of sexual desire in himself. I'd drop the hint, let it take hold, and leave him alone to please himself as he saw fit.

When neither movement nor music nor masturbation sufficed, I knew Seva was in a rough spot. At these moments I had recourse to my best aid, the oldest human sense—smell—which can sway any mood. To Seva's nostrils I'd introduce first the slight sharpness of ripe currants, then the dulcet scent of just-picked strawberries. Instantly he'd be transported to the countryside near Penza, to the Sura River and the fields in Oukhtomovka, where as a boy he used to chase swallows. He'd exhale a sigh of relief.

I made sure, however, never to bring to his nose the scent of *Solanum dulcamara,* a climbing vine with delicate purple flowers and bright red berries that grows across much of Europe and parts of Russia. A member of the nightshade family, it looks enticing but is actually deadly; ingested, its berries can quickly poison a person. It's called bittersweet. Seva, I knew, would be drawn to it because of its name.

I could see dimly where things were headed, and I didn't want to give Seva any ideas. His world was in a bad way. Just how bad I couldn't have known; I'm no clairvoyant.

WHEN MEMORY brings me to this juncture—to those magical afternoons with Seva in the theater, just the two of us, the air backstage redolent with the scent of red berries—I become a little desperate and must switch gears. Otherwise I start thinking about my burden of failure, about how I should have made Seva say something at the trial—something that would have redeemed him in their eyes—though for the life of me I don't know what that would have been, what might have worked, what could possibly have swayed them . . .

Enough, then. Nothing further needs to be said now about my former partner or our partnership. Back to where we left off! Reenter Camilla, into whose next dream her father was once again inserted. Along with Seva, for a brief cameo at the end.

TWO

LITTLE OBJECTS *are whirring in a circle around the man's face, which, like the rest of him, is harshly backlit. The blurred movements around his head distract me; I can't make out any of his features. I am alone at the rear of the theater, staring at the stage.*

Stuart, I call, is that you?

No, answers the man as he keeps juggling. How disappointing. You fail to recognize your own father!

I move closer. Now I see: it's Jordan in a tux, his pale face slathered in greasepaint, his eyebrows and lips etched in black and red. His hands are white-gloved, and he sports a yellow cummerbund and patent-leather slippers. His hair's slicked back. He isn't wearing glasses.

How can you do that without your glasses, Jordan?

Practice, my dear. Years of practice. He speeds up his tempo slightly; the shapes make a soft whistling sound as they orbit. They're not balls, but I can't yet tell what they might be.

But you never learned—

Correction: I never studied. I learned—I taught myself! A true vocation requires dedication. You and I are both obsessive. Takes one to know one, doesn't it?

I'm still trying to discern the shapes he's juggling, but they're spinning too quickly. Slow it down a minute, I say, getting up from my seat and climbing onto the stage. I want to look.

He obliges, plucking each object from the air, one by one, until finally they're all resting in the crook of his left arm. Moving to a spotlit area of the stage, he arrays them gently on the floor. We crouch together and examine the objects glinting at us.

They're perfume bottles—seven in all. Some are sharply faceted; others have voluptuously swollen edges. The bottles vary in size, though none is larger than a woman's fist. Some of their stoppers are elongated, some flat topped. Several have been ornately worked into the forms of serpents, bees, or vines. The necks of the bottles are wrapped with delicate gold, silver, or black cord. None of the flacons has a label; all are empty.

Why are there seven? I ask Jordan.

One for each day of the week, he says.

Whose are they?

Who owns them, you mean? Or who designed them? I do. I did.

And their fragrances? Why are they all empty?

Kneeling, my father picks up two bottles and starts juggling them. He adds a third; slowly, sure-handedly, he swipes each of the remaining bottles from the floor and puts them into play, gradually elevating the entire cluster of seven while raising himself from squat to upright.

The fragrances . . . The bottles whiz around his head. Ah, I wish I knew what happened to them, my dear! It's so mysterious. Apparently I can have one or the other—scent or bottle—but not both. Yet without its vessel, the scent vanishes; and without its scent, the vessel is an echo, not actual music, merely an empty echo . . .

He continues juggling for a moment, then lets the bottles drop, one by one. Seven smashing sounds later, my father is surrounded by shards. The spotlight scatters rays of light everywhere.

Jordan, I call, squinting. I can barely make out his form. The light is blinding me. Now what'll you do?

Nearly invisible now, he sings back at me that old Irving Berlin tune: "What'll I do when you are far away . . ."

A quick incandescence (in the midst of which I think I see, off in the wings, a tall man in a dark cape), and my father is gone. I smell his absence, a whiff of bitter chocolate.

⅍

TWO MESSAGES blinked on my answering machine when I arrived home. The first was from Danny, who'd called from the subway. She would stop off at BAM, she informed me, and pick up two more tickets, in case Stuart and Carl could join us. They'd surely enjoy a Robert Wilson outing. If they couldn't make it, no problem—we'd scalp the extras before the performance.

I left her answering machine a grateful response, suggesting we meet at a bar in Fort Greene beforehand; I'd call Stuart, I added, and let him know the plan. Then I listened to my second message.

It was from Nick: the Paramour, as I called him. He'd been in the neighborhood and wanted to stop by for a visit. I pictured him calling from a phone booth, bouncing lightly on the balls of his feet as he spoke into the receiver, all that male energy coursing through him. I could beep him, but it was getting late. He'd probably gone home, and that's one number I didn't dial. Not that it mattered. I'd see him soon enough.

NICK WAS the only man other than Stuart or Sam whose presence in my life I'd have described, then, as continuous. A steady. An odd sort of steady.

He lived on Avenue B in the East Village, in a brownstone he'd bought two decades earlier. The house had high ceilings, long windows, several fireplaces, and four floors of space, one of which Nick rented to a pair of artists who, like him, had lived in the neighborhood forever. He'd been married almost thirty years—to a nurse practitioner—and had two grown sons, both living in Queens. I envisioned a pair of good-looking, humorous guys, very like their father. Though Nick's extended family was massive, his father was the only one I met, not long before he died of a heart attack. He was a shorter, thinner version of Nick, with a gusty laugh and one of those great accents you hear among Brooklyn old-timers—he said "burler" for boiler and "toidy" for thirty.

His death came, I knew, as a blow to his son. Nick and I didn't talk much about it, though. Our conversations rode a different set of rails.

WHAT NICK most liked talking about was his work.

He restored the exteriors of old residential buildings—only old ones; he deplored the construction of new ones. Nick could do amazing things with brownstone, limestone, terra-cotta, and brick. He repaired keystones and capitals and designed ornamental reliefs. Carpentry was a snap for him; he'd been mouthing nails and wielding saws and hammers since he was a kid. The only material he didn't work with was marble—"a whole other ball game," he once said to me cheerfully.

I met Nick while he was repointing some bricks and fixing the façade of a three-story brownstone next to my apartment building. The first time I spotted him, he was up on a scaffolding at the building's roofline, his baseball cap turned backward as he poked a crowbar around the cornice to determine the extent of its damage. When I asked him what he was doing, he looked down at me, turning his cap around before answering—to shield his eyes from the sunlight, he later told me, so he could see the face that went with the voice.

He was a chatterbox. We got to talking, and I noticed his body right away. Heat rayed off him, nearly visible. I've seldom picked up on that kind of sexual force so directly without feeling an accompanying hint of threat, but it was soon obvious I had nothing to fear from him. And I wanted him. He was lean and altogether virile in the best way, without self-consciousness. I'd been without a lover for quite a while; intimacy seemed beyond my reach—no, beyond my ken, really. I'd come to see myself as unschooled, unfit. But here was someone who prompted no memories of marital love, a man who had nothing to do with the life of the heart or mind but plenty to do, evidently, with that of the body. He combined a dog's easygoing nature with a panther's lithe prowl, that coiled force in the hips and thighs. This, I thought, was a nice animal indeed.

We started sleeping together—always at my place, usually in the late afternoon or early evening, when he was supposed to be getting supplies for his job or working out at the gym. Soon a week didn't pass without a visit, often two or three, from Nick. He took to calling me every day, just to check in. Who'd have thought adultery could become so reliable, so nearly domestic?

The Paramour got what I was doing at The Fourth Wall, quickly revealing a keen sense of what was and wasn't collectible. Nick noticed things that escaped everyone else's attention, mine included. A few months after we became involved, he found an antique silver dollar at the corner of West Fourth and West Tenth—a good omen, he claimed, because that intersection is so improbable it's bound to bestow luck. On the windowsill of a building he was restoring in the East Village, he picked up a green plastic disk that looked like a coin and was lettered in Cyrillic. I showed it to Stuart, who determined that it was a token intended for use in Moscow's metro system. When I informed Nick, he was skeptical at first, then pleased at having found something so exotic. One day he entered my shop, put his arms around me from behind, and slipped the token into the front pocket of my jeans—a gift. Into the other, he tucked a black silk thong.

BEFORE MEETING Nick, I'd never asked anyone to help me out on my collecting missions for the shop. Even Sam seldom accompanied me. But occasionally, if Nick had a spare hour or two, I'd take him on a hunt for new inventory. Whenever he went with me, we'd find something unusual to add to my stock.

Even Sam. That phrase came to me often at the start of my affair with Nick. Even Sam hadn't shown such excitement at the sight of spiked heels; even Sam hadn't lapped at me greedily, like a single-minded cat, every time we went to bed. But even Nick couldn't carry away with him, each time he left, the solitude that would surround me afterward, as I lay amidst sheets damp with his sweet saltiness. That solitude—saturated, effulgent, like early-morning air after a night of rainfall—was wholly familiar to me. I'd known it since childhood. To me it was fragranced, and its scent was so singular, so fully mine, not even my father could have identified it.

Looking back, I see Nick and myself playing a kind of hide-and-seek: the hiding, sex; the seeking, its solace. Yet though we did give and take our pleasures, I didn't find him, nor was I found. The game wouldn't work that way.

STUART CALLED me just as I was climbing into bed, reminding me that we needed to enact a recently made deal. I was supposed to hand over to him a small box of old books (mostly plays, along with a few works of criticism), which one of my clients had given me before moving to Europe.

As it happened, I'd come into a mini-treasure. My unwitting benefactor hadn't realized that among the dozen or so books in the box were several rare titles. He also hadn't left a forwarding address. Spoils of war, said Stuart when I told him. He'd offered to sell the books and split the profits with me. Several of his customers were potential takers, he said, and he'd tap them right away.

We agreed to meet at ten-thirty the following morning for the box handoff. Stuart wished me pleasant dreams. Hanging up, I flashed onto the cartwheeling man from my first dream, the one set in St. Petersburg. I could see his sinuous form and masked face, yet I couldn't get the bell in my memory to ring.

AT THE appointed hour, Stuart and I met up at a café midway between our shops and ordered our usual snack of milky coffee and brioche.

Stuart babbled for a while about a party he and Carl had recently attended. Listening to his witty account, I felt a rush of gratitude that we'd managed to stay close for so long. That I had, still, a best friend. He and I had endured tense times, patches of mutual anger and disappointment, but we'd pulled through; I could observe whatever conflicts arose now through a lens of surety. Having failed to master the art of close friendship with anyone else, I felt fortunate to experience with this man a quiet trust in trust itself.

He circled my left wrist with his long fingers. Pulling my hand toward him, he leaned over to examine the bandage covering my thumb.

"What's this?" he asked. "An injury, or some new fad in adornment? Maybe there's a tattoo under here?" He poked gently at the Band-Aid. "Unserious, I presume. And how did we do this to ourselves?"

"It's healing up nicely, thank you."

"Not an answer to my question."

"Food prep," I said. Any mention of sardines would prompt a sarcastic lecturette about eating too healthily.

"Don't tell me," Stuart went on. "You whacked your thumb on a day-old granola bar?"

"*You're* the hypochondriac," I said. "If you ate better, you'd have fewer complaints, real or imaginary."

He performed an exaggerated shrug, the tips of his shoulders nearly touching his earlobes. "Oh wel-l-l-l," he sang, splaying his hands. "At least I'll be able to tell Saint Peter I enjoyed my last meal. Unlike some people who're so damn *renunciatory* . . ."

I cocked an eyebrow at him. "Change of subject," I said. "Do you ever dream about your father?"

"My father?" Across his face flitted a fast shadow, some rogue emotion. "Very seldom. I dream about a lot of other relatives, though. Including my mother, and both my grandparents, and even my second cousin Wendy, whom I haven't seen since I was, oh, maybe ten. So that should tell you something, though I'm not sure what."

He swabbed butter on the remaining half of his brioche and popped it efficiently into his mouth.

"Do you *wish* you dreamed about your father?" I asked.

He shook his head vehemently, then swallowed before answering. "God, no! There's limited time for dreaming—why waste it on *him?*"

Stuart's father had walked out on the family when Stuart was six, leaving an irate mother and an even angrier son. His reaction to my question didn't surprise me.

"But that's not a choice, is it?" I asked.

Stuart pondered this. "You know," he responded finally, "I used to think dreams just happened, and you couldn't assert any control over them, couldn't alter their content. But then I read about lucid dreaming—that's when you're dreaming and you realize it while you're actually inside the dream, you know? And you can change the progress of the dream as it's happening. It's fascinating. We're tinkering much more often than we're aware of, but at the unconscious level, not with our waking minds." He shook his head. "Who knows, maybe I'm dreaming about my father every night." This thought seemed to displease him. "Why'd you ask?" he added.

"I dreamed about my own father last night," I said. "Second time in a row, in fact. Very strange. In last night's dream, it was as though I'd conflated you and him. Jordan was a juggler. He was on-stage, juggling perfume bottles, and he broke them all. Deliberately."

"Jugglers," Stuart said sternly, "are *not* mimes. Jugglers are a bunch of prima donnas. I've seen them throw tantrums and squeal like babies when they're rehearsing. Somebody sneezes, and they fuck up, and then they yell, *Oh my God, you just ruined my whole routine!* Can't stand jugglers. Silly little show-offs." He agitated his coffee with his spoon.

I let him compose himself before continuing. "It was quite weird, this dream," I said. "I mean, all those perfume bottles shattered on the floor. And they were empty, too."

"Well, think how your dream would've smelled if they'd all been full!"

I had to laugh. "Hadn't considered that," I said. "But what stayed with me, when I woke up, was how frustrated my father was. It was hard for him to design bottles, actually. He never liked the packaging side of the business."

Stuart flagged our waitress, who produced a check. He paid, left a generous tip, pocketed his change, and stood up. "Most of your dreams don't involve people you know personally, do they? Which is why I like hearing them—they're so inventive! You know, I loathe it when people throw a bunch of glib psychobabble at their dreams—'Oh, this one was definitely about my submerged libidinal feelings for my dog . . .' Why'd you say you dreamed about your father, by the way? Maybe you were dreaming about *me?*"

"Trust me," I said. "This was definitely about Jordan."

He widened his eyes in fake disbelief. "Fine. I'm not hurt."

As we left the café, Stuart took my hand and swung it broadly. At the corner of Washington Square, we paused. Stuart was about to head north, I was going west.

"Well?" Still holding my hand, he gave it a little squeeze. "What'd you find out about him?"

"About Jordan? I'm not sure that's the question," I said. "I'd like to know what the dream's saying about *me.* There I was, in the audience, watching him, and I actually climbed onstage so I could see what he was juggling. I even asked him to stop so I could take a closer look at the bottles."

Releasing my hand, Stuart licked and then twirled one finger in the air as if testing the direction of the breeze. Using the same finger, he reached over and lightly chucked the tip of my chin.

"Very interesting," he said. "You're a spectator but also an actor. The one under the spell and the one creating the spell . . ."

"That's a bit complicated, buddy."

"Oh, I think not. Not for *you.*" He tapped me on the temple. "You need to remember more of your dream. Usually some missing piece lurks right at the edge of memory. Some detail that's being suppressed. When I first wake up, I often can't recall anything I've dreamed, but then it shows up later, when I least expect it. Like, *Oh no, not* that! *Don't wanna think about* that!" Clamping one hand around his throat and the other over his eyes, he made a strangled noise.

"I know the feeling," I said.

He grinned and turned away, waving. "Bye, darlin'. Be good. Thanks for the theater invite—see you Wednesday! I'll meet you at that bar in Fort Greene beforehand, right? Oh, by the way, did you talk with Danny?"

"Yeah. I'll tell you about it at some point. After I check in with Sam."

Stuart shielded his eyes.

"Cut it out," I said. "And tell Carl I'm sorry he can't make it to BAM." On Wednesdays, Backstage Books stayed open late. Carl had volunteered to stay at the store so Stuart could attend the production.

"I shall tell him," said Stuart. "But don't feel too sorry for him. Last week I spelled him so he could dine with his sister—not the nice one, the witch, the one I detest! See what a good mate I am? Oh, and next time you speak with Danny, tell her I'll give her a check for both tickets. Ciao!"

He hadn't gone far up the block—I could still see his back—when the scent of chocolate came, not to my nose but to memory. *The missing piece,* I nearly called out but didn't. Odd, I thought, to be recalling that scent, so bound up with memories of my father's death. And for Jordan to arrive so vividly in a dream of mine, when he'd been offstage for so long.

As I was opening my shop, the phone began ringing. I caught it just before the answering machine picked up.

"Cam." It was Danny, sounding purposeful. "I've been thinking—are you alone, have you got customers?—I wanted to ask you a favor. Would you go to Ithaca with me next weekend?"

"Ithaca?" Thinking she was referring to either a play or a restaurant, I tried to remember whether I'd heard of either one. Nothing came to mind.

"You know, upstate. Where Cornell University is—where Mom used to live. I'd like to drive up there and do a little research."

"At the university?"

"No. I'd like to talk with someone who lives there."

"Oh," I said, confused; my inner warning lights hadn't begun to flash. "Like a friend from college or something?"

She hesitated a beat before answering. "I'd like to talk with Billy Deveare's sister."

The lights started blinking now. I put down my bag and key ring and sat at my desk. "His sister?"

"Yeah. When I was cleaning out Mom's desk, I found something tucked at the back of a drawerful of stuff—mostly junk, which is why you and I missed it the first time around. It's an invoice from the hospital where I was born. For a procedure Mom underwent a year before my birth. A little less than a year, actually—like about nine months. She was artificially inseminated, Cam."

"You're kidding," I said, though I could tell from her tone that she wasn't.

"Nope. The sperm donor isn't named on the invoice—I guess that's to protect his privacy. But since Billy's on my birth certificate as my father, he's obviously the one."

I was silent for several moments, trying to decide which of my multiple questions to ask. "Danny, what exactly do you want to find out in Ithaca?" I said at last.

"I called directory assistance in Ithaca and found a J. Deveare," she replied. "I dialed the number and a man answered. When I asked if he was related to the late Billy Deveare, he said his wife, Judy, was Billy's sister. Then he asked why I was calling. I hadn't given my name or anything, and I didn't know what to say, so I hung up."

She paused. When she resumed, her tone was more urgent. "But I got the street address from an Ithaca phone book, so I know where they live. Cam, I want to go up there and talk with her. I want to find out if she knew her brother had a kid. I want her to describe Billy to me. And their deal. Mom probably told you what she told me: as soon as she learned she was pregnant, she dumped Billy. And then he died. But what if that wasn't true?"

"That he died?"

"No, of course he died. . . . But I want to find out whatever I can about him, Cam. That means starting with the sister."

I considered my options. If I were to try talking Danny out of her mission, she'd balk. She was obviously determined to go up-state, with or without me. She wouldn't shelve her plan for lack of a companion. And actually, there was no good reason Danny shouldn't go. She'd been told almost nothing about her father. It made sense she'd want to learn more about him at some point. And since the only other person who could've described him—Eve—was gone, Danny was justified in believing that a trip to Ithaca was her best shot.

I CLOSED my eyes. Out of nowhere the masked man from my first dream returned again to my memory. There he was, traveling across the stage with such elastic ease. As soon as he was done, another image arrived, equally unexpected: Eve in her hospital bed, a few hours before her death.

The memory surged, potent and irresistible. I'd been sitting in a chair drawn up to her bedside. No one else had been in the room; Danny had stepped out to speak with one of the nurses. Eve's breathing was labored, and a slick gleam coated her skin, across which the septicemia would shortly travel. She'd smelled stale—this woman who'd worn perfume all her life now gave off a spoiled odor.

After a few minutes alone with her, I'd slipped out of the room and gone to a restroom down the hall, where I'd vomited, wept, and vomited some more. A nurse had fetched me, and I returned to Eve's room just in time to see the rash spreading over her body—a weirdly beautiful, purplish blooming, like a child's finger painting of a lilac tree. Danny had begun crying in short, staccato gasps that didn't cease until Eve herself stopped breathing, an hour later. At that point Danny had fallen completely silent, refusing my moves to hold her, not even allowing me to take her hands in mine. I remembered staring at Danny's hands, then at her mother's, then Danny's again, imagining the difference in their temperatures—Eve's cooling, her daughter's warm.

I OPENED my eyes, aware of the phone at my ear.

"Cam?" Danny was saying. I had no idea how many times she might have repeated my name.

"Is it okay if I give you an answer tomorrow?" I asked.

"All right," she said, clearly disappointed. She'd expected an immediate yes. "I'll call you."

After hanging up, I looked at my left thumb. While cradling the receiver between my shoulder and jaw, I'd fiddled with the bandage until it was twisted, useless. I pulled it off. Time to let the air heal my little wound.

I'D CUT myself in the same place on the same thumb, nineteen years earlier. Closing an old manila envelope, I'd slid my thumb across the back, and a brass prong, surprisingly sharp, had slashed me. A bit of blood had soaked into the yellow-brown envelope, leaving a stain. The slit was nasty, definitely more than a paper cut.

The envelope had been lying among heaps of manila folders and files that filled several large cardboard boxes in Jordan's attic. When my father died, Stuart had offered to help me with the task of sorting and disposing of his belongings. A few days after Jordan's cremation, he and I rented a small van and drove out to Frenchtown, New Jersey, where Jordan had lived for the final ten years of his life. There we spent a humid September weekend rummaging through his possessions.

I'd been surprised to find so much paper. Apart from the usual personal records, Jordan had kept a lot of information on the perfume industry, some of it three or four decades old. I discovered several letters from French colleagues, thanking him for his assistance and urging him to visit again. He'd also maintained numerous files on the theater, crammed with program notes, reviews, and articles about actors, directors, and productions.

My father loved theater. I suppose I could say my own love of it came from him, but in a passive, indirect way, not through any conscious incitement. Going to the theater was our only shared pastime, but our tastes were frequently at odds. Still, Jordan had passed along to me an instinctive leaning toward theater as nourishment unattainable anywhere else—not in books, certainly not onscreen.

Like everything else in his attic, Jordan's theater files were covered with dust. Flipping through them, I felt a little giddy with sadness, imagining all the hours my father had sat by himself in theaters around the world. Wherever he went—Brazil, Japan, Egypt, Finland—he'd attended stage and musical performances of all kinds. He would have dressed impeccably, wearing his wire-rimmed glasses to catch those sorts of small details that other people miss even after several viewings of a performance.

As I was stuffing the theater files back into a box, Stuart discovered a smaller carton, labeled "Russia," tucked behind a steamer trunk filled with yellowed sheets and towels. From it he extracted a handful of manila envelopes and flapped them in front of me.

"Recognize these?" he asked.

I took a quick look at one of the envelopes, which contained materials related to a visit Jordan had made to Moscow and Leningrad, five years earlier—one of his last trans-Atlantic voyages. Before that brief trip, Jordan had never been behind the Iron Curtain. He'd gone, he said, to satisfy his curiosity, and he'd returned home without much to report. Moscow's metro system with its beautiful mosaics and lighting fixtures had fascinated him, and he'd praised the perfume bottles he'd seen in the Hermitage Museum in Leningrad. The ballet was excellent, the theater iffy—though he'd seen a revival of a satirical play by Vladimir Mayakovsky, *The Bedbug,* whose staging he'd pronounced masterful even given that he understood none of the words. Apart from those highlights, the Soviet Union hadn't impressed him. He'd returned with a few bars of unpleasant chocolate and a little gift for Eve and me: we each got one of those painted dolls with a set of smaller dolls inside them.

"Never saw this stuff," I answered Stuart. "It's from Jordan's trip to Russia."

He returned to his packing, and I glanced at the remaining contents of the Russia box. As far as I could tell, its envelopes contained tourist information: articles from travel magazines, brochures on the Kremlin galleries, a catalog from the Pushkin Museum. Several flyers advertised hotels that looked like hideous concrete bunkers.

Reinserting these materials into their envelope, I cut my thumb. I remember wrapping it in some paper towel and securing the pseudo-bandage with brown packing tape. Afterward Stuart and I filled up the van and drove to the Salvation Army office in Somerville, where we dropped off all of Jordan's clothing and several pieces of furniture. A nice woman at the Salvation Army gave me a smaller bandage for my thumb so I could drive back to the city with a firm grip on the wheel.

Soon thereafter I looked over all of Jordan's theater files. As I'd suspected, they contained nothing noteworthy, nor anything I wished to keep, so I threw them out. I decided to examine the Russia files some other time; that carton went into my basement storage bin. Occasionally, as the years passed, I'd remember it was still there and wonder if a few theater or concert programs might be tucked away in it—maybe even something signed. Or Jordan might have jotted notes on performances he'd attended at the Bolshoi and the Alexandrinsky. Possible, but unlikely. Jordan hadn't kept records of his travels; he didn't own a camera or photo albums. He wasn't the type to leave traces. That, he would have said, is what fragrances are for.

MY FATHER'S perfumes melded coolness and warmth, elegance and carnality. It was impossible not to feel drawn in by them. They operated at a deep level of sublimation, a place where safety and risk mingle and cannot be untangled.

For Jordan, perfume was more than anything else an acknowledgment of impermanence. Fragrance is time-bound: it ends in decay. Rather than attempting to deny or overcome this reality, Jordan found ways of exploiting it. He orchestrated his fragrances' life spans like beautifully shaped musical compositions. Magically mobile, they registered in the mind like a dream.

He taught me the basics of perfume making when I was young—enough for me to gain a dim sense of what he did in his lab, and to appreciate the ways in which his efforts resembled those of a painter or a composer. Jordan worked with a remarkably broad palette, celebrating even the most familiar pairings, such as rose and jasmine, or lily and narcissus. The harmonies of his perfumes were complex, and the extraordinary range of their textures—from airy to dense, silken to flinty—sparked envy among his colleagues. Gradually I came to understand that Jordan's scent-notes met the nose as an arpeggio meets the ear. They were successions of olfactory sensation, always quick and light, in perpetual motion.

Once I asked my father why the same fragrance didn't ever seem to smell the same way twice on the person wearing it. Jordan replied that I must have a good nose: not many people were aware of what I'd noticed. This bit of praise I relished for its unexpectedness. Then he went on to describe the complicated interplay of fixatives (chemical agents added to a perfume so it could "cling" to its wearer) with the wearer's own unstable skin secretions and body temperature—both of which made it impossible for a perfume applied on one day to smell just as it would if reapplied on another.

Perfume's like a song, he concluded. Or a play. Each time it's performed, it gives you something different.

Jordan was a master of forest scents culled from ferns, mosses, lichen, roots, bark, and resin. He harnessed their shade and smoke to the sweetness of hyacinth and violet, or the assertive spiciness of sandalwood and patchouli, creating perfumes that were overtly lush and serene but covertly turbulent, their sensuality in constant flux. He was one of the few perfumists of his generation who could handle fruits with real authority, using their essences to generate spritely top notes in fragrances buoyed by grassy or floral layers and underpinned by a calming basis of oakmoss and musk. Jordan's fruity fragrances managed to convey what few in that category do: an unmistakable erotic charge, at first innocent seeming but soon enigmatic, insinuating, unnerving.

And with the "orientals"—opulent scents such as amber and vetiver—Jordan created fragrances that were provocative without ever resorting to vulgarity. Theirs was a lingering touch that imprinted itself on memory yet tricked memory, too, for it couldn't be duplicated. I think of Jordan's perfumes as secret passwords each wearer decoded on her own.

I HAVE my own theory about fragrances and how they work. Perfume disturbs self-recognition, and this disorientation is deeper than the confusion brought about by, say, wearing tinted contact lenses or someone else's clothing. Suddenly the perfume wearer co-exists with a person who looks, sounds, tastes, and feels to the touch exactly like herself or himself but *smells* different. And this gives the perfume wearer permission to *be* different—not necessarily in an alarming or radical way, but still, the capacity has been activated.

My father loved creating substances that possessed the power to redirect personalities. Fragrances allowed him to play an endless game of possibility in the theater of desire. And then there was that other theater, death's. As any undertaker can attest, fragrances are excellent not only for enhancing a romance but also for disguising the smell of decay. Especially fragrances featuring Jordan's favorite white flowers: orchids, lilies, narcissus, and gardenia.

Most people can't imagine the death of a loved one without the presence of bouquets of white flowers. Tranquil and reassuring, these blossoms often show up on coffins and in funeral processions. My father, however, spurned this use of scent for himself. He wanted his long and intimate relationship with fragrance to terminate with his own ending. The day of his death, I found a note under his pillow, written in a spidery but legible hand. *Cremation*, it read, *and no flowers, please*.

IN MIDAFTERNOON, I hung my BACK IN TWENTY MINUTES sign in my window and made a quick delivery to the townhouse of a client on Barrow Street. The day was mild, my fast walk revivifying.

A few days earlier, this client had purchased from me a photo of an old theater in Dorchester, Massachusetts, which had been renovated in the 1970s. The picture (which I'd found in a piano bench in a Union Square antiques dive) showed the theater's unrenovated interior. My customer had been involved with a performing-arts center housed in this theater, and although she had plenty of pictures of the refurbished space, she'd never seen a photograph of the mess it had once been. I offered to frame one of her "after" photos along-side my "before" photo, and to deliver the pair to her in time for a dinner party she was to host that evening. For this she'd compensated me handsomely.

After running my errand, I returned to The Fourth Wall. A little decal was affixed to the glass of my shop's front door. It was a clown, brightly costumed, beneath whose outstretched hands a folded note had been tucked.

Stuart, I thought. But when I pried the note away from the decal's sticky backing and opened it, I saw it was from Danny, thanking me for hearing her out. Would I please set aside whatever qualms I might have and take a ride with her to Ithaca?

Refolding her note, I caught from it a quiet whiff of Danny's perfume. The little clown would be tricky to peel off the glass; its adhesive resisted my thumbnail. Leave it, I decided, pressing the decal back on the door with my forefinger. And go to Ithaca with Danny. Why not?

INTERLUDE

CAMILLA'S FRIEND Stuart is too hard on jugglers. Seva always held them in high regard, and I agree with his assessment.

A fine juggler isn't an entertainer, after all, but an artist who works in the most challenging medium of all: air. I'd say Stuart is rather competitive, which is only to be expected. The tension a mime generates onstage derives entirely from his physical presence. If he wants to incorporate objects into his act, he must evoke them himself, inciting the viewer's imagination. His is the art of making the immanent actual, which is even more difficult than keeping multiple balls afloat at once.

Stuart's a good mime, though lazy. He's physically elastic and possesses a sharp eye for details. He's also got a sense of humor—and he's a theater man, so he knows his antecedents. More centrally, he's aware of his vulnerabilities yet not ensnared by them.

Weakness acknowledged is a performer's most renewable resource, the wellspring of his power. This paradox happens to be as valid offstage as on, a fact I emphasized to Seva on numerous occasions. He and I never saw eye to eye on the question of self-exposure. When he was imprisoned, I tried everything in my power to get him to pretend compliance—to think pragmatically, in other words—but his love for Russia had by then gotten all tangled up in his love for his work. Was my failure to allow for this ultimately responsible for what finally happened? Or by the time he got to Butyrka, was it already too late for a different outcome?

Occasionally I bring to mind a speech that Niels Bohr, the Danish theoretical physicist, gave to an audience of his peers, back in the mid-Twenties. Bohr was describing something he called the complementarity principle, which he applied to quantum systems. For any quantity that can be measured, Bohr explained, there is another, "complementary," quantity—and the more accurately you measure the one, the more impossible it is to measure the other at the same time.

As might be imagined, this idea took some digesting, though

Bohr explained it elegantly. At one point somebody asked him rather provocatively, "What is complementary to truth?"

"Clarity," Bohr answered, without missing a beat.

Amen to that. Too bad Seva wasn't there to hear him say it.

CAMILLA WASN'T at ease with her decision to go to Ithaca with her cousin's daughter. And for good reason: Danny's father-quest looked to be a fraught undertaking.

I predicted that when things boiled over (as they were bound to do), Danny would have a harder time of it than Camilla. She seemed a bit of a golden girl, untested by difficulty. She might require serious babysitting.

Yet before long, I began viewing her situation differently. The chief challenge she faced wasn't finding herself suddenly alone after her mother's death, but rather being forced to manage unwieldy emotions. Not everyone handles improvisation with aplomb! Even good actors can be thrown by it.

Seva used to assign each of his players a set of *praktikabli,* prepared places on the stage. Sometimes the cast members would fall apart completely when their *praktikabli* were altered without their foreknowledge. Watching Danny get tossed around by anger, grief, and confusion, I revised my opinion of her. She was handling her assignment just fine, all things considered.

BUT I spin ahead of myself—rather, of the two road-trippers . . .

The first of Camilla's nighttime dramas provided her father with a minor role; the next placed him front and center. Not yet encountered on Camilla's dream-stage, however, was her mother. *That* crucial personage, I decided, would have to make an appearance before Camilla left for Ithaca. No point delaying the encounter.

So for our third co-production, I prompted my collaborator to return to her earliest theater—that apartment on Ninth Street where she was raised—and unlock its doors and enter. Once inside she'd find everything topsy-turvy: the perfect Meyerholdian set, in other words!

THREE

THE KEY to the building's front door is the large brass one. I put my left shoulder to the door and turn the key in the lock. The door gives way, as it always used to do, with a little groan. Passing through the tile-floored vestibule, I walk down the familiar hallway to the stairs on the right, ascend three flights, and proceed a few paces until I'm standing in front of the door to the apartment.

It swings open noiselessly. Instead of finding myself in the front hall, however, I see I'm somewhere else altogether: in an enormous laboratory. Small vials arrayed on large chrome racks line the vast room's walls. The space smells of nothing at all, the perfect absence of odor.

Thinking it impossible that I could be smelling actual nothingness, I turn to my father, who is standing at my side. Underneath his white lab coat (I too am wearing one, its cotton stiffly clean, its cuffs neatly folded back), Jordan is sporting a tuxedo. His shoes are black patent-leather loafers, very dressy.

I sniff loudly, then raise my eyebrows questioningly. Jordan says nothing, though I know he's understood my query: Why no smells?

I begin inspecting several vials lying on the huge worktable in front of me. The table's gray surface looks like a slick metallic sea, so long and wide that I can't make out whatever's on its opposite side. Each of the vials before me has been labeled in my father's meticulous hand. Their contents appear to be powders in various neutral shades. Some look like dust, others like finely ground mica, still others like cornmeal, sand, or flour.

Jordan hands me a large mortar and pestle, and I empty several vials into the mortar's deep marble well.

Did you read their labels first? Jordan asks.

No, I say. Why should I? What difference does it make?

It makes a big difference, he snarls. Stop acting like you haven't a clue what you're about to do.

Oh come on, I respond, my tone placating. This isn't the time for you to start picking on me about the details. Be glad I'm here! How would you do this without me? Smiling, I wag my forefinger at him. I'm it, Jordan: your one and only! Show me some gratitude, why don't you?

He nods brusquely. Get on with it, he orders. Mix in some of that— he points at another vial—and then add this beaker of water. He hands me a clear plastic cup filled to its brim, and I pour the water into the mortar after adding the vial's contents.

Now swish it all around with the pestle. Make sure you break up any lumps, he says.

I do as I'm instructed. The mixture gives off an unfamiliar smell; my nose wrinkles. Whew, I say. Strong.

Jordan nods. Solanum dulcamara: *bittersweet.*

He loosens his silk bow tie, which I recognize. Eve gave it to him for his birthday—which one, fiftieth, sixtieth? I can't recall. Everything that's come before this moment is a blur; all I know is I'm in this lab with my father, assisting him.

Now the pudding, says Jordan.

I open the door of a refrigerator behind me and pull out a small crystal bowl filled with a jelled brown substance. A silver spoon stands upright at its center. As I hand the bowl to Jordan, the spoon wobbles slightly.

Follow me, he states. And don't forget that, he adds, pointing at the mortar.

He climbs onto the table, still holding the crystal bowl. I manage somehow to climb up as well, mortar in hand, and seat myself in front of him.

We're now in a small sailboat whose rudder Jordan grasps with his free hand. We are sailing across the gray sea of the table, cutting swiftly through the placid waters, our bow aimed directly at a dark object on the other shore. A steady wind is strong enough to propel us forward without rocking us. Although only one sail is up, we're making good progress. The table edge from which we've departed recedes, nearly vanishing as the upcoming shoreline—the opposite edge—comes into view.

What's that? I ask, pointing at the object on shore. Seen from our vantage point, it looks to be a fairly narrow wooden box about six feet long.

Grasse, Jordan answers. In France. Near the Riviera.

I didn't ask where, I asked what.

Don't be peevish, he retorts. You always wanted to go to France with me, and now I'm taking you. Aren't you glad?

It's a little late for that, I say, turning around to glare at him.

His smile is sidelong. Ah well, some daughters are just hard to please.

Hard to please? I say, incredulous. Are you out of your mind? No, I get it—you're trying to guarantee my final memories of you will be angry ones, aren't you? Aren't I right? I stand, but the boat nearly tips, so I sit down again.

Calm yourself, Cammie, Jordan says. We're almost there.

He brings down the sail, and we continue drifting toward the box. In a few moments we pull up alongside it and hop out of the boat, which promptly disappears.

We approach the box. I am following Jordan, who walks with his usual gracefulness, though I notice his gait has changed: it's slightly wolfish, as though he were stalking prey. He's no longer wearing a lab coat, nor am I. I'm in an elegant suit with a closely fitted peplum jacket and knee-length skirt, very early-Dior and lovely. My father's tux is cut like the one Humphrey Bogart wore in Casablanca. *We look like a French couple from the 1950s.*

Reaching the box, Jordan moves to one of its sides; I stand at the other. He lifts its lid, hinged on my side; I feel it graze my kneecaps. We both stare in.

A woman is lying on her back in the box, her eyes closed. Although her face is heavily veiled, her naked body is swaddled in a layer of sheer fabric—muslin, it must be—through which I can perceive her full breasts and hips, the red polish on her fingernails and toenails, the dark hair of her pubis. She is at rest on a white satin coverlet. Next to her is an empty space, lightly indented.

Jordan steps into the box and settles into the awaiting space. Sitting upright next to the woman, he tenderly places his palm on her thigh for a moment, then stares up at me. He is still holding the crystal bowl with its erect spoon.

He points at my mortar. Time for administration, he says. But first the chocolate pudding.

He ladles the bowl's contents into his mouth so rapidly I can't imagine how he's had time to swallow. Then he extends one hand toward me, beckoning me closer.

Ready? I ask.

He nods, and the sudden change in his expression—it's now utterly gentle—astonishes me. Removing the spoon from Jordan's bowl, I dip it into the mortar. Jordan opens his mouth; I feed him slowly, using the spoon's rim to catch small dribbles. The potion must taste dreadful, but Jordan's expression never changes. He is gazing at me blissfully, gratefully. Neither of us speaks until he has swallowed his last spoonful. Then he lies down, closing one of his hands over the wrist of the woman lying next to him.

Now, he says to me quietly. Close it.

Can I get in, too? I ask.

He shakes his head, a tender negative. No room, he says.

As I begin closing the lid of the box, I hear his voice again, very low. I hover over the two of them, Jordan and the woman, straining to hear.

Enfin, Camilla, he is murmuring to her as the lid drops. At last.

⁜

THE LITTLE clown Danny had affixed to my window remained on my mind as I closed my shop on Tuesday afternoon and took a walk up to Eve's old garden store in Chelsea. I hadn't visited since we'd sold it and was curious to see if it was as attractive as it had been under Eve's management.

En route I passed a kitchen supply store. Its windows were nicely dressed. Blue-and-white checked tablecloths had been hung as backdrops for a display of kitchen implements—everything from whisks and workbowls to soufflé dishes. Among them was a small mortar and pestle.

Noticing it, I paused and stared, and something in my mind dislodged like a piece of fruit falling from a tree. Jordan, in a dream (had it been only last night?), the two of us mixing a concoction in a lab, then getting into some kind of boat . . . The scenes blurred as soon as they arose. I could remember nothing clearly except for a bowl of chocolate pudding, the thought of which launched a bright flare of anxiety.

I couldn't shake the notion that I'd somehow journeyed to the site of my parents' deaths. Hadn't there been a box, coffinlike, into which Jordan had climbed? And hadn't my mother been in that box, veiled, her features indiscernible? I saw the slow, tender shake of Jordan's head as he refused to let me join the two of them. Then I let the dream go.

A FEW blocks later I found myself in front of Eve's shop. Its storefront window now sported an uninspired sign—CHELSEA GARDEN SUPPLIES—in place of Eve's THE MAD GARDENER. The banality of the new sign irritated me, and I couldn't make myself enter the store.

Eve had taken her shop's name from *The Mad Gardener's Song,* a tale in verse by Lewis Carroll about the hallucinations of a crazy horticulturalist. When Jordan was sick, he'd read that funny tale aloud to Danny, who'd loved the delightful black-and-white drawings. Standing outside my father's study one morning, I'd heard their two voices (Jordan's low and weak, Danny's high and strong) reciting the lines in unison. Jordan had explained to her that the Mad Gardener lived in a country called England, whose capital was London. He'd then described St. James's Park—his favorite spot, he'd said, in that city. Years earlier, he told Danny, he'd taken a memorable walk in the park, a long stroll on a damp June morning during which the air had turned the most beautiful pearly-gray color he'd ever seen.

Overhearing Jordan, I'd convinced myself it was a good thing he was telling six-year-old Danny such stories. Having made myself think this, I'd turned away, finding the thought too painful to maintain. Here was my father, talking freely with a little girl he barely knew. . . . When I was Danny's age, Jordan hadn't ever recounted to me anything remotely as tranquil as the tale he'd told her. In the past *I'd* heard about, there'd been no peaceful early-morning strolls. There'd been perfume and Paris; work and the unacknowledged presence of my mother.

FOR ALL Jordan's travels, France was the country he knew best. Paris was nearly as familiar to him as New York, and equally as important professionally.

He made his first trip to Grasse, the flower-growing region in France where some of the world's best perfumes have originated, in 1929. One of the few American chemists of his generation to visit Grasse regularly, he got to know it well. Back then, before World War II, Grasse led the industry. During the war the region was cut off from clients and suppliers, and by 1950 large foreign investors had already started moving in.

When I was a little girl, Jordan told me that scientists were kicking the flowers out of the picture. I didn't understand what he was saying, and imagined a group of men in heavy boots, stomping on roses. What he'd meant, of course, was that natural aromatics—the industry's name for the stunningly scented flowers and herbs that grow so abundantly in Grasse—were soon to be eclipsed by the cloned cells with which chemists could now make artificial flower oils. As far as perfume was concerned, the French Riviera would never be the same.

"With perfume, everything comes back to natural ingredients," Jordan said to me once. He was praising his French colleague Edmond Roudnitska, the *parfumeur* who developed Femme and Diorama, for refusing to jump on the bandwagon of synthetics. "Roudnitska keeps telling these corporate guys, yes, you can use amyl salicylate to mimic certain fern or floral notes—it's cheaper. But if you substitute too many synthetics, you'll end up with average perfume for average noses. Like a plastic fern plant. That's where things are headed."

There aren't many truly gifted "noses," olfactory artists. This helps account for the mystique of good perfume. To meld and balance scents, a nose has to discern the subtlest of differences among thousands of smells, as well as among ever-so-slightly-varied batches of the same elements. For all but the best perfumists, this is extremely difficult to do. If, say, the night-blooming jasmine in Grasse reaches its peak earlier than a manufacturer has anticipated, the perfumist must be able to identify jasmine from elsewhere—a crop that, when substituted for the original, will ensure a consistent personality for the perfume being produced. Mistakes are costly.

MY FATHER enjoyed a long, internationally active career in fragrance. Although his official retirement took place when he was sixty-five, he continued to play an advisory role in several companies, both American and French, which had employed him over the years. He didn't stop working until he was seventy-four. Younger biochemists were frequently impressed to learn that Jordan Archer had been in the business long enough to have worked for Coty before World War II.

Shortly before he retired for good, Jordan helped design a glass device resembling a fortune-teller's crystal ball, which he dubbed "the smell trap." Its purpose was to capture floral aromas so they could be transported over long distances. Jordan's colleagues knew of his artistry but hadn't realized just what a fine scientist he'd always been. The smell trap was a memorable finale for his career.

Yet my father never became a top-level corporate man. He must have communicated to his managers what I'd learned about him when I was a child: Jordan was a solo player. And although he earned a good living, he wasn't a big consumer. The only things of real value in his apartment were several works by the German artist Max Beckmann, which Jordan had acquired during his first trip to Paris, in 1925. That year, Galerie Druet, a showcase for emerging artists, held a show of contemporary painters; viewing it, Jordan sensed that Beckmann, already popular, would become a major talent. He bought an oil painting and several sketches—one of which was a study for Beckmann's famous portrait of an actor in circus acrobat attire, a thin man who looks Mephistophelean. I've had several generous offers for this sketch, which hangs in my shop, but I'll never part with it.

JORDAN STAYED with Coty for over twenty years. He knew the key players in the major French firms and was on a first-name basis with the much-revered Henri Almeras, who had worked for Poiret at Parfums de Rosine. I imagine my father must have been a popular guest at Parisian dinner parties: smart, suave, and amusing in his spare, understated way.

It was in 1928, while he was in Paris on an assignment for Coty, that he met my mother, a young American expatriate. They didn't marry until 1949, though—a few months before her death, after which Jordan resigned from Coty and returned with me to New York. There he took a job with Jean Patou.

This change of employers had no noticeable effect on his traveling, which remained frequent. During my elementary school years, my father made a great many trips to Patou's headquarters in Paris as well as to Grasse. I used to pester him to take me with him to France so I could see my birthplace, but Jordan always refused, brooking no arguments. His absences made me panicky. On days when he was preparing to leave, I would try to barricade the apartment's front door, and Dan or Sarah would have to restrain me. I still remember my rage at all three adults; it flits over me from time to time, a shadow feeling, shapeless yet palpable.

Jordan switched employers again when I was in high school, this time basing himself permanently in New York. He still traveled, but he seldom went anywhere except France for business. The rest of his trips were for his own pleasure, and he always took them alone. I stayed home with my uncle and aunt. They put up with Jordan's shirking of his paternal duties because they were dependent on him financially.

IN THE family apartment, Jordan sometimes stayed up all night. He'd sit in a chair in the living room, his feet on the floor, his fore- arms and hands on the chair's armrests: a formal pose, as if for a photographer. His eyes were open, I assume, though I can't swear to this. I also assume he was ruminating, remembering, regretting. I can only guess at the mix.

I discovered this nocturnal habit of my father's because I was wakened occasionally by nightmares. Now and then, I'd get up around three in the morning, unable to speak a word, my lips pasted shut. My bad dreams weren't of monsters or other dangers but of speechlessness. I'd scramble out of bed, and gradually, as I stood in- haling and exhaling noisily through my nose, my panic would abate and I'd be able to open my mouth. Then, gulping air down my throat, breathing but still not able to talk, I'd make my way slowly down the dark hallway toward the living room, hands outstretched at either side, checking for the walls.

The living room had a green-and-cream rug whose fanciful Art Nouveau pattern enchanted me. I loved to sit cross-legged on it, tracing its stylized vines beneath the tips of my forefingers. At night, if a bad dream roused me, I'd go to the living room and curl up on the rug, pretending it was my hammock, imagining myself safely bowered in a canopy of vines. Slowly my body would uncoil and I'd fall back asleep. Early in the morning, hearing my uncle open and close his bathroom door, I'd get up and pad quietly back down the hall to my room so no one would know where I'd been.

Jordan knew, though. Sometimes as I lay on the living room floor waiting for the room's serene darkness to rescue me, I'd hear a low-voiced question: *You all right, Cam?* The first time this happened, I was completely startled. I told my father I was fine, just couldn't sleep. *You'll get there,* Jordan murmured, and we both stayed put, he in his chair, me on the rug.

After that initial shock, I was prepared to find him in the living room, whether he spoke or not. His dimly silhouetted form no longer startled me, nor did his presence prevent me from falling asleep. I knew he'd be gone when I awoke. A blanket would cover me, the sole evidence I hadn't dreamt him.

WHEN I was three, I was told by Jordan that my mother had become sick in Paris and had to stay there after I was born. Once I became old enough to grasp the notion of death, the story was emended: Camilla had actually died in Paris, which was why she hadn't returned to New York to live with us.

I remember groping to understand this revision. My mother was no longer in an apartment in Paris, stricken and weak, like Sleeping Beauty under a spell. She was several feet underground, wearing a nice dress.

It was sixteen-year-old Eve, not Jordan, who told me the full truth about Camilla's death. This revelation took place in the bathroom. Having clumsily knocked my toothbrush off the side of the sink and into the wastebasket, I'd decided to use Eve's, and she'd caught me in midact. My unauthorized usage of her toothbrush angered her, and she hissed something to the effect that I was the real reason my mother wasn't alive. Camilla hadn't gotten sick—that was a fib. It was childbirth that had done her in.

Those were Eve's words: "done her in." She must have heard that expression in some gangster movie. I didn't know what the phrase meant, but it sounded final. After rapidly piecing together the little I'd heard about the delivery of babies, I came to a disturbing conclusion.

You mean, I asked, my mother *died* pushing me out?

Yep, said Eve.

After a moment of stunned silence, I dropped Eve's toothbrush on the floor. Her eyes went wide with disbelief, imagining I'd done it on purpose. She called me a little witch then, and I didn't defend myself, because I knew she had to be right: *I* was the reason my mother had died. I began crying, and Eve pulled me into a brusque hug.

I'm sorry, Cammie, really sorry, she said, rubbing my back vigorously. Then she hustled me down the hall and into my room, away from the kitchen, where Sarah and Dan were having an after-dinner coffee. Jordan was in France.

Eve tucked me into bed. Sitting next to me, she ran her index finger lightly over my eyebrows. The sensation of her fingertip repeatedly stroking my brows from inside to outside reassured me.

Listen, she said. You had to find out sooner or later that Camilla wasn't just hanging around in Paris. You understand? It's not such a big deal.

She gave my shoulder a little shake, and I nodded affirmatively. I actually did feel better. Camilla remained a pale beauty lying in a lovely coffin. Nothing about this vision would require alteration.

Plus, said Eve, I'm like your mother now! Aren't I?

I thought Sarah was like my mother, I said.

Eve made a dismissive gesture. Sarah's my father's wife, that's all. She's not like either of our mothers! It's much better if you think of me as Camilla. I look like her, don't I?

She did. I'd often noticed that the one photo of Camilla in the family apartment—a portrait taken during my mother's final year of high school—revealed a strong resemblance to Eve.

But I thought you were like my sister, I said.

Well, I'm that, too! But mostly I'm like your mother.

This pleased me enormously, and surprised me, too. It made me feel I was special to her, and except for Jordan, there was no one but Eve for whom I wanted to be special.

Good, I finally managed to say.

I'll tell your father you know what happened to Camilla, Eve said. That way, you and he won't have to talk about it. Okay?

Okay, I said, nodding.

Eve must have done exactly what she said she would do. Or so I concluded. Twenty-five years passed before my father and I spoke directly about my mother's death.

I RETURNED home from my nonvisit to Eve's store and hopped in the shower, in need of a cooldown after my brisk walk to Chelsea and back. I'd just finished toweling off when my buzzer rang.

There stood the Paramour, holding a present: a blue box tied with a bold orange satin ribbon. From it spilled a collection of new playthings, the most outlandish of which was a black lace-up corset trimmed in velvet. Everything was just the right size, I could tell.

Nick grinned like a boy in a firehouse. "Equipment," he said.

"You've outdone yourself," I replied. I motioned him to follow me into my bedroom, where he undressed while watching me outfit myself in my new gear. Then he proceeded, in his usual languorous, attentive, and well-paced manner, to strip me of each of my just-received gifts while administering others. I returned the favor, our bodies a fine entanglement.

When we were done, I turned on my side to face him. He began idly running one of his large, coarse-skinned thumbs across my forehead. "What's news?" he asked.

"Not much," I answered. "Except for the fact that Danny seems to be losing it."

"Losing it?" Nick had met Danny once or twice. I'd never introduced him to Eve, though she'd asked to meet him. I hadn't wanted to watch her perform a seduction, as I'd assumed she would, nor had I wished to see Nick succumb, as I'd suspected he might.

"You mean Danny's not going to work, not eating, something like that?" Nick added.

"No, she's functioning all right. It's just that she's decided she wants to find out more about her father. She never knew him—he died when she was a few years old."

Though varied, Nick's facial expressions were easy to interpret. He gave me one of his "So?" looks.

I filled him in on Danny's plan. I'd agreed to go to Ithaca only because I didn't want Danny to feel abandoned, I said.

At this, Nick propped himself up on one elbow. "But you have to go with her if she wants you to," he stated. "You're all she's got. There aren't any other relatives, right? You're basically her mother now."

I sat up. "That's not true," I said, hearing, as soon as I'd spoken, the tightness in my voice. "The fact that Eve's dead doesn't change a thing in that department."

Nick raised one eyebrow. "Be realistic, Cam. The girl's what, twenty-five? And she has no parents, no siblings, no aunts or uncles or cousins. Only you, right?"

"And my ex," I said. I walked to my closet, pulled out my robe and moccasins, and put them on briskly. "Danny's close to Sam and his family. She babysits for his kids fairly often."

"Whatever. The point is, *you're* the only person Danny can really rely on now. Everyone else is secondary."

I turned to face him. "Actually I'm feeling a little secondary myself. Here I've agreed to run up to Ithaca on a wild-goose chase for some guy who's been dead for years. Kind of silly, don't you think? It's not like I have all the time in the world for a road trip."

"Well, what else is biting into your schedule?"

The delivery of the question was neutral, without a hint of sarcasm, yet it felt like a laceration. "This little jaunt isn't something I feel like doing, Nick," I answered. "But I'm going with her anyway. So let's give me credit for that, okay?"

He got up from my bed. "I just don't think it's that big a deal, baby," he said quietly, as he began to dress. "Maybe if she learns something about her other parent—the one she never got to know—she'll feel better."

"And if he turns out to have been a real loser?"

Nick carefully folded the corset and rolled the stockings into a neat wad before handing the lot to me. "Knowing something's better than knowing nothing," he said.

"We'll see. And now you need to go, bud—I have things to do tonight," I lied, wanting suddenly and fiercely to be alone.

"Okay," he replied gamely. "I'm off to the gym, then."

AT MY front door, he embraced and kissed me. I smelled his familiar scent, a mix of lovemaking and aftershave, and a little war erupted in me: *stay—go!* After ushering him out, I listened to the sound of his footsteps diminishing, then leaned against the door, exhausted.

I hadn't actually had a solid night's rest, I realized, since Eve's death. Rousing myself, I pushed off from the door and headed down the hall, lured by the thought of a bath. As I drew the hot water and added a handful of gardenia-scented bath salts—another gift from Nick—I pictured a recumbent figure, a woman swaddled in something like sheer muslin. Now it returned: the dream of the boat and the box.

Settling into my tub, I inhaled the perfumed vapors, aware of the tension knotting my neck. Nick was right, I had to admit. Nobody else in Danny's circle knew the cast of characters or the earlier acts as I did. We'd go to Ithaca, and Danny would find her father—intimations of him, anyway. Maybe some clues, a few hard facts. But Eve would elude us, and Danny would feel frustrated without knowing why.

AT THE start of 1980, when Danny was six, Jordan was diagnosed with cancer. I began going out to his house in Frenchtown on weekends; Eve and Danny visited regularly as well. Danny entertained Jordan—they played checkers or read stories—while Eve gardened and I cooked for him, stockpiling his refrigerator with meals. Eve told Danny something about Jordan's condition, and I stuck to the bare facts: Jordan was ill, he tired easily.

His cancer spread aggressively. In April his doctors determined that surgery and further chemotherapy would be pointless. The endgame wouldn't be protracted, we were told, and Jordan would be best off at home, with nursing help when necessary.

He took the news squarely. I hired several attendants from a private agency; on weekdays they prepared his meals, helped him bathe, and administered his medications. I came out on weekends, which was enough for him, he said, and for me as well.

By June he was sometimes in a dopey haze. His will, he'd told me, stipulated that half his money and all the proceeds from the sale of the Frenchtown house would go to me; some money would be left to Eve, the rest to Danny. He'd already surrendered his trusty Volvo to my cousin. But he wasn't able to give me clear instructions about what to do with the rest of his possessions; he didn't care how I disposed of them. He'd already set up a living trust to protect his estate from undue taxation. With practical matters, my father was fastidious.

It was during that summer, as he steadily weakened, that Jordan and I began finally to converse in detail about the past. His, that is, not ours; he and I didn't have much of one. Mostly he talked about his perfume-making and theatergoing experiences. Other people, I soon realized, didn't figure strongly in his narrative. A few weeks before his death, on an overcast morning in early August, I heard at last the story of my mother.

THAT STORY was initiated by another: the account of Jordan's chance encounter with Vsevolod Meyerhold in a small Paris hotel at which both men happened to be staying.

I was naturally quite surprised when Jordan mentioned the Russian theater director's name. I knew well who he was, having read about him over the years. Emboldened by my enthusiastic response, my father began reminiscing about the brief time he'd spent in Meyerhold's company.

He'd had drinks, he said, with the director and his wife at the hotel's bar, then invited the couple to join him for supper the next evening. They'd had a few more meals together, including a final dinner at which Jordan spent a small fortune on a bottle of Chablis.

It had rained lightly that night; Jordan lent Meyerhold his umbrella so the director and his wife could take a post-dinner walk through the damp streets.

I pressed Jordan to describe the Russians' appearance. Meyerhold was tall and rumpled, his gaze intense; the wife was sharp-tongued, full-figured, and lively—an actress through and through, but likeably so. They were both witty observers of Parisian society and culture. The wife loved to eat. She'd expressed a greater infatuation with France than did her husband, who struck Jordan as being homesick.

At one point during his narration (I was standing near his bed, folding his laundry), my father paused to sip ginger tea—to settle his stomach, routinely distressed by his pain medications. Then, without any preface, he brought up Camilla.

I FIRST saw your mother, he said, on the same street where I met the Meyerholds.

Hearing this, I pushed the laundry basket aside and sat in the chair by Jordan's bed. My entire body felt warm, as though my temperature had just risen a notch. I wondered if my face looked flushed, and if my father would notice.

When was this? I asked quietly.

In 1928. She was gazing at the window display of a little shop a few doors down from my hotel. It was an exclusive *parfumerie*— I'd already cased it, so I knew it sold only the best fragrances. The owner was a really haughty homosexual. He must've been at least seventy, beautifully dressed. This man knew his perfume, and he had an attitude to match. Eventually I wore him down, though. He showed me a nice collection of Lalique bottles and one unusual flacon of a Poiret perfume called Le Fruit Defendu.

What did it look like?

Quite a vessel, that one! It was shaped like an apple. It lay in a silk-upholstered silver box with jungle foliage embossing—fronds and vines and so forth. Sort of opulent and humorous at the same time. Nothing like an appeal to original sin to get a female buyer's juices flowing! Or so the thinking went, I guess.

And Camilla? What did she look like?

Your mother wore a skirt that was long and nicely tailored but not altogether clean. She'd dragged part of its hem on the ground. Actually, her entire outfit looked like it needed a good shaking out and pressing.

He yawned, not out of boredom, I could tell, but because he was short of oxygen.

She had very little money, he continued. She was living on what she'd borrowed from Dan to get herself to France, and there wasn't much left over for clothing. At that point she'd been in Paris for maybe six months. She'd found two little rooms in an apartment near Montparnasse that belonged to a retired civil servant and his wife. They weren't fond of Americans, but they put up with Camilla because she minded her own business.

He adjusted his position in bed; I saw him wince softly as he did so.

Anyway, there she was, staring at bottles of perfume in a storefront window. Not quite what I'd call the picture of elegance. But her skin, her hair—everything shone . . .

Shone? I repeated, not sure I'd heard him right.

I don't know how else to describe it. She was one of those women who give off a kind of gleam, regardless of how they're dressed or coiffed.

Was she wearing perfume?

Oh yes. She was wearing Coty's Narcisse Noir, a scent I'd always liked. In the trade it was considered a real keeper, a fragrance that would last. A man named Daltroff developed it. He was a Russian who'd made perfumes for the czar's family before emigrating to France, and he was talented. I'll tell you what, though: that fragrance wasn't something just any woman could wear! Especially not a nineteen-year-old. It tended to come off as heavy, even a bit oppressive. But on Camilla it was something else . . .

So how did you actually meet her?

I just went up to her on the street, and we stared at the window display together. She didn't seem at all perturbed that some strange man was standing beside her. I spoke to her in French. Quite a bottle, isn't it, I asked, pointing at it—at Le Fruit Defendu.

Camilla rolled her eyes at me. You aren't kidding, she answered in English. I must have looked surprised at her switching languages on me like that, because then she said, Takes one to know one—your accent gives you away! I had to laugh at that, since she was right. She laughed, too. She had a nice strong chuckle.

What's it smell like, do you know? she asked me. I told her the scent was dominated by Bulgarian rose, which would make it expensive, apart from the packaging. Of course, *that* would also raise the price considerably, I said.

She wanted to know why Bulgarian rose would make it costly. So I launched into a lecture. Getting the oils from the roses, I told her, is a very labor-intensive process. First you've got to separate the petals from the green sepals at the base of the flower. That's a major job right there. Then it takes multiple distillations to separate out the oil. Peasants do that by hand.

Where—in Bulgaria? she interrupted. I explained that most of Bulgaria's roses are grown in a place called the Kazanluk Valley, but a similar variety of rose has also been cultivated in Russia, on the Black Sea. It takes a whole lot of them to make even a small amount of perfume, I told her. Four thousand flowers yield only about a kilogram of oil.

She whistled at that—a loud whistle, like a man's. And then she turned from the window and stared directly at me. Her eyes were dark blue, like yours only bigger, with dense black lashes. I couldn't place her; she was clearly an American, but physically she could've been French or Italian or Greek. And she was so young!

You work in perfume, don't you, she said. I could hear the interest in her voice; it was genuine, not just a way of keeping the conversation going.

Yes, I said, I make it.

She nodded, and that gleam of hers seemed to intensify. Hard to describe—but when it happened, you couldn't miss it.

Good, she said. Then maybe you can tell me where I might look for a job. Because I want to work with perfumes. Not in a shop like this—I don't want to sell them, I'd make a lousy salesgirl! I have ideas about packaging. There's a line between gorgeous and silly, and I know when it gets crossed.

She paused. I love perfume, you see, she added, very slowly and emphatically. That was it—she *had* me . . .

Had you?

This was somebody I needed to get to know. Very few women at that time were trying to get into the perfume business. They wanted to wear it, not make it or market it.

So then what did you do?

I gave her my business card and pointed at the hotel's awning, a few hundred yards away. That's my current address, I told her. Then I asked her to join me for a drink the next night at the hotel bar. She nodded at me again—seriously and unseriously at the same time, if that's possible. Like she meant it but found the whole thing amusing anyway. She held my card at eye level and read aloud Coty's addresses in New York and in Paris. Then she extended her hand to me. Its grip was surprisingly warm, I remember. She said her name, and then she turned and walked away.

Did it occur to you that you might never see her again?

Jordan paused before replying. For as long as I knew your mother, that thought was always occurring to me, he said.

HE TURNED on his side, exhausted. In a minute, he was asleep.

I picked up the laundry basket, carried it to his bureau, and distributed its contents in various drawers. The sheets I carried to a linen closet in the hall. Folding them, I noticed they were suedelike to the touch. Because Jordan had purchased them, the sheets were of the highest quality, and they'd softened beautifully over the decade he'd lived in Frenchtown.

Stacking them on a shelf, I realized I was feeling glad. How could I not be? Against all expectations, my father's and my silence was buckling at last. I sensed that there would be more: he'd fill in the blanks, paint a verbal picture of my invisible mother.

Yet in its strange quiet, its sobriety, this gladness I was experiencing was unlike any I'd known before. Why, I wondered, had my father and I waited until now to talk about Camilla? Having had all along so little connection to risk, why hadn't I taken a chance and forced the issue with him a long time ago?

Better silence than separation: that had been my strategy. And although in a sense it had been successful, my fear of losing Jordan had remained unexpunged. *Did it occur to you that you might never see him again?* Yes, that thought was always occurring to me.

DRYING OFF after what had turned out to be a very long bath, I saw that the water's heat had mottled the skin on my belly. Slathering myself with lotion, I visualized Eve's skin as her blood toxified and the purple blush spread across her.

After her death, neither Danny nor I had referred to that eerie final hour. Nor had we spoken of Eve's symptoms prior to her hospitalization. Yet although these things were unavailable for discussion, they definitely weren't gone from memory—mine, anyway.

As I dressed and poured myself a vodka, I pictured the last time I'd seen my cousin in her apartment. She'd been in bed all day, the curtains drawn, her temperature elevated. Eve's assistant at The Mad Gardener had called Danny to report that Eve hadn't come to work that day or the day before. Danny had then called Eve at home, and after hearing her mother's abnormally groggy voice, she'd phoned me, asking if I'd mind running over to Eve's with her that evening. Something was up, she said. Reluctantly, I'd agreed to go with her—mostly because I knew how rare it was for Danny to display concern about her mother's well-being. Normally she maintained a wary distance.

I'd then called Stuart to bow out of a film date we'd made for that evening. After inquiring about Eve's symptoms, which apparently included a stiff neck, Stuart announced she might have meningitis. No way, I responded—that was far too exotic. It was predictably hypochondriacal of Stuart to imagine something so extreme.

AT EVE'S that night, Danny made a pot of tea, but Eve wasn't interested. Danny and I tidied up her room while she lay in bed, listless.

She hadn't wanted us to hang around. Several times we tried persuading her to eat something, but she wouldn't take more than a few sips of water. She said she felt achy, as with the flu.

After about an hour, we said good night to her. As I was pulling the bedroom door closed behind us, Eve called my name.

"There's something I want to ask you," she said, her voice so low it was barely audible.

I stepped back into the bedroom while Danny headed toward the kitchen with the teapot and mugs. Eve spoke without turning her head toward me. I remember thinking it was odd she didn't turn to face me, not realizing it was too physically painful for her to do so.

"Danny's worrying," she said. "I don't want that, Cam. Remind her I've talked with my doctor, okay?"

"We're not used to seeing you like this," I said.

Eve nodded a little; the action seemed to cause her discomfort.

"Eve," I asked, "does your neck still hurt?"

"Some," she replied. I could hear her inhaling and exhaling slowly.

"You know," I said, "Stuart told me a stiff neck and a severe headache could be a sign of meningitis."

Eve said nothing.

"Does your head hurt now?"

"Yes."

"Did you tell your doctor about your neck?"

"No," she answered without heat.

"Well, why don't you?" I said. "I mean, there's no reason not to mention it to him—"

"Cam," she broke in, "leave it alone, okay?"

It was my turn to say nothing. The silence between us felt charged. "All right," I answered at last.

"I mean it," she said, her voice low but willful. "Don't talk about my symptoms with Danny or anyone else. It's nobody else's concern." She paused. "Promise me."

"All right," I repeated. "But let your doctor know if your neck keeps hurting, won't you?"

Eve stayed silent for a little while. "I'm tired," she said finally. "You'd better go now. I need to sleep."

"Cam?" Danny called from the hallway. "You ready?"

"Go," Eve murmured.

Her stubbornness was frustrating but unsurprising. "Be right there," I called to Danny. Then I gave Eve's forearm a squeeze. Her eyes were closed; I figured she'd fallen asleep. On tiptoes, I crossed the floor and shut the door behind me.

Danny and I headed down Seventh Avenue and across Bleeker Street. I said nothing to her about my conversation with Eve; she didn't ask. At the West Fourth Street station, I saw her off to Brooklyn. Before descending the subway stairs, she told me she was sure her mother was having a migraine headache, and I agreed. There was no need, I decided, to contravene Eve's request by telling Danny or anyone else about her neck. That was her business.

The ambulance came the next morning, after Danny, getting no answer when she phoned Eve at nine, obeyed her intuition yet again and went to her mother's apartment. She found Eve unable to move. By that time (though no one knew it), the conclusion was foregone.

AFTER MY vodka, I had a light supper, did a bit of reading, and awaited sleep with trepidation. What lay in store? Previously my dreams had been either transparently simple or obscure in an amusing way, like something the director Richard Foreman might devise for his smart and silly Ontological Theater. I wasn't used to having dreams that seemed to require investigating, yet resisted memory so effectively.

When at last, drowsy but still awake, I made myself shut my eyes, two pictures appeared (superimposed, as if projected simultaneously) on the blank screen of my closed eyelids. One was of my father on the final morning of his life; the other was of Eve, unconscious, a few hours before blood poisoning took her down. Jordan, terminally ill, had been ready to go, had wanted out. But Eve? On that evening in her apartment—the last time we'd spoken, when she'd demanded my silence—had she hoped to be saved, or trusted she wouldn't be?

I fell asleep with that question unanswered, as it had been nightly since her death.

INTERLUDE

THE BIRD'S feathers were by now rather ruffled!

Well, that was only to be expected. How best to put it? When I first began playing on her dream-stage, I'd have said Camilla was someone for whom consternation was inevitable.

I'm speaking not of ordinary vexation but of something more purely existential, which in Camilla's case displayed itself chiefly with respect to her family. And here I'm reminded of a letter Anton Chekhov wrote to Seva, in which he made the following observation:

> Nowadays, almost every civilized person, no matter how healthy he may be, never feels so irritated as when he is at home among his own family, because the discord between past and future is felt primarily within the family. The irritation is chronic . . . It is an intimate, family irritation, so to speak.

All the questions surrounding Camilla's recently departed cousin were related, it seemed, to this intimate irritation. And if I were to continue agitating Camilla's night-mind? Eventually her waking self would recognize that the discord she was experiencing was merely improbable harmony: harmony masked, in disguise.

THE YOUNG American chemist whom Seva met in Paris had left an indistinct impression on me.

Not that Jordan Archer was bland. He was good-looking (if slightly anemic), with a lean sense of humor his French colleagues clearly enjoyed. No, he wasn't dull; if anything, he was a bit *louche*. But he had none of the effervescent energies of so many of Seva's associates. Jordan simply wasn't a theater person, though he certainly was a dedicated spectator.

He had an avid interest in all things related to perfume, as well as a knack for turning up wherever Russians were to be found. Looking back, I give him credit: this was a man with good instincts for cheap talent. In Paris he zeroed in on exactly that group of people who might help him come up with fresh ideas for the packaging of perfume—a task he found burdensome. Russian artists and performers have often been short on cash, hence willing to sell their creative talents for next to nothing. Jordan had a sharp eye for other people's susceptibilities.

ZINA TOOK a shine to *l'Americain*: he brought out the maternal side of Seva's wife. I can still see them sitting in the hotel restaurant, sharing their first meal together.

Jordan pecked at his dinner like a listless sparrow while Zina tucked greedily into hers. Suddenly she noticed that Monsieur Archer wasn't eating very much. This set her off—Zina could never stand seeing someone pass up good French food. *Mange!* she ordered, pointing her fork at his plate.

Jordan gave her a wan smile and nibbled a little, but he didn't make more than a small dent in his dinner. From that point on, Zina decided that her mission was to fatten him up. They dined together on several occasions, and each time she cooed at him appreciatively whenever he managed to finish his meal.

It must've been a struggle for Jordan to acclimate himself to Seva and Zina; their unruly appetites roughed up his own. Although he shared the Meyerholds' enthusiasm for red wine and brandy, Jordan was physically incapable of overindulgence. He never smoked, claiming tobacco was bad for his sense of smell, and he shunned garlic. (This refusal shocked a French waiter who, upon serving Jordan a plate of snails dripping in garlicky butter, was politely ordered to rinse off the snails and return them dry. *Mais, monsieur,* the waiter sputtered, *ce sont des escargots!*—to which Jordan replied coolly: *Ça n'importe pas.*)

He was certainly someone who knew what he wanted. Jordan's encounter with Camilla *mère*, however, must've stopped him in his tracks: meeting her, he'd met his match. After a long, taxing courtship, he and his lover finally managed to make peace with each other and their bond. But then Camilla *fille* was conceived, and Jordan's future abruptly rerouted itself. A daughter's birth, a wife's death—a brutal confluence. . . . Jordan took what happened as evidence of his own wrongdoing. *If I hadn't impregnated her, she wouldn't have died.* There was no one with whom he might have shared this awful notion. He kept it at bay, barely—waiting for the day his guilt (lupine, determined) would rush in and savage him.

CAMILLA FILLE knew her father felt responsible for what had happened. Knew, too, that she was somehow the underlying source of his torment. Children sense such things and carry their sensing with them, even into adulthood, as a kind of chronic foreboding. This I picked up on. The hum of anxiety—nameless, pervasive—was familiar to me.

When in June of 1939 Seva traveled to St. Petersburg (then Leningrad), I'd known something was wrong, though I couldn't have said what. The weather had played its part. At that time of year, the sun sets extremely late; people go out strolling along the Neva and its canals at midnight or later. This lends the city an air at once festive and friendly. But that June the White Nights held an oppressive, nearly electrical charge—like what you'd feel in the air just before a thunder-and-lightning storm breaks out.

Seva had been jumpy, ill-humored, and distracted for weeks, and Zina had urged him to take a much-needed break from Moscow's hothouse environment. He'd hopped on the overnight train to Leningrad, arriving at its central station after an uneventful ride. Although it was only eight in the morning, Nevsky Prospect (at that time called Twenty-Fifth of October Prospect—ah, those absurd name changes!) was bustling.

Seva took a streetcar for a few blocks, crossing the Fontanka; then he disembarked and strolled for a while. At the Griboedova Canal, he paused to watch the gray-green water flow lazily beneath the bridge of the four griffins. For the first time in far too long, he inhaled a long breath of contentment. Then, having had his fill for the time being of the city's visual attractions, he made his way to the flat on the Kharpovka Embankment where Zina's sister and her husband lived.

The night of June nineteenth, he visited friends and stayed out very late, drinking, eating, and gabbing. He didn't return to his sister-in-law's flat until about seven in the morning. The walk home did him good; the air was cool and clear, and Seva gulped it appreciatively. As soon as he turned his key in the building's front door, a black crow fell headfirst into the canal. I don't think Seva witnessed this peculiar sight; he was caught up in remembering the evening's lively conversations. The occurrence struck me, however, as irregular and inauspicious. Sure enough, the NKVD officers arrived two hours later with an arrest warrant . . .

BUT I'M ignoring my timing. A director's most important task (Seva always claimed) is to impose a rhythm on a performance. No more peeking ahead! Back to where we belong: in Camilla's theater.

And for our next act? It was time, I decided, for the masked man to identify himself. Thus Meyerhold steps out from the shadows and puts Camilla on notice: *Think you can slack off? Not on this stage, you can't!*

FOUR

TALK TO me, my father says.

We're in a city, and it dawns on me that this must be Paris, where I was born. I have never visited there; I know it only from photographs. We're near a river, I can smell it.

Across the street from us is a church. I've seen it on postcards; it's not Notre Dame but another one, smaller and lovely. Faint sounds of singing emanate from it. I picture its interior, drenched with colors filtering through stained-glass windows on which the midmorning sun is raying hard.

Jordan is staring at me, waiting for me to answer his request.

Come on, Cam! he wheedles. You don't have to make it so hard. Just talk to me a little! You don't have to tell me anything important . . .

He looks the way he always used to look, ever the same: his brown eyes (irises flecked with gold) alert behind his wire-rimmed glasses, his thin lips pulled back from slightly crooked upper teeth. He's brushed his hair back from his face; it gleams in the sunlight. He's wearing a beautifully cut gray suit, a pale blue shirt, a handsome tie, elegant black loafers, a belt with a tasteful silver buckle. He's slender and tall, topping six feet. He doesn't look like a businessman or a chemist; he looks like a sensualist, which he is.

I reach toward his face. My hand goes up to his left ear, my forefinger stroking that spot just below the lobe where perfume is applied. As I start to withdraw my hand, Jordan catches it with one of his own, his fingers lightly encircling my wrist. My forefinger is still extended as though I were wagging it at him. He stares at its tip for a few seconds, smiling; then he blows on it, a warm hit of air, and fragrance is released—an exquisite misting of white flowers whose scents arrive in succession: gardenia, narcissus, lily of the valley. After the sweetness something else, darker and muskier, begins to assert itself, modulating the soft whiteness into a lower register.

Ah, the smell of earth, Jordan says, inhaling. And I should know, because I'm dead. So I can be objective about these things. Can you?

I'm trying to remain quiet, but Jordan's question provokes me. No! I yell. What do you expect?

I expect you to be able to converse with your old man for a couple of minutes, Jordan answers. It's not such a hardship, you know.

Actually, it is a hardship, I say.

Still hung up on those final moments, aren't you, Cam? The pills, you're remembering me forcing them down with the pudding, right? You make an awfully good chocolate pudding, by the way. Merci, chérie!

His French accent is perfect. He bows from the waist, like an actor. Standing to one side, I start coming unstuck.

You bastard! I shriek. I should be thrilled because you're taking the time to show up, right? But guess what. You don't have a clue who you're talking to! You never have, Jordan. You don't know me from fucking Adam!

Please, my dear, he says. I've never cared for the adjectival use of that obscenity. It's a verb, Camilla—it has a verb's force. You should use it accordingly. You could say, for instance, Fuck you, Father!

I fly at him. I leap onto his chest and plant my knees on his col-larbones. He wraps one arm around the calves of my legs, supporting me; the other arm he raises high, as if he's about to hit me. Lifting my own hand, I grasp his forearm, pushing forward, hoping to topple him.

We're locked like this, swaying unsteadily, when a man in a black cloak emerges from the shadows. He strolls over to us, proceeding with an elegant elasticity. In the background I hear piano music, a song like a circus tune or the saccharine, repetitive medley of an ice-cream vendor.

Tsk, tsk, says the man, so softly I can barely hear him over the noisy piano. You two seem to have forgotten everything I taught you. Your knees go to the chest, *remember? Not so high up as this!*

He points at my kneecaps, which are lodged just below Jordan's neck, and frowns at me.

You've practically got your knees in his throat! And as for you (now he addresses Jordan), you're not arched back far enough. Why have I bothered instructing you if you're going to flout the rules? This is real theater, not just a bit of gymnastics! You're each playing a part, *remember? You two are in a* relationship *here.*

The man yawns, stretches his arms high over his head, waves them indolently from side to side, and lets them fall, slapping his sides loudly with both hands.

Aaah, he exhales, it's like I told that journalist, way back when. Talent always experiences a role deeply, whereas mediocrity merely en-acts it.

He turns to Jordan and me. I mean it, he says in a low, hard voice. You aren't dealing yet!

Abruptly Jordan drops me. I land in a heap, pick myself up, dust myself off.

The man gives Jordan a dark look. Va! he shouts.

A trampoline descends from above and lands with a clatter a few yards away from us. Jordan eyes it, gauging the distance. Crouching, he bounces lightly on the balls of his feet; then he takes a few brisk hop-skips and springs forward, leaping and landing directly on the trampo-line's center. He jumps, jumps, gaining momentum and height, his necktie flopping. Then he does a midair flip, lands straight-legged on both feet, and pops off at an angle, vanishing into the wings.

Standing to one side, I stare at the empty trampoline. The man is looking at me now, his lips pulled back in an enigmatic smile.

As for you, he says, it's not enough—it's never enough!—to simply do the exercises. Roles, one must always be thinking about roles. Ask yourself what parts this father of yours played. And with whom, for whom? Do you know? Or do you only think you know?

Who are you? I ask, turning to him.

Vsevolod Meyerhold, he says, bowing. At your service.

"MY WORD," said Stuart, "what *are* we wearing?"

We were sitting in a bar near the theater, awaiting Danny. The bar offered a grand array of beers. Stuart was drinking a local brew called Brooklyn Black Chocolate Stout, which he described as malty and smoky; it had a thick, creamy appearance, as though its ingestion required a spoon. To his dismay I'd ordered a Molsen, which in Stuart's book is like ordering a glass of fruit juice in a winery. The bar was crowded. As Stuart pulled in his seat, leaning toward me to allow another patron to pass behind him, his eyebrows rose with curiosity.

"Wearing?" I repeated. Looking downward, I inspected my white T-shirt, blazer, and black jeans. "Seems to me I'm wearing what I always wear. Maybe you need new glasses?"

He'd just bought new ones (they had thin red wire-rimmed frames and looked rather like those of Abby, Sam's daughter, as I'd already teased him), and he scowled at me now through their oval lenses. "Not your clothes, dumbo," he said. "Your *scent.*"

"Ah," I said. "It's something new. They sell it at that Japanese department store in Midtown—the chic one." I waved my wrist before Stuart's nose. "Nice, isn't it? It's the only one I've worn that isn't one of my father's."

He placed his cheek against mine, sniffing deeply at my neck. "Fabulous. And does the lover-man approve?"

"Yes, the lover-man approves," I answered. "He is exceedingly easy to please."

"Easy to please," echoed Stuart, pensively. "I'd say your lumpenproletarian has done you some good after all."

"My what?" I jeered. It was an open secret that Stuart fancied Nick, whom he'd met once or twice.

"That handsome representative of the working class! Your woika," said Stuart, sliding into a Brooklyn accent. "Your *hard* woika," he added, chuckling. "I can well imagine how you exploit *him.*"

"Keep your dirty mind off my guy," I said.

"Yes, ma'am." He mimed a schoolmaster's rectitude, crossing his arms at his chest and drawing himself upright. Then he relaxed, reaching across the table to squeeze my forearm gently. "Glad you're enjoying yourself, Cam," he said. "I have to say I didn't think you still would be. After the initial kick wore off, that is. I wouldn't have pictured you in such a long-running movie. It's very French. Only *you're* not very French. Nor is the man himself, needless to say."

"Oh, come on—Nick's a good pal," I said. "I seem to require a degree of loyalty in a man, and I get it from him. Despite the fact that he's married to someone else."

"No," said Stuart. "You get it *because* of that fact. Let's not make too much of the adulterer's fidelity."

"Have no fear," I said. "Let's not forget who the adulterer's mistress is. She's not exactly waiting for the adulterer to declare his intention to marry her."

"True." He sipped his beer and smacked his lips approvingly. "You know," he went on, "Carl's spoiled me. We spend so much time together, and he hasn't once tossed me out the window. He's an absurdly decent person. How did I end up with an absurdly decent person?" His face contorted into a parody of bewilderment, all raised brows and widened eyes; then his expression resettled. "Dunno," he said softly, his tone serious now. "Not a clue. Lucky stars."

I imagined Stuart in his lover's arms, his self-doubt edged to one side by Carl's steadfastness. The mental picture comforted me for a moment; I felt as though Stuart's domestic tranquility were somehow rubbing off on me. His next words, however, dispelled this.

"A question. Are you fixing on spending the rest of your life in the company of a married man? Just *asking,*" he added as I started scowling. He reached over and pinched my chin between his thumb and forefinger. "Thing is, you've been involved with Nick for five or six *years* now, right? You're stingy with the details. I'm not talking sex, I'm talking"—he thumped his heart lightly—"*this*. Seems to me you've been treading water, Cammie. Nick's a nice guy, fun guy, good guy. And? But? Well?" His head clicked back and forth with each query. "I mean, the man's not planning on divorcing the wife— fine, I'm not lobbying for that! But the thing is, you don't seem to have upped the ante. Know what I mean?"

His gaze was warm and undeflectable; I could feel the years of our friendship behind it. "Lately, whenever I've tried asking you about this—and about Eve, too, while we're at it—I feel like I'm being put on hold. *One moment, please,*" he mimicked nasally. *"Please be assured that your call is very important to us . . ."*

He lay a hand on his heart, lightly lifting and lowering his fingers, registering its beat. "Are you open for business?" he asked softly.

Something stirred in my memory. Jordan and me—in Paris? And a cloaked man. Yes, it *was* Meyerhold . . .

"Yoo-hoo," said Stuart, lifting his hand off his chest and passing it back and forth before my eyes like a windshield wiper.

"I'm just remembering a dream I had last night," I said. "A Russian director was in it—Meyerhold. You know who he is, right?"

"Please, Camilla. My bookshop is devoted to *theater,* remember?"

"Sorry. So in this dream, my father and I were in a city, I think it was Paris—"

"Another father dream?"

I paused. "Recently, all my dreams have involved my father," I said.

"The ones you remember, that is."

"Are you finished?"

"Mais oui. Do go on."

"Jordan and I were having a fight—not like boxing, more like wrestling—and then this guy showed up, wearing some sort of cape. He introduced himself as Meyerhold, and his accent was Russian, so I knew he was *the* Meyerhold."

"Well, *that's* original," Stuart drawled. "Better than Peter Brook! So what happened?"

"At one point I'd actually climbed onto my father's chest, and he was leaning backward, and I was about to knock him over, when all of a sudden Meyerhold started scolding us as if we weren't following his instructions properly. I'm not sure about the rest—something to do with a trampoline. Then my father disappeared."

"Majorly trippy." Stuart took a long, loud pull on his beer.

"You're making disgusting sounds," I said.

"Deal with it," he said. "I think I'm still waking up, actually. Carl and I had raucous sex last night. Didn't sleep much."

"Keep your sex life to yourself."

"What good would it do me *then?*"

"Spare me."

"But I *do,* my dear, I do! Can you honestly say I talk frequently with you about sex—mine, yours, anyone's? I'm a paragon of privacy. So if once in a while I make a tiny, trivial allusion—"

"All right." I caved in. "Of course I don't want you to feel like you can't say anything about it."

"Oh, I don't feel that." His voice sounded soothing, but I waited for the sucker punch. It came, not too hard but well aimed. "What I feel is, you'd mind less my saying something about my existence as a sexual being if you had something to say yourself. Lately you've been rather, um, withheld—"

"Discreet is maybe the word you're looking for."

"Like most adulteresses. But I believe the word *is* withheld. Anyway. Funny you should ask about Meyerhold." Stuart was signaling an end to putting me on the spot and a return to a familiar, easier topic: theater. "Some books arrived in today's mail, postmarked Paris. I'm on the mailing list of a theater bookstore over there, and occasionally we send each other titles. One of the books in the batch they just sent is a biography of Meyerhold—in Russian, no less! I've seen books about him in English, and I've heard there's one in French, but I didn't know about any Russian bios. This one seems to be a reissue of a volume originally published in the mid-1950s. With some amazing photos."

He took a swig of beer. "Anyway. So tell me what *you* know

about Meyerhold. I know the basics, not much more. He started out as an actor, right? And he did very cool things with sets and lighting."

"Yes. And then he went on to revolutionize the theater in Russia. The Communists couldn't deal with him, though. Way too quirky."

"When did he die?"

I had to think for a moment. "In 1940. They tossed him in jail for a while, then shot him."

"Nice."

I paused to sip first my beer, then Stuart's. His was definitely tastier. "The funny part about my dream is that Jordan's and my movements came straight from Meyerhold's system of biomechanics."

"Biomechanics?" Stuart said. "One of my mime teachers talked about that, years ago. Refresh me."

"Meyerhold invented a set of training exercises for his acting students, to loosen them up physically and mentally. Biomechanics was a lot like mime training, actually."

"How did it work?"

Again I had to stop and think. "His students had to do everything in pairs, so they'd figure out how to respond to one another in an instinctive way," I said. "Plus they would learn about rhythm and timing: pauses, rushes, and so forth. Meyerhold gave them funny names—the exercises, I mean. Things like Slap in the Face and Taking the Partner Aside. I remember the exercise my father and I were doing in the dream was Leap on the Chest. It's supposed to force the pair of actors to coordinate their movements as the center of balance swings back and forth between them. There has to be mutual reliance for it to work. Otherwise, both people will fall down."

I stopped, trying to assemble more memories of what I'd read about Meyerhold's techniques. "If I'm not mistaken, that particular exercise usually included another one, called Stab with the Dagger. The person who'd been leapt upon had to arch backward and hang his arms down as if awaiting his own murder."

"Well, well," Stuart said. "Not sure what to make of *that*. But keep dreaming—and report back to me. This is starting to look like a Daddy mini-series!"

THE EVENING proceeded entertainingly. Danny showed up, Stuart bought her a drink, and she regaled us with tales from her workplace. I was struck by her poise. She wasn't behaving at all like the distraught girl who'd lobbed things around my shop a few weeks earlier. Perhaps, I thought, the worst really was behind her.

The Wilson production was predictably long and provocative. Some members of the audience left partway through, and during intermission Stuart imitated their long-faced disapproval—to the amusement of the people sitting on either side of us, who were enjoying the show as much as we were. After the performance ended, Stuart, Danny, and I returned to the same bar at which we'd met and had a snack. I got home around two in the morning. Almost as soon as I entered my apartment, the phone rang. It was Nick.

"You all right?" I asked, entirely surprised to hear his voice. He'd never called me after midnight.

He was fine, he answered. Just awake, watching cable TV.

"And the wife?" I asked.

She was upstairs, asleep.

I tried processing this information. It computed at the fact level, but something wasn't registering.

"And you're calling me because . . . ?" I asked.

"Nothing urgent," he responded. He'd tried me at midnight, knowing I was out with Danny and Stuart, figuring I might arrive home around that hour. When I didn't answer, he'd tried again at one o'clock. He'd been about to give up on me but decided to give it one last shot. "Nothing urgent," he repeated. "Just wanted to say hi."

"Oh," I said. "Bored and lonely?"

"Umm, something like that," he answered.

The picture finally cleared. I saw him sitting in his living room, listless but not yet ready for bed, watching some movie but not paying much attention, thinking instead about fucking me. On the phone, that is, no other venue being possible, given the lateness of the hour. And the woman upstairs. A hot bedtime story, something to get him off: that's what he wanted, though he wasn't going to say so. He'd make *me* say so. And offer to do something about it, too.

On another evening, in another context, perhaps I might've had a different response. But on that evening, at that hour, I could find no way around my perception of our conversation as pathetic. Cornered, I was finally provoked.

"And what if I were with someone?" I asked. "And that's why I wasn't picking up the phone?"

Though the tone of my voice hadn't changed, the words sounded like spat-out nails—to me, anyway. Nick, obviously taken aback, didn't reply. We'd never aired anything like this before; there'd been no reason to. It would have seemed like a waste of time. We both knew I was a woman without prospects: a disbeliever in them, which amounted to the same thing.

Are you open for business? Recalled, Stuart's question had a knife's thrust. Holding the phone receiver in my hand, I listened to the sound of *no no no* pelting in my head, furious as hail.

"Camilla?" Nick's tone was steady, but I could hear his uncertainty.

I let my forefinger rest lightly on the receiver's button. "Go fuck yourself," I answered in the same mild tone I might've used to suggest he eat a sandwich. After listening for a moment to the sound of his speechlessness, I pressed the button and he was gone.

I SURFACED the next morning, blearily, to the buzz of my alarm clock. Though I tried, I couldn't summon my exchange with Nick; it kept slipping away, refusing to cohere. I knew it had happened, it would have consequences, yet none of it came into focus.

I showered and dressed, then sat in my kitchen sipping strong coffee in rapid gulps to wake myself up. My thoughts wandered, not to Nick but to Danny. We'd take her car—Eve's old Volvo wagon— to Ithaca. The Volvo, which had originally belonged to my father, was still in good running order. Its interior gave off an interesting scent: part potting soil, part leather, part something else—perhaps a trace of Jordan's aftershave, with its pleasing strain of bergamot.

I was looking forward to being in the Volvo again. Pulling out my day runner, I jotted a reminder to myself to check the Web for cheap motels near Ithaca. We'd need rooms for Saturday night.

AS I was pulling on my jacket, the phone rang. Letting the machine pick up, I stood by the door, listening to Nick's voice as he left a message. *Just checking on you, Cam. Not quite sure what got your back up last night . . . Didn't mean to offend. I guess I thought . . . well, anyway, I didn't intend anything, uh, awkward. Hope I'm forgiven.*

There was a pause before another word, spoken quietly but clearly: *Love.* Then the machine clicked off.

I locked my door, went downstairs, stood outside, and began to cry. My tears weren't profuse, nor was I at all sure what was prompting them. I knew only that I wanted to grip Nick's face between my palms and feel his stubbled skin, the glossy coarseness of his eyebrows. Wanted to order him never to say that word again. No pointlessness, I wanted to tell him. Just keep your hands on me. Play your part and I'll play mine.

THE FOURTH Wall's main source of light—a big chandelier from the set of a 1909 revival of *The Importance of Being Earnest*—didn't work when I arrived and flipped the switch.

I got up on my stepladder and checked the bulbs and my fuse box, to no avail. The culprit, I decided, was either the lamp's antiquated wiring or the outlet. In my back office, the fluorescent overhead was working fine, so I wasn't completely in the dark. I called my electrician, Martin, who promised to come over soon.

Then I phoned Danny and invited her to stop by after work. She was in a cheery mood. Our night out, she said, had done her good. And had I managed to get a few hours' sleep?

To this I answered yes, recalling Nick's voice on the phone in the small hours of the morning, and wondering how long the unpleasantly constricted sensation in my chest would last.

MARTIN TOOK longer than promised. Waiting for him, I rummaged around in one of my display cases, looking for a theater program I'd been saving for Danny: the playbill for a performance of *Threepenny Opera* directed in 1976 by Joe Papp. That production had featured Raul Julia, not yet known as a movie star but already a talented stage performer.

After some hunting, I located the playbill and was relieved to find it in good shape—no tears or wrinkles, no smudges. Beneath a photo of the actor was his signature, a bold flourish. I'd bought this playbill right after the play closed, thinking it'd make a good gift for my cousin. After attending the first Broadway performance of Julia's career (a clunky vehicle called *The Cuban Thing*), Eve had become an admirer. In 1972, when Julia was nominated for a Tony Award for his performance in *Two Gentlemen of Verona,* Eve was hugely irritated that he didn't win.

Danny became a Raul Julia fan, too. She saw *Kiss of the Spider Woman* when she was in middle school, and the film made a strong impression on her. The first Addams Family movie sealed her high regard for Julia. He *was* Gomez Addams; nobody else could possibly play that part ever again, she stated.

I never got round to giving the playbill to Eve. Why not offer it to Danny now? She'd get a kick out of it. I put it on my desk, where I wouldn't forget about it.

THE CHANDELIER was repaired by noon—just in time for a steady stream of clients, the last of whom departed at around five. I toted up my earnings. A few walk-ins had spent lavishly; I was ahead of my projected take for the month.

Danny showed up at six, having called beforehand to say she'd been assigned a last-minute task and would be running late. As soon as she came in, she pulled a map out of her backpack. Leading her to my office, I asked her if she wanted a shot of vodka and told her I'd reserved us two rooms at a motel on the outskirts of Ithaca.

"Good—and thanks for making those arrangements, Cam. Ching-ching," Danny toasted, tapping her shot glass against mine. "Oh, before I forget: I've decided against letting Judy Deveare know we're coming." She drained her vodka and settled into the chair across from my desk. "It's better if we just show up. Something tells me she'll be there."

"It's your call," I said. "Have you thought about what you want to say to her?"

She nodded. "I'm going to ask her what she remembers about Mom. Assuming she knows who Mom was. I just want her general impressions. I'll also ask if she knows anyone else who's still in Ithaca and might have some memories of Billy."

"What if Judy doesn't believe you're Billy's daughter?" I asked.

"I'm bringing that document from the hospital. But I doubt I'll need to show it to her. I have a hunch that Judy won't be all that surprised to see me."

"Well," I said, "we're riding a bunch of hunches here."

Danny fixed me with a stare. This trip would happen along the lines she'd devised, so I should stop suggesting otherwise: this was the message she was sending. "I'm also hoping for a short visit to Cornell. I'd like to see where Mom went to college," she stated.

"Actually I'd like to see Cornell, too," I said. "Because of my father."

Jordan's parents had both taught in the university's math department. They'd died in a car accident when he was seventeen, at which point he'd been given a full scholarship for undergraduate study. He received a B.S. in chemistry and stayed on for a master's degree, switching to Columbia University for his doctorate. Cornell retained a warm place in his memory, having served as his family at a critical time. Over the years he'd made several generous contributions to its chemistry department.

Jordan had also paid for Eve's undergraduate tuition at Cornell. When he pushed her to apply because the university had a reputable horticulture department, she'd been happy to do so. Attending Cornell meant getting out of the family apartment, out of the city, out of sight of her parents. Dan and Sarah readily accepted Jordan's offer to cover the bill. They couldn't have handled it on their own.

"I FIGURED it'd be good if we could go to Cornell together," said Danny. "You could see what your father did for the chemistry department. Mom told me they used his money to buy new measuring devices—you know, fancy scales and instruments and whatnot."

"I always wondered where the money went," I said.

"Mom was impressed by the chemistry labs when he showed them to her."

This pulled me up short. "When Jordan showed her? You mean while she was a student there?"

"Yeah. During her junior year, when he visited. She told me she'd been eating nothing but lousy college food, and there was your father, plunking down for an expensive meal at the best restaurant in town." Danny hadn't yet noticed my bewilderment. "Jordan must've seemed like a one-man rescue squad."

My father had never mentioned to me any visits to Cornell during Eve's college years. Even when young, I always knew where Jordan was traveling. He'd gone to Ithaca once, I recalled, for a reunion of Cornell chemists, and he'd probably seen Eve then—yet that was in the late 1960s, when she was long out of school and managing a gardening business near Ithaca. But before that?

"Are you sure Jordan visited your mother while she was in college?" I asked. "He made a lot of business trips during those years, but I don't think any of them took him upstate."

"I'm sure." Danny was finally taking note of my disbelief. "I definitely remember Mom talking about that meal he treated her to." She paused, considering. "Maybe he was en route to Montreal or something?"

"Maybe," I echoed blandly.

Danny shouldered her backpack. "So how about if I pick you up at around eight on Saturday, Cam? Is that too early?"

"That's fine," I said. "Just ring. I'll be ready with a thermos of coffee and some bagels." I picked up the playbill that lay on my desk. "Here, I've been meaning to give this to you. Actually I'd meant to give it to Eve a long time ago, but I never did."

Danny took the program and stared at it uncertainly, then flipped through its pages until she came across Raul Julia's photograph. "Oh my God," she crooned. She glanced again at the cover. "He was in *this?*"

"Yep. Your mother saw the play and said he was great. She always liked him so much more than any other male actor."

"Where do you think I got *my* Raul Julia fixation? He wasn't exactly a typical love object for the average ten-year-old girl! Remember when Mom took me to see *Spider Woman?*"

She paused. "Mom almost never took me to the movies. That was your job—yours and Sam's. I remember the conversation she and I had after seeing that movie. She said it was a love story, about the kind of love that comes out of left field. You're helpless in the face of it, she said—there's nothing you can do . . . It's like an accident."

Her expression shifted so quickly that it took me a few moments to realize what was going on. Her face grew suddenly flushed, and her eyes filled. If I hadn't known her well, I'd have thought she was having a sudden attack of hay fever. She wasn't, though, and we both knew it. This was as close as she'd get to crying—for now, and in front of me.

She pinched the bridge of her nose, sniffed sharply, and wiped her eyes dry. "It was always like that with her. She'd drop a few clues, and I'd sit around for days trying to figure them out . . . I used to think if I didn't ask too many questions, she'd spend more time with me. Even though I knew it didn't work that way."

She was right: it hadn't worked that way.

"Cam, when you lived with Mom on Ninth Street, did she ever do her vanishing act?"

I squinted at Danny as if I hadn't understood the question. Her tone had altered; it was urgent now. There was something she wanted—needed—to hear from me.

"You know," she said. "Like when she'd shut her bedroom door and that'd be the last you'd see of her for three days in a row?"

I kept silent, waiting for her to elaborate.

She twisted one of her rings around her finger. "I swear, Cam, she didn't *once* exit that room."

Hissing in frustration, she wiped her face with the backs of her hands. Her tears were falling freely now, and noiselessly. "Mom wasn't negligent—I mean, there was always food in the apartment and a phone I could use. But I was on my own. Nobody ever called to find out where she was. She must've told her assistant not to expect her, and I guess she banished all the fuck-mates . . .

"The only sound I'd hear coming from her room—the only sound for three solid days!—was her crying. She had this way of sobbing very quietly, in the early morning. She'd drag the air up into her lungs, and it was like her sobs were a series of short steps, and at the top there'd be this incredibly long silence. I'd stand at her door, listening to it, to the silence. Then she'd exhale, and the sound would be like a wave—not the crashing kind, the rolling kind . . . Sometimes I'd pretend she was ill. Even though I knew she wasn't."

She gazed at me, her eyes dry now. "Did you know Mom needed to cry for three days at a time?"

I reached for her, pulling her to me. "Nobody understood Eve," I said, wrapping my arms around her. Her fragrance rose off her, an iris-and-vanilla emanation, light yet penetrating.

Her shoulders stiffened. "But you grew up together."

Taking hold of her upper arms, I gave her a little shake. "Danny, she left for college when I was eight, remember? She stayed upstate more than fifteen years, till you were born. *You* were what linked us, when she came back to New York."

She didn't move, but I felt her body relax a little. I'd last held her at Eve's memorial service; since then she'd restricted our physical contact to quick kisses on the cheek. It felt good, and strange, to be so near her. After a few more moments of silence, she extracted herself from my embrace and took a step backward.

"Mom thought I was a great kid," she said quietly, her voice holding bitterness and longing in a tense, fragile balance. "She just didn't want to *be* with me."

"She didn't know how." My words were, I knew, patently inadequate.

"Uh-uh." She was refusing my refusal to engage. "Something happened to her—pertaining to *me*." Moving to the entrance to my office, she leaned against the doorframe and banged the back of her head against it lightly, repeatedly. "Why'd Mom have me and then *not* have me, Cam? How'd she pull it off—being my mother yet not being my mother, year after year? Why didn't she go nuts?"

"Nobody can answer that."

The look she threw me communicated an unmistakable accusation: *You're not telling me what you know!* Slipping an arm around her waist, I began steering her toward the front of my shop. "Let's see what happens in Ithaca," I said as we stepped out onto the sidewalk. "I'll look for you Saturday morning, okay?"

She nodded, but her skepticism hadn't receded. It was there in the back-of-the-hand wave she gave me as she walked off.

AFTER DANNY'S departure, I tidied up my office. Mulling over our talk, my insufficiencies replaying in my head, I found myself remembering my most recent dream—the one in which I'd been sparring with my father.

Over what, exactly? *Roles,* Meyerhold had said as he appraised Jordan's and my performances. Did I know which roles my father had played, and for whom?

No, I did not. The stories Jordan had recounted to me at the end of his life had been truthful, I believed, yet I wasn't sure what they signified. And who could say what he or I might have altered in the telling, the listening? There'd been moments of pure puzzlement, too—as during one exchange, uncharacteristically philosophical, which took place days before his death.

You know what experience is, Cam? he'd asked.

No. Tell me.

It's a web spun by a spider.

Oh? I said, trying not to sound either flippant or serious.

The mind's the spider. You know what the spider's like?

Tell me, I said.

It's ravenous but also cautious. It snares only what it thinks it can devour safely.

His thin lips were pulled back from his teeth. In that moment, the pale gauntness of his face so disturbed me that I could hardly bring myself to look at him.

Devour? What do you mean by that? I said.

The spider feeds on prey, he answered. Things it wants to incorporate. Ideologies, theories, beliefs . . .

He stopped, his breathing labored. After a few moments, he resumed, his voice muffled now by fatigue.

But the spider avoids truly dangerous prey, he said.

Dangerous?

Things it feels menaced by. Certain ideas, fantasies . . .

He shifted position, inhaling sharply. I knew I shouldn't be pressing him, yet I felt compelled to ask another question.

Tell me, I said, what the spider needs most.

Once again Jordan inhaled, very softly now. He became so still I thought he'd stopped breathing altogether.

Drama, he exhaled at last. Someone to applaud . . .

He spoke another word, and I bent closer to hear him. *Camilla,* he murmured, *Camilla, Camilla.* He wasn't calling for me: he was crooning my mother's name.

WHEN MY parents were a couple, they were apart a great deal, Jordan told me.

Their love affair lasted twenty-one years; during that time, my mother did not once go to New York. She'd made a firm decision never to return to the United States, and no one was going to make her change her mind.

So between 1928 and 1949, Jordan made regular trips to France—partly for his job, partly to see my mother. Proximity turned out to be double edged. For its momentum, their relationship depended on repeated separations.

As the 1920s drew to a close, Jordan begged Camilla to marry him, but she declined. Then, during the mid-Thirties, she begged him to move to France, and he refused. At the start of the war, they both played the infidelity card—seeking to humiliate each other, I suppose, and hoping thus to recalibrate the delicate balance of power between them.

When the war came to an end, their private battle lulled. During those summer weeks in 1980, as I folded my father's laundry and listened to his recollections, I sensed he was narrating an inevitability, a story with only one possible outcome. Beneath all the repeated administrations of hurt, a deep mutual need had bided its time.

THEY READIED themselves without realizing it.

Camilla was by this time working for Coty as one of its marketers; my father had ascended to the post of senior chemist. Work was a safe haven, the one arena in which they'd always be able to interact contentedly.

We had a ritual, Jordan said to me one afternoon.

Ritual? I repeated, not sure I'd heard the word correctly.

Involving perfume.

Please describe it.

Camilla and I weren't company people, you see. The only thing that mattered to us was perfume. She was like me—she never got tired of it . . . She was good at marketing, but what she really loved was spending time in my lab.

How was her nose?

Very refined. She could identify false or weak notes in any fragrance. And she was an excellent judge of staying power. That's harder to appreciate—it takes a certain intuition.

What was that ritual of yours?

Ah . . . a little perfume-testing thing we did together. Whenever I was developing a new fragrance, I'd apply it at the base of

Camilla's throat, behind her earlobes, and on the insides of her wrists. Then I'd wait a few minutes, close my eyes, lean in, and inhale. To check the harmonies.

Harmonies?

The way the notes unfold. A scent plays out, like music.

And then what would happen?

I'd ask Camilla for her reaction. She wouldn't say it right away. First she'd tussle with me for a few moments on the sofa, or run down the hall, to elevate her body temperature. That's how you bring out the full range of a fragrance, by warming the skin. And then she'd sit next to me, inhaling and exhaling, smelling the fragrance on herself . . .

Did she always tell you what she really thought?

He gave a nod. Always, he said.

IN THE autumn of 1948, entirely by chance, they conceived a child. Camilla had never before been pregnant. She was about to turn forty.

With the pregnancy, something opened between them—perhaps because neither could pretend to be young any longer, perhaps because their mutual dependence could finally be acknowledged. Jordan offered no explanation. They were simply relieved, he said, that all the battling was finally behind them. Years of friction had yielded a burnished tenderness—or so I pictured it, needing to envision their feeling for one another. It had a sheen, I imagined, like that of old brass.

In the sixth month of the pregnancy, they decided to marry. Jordan negotiated with Coty to be posted permanently in France. After relinquishing his New York apartment and packing up his few possessions, he flew to Paris. Camilla met him at the airport, and they took a cab to the *bureau des mariages;* at the threshold, Jordan hoisted Camilla and carried her over.

The wedding took all of three minutes, and the resulting *certificat* listed the wife as Camilla Archer, née Pell. Her pregnancy was not officially noted, though it was plain for all to see—and warmly toasted by the enthusiastic patrons of Le Trianon, a little café near the Place des Vosges, where the newlyweds repaired after their civil ceremony for a celebratory glass of champagne.

As they sipped their brut and received their toasts, Jordan and Camilla were holding hands. They held each other's hands a couple of months later, too, when Camilla's labor began. And they were still holding hands, my father said, when it ended.

YOUR MOTHER was a loner.

Jordan spoke to me from his bed, where he lay resting after one of his slow, difficult walks to the bathroom. I stood near the bed, a basket of clean clothing and towels before me. This had become our pattern: Jordan talking, me folding and stacking laundry.

He had two more weeks to go. The date had been chosen, though we hadn't refined the details. In the time remaining, I'd told him, I wanted him to recount as much of his and my mother's stories as he could. He'd agreed to talk, but reminded me that we'd need to set aside some time for planning—rehearsing, he called it. As if this were a one-act play and I his stagehand.

How long had Camilla been in France when you met her? I asked him.

About a year. She was only nineteen. But she always struck me as being older than she really was. She had some gray hair even in her twenties. And lines at the corners of her eyes. But she was one of those women who age beautifully.

Her parents? What were they like?

I never met either of them. Your Uncle Dan said their father was a heavy drinker, always antagonizing people. The mother was a silent type, rarely showed her hand. Didn't like outspokenness—it scared her off.

So Camilla scared her off?

He gave me a thin smile. Camilla scared off most people, he said.

And why France?

I told you, she was a loner. And she was tired of America. You know, the Roaring Twenties—too many people getting fat too fast . . . Dan had loaned her some money for a trip abroad; their parents weren't about to sponsor any travels. Camilla had read about France and thought it sounded like a nice place.

He paused to sip water. He'd been dehydrated for several weeks, unable to stomach most liquids. I was glad to see him drink.

So off she went, he continued. And then she refused to come back. Dropped out of sight completely for several months, then called home and announced she was going to make a career for herself. She'd already learned to speak pretty good French, and she'd landed a job at a small Parisian perfume company with production facilities in Grasse. Near Cabris—that's the town where Edmond Roudnitska had his house. Everyone in the business used to drop by his place. It's beautiful there . . .

I could feel him migrating backward in time. His face softened a little.

How did her parents react?

Well, they'd never heard of Grasse. And Camilla's move to France was like a fire alarm—it scattered the whole family. After a couple of years, the parents left the city and moved back upstate, where they were originally from.

Near Ithaca?

No, near Albany. But far enough away that Dan hardly ever saw them. He stayed in the city, of course. You would've had to crowbar that guy out of Manhattan.

Did he visit Camilla in France?

Dan? You kidding? He never went further east than Long Island! No, he and Camilla settled into an arm's-length sort of thing. They had nothing in common. She rarely mentioned her brother to me.

He rubbed his eyes with one hand. I had to look up Dan's address in the phone book when I called him after . . . when you were born.

AT MY BIRTH—once the doctor had arrived and my mother's body had been removed—one of the two midwives asked Jordan what my name was. Camilla wasn't a name he and my mother had chosen; it was simply the only name he could summon.

With no close friends in France, he was effectively alone. A few of his dead wife's colleagues tried reaching out to him, but he rebuffed them. His loss numbed him; he could scarcely feel it. It frogmarched him through his days.

I wasn't yet real to him. He'd hired a wet nurse; she and I occupied the apartment's bedroom. Jordan spent his nights in a living room chair or on blankets piled on the floor. At seven each morning he went to work, staying there till eight or nine in the evening. He began really to notice me, to pay attention, only when my nightly crying changed from a helpless mewling to something fiercer, more assertive. All that shrieking and squalling became suddenly articulate. My cries, he said, were telling him Paris wasn't where we should be living.

And the trip home, to New York—what was it like?

He didn't answer me; he'd fallen asleep, cut off by exhaustion. I was left to imagine that return. A six-day trip by ocean liner; disembarking at a Midtown pier; a cab ride to an unfamiliar address in the Village; a buzzer at the door. Someone (Dan, Sarah?) had listened incredulously to my father's self-introduction. Staring at the small bundle in the traveling bassinet.

Eve would have stared, too. At these strangers, two would-be members of her would-be family. She was ten, precociously attractive. No longer a child, if she ever had been. Seeing Jordan and his baggage—four suitcases and a baby—what had she said to herself?

ON THE corner of Sixth Avenue and Eighth Street, I bumped into Stuart.

A bit jumpy after Danny's visit, I'd closed The Fourth Wall earlier than usual and had just crossed Sixth Avenue, intending to drop off a deposit at my bank, when Stuart materialized out of nowhere. He was en route, he explained, to a nearby pharmacy, to get some medicine for Carl.

"Anything actually wrong with him?" I asked.

Stuart fake-smacked me with the flat of his hand. "Care to re-phrase that? Like, 'Oh, is Carl all right?'"

"Sorry," I said. "I do hope he's all right." We'd had versions of this exchange before; Stuart's touchiness wasn't merely a reaction to my seeming lack of concern. It did no good to remind him that he'd always been a committed fabricator of worst-case scenarios; he couldn't shake his anxiety.

Now he rolled his neck and shoulders: de-kinking, he called it. He'd spent his day going up and down a ladder, restocking the high-est shelves of Backstage Books. I mimicked his movements and he mimicked mine, exaggeratedly. We drew amused stares from several people walking past our mirror-image improvisation.

Then we traded a few shop tales. Admiring the amount of the check I was about to deposit, Stuart commented that I was getting harder-nosed about pricing.

"This," I said, waving the check, "is for that photo-framing thing I told you about. It'll cover the motel room this weekend."

"Well, Danny will be grateful—her salary's a disgrace! How's she doing, anyway? And are *you* ready for this jaunt to Ithaca?"

"As ready as I'll get," I said. "I'm worried about Danny's expec-tations, though. She thinks she'll find out all sorts of things about her father, but I have my doubts."

"Her father? Billy?"

I nodded. "She's hoping to speak with his sister, and maybe some other people who knew him. We're going to Cornell, too. First time I've ever been there. Jordan never took me."

"Well of course not! If your father couldn't get his head around the idea of taking you to *Paris,* why on earth would he drag you *upstate?*"

I was about to respond to his remark when I felt a hand on my shoulder. Stuart's eyes widened.

"Ho, ho!" he exclaimed, pointing at Sam, who stood by my side. "Twice in a matter of days!"

Sam smiled at him. "You know, I can go months without seeing somebody in this town, and then I'll find myself sitting beside that person on the subway every day for the next week."

"Ain't it the truth." Stuart clucked his tongue.

"The Village is the worst," I said. "If I want never to see someone again, I can be sure I'll run into them on Sixth Avenue."

"Gosh, Sam, I'm sure she didn't mean *you*," said Stuart.

Sam rolled with it, still smiling. "So what convenes this meeting?"

"Actually," I said, "we were talking about Danny. Did you know she and I are going to Ithaca this weekend?"

I'd guessed right: Danny had told him. He nodded. "Well," I continued, "I was just telling Stuart I hope her expectations aren't too high."

"She'll be all right," Sam responded. "I'm en route to meet her right now, as a matter of fact. We're having a drink."

"Oh," I said. It was Thursday—the day he'd said he'd be seeing her. She hadn't mentioned their date to me. Did she know I knew about it?

"Maybe we could have lunch tomorrow," Sam added. "Because I don't really have time to talk right now."

"Tomorrow would be fine," I said after a moment. "I'll call you in the morning."

"Good." He waved both hands—one at me, one at Stuart—and turned away. Watching his retreat, Stuart sniffed loudly.

"What's your problem?" I said. "Because you do seem to have a problem."

He shrugged. "I would say I am having a trust issue. I have frequent trust issues where men and their dependents are concerned. Chalk it up to my father. You know, that nice fellow who dumped my mother and me when I was a lad?"

"Danny's not Sam's—"

"Cammie, this threatens to become one of those merry-go-round arguments, doesn't it? So let's drop it. I am, however, a bit concerned about *you*. This road trip? I'm not hugely in favor of it. Not that it's any of my fucking business. But adventures like this can yield unpleasantness . . . You'll call me if need be?"

"Of course. Thank you ever so much for offering your counseling services," I minced.

"All right, then, off we go." He reshouldered his bag. "Don't talk to any more strangers on the street."

"Tell Carl to feel better," I called after him.

As I moved to the crosswalk, preparing to make my way back across Sixth Avenue, the light changed in my favor and a familiar-looking pickup truck honked at me. Pulling over, Nick opened the passenger-side door.

"Oh good grief," I said as I climbed in.

He gave me a half-alarmed stare.

"It's just that in the space of ten minutes," I explained, "you're the third friend I've run into, right on this corner."

"Ah," he said, easing the truck into a just-released parking spot. "So is this 'three strikes and you're out' or 'good things come in threes'?"

"In your case," I said, "the jury's still out."

"You're here, right? So I guess I've been—what's the word?—acquitted." He leaned over to kiss my cheek. "I've just finished for the day. My job site's a couple of blocks from here."

I leaned back against the door and pointed at him. "You have some more repair work to do."

"That's no surprise," he said. "I do it for a living. People say I'm good at it, too."

"I'd like—"

"You're the boss, Camilla," he said quietly. There was no suggestion of either sheepishness or defensiveness in his manner. If I was game, he was saying, we might forget last night. It was my call.

"I'll be away this weekend," I said. "In Ithaca. When I get back . . ." I clambered out of the truck, glad for his inquiring gaze as I retreated, leaving the sentence unfinished.

INTERLUDE

TIME OUT. A brief break, in which I'll do some necessary clarifying—and a bit of confessing as well.

How did the paths of Jordan Archer and Vsevolod Meyerhold recross after their first serendipitous meeting in Paris? To answer, I must briefly sketch the ups and downs of Seva's career during the Thirties—that parlous decade . . .

TORN BY his multiple talents, Seva sometimes wondered whether he should have renounced acting altogether, in favor of his directing career. There was always the lure of music, too.

He envied Dimitri Shostakovich's ability to mess around on the piano as if it were a toy. Mitya, the theater's in-house music man, led Seva's actors through their warm-up exercises, spurring them on with witty renditions of Russian folk tunes. These he transposed from minor to major and back again, pounding them out at an incredible clip, like a carousel gone berserk.

Seva liked to sketch, too. He undertook little studies in pencil for his own entertainment, and he drew Zina in all manner of poses and costumes—as well as naked, of course. He'd scribble zestily the dark thatch between her legs, the equally dense tufts under her arms, and the errant curls on her head. (The two of them shared a dislike of hairbrushes; Zina was well coiffed only onstage.)

I began noticing that sketching was therapeutic for Seva after he and Zina returned from touring in Germany and France in 1928. Seva was vexed because Glaviskusstvo, the state arts authority, had demanded that Comrade Meyerhold come back to discuss the financing of his theater. Upon his return he gave them an earful. "Let me remind you," he wrote in an acrimonious letter, "that fewer than half the seats of the Zon Theater are usable. Is it your wish that our patrons end up on their literal asses while watching our productions? If not, then get me some real seats and rehearsal space!"

To relieve his stress, Seva took up drawing on a regular basis. Its physicality calmed him. Drawing helped him handle the news of

Trotsky's ouster in 1929, and it proved crucial in 1930, when two deaths rocked Seva: Volodya Mayakovsky's and Sasha Golovin's.

BOTH MEN died that same April: a cruel month indeed.

Volodya's suicide devastated Seva. After receiving the dreadful news, Seva couldn't speak about his friend. It was several days before he broke his silence, and then only with the tersest of comments.

Sasha Golovin's death was less shocking. A well-regarded painter, Golovin was also a gifted set and costume designer. Seva and Sasha's last duet in prerevolutionary St. Petersburg was Lermontov's *Masquerade,* a lush, dark drama about a doomed gambler. The two artists had an excellent time putting the production together.

To stage it Seva had called on me for inspiration. I'd urged him to go to the wide mirror at the back of his studio and stare at himself in it. *Multiply,* I'd prompted him. He'd nodded slyly, then trotted to his personal prop kit and fished around in it for an old hand mirror. Returning to the larger mirror, he'd raised the small one to the side of his face—the glass turned outward—and watched himself smiling at himself smiling at himself smiling at himself, the mirrors' regress continuing past the point of visibility.

"Perfect," he'd murmured. "We'll make the audience and actors see each other *and* themselves."

The next day he'd ordered his stagehands to cover a big set of doors at the rear of the stage with mirrors. Sasha Golovin then created five layers of curtains that parted sequentially during the performance. The last was made of black netting, like a mourner's veil—marvelously spooky!—and the audiences yelled their approval.

Not everyone was pleased. One snide commentator remarked that Meyerhold had staged "a Babylon of absurd extravagance." Seva was used to this sort of venom. A few years earlier, an influential critic had called another Meyerhold-Golovin spectacle at the Alexandrinsky Theater a mere fairground show. Now *that,* responded Seva, was the best compliment he could've received. Mimicking his detractors ("Meyerhold? He's a lost cause; he's obsessed with *commedia dell'arte*"), he'd retorted that he was indeed inspired by *commedia* characters such as Pantalone, the deceived and deceptive merchant, and his daughter, Columbine. And clown figures like Pierrot, he said, were always blends of foolish and shrewd, hence excellent starting points for depictions of modern people.

Elements of *commedia* personages exist in every character, Seva wrote in response to his critics: "It's simply a matter of finding them." True—and I had cause to remember those words when Seva was in prison.

THE SUMMER following the deaths of Mayakovsky and Golovin, while in Paris, Seva became fixed on the idea of taking Volodya's *The Bedbug* to New York. The biting humor of the play, a futuristic comedy, had made it a hit in Moscow, and Seva was convinced it could do well in revival—especially in a city whose tall buildings would inspire fresh ideas for staging.

Seva wrote to Glaviskusstvo, requesting permission to take Mayakovsky's play abroad "for the edification of the American masses." Before long he received a reply: *The Bedbug* wasn't going to the United States or anywhere else. This time, Seva wrote directly to Comrade Bubnov, Commissar for Enlightenment, who responded with a brief note in which he ordered Meyerhold to return home, pronto.

Seva was furious: this was the second time he'd been told to leave Paris. Back in Moscow, he spent several sleepless nights at his theater, pacing and smoking and breaking into angry rants. Finally he stopped pacing, holed himself up with a pad and pencil, and began sketching.

First he did a set of funny caricatures of bureaucrats with human heads and the bodies of insects. Starting with Comrade Bubnov as a bedbug, he moved on to theater critics, whom he depicted as lice and cockroaches. A few days later, after downing countless cups of black tea sweetened with jam, he started on a series of fantastical bugs, several of which were quite scary-looking. Casting around for sources of inspiration, he began pulling books and journals off his shelves. Someone had recently given him a copy of Franz Kafka's *The Metamorphosis,* which he'd read with admiration. Flipping through its pages once more, Seva decided it was hopeless to think about sketching a bug like *that.*

SEVA RENOUNCED his insect fixation after a few days. It had served its purpose, releasing some of his pent-up rage and sadness. Moreover, sketching had allowed him to see himself as someone who could handle a pencil.

Advertising and packaging had always intrigued Seva: they were cousins of set design. He admired the clever wrappers of the Nozhnitsky tobacco he purchased weekly, along with the slender boxes containing Epokha and Reklama cigarettes. Yet until his run-in with the Glaviskusstvo authorities, Seva had been unaware that he faced an opportunity at once amusing and potentially lucrative—the design of a perfume bottle.

Indeed, he'd barely registered a request for creative assistance made by the young American perfumist he'd met in Paris. Seva's memory of Jordan would have languished in the cellar of his consciousness had I not remembered that Mr. Archer's business card lay somewhere in the jumble of papers on Seva's desk. Responding to the American's plea might, I decided, provide my partner with a good outlet for his inchoate feelings.

SO I began jogging his memory.

First I stirred up some relevant specifics. The American had described himself as a regular theatergoer. Jordan had chatted intelligently with Seva about his favorite plays, especially those of Shakespeare, and he'd been curious about Strindberg, Brecht, and Chekhov. (Upon hearing that Seva had worked with Anton Pavlovich, Jordan had asked, "What was he like?" To which Seva had replied, "He coughed all the time, and was one of the funniest men I've ever met.")

Now, helped by my promptings, Seva began remembering that the American had told a few tales of his own. Jordan had known a great deal about his perfume-making forerunners and peers, everyone from medieval alchemists and herbalists to present-day manufacturers. Gradually I guided Seva's memory toward the chemist's request for help. It had come at the end of a lovely dinner whose cost the American generously offered to cover. Over a concluding glass of wine, Jordan had pulled out a notebook containing photographs of perfume bottles. He and the Meyerholds had examined the pictures together.

THE FIRST was of a bottle of Molinard's lovely Xmas Bells fragrance. It was an extraordinary vessel: a black glass bell decorated in gold, like an exotic Christmas tree ornament. Molinard's perfumes, Zina told Jordan, appealed strongly to wealthy Russian women. She knew a few (formerly aristocratic but now living in reduced circumstances) who still owned a bottle or two of Molinard— but nothing like *that,* she'd exclaimed, pointing at the photo.

Another picture showed a Guerlain crystal flacon in the improbable shape of a turtle. A different Guerlain bottle, designed in collaboration with Baccarat, had a delicate hollow stopper shaped like a heart. Yet another (exotically named Djedi) was in the shape of a faceted crystal; it looked as though it had just emerged from a cave. A Baccarat-designed bottle resembling a glistening snail had been hand painted in eighteen-karat gold. The opulence of each design was astonishing.

Seva had sat quietly, a polite but less than avid viewer, while Zina oohed and aahed at the photos. But one of Jordan's pictures had grabbed Seva's attention: that of a clear glass bottle created by René Lalique. The bottle's stopper took the form of a woman. One of her arms crossed her breasts; the other covered her crotch. Her face, over which her hair fell loosely, was tilted to the right, and her expression, visible even in so small a photograph, was nearly despairing.

This photo was the one I now led Seva to recall. That arresting mix of sensuality and desolation had struck him then, and I figured it would do so again.

"Volodya," he whispered.

I was expecting this reaction. Mayakovsky's eros, as Seva knew well, had been liberally spiked with Thanatos. Orgasm had been mordantly beautiful to Volodya, its shudders very like those of terror. (*Love has inflicted on me a lasting wound—I can barely move*: his poetry was full of such claims.)

Seva was remembering; then he began imagining. His forehead creased the way it did when he started to get ideas.

"Let's play with this perfume-bottle thing," he said finally, smiling a little. "I'll send a few designs to that Archer fellow."

So I knew we were onto something, and it would be curious.

RETROSPECT LENDS these droll, minor-seeming events—the Russians' stay at a certain Parisian hotel, the American's quirky offer of collaboration—their luster. For if these things hadn't taken place, Meyerhold's quintessence would never have found new lodgings in Camilla Archer.

Yes, quintessence!—that's my word for it. Call it spirit or *esprit*, whatever you'd like. I'm referring to those incorporeal energies dispersed at every human being's death.

Some people call this process the transmigration of the soul, or the unfolding of karma. Others think of it as the passing on of a legacy, or simply the procreative force of memory. Yet however it's labeled, the phenomenon's the same: at death, a person's mental energies are dispersed like an invisible mist—a scent potently fragrant for certain receptors . . .

Being an agent of this dispersal after Seva's passing, I began by appearing occasionally in the dreams of various individuals with whom he'd worked. Over a period of many months, I infiltrated all manner of nocturnal dramas: dreams about St. Petersburg, socialism, sex, the muted sound of footsteps on heavy white snow . . . Although it was entertaining to see Seva's mental ashes scattered in this way, I wasn't satisfied. Remorse gnawed at me. I'd encouraged my late partner in his fidelity to the Revolution, that utopian sinkhole. Then I'd let him believe art could inoculate him against history. Hadn't I effectively spurred him toward a brutal, needless death? What mea culpa could I now offer, what remediation?

An answer took decades to arrive. For starters, the mental scent of someone as complex as Seva doesn't disperse quickly. Moreover, I was seeking a particular receptor—someone with a deep love of theater, hence susceptible, though not an actual professional. An individual with conflicted emotional loyalties, adept at self-concealment. The person I had in mind needn't be buffeted, like Seva, by political winds. A family crisis would do as well. It would present similarly fierce challenges to this individual's self-definition.

Only this really mattered: once singled out, my collaborator would have to play his or her scenes without a script, and improvise without holding back. She would need to learn that the wearing of masks and costumes isn't expedient but essential, a necessary risk. And would require a full reconnoitering of the human heart pounding beneath the disguise.

IF THIS learning were to happen, perhaps at last I might feel I'd atoned for failing to help my Russian partner. But would Camilla prove herself worthy?

As of our fourth co-production, I was feeling guardedly optimistic. Things were heating up nicely. It was time to insert the ex-husband into the next dream, along with Jordan—and Seva, too, of course. Before long, Camilla's carapace of denial would start cracking, and she and I would both have a shot at some relief.

FIVE

SAM AND I are in bed. A silvery pool of moonlight spills on the floor beneath our open window. The night is mild, calm.

The light looks like mercury, Sam says as he points to the floor. Like rain in an Atget photograph. Or like you.

Me?

I am at his side, one forefinger on his chest. Where his pectoral muscle and rib cage meet, the hair grows shorter, finer, sleeker, not curly and coarse as in the dark mat sheltering his breastbone. Following the slope of his chest, my finger runs a circle around one raised nipple, returning to the smooth side, where his ribs form a staircase that curves around to his back.

Here, he says. His fingers descend; the middle one parts me. He presses gently, then begins slipping downward. His finger's still in me. Now his chest is at my pubis; our hairs mingle. The soft bristle of his chin makes me pulse hard, and I tighten around his finger.

He's on his belly. His eyes close, then reopen. They're in shadow, but I catch their gleam. Pale moonlight washes his back. He presses one cheekbone against my inner thigh, then does the same for the other, his head swaying back and forth, his breath warm, roving. I begin arching, and his mouth plays me. I clench and clench until the chord spends itself.

Through our window wafts a scent. It swirls densely, though it smells nothing like smoke. It smells like a man and a woman mingled, a malty, piquant tang. The swirling thickens, solidifies, and assumes the shape of a man in a tuxedo. He's tall and lean, his dark hair tousled. He wears a black eye-mask and white gloves. In one outstretched hand, he holds a small glass bottle shaped like a whale, its spout glinting in the moonlight.

The man's fingers squeeze the whale bottle gently. I see a scent emerging, a fine, full spray.

Sam sits up. Are you something like a genie? he asks the man in a tone of helpless awe.

Something like that, answers the man. He speaks with an accent— a Russian accent, I now realize. The timbre of his voice is reedy, seductive.

Actually, he adds, I am more like a conjuror.

Can you conjure children? asks Sam.

The man's eyebrows dip into a frown. Children? Nyet! *Too complicated! As Mayakovsky said: "Who can control this? Can you? Try it . . ."*

I sit up. I've figured out who this man is: he's my father in disguise. I begin yelling, my voice loud and hoarse.

You're quoting Mayakovsky? He was talking about love! Remember what that *is, Jordan?*

Of course I do.

No you don't! You don't know a thing about it!

Please, my dear. It was time for me to exit. As you were well aware—you helped me off the stage! Let us not forget the facts.

Paying no attention to our exchange, Sam gazes earnestly at Jordan. Try, he pleads.

Try what? asks Jordan, perplexed.

Try conjuring a child!

Ah, my poor friend, says Jordan, his tone indicating he's just figured out what Sam is talking about. For that, you will need a different partner. This one here (he points at me) is following another path! I respect this—after all, I never intended to become a parent myself. It happened entirely accidentally. This daughter of mine has made her choice: no children. Yet she's left with a residual feeling of—oh, what's the English word? Ah yes, gloom! *How to cheer her, reassure her? How to tell her—*

Oh, fuck off, I interrupt in disgust.

He gazes at his whale bottle, then leans over and begins murmuring to it.

She doesn't understand, my darling, he says consolingly. And now she's angry, our daughter's so angry with me! Camilla, chérie, *what should I do?*

Get lost! I shriek at him.

Lost? He smiles wanly at me. But I already am, my dear. I already am.

There's a swirling of opaque light. Now Jordan is wearing a white eye-mask whose contours are ringed with rhinestones—only he's not Jordan anymore, he's Meyerhold. The disguise has been dropped.

The director shakes a long forefinger at me.

You did indeed help your father off the stage, he says, his tone coolly admonitory. And it was your decision to do so.

He wraps his cape tightly around himself. I cannot see his eyes, still concealed by the mask, but I sense the heat of their gaze.

And don't make the mistake, he adds, of thinking your father wasn't grateful for your assistance. He certainly was! But he was silenced by his need for privacy. Ask yourself this: Is disclosure your natural instinct? Might you not extend a little sympathy for the old man's failure of nerve? Yes, he should have told you about Eve . . . Yet on that score, you're not the only person owed an explanation, after all! What about Danny?

Another swirl of light and I awake.

HAVING ENCOUNTERED, on the same street corner within a ten-minute stretch of time, the full complement of men in my life, I returned home both stimulated and fatigued. I ate supper, went to bed early, and fell immediately into a deep sleep.

Awaking the next morning to an indefinably charged scent, I realized I'd had another strange dream. Sitting on the edge of my bed, still drowsy, I made myself focus as hard as I could. In the dream there'd been some sort of altercation with Jordan. Sam had also been there; something took place between the two men. And Meyerhold had been onstage as well. He seemed to be turning into a regular presence in my dreams.

I made up my mind to borrow from Stuart a couple of biographies I'd read years ago. It was time to reacquaint myself with the Russian director's ideas about theater. About the pleasures and perils of disorientation. And theaters as sites of dreams.

I SHOWERED and put on my work uniform, as Stuart calls it. Every day I wear the same thing: chic black jeans, a white T-shirt (V-necks, in fine cotton or silk), a blazer (linen in summer, gabardine in spring and fall, cashmere in winter), Italian loafers or boots, and gold jewelry. I carry a small, elegant knapsack. My uniform's expensive, but the expense is part of my cost of doing business. When you're a dealer in inessential and costly objects, dressing scruffily is not a good idea.

Heading out the door, I remembered that I had a lunch date with Sam. At The Fourth Wall, I phoned him and left a message suggesting a time and venue—relieved that he rarely answers his cell phone, preferring to treat it as a beeper. He needn't call me back, I told him, unless there was a problem.

At ten (early in my business—most collectors are night owls), a young actor came by with a collection of stage properties from various productions that had been mounted in London in recent years. He'd just broken up with his British boyfriend, he said, a professional props man (and, it seemed, a likely pilferer), from whom he'd received a small treasure trove of props that he now wished to trade for fast cash. I ended up taking the whole terrific lot, including a beautiful crop and bridle from a Broadway run of *Equus*. (These items, I saw, were authentic; they bore the PT stamp of the Plymouth Theater. I figured they would impress a client of mine who, being heavily into both theater and horses, considers *Equus* the best play ever written.) The deal was concluded affably and in my favor.

An hour later I sold a wide-brimmed black hat to a client who's an obsessive collector of Samuel Beckett memorabilia. The hat entered my shop on the head of a woman who looked to be around sixty. After introducing herself, she told me her story. Apparently Beckett's *Ohio Impromptu* (a wonderful little stage piece with two characters, a Reader and a Listener) had premiered at Ohio State University in 1981, and this woman had been in charge of props and costumes. One of the props (there were only two) was a hat; the other was a book that lay open on a table throughout the performance. (They'd used a French dictionary, an amusingly Beckettian touch.) Would I, she asked, be interested in the hat?

Her story had to be true, and her hat was in mint shape. I made her an offer that she happily accepted, evidently feeling no strong attachment to her headpiece. Then I called my Beckett-besotted client, who showed up within minutes, checkbook in hand, and paid me very handsomely for the hat.

I phoned Stuart to brag about my morning's take. After congratulating me, he told me I'd missed a golden opportunity: I should've asked the seller if she still had the dictionary as well. Or perhaps she'd kept one of the long black coats worn by the play's speakers? I got off the phone and kicked myself for not doing exactly as he'd suggested.

THE IMAGE of a black coat, however, prompted me to recall a few more details from the previous night's dream. In it Jordan had been whispering something to a small perfume bottle. Whale shaped, it had actually spouted its scent—a nifty bit of bottle engineering.

The whale bottle in turn reminded me of a conversation with my father that had taken place when I was in sixth grade. It concerned a report on sea creatures that I was writing for science class. I'd asked Jordan what made dolphins and whales so special.

I don't know about dolphins, he'd answered, but ambergris is one thing that makes whales special. Sperm whales secrete it. A very heady scent. Makes some people a little dizzy.

Like ammonia? I asked.

No, in a nice way. (He didn't add—I would have been too young to understand—that ambergris is said to smell strongly like a woman's secretions.)

How do you get it out of the whale? I asked.

You have to kill the whale, he said. Which is why ambergris is rare and expensive. Most ambergris these days is artificially produced—except in Russia, where they get it straight from the source.

I expressed outrage at the idea of Russians hunting and killing sperm whales, and Jordan shrugged.

Whales aren't the only animals in Russia that produce scents, he said. There are Russian beavers, whose glands produce castoreum. It has an earthy, leathery smell. Makes an excellent fixative. But getting the oil from the beaver is tricky, because its sweat glands are located right between the anus and the genitals in both the male and the female.

This embarrassed me, but Jordan seemed not to notice.

Canada, he continued, produces a better castoreum. But there's one thing from Russia that nobody can beat: birch tar oil, from the birch trees that grow over there. It's used to make the *cuir de Russe* fragrance, Russian leather. The Russians also do a nice harvest of roses. And clary sage, and certain umbellifers. Those are weeds—at least that's what *we* call them. In Russia not everything we consider a weed is a weed. Over there they have different ideas about things.

I'd gathered as much from my social studies class, but I said nothing.

Russians, Jordan continued, have been involved in fragrance for a long while. Actually it was the Venetians who first brought the

Russians into the European perfume market. Venice had a trade triangle going between southern Russia, Egypt, and Venice. The Venetian merchants used to nab teenaged boys from the Black Sea area and sell them off in Egypt, to serve in the army. The Venetians probably swapped perfume for those boys in Odessa or some other Crimean port. Clever people, the Venetians! Excellent traders.

For the first time, I'd realized how well informed about perfume my father was. He'd acquired most of his knowledge while working for Coty, which had its own Russian connection: Ernst Beaux, the St. Petersburg–born creator of Chanel No. 5. Beaux was a technical innovator whose formulas made use of newly created aldehydes— molecules that smelled something like a hot iron on damp cotton. They could spur raw materials to greater depth and loveliness, and they gave the entire perfume industry a boost. (Beaux was rumored to have developed Chanel's famous scent while working for Coty. A few years after No. 5 appeared on the market, Coty began selling a fragrance called L'Aimant that bore a powerful resemblance to Chanel's perfume, although nobody was ever able to prove that the Russian had tricked anyone.)

Jordan knew all about Beaux's aldehydes, but they weren't his passion. What riveted him was the paradox of a perfume's birth. That birth always begins with a death—"the agony of the flower," as his French colleague Roudnitska called it, which occurs during its harvesting. After a flower is cut, its scent goes through moment-by-moment transformations that make it highly unstable and unpredictable. For the perfumist, the challenge lies in capturing the right smells from this rapidly shifting spectrum before they evanesce altogether.

This obviously requires considerable technical skill. A good perfumist, however, begins not by manipulating molecules but by recollecting unusual and powerful experiences. Distinctive perfumes require distinctive origins, said Roudnitska. Feelings first, science second.

My father satisfied Roudnitska's requirements. He could recollect in its entirety an experience utterly foreign to his peers: that of watching a wife expire in a room filled with the smells of parturition. The flower's agony.

THOUGHTS OF Jordan and the dream had led inexorably to my mother. This time, though, instead of feeling what I normally felt when confronting her in my mind—guilty, glum, and alienated all at once, like a child scolded for not crying at the funeral of a relative she didn't actually know—I felt anger, a sudden gust of it gyrating across me.

I pulled aside the curtain concealing my dartboard, opened my drawer of photos, and contemplated my options. Choosing a pair of head shots, I fixed them to the board and began tossing my darts. I took aim first at my mother (whose picture I'd photocopied for this purpose) and then at Eve—Camilla, Eve, Camilla, Eve—hitting them over and over, hard, until I'd covered both their faces with tiny pricks. Then I removed the targets and sat at my desk.

What, I wondered, would Stuart think if he were to walk in and discover me engaging in this secret pastime? This is how you've chosen to pay for being an understudy, he'd say. You see yourself as second fiddle, and you're paying with resentment! That's one thing you've got oodles of, isn't it?

ALMOST NOON: time to meet Sam. My dart tossing had let off some steam, and my mind felt nicely vacant.

As I made my way east, yet another detail from my latest dream came to me. Jordan had been wearing a tux, just as he had in the juggling episode. Although I'd never actually seen my father in formal attire, I knew he'd been no stranger to it.

I recalled the sight, in my dream, of his white-gloved hand around a whale-shaped bottle of perfume. And his odd accent—but wait, no, that hadn't been Jordan—it was Meyerhold. He'd impersonated my father, pretending to be Jordan before revealing that he wasn't.

The tumblers were falling into place now. Sam, perturbed, had asked Meyerhold to conjure a child. *For that,* the director had replied, *you will need a different partner.* And hadn't Meyerhold said something about an explanation owed to me, and to Danny as well? About Eve?

"Cammie?"

Sam's voice startled me. I'd arrived at our appointed spot on Grove Street, unaware that I'd actually stopped walking.

"You look zoned." Sam gave me a hesitant smile.

"I am, a little," I said.

"Well, do you want to go in, or would you rather collect yourself first?"

I stared at his face, which remained more familiar to me than anyone else's; I knew its every mark and line. "I'm getting collected," I answered after a moment. "Though I'm not particularly hungry."

"That makes two of us," he said. "Don't know why I have no appetite—maybe it's the balmy weather?"

I scanned Grove Street, seeing as if for the first time the recently budded pale-green leaves, their tracework shadows spilling over the sidewalks.

"Let's—"

"—walk," Sam finished with me, our voices landing on the word at the same time.

We began strolling westward in easy adjacency, our knapsacks slung over our outer shoulders so they wouldn't collide. As we walked we chatted. I heard about Lila's volunteer work at Abby's school, about the Williamsburg gallery's increased insurance premiums, about Sam's newest photo-book projects. His favorite, he said, was a Wegman-style collection of pet portraits featuring not dogs but birds—in particular an irascible mynah bird named Cockpit, whose owner (a former pilot) had captured the bird's antics in a stunning series.

From me Sam heard about The Fourth Wall's latest acquisitions and sales. He was also told about several plays I'd seen during the spring, about Stuart's computer problems, and about the garden store that had replaced Eve's. He did not hear anything about Nick.

Sam and I never discussed the Paramour in any but the most cursory terms. Ditto for Lila. No sand in the crankcase, Stuart had once said, and Sam and I obeyed that rule.

TALKING, WE wound our way up, down, and across streets we'd walked countless times: Hudson, Commerce, Barrow, Jones, Morton, Leroy, Carmine. We covered the length of Bedford Street (past The Fourth Wall, at which we both cast a proprietary glance), finally turning east on Christopher Street.

In Sheridan Square we settled into a booth in a café. Neither of us alluded to the fact that we were spending not just a lunch hour but the better part of an afternoon in each other's company. By the time we'd ordered our second iced coffee, we'd dispatched a good many topics, though Danny wasn't among them.

I was the one to insert her obliquely into our conversation. After hearing about Sam's latest car, a secondhand Audi, I mentioned that Danny and I would be driving Jordan and Eve's old Volvo wagon to Ithaca.

"It's still up and running. Which is unbelievable, really, considering it's over twenty years old," I said.

"So you're making Danny do the driving." Sam was putting his toe in the water.

"I hate to drive unless I have to, as you know. This whole idea's hers, remember? I'm just going along for the ride."

Sam gave a short smile. "Oh, I suspect it's somewhat more complicated than that."

"But of course." The smile I returned was similarly brief. "With her it tends to be, doesn't it?"

Sam waded in a bit further. "We talked last night. She told me about Eve's having been artificially inseminated." He paused. "What sort of arrangement do you think Eve might've made with that guy—what's his name, Bobby?"

"Billy. Billy Deveare, Danny's father."

"Yeah, I suppose."

My face must've registered my confusion. "There's no way of

knowing for sure that he was the father," Sam said. "All Danny's got is a piece of paper stating Eve was inseminated. The donor's not listed."

"But Billy's on the birth certificate," I said.

"Which means only that he agreed to sign his name. It's not proof."

"What are you saying? You mean Billy didn't—but why would he do that?"

"Who knows?" Sam answered. "Money, maybe. Or perhaps he just wanted to lend Eve a hand in a tough situation. Maybe he felt sorry for her and agreed to be the father, but on paper only. Maybe she had some other guy in Ithaca."

I shook my head. "Too complicated, Sam. There's a much simpler scenario. Eve decided she wanted a kid, and Billy was willing to be the father in the physical sense—and legally. But they weren't actually lovers, so she borrowed his sperm."

Sam shrugged. "That may be what happened, but nobody knows for sure. No one *can* know, with Eve. You know how it was—always plenty of men in her life . . ."

OUR BOOTH felt suddenly confining; I nearly signaled the waitress for a check, then thought better of it. There was more for us to talk about.

"Well, your ideas sound far-fetched," I said. "And I bet they sounded that way to Danny, too."

Leaning forward, Sam put his elbows on the table. "Stuart's right, you know—what he said, the other day. About Danny being in a messy place. And there's something else. She seems to have this idea that you're holding out on her, Cam."

Something like exasperation coursed through me, a similar jazzing of my nerves but more distressing. Out of nowhere came a memory of Eve in Frenchtown, the summer of Jordan's death. Eve tending his backyard with a spade and a trowel, weeding, watering. Acting like the woman of the house.

"As far as my cousin was concerned," I said, "her lovers were never any of my business. That includes Danny's father."

Sam's left hand pumped an invisible brake. "I know. And I've told Danny she's got to accept that you might not want to talk about certain things."

"Such as?"

"Such as *your* father." His gaze held mine steadily. "I don't know what you've already shared with her . . ."

I shook my head. "You and Stuart are still the only people who know how Jordan died."

Again he frowned. "Yes, but you need to realize something, Cam. Danny's got pretty clear memories of that day. She was six years old, it's not just a big blur to her. She's got specific recollections and questions. And she feels you've been keeping secrets about that. As well as about Eve."

Another tap dance of my nerves. "Well, I guess she'll just have to be mad at me, then," I responded. "Because I made a promise to my father, and I don't plan to break it—especially since Eve was involved. Don't push me on this one, Sam."

He lay a hand over both of mine, his touch less reassuring than strange; I couldn't remember the last time my fingers had been cupped in his.

"I'm just disturbed that she'd be thinking of herself as having somehow failed," he said.

"Failed at what?"

"Dealing with Eve. Accepting her as she was—a lousy mother, an unhappy woman. I think Danny's worried that her anger made Eve all the more withheld. She always longed for Eve to be open with her—"

"I know that. But Danny would never have gotten what she wanted. Eve was incapable of being open with anyone."

"Except your father, maybe?"

"Perhaps," I answered. "I have no way of knowing. Eve certainly couldn't be open with *me*. Or with Danny. Or you, for that matter."

He looked away, and when he spoke again, the pain in his voice was palpable. "Did you and I do enough for Danny?"

"We stepped into the breach. And we can keep doing that, Sam."

He nodded. "You're right. And it's ended up good for both of us, having her in our lives. Don't you think?"

I heard no uncertainty in his voice. He wasn't looking for a confirmation of his own belief; he wanted to know what I felt.

"I think so. Now."

"We needed a kid."

"It didn't help." The old heartbreak, not yet dispatched. Dormant, it could still be jostled into stinging life. "You can't *will* such things, can't order yourself to want your own child. I wish I'd known that, for your sake. Having Danny in our life was enough for me. But for you . . ."

My sentence required no finishing. Something like embarrassment, a deep surprise at the unexpected rawness on display, came over us. We stared off into nowhere until a waitress slid a check onto our table.

MY AFTERNOON with Sam triggered memories. Most were of Eve after her return from Ithaca to Manhattan. Random details: her answering machine's jingle (the tune from the Yogi Bear cartoon series); a set of framed botanical prints in her bedroom; her enjoyment of macaroons and marzipan (the stickies, she'd called them, licking her fingers while eating them). And an amber necklace I'd found on the sidewalk when I was five, which I'd given to her. I could still recall my fierce pride when I'd presented it—how pleased I'd been to make her blush in happy surprise.

Eve hadn't been one for verbal acknowledgments. She'd had other ways of signaling thanks: with a bunch of fresh rosemary tied in twine, or an African violet in a clay pot. And her own way of laughing, too: a low, skittish trill, at once alluring and evasive. It was the laughter to which she'd treated Sam and me while commending us for rescue work performed on her behalf.

We'd done plenty of it. Within a few months after Eve's return from Ithaca, my studio apartment had become Danny's second home. Then, after I met and married Sam, our apartment became the place where Danny could most often be found when she wasn't in school. Eve's garden shop was in Chelsea, and her landscaping clients lived all over the city and on Long Island. She was incessantly, aggressively on the go. Gradually her busy schedule began edging Danny out.

There were, of course, day care centers and after-school programs where a single mother could deposit a young child, and Eve took advantage of these—but she also had a cousin nearby. When all else failed (and it frequently did), Sam and I were there to pick up the slack. Eve had no real friends, no one else to ask for help. So Sam ended up keeping track of Danny's pediatrician and dentist appointments, and I took her shopping for school clothes, books, toys, and games—always with cash supplied by Eve, who was careful never to incur any financial obligations to me. Sam and I both attended Danny's school plays and athletic events. Our work and social schedules were flexible and seldom jammed. We liked hanging out with Danny, and we usually had room to maneuver when Eve found excuses for not maneuvering herself.

Beneath the issue of our availability lay something more basic. Sam and I wanted what Danny offered us: regular doses of warmth, and a mix of silliness and verve to which we both grew addicted. Occasionally we'd wonder aloud what Danny herself was making of Eve's unmotherly behavior—how it was affecting her at some hidden level. But of course neither of us spoke about this with her, and I knew there'd be no speaking of it with Eve.

THESE MEMORIES linked with others. Of being married and coming unmarried, as in unglued.

When Sam and I finally got round to confronting the issue of parenthood, sometime in the fifth year of our union, I was overwhelmed by ambivalence. Or so I called it, though my version seemed more intractable than that of other women I knew. Sam, I suddenly understood, was expecting me to convert without angst to his way of seeing things. For him, having a child was an inevitability, not an option. How had I managed to overlook something so obvious? And how had he failed to plumb the depths of my uncertainty? Beneath love lay bewildered incomprehension.

Meanwhile there was daily life to attend to. The Fourth Wall was earning a steady income, but after a time, Sam grew less gung ho about it than I was. He left the running of it to me, instead pursuing his central enthusiasm—the photo-book projects he'd begun undertaking as a freelancer. And because he was also thinking about opening an art gallery, he spent his spare hours making visits to potential spaces and developing contacts with artists and dealers.

One of his dealer friends employed Lila as an assistant. Sam didn't pursue her until he and I were divorced, but she was there: an alternative future, with full-time parenthood built in.

BY THE time he and I did begin trying in earnest to conceive, I was in my late thirties. Months went by and nothing happened. I didn't become pregnant, nor did either of us make an appointment to talk with a doctor or explore other possibilities for "starting a family," as the antiseptic saying went.

Near the end of a long stretch of scheduled copulating, my resolve gave out. One evening in the fall of 1990, we both gravitated toward separate beds. Sam threw a sheet and blanket on the living room sofa, and I headed for the daybed in our small guest room. The next morning I arose and walked into the bedroom we shared, expecting to find my husband there. Our bed lay empty, its spread pulled over its pillows. I remember exactly how it looked, unrumpled and unremonstrative, as smooth-faced as a confessor.

Sam entered the room right behind me, his surprise at the sight of the pristine bed as evident as mine. Later that week, after we'd both dumped buckets of tears (Sam wasn't the crying type, and the sight of his sobbing was at once oddly beautiful and heart-stoppingly sad), we separated.

We were divorced on a beautiful morning in May, the kind that brides-to-be pray for. We took the subway downtown to the municipal building, where we sat in an open courtroom with a half-dozen other couples. Waiting patiently to be sundered, we held hands the entire time. When our moment arrived, the judge, a woman, threw a puzzled glance at our interlocked fingers. Were we sure, she asked, that we wanted to do what we were about to do? Her question, so like the one posed by the person who'd married us, drew a wan smile from us both. We nodded like a pair of well-mannered children too shy to talk.

The judge pronounced and gaveled, then signed our rupture into reality. We got back on the subway and returned to the Village, where we entered a café and drank coffee dazedly, like two people who'd just walked away from an explosion. I remember Sam's and my parting: the two of us on the sidewalk, smiling bravely. Sunlight glinting everywhere. A swift embrace of hands. A prickling sensation in my fingertips afterward, which lasted hours and felt purposive, like a code, though I couldn't crack it.

OUR MARRIAGE was over, yet Danny was still in it.

Sam and Lila were married in July of 1996. Eve, Danny, and I attended the wedding. A party took place after the ceremony, in a large, ramshackle loft belonging to a painter friend of Lila's.

At the request of the bride and groom, Eve had decorated (transformed, really) the loft. There were rose petals all over the floor, as well as quantities of red roses strewn on a bed pushed into one corner. A lamp above the bed illuminated the entire garnet-colored mass. It was so attractively done, I remember thinking. Tasteful and amusing at once—just what Sam would want.

At one point during the party, I found myself standing with Eve off to one side, near the rose-covered bed. People were dancing; the party was in full swing. Eve turned to me, raising her champagne flute.

"Cheers," she said, and we tapped glasses. She wore a long green dress, deeply V'd in front and back, which showed off the column of her spine and her strong collarbones and décolletage. Several men did double takes as they walked past her. Her fragrance, Lune, surrounded her lightly, a sublime aura. Inhaling it, I felt as if I'd entered an invisible chamber; the fragrance wasn't only in the air but also, and perhaps chiefly, in my memory. Lune *was* Eve, the woman I'd adored and raged at (silently, fiercely) since the day she'd first started wearing my father's perfume. Since she was fifteen.

"I just had a flash," she said, "of the fathers. Ours."

"Jordan and Dan?" I asked, nonplussed. Eve rarely mentioned either man.

She chuckled softly. "Can you believe Dan's been dead twenty years? And how many has it been since Jordan died?"

I counted. "Fourteen."

She nodded. "Ever miss him?"

Possible answers sparred within me. "Sometimes I'd like to ask him a few questions," I said.

"About?"

"Oh, theater, his travels . . . Things he's seen and done and smelled."

That low trill. "You make him sound like an old dog."

"He was, in a way."

"No, *Dan* was an old dog. Jordan was someone with an excellent nose. And a need for privacy."

I'd never heard Eve state such things about my father. "He did keep to himself," I said. "And he wasn't into memorabilia, that's for sure. Ten years in that house in Frenchtown and almost no possessions. It was easy for Stuart and me to clean the place out after he died."

"Nothing to give him away."

I glanced at her. "I guess so."

"You think that's how he wanted it?" Her question was uninflected by any emotion I could detect.

"I guess," I repeated.

"Me, too. But you'd know better, being his daughter." She set down her glass of champagne. Returning her gaze to the dancers, she extended one hand, gesturing lightly. "Why didn't you have one with him, Cam?"

I followed the trajectory of her forefinger. She appeared to be

pointing at Sam, who was dancing with Danny to an upbeat number that had brought lots of people onto the dance floor. "Have one
what?" I asked.

"A kid," she answered.

I turned to stare at her, wondering if I'd heard her right.

"I mean, would it really have been such a hard thing to do?" she
added.

"I suppose I didn't want it enough," I replied. "It was always hy-
pothetical for me."

Eve said nothing, and we sipped our champagne and stared at
the dancers. Then she lit a cigarette. She smoked infrequently and
only at parties, when enough other people were doing it. She lev-
ered her cigarette up and down with her thumb, using it as a
pointer.

"Do you know if he's slept with her?" she asked.

Again I followed the gesture's trajectory, the lit tip of the cigarette. My astonishment was so large I could barely say the two
names.

"Sam?" I asked. "Sam, you mean—with Danny?"

"Yes," said Eve, "that's who I'm talking about."

Her face told me nothing. "Eve," I said, "are you really asking
me if while Sam and I were married, he ever—"

"No," she broke in, "of course not, Cam! Not while you were
married. Danny was too young then! I mean sometime later. Like
during the past year or so."

For a moment I wondered if she was drunk, though I knew that
was highly unlikely. She'd probably had no more than a glass of
champagne all evening.

"What on earth are you talking about?" I said. "What sort of a
man do you think Sam is? And have you forgotten he started dating
Lila over a year ago?"

"No," she responded, "I haven't forgotten. But he and Danny
did take that trip to London a few years back."

For her twentieth birthday, Sam had offered to accompany
Danny on a five-day trip to London. It was her first journey abroad.

They'd gone to a bunch of plays and galleries, and she'd had an excellent time.

"Listen to me," I said, putting down my glass. "I met the two of them at the airport when they returned from that trip. And I can tell you they didn't sleep together while they were over there. Because I would've known right away—"

"I believe you, Cam. But admit it. You weren't entirely sure until you saw them. Aren't I right? There'd been a little question in the back of your mind . . ."

For a moment I felt as though she'd placed her hands over my eyes and whispered something malevolently irresistible in my ear. "As soon as they walked through the gate at JFK, I knew nothing had happened. *Nothing*," I repeated.

The smoke from her cigarette formed a pale gray wreath around her head. "I expect that's true," she replied. "Nothing happened in London. It's afterward I'm thinking about."

"Afterward?" I came unstuck. "This conversation's absurd," I snapped. "Sam's been like a father to Danny, and she's like a daughter to him—and *you* ought to know that better than anyone else. Why are you saying these things?"

Before I could add anything else, she'd taken my hand, pulling me behind her. We were headed, I saw, straight for Sam and Danny. Reaching them, Eve released me and took one of her daughter's hands, pivoting Danny away from Sam and leaving him to me and me to a shocked silence that Sam mistook for my usual unruffledness.

He and I danced together briefly. When the tune ended, he kissed my cheek, handed me off to Carl (who received me graciously), and went off in search of another partner—his bride, in all likelihood, since he'd scarcely seen her all evening.

MY COUSIN and I did not revisit that conversation. For several weeks after the wedding, I avoided her. I was too angry to deal with her even perfunctorily. As I saw it, she'd set out deliberately to provoke and distress me.

This had nothing to do with Danny, I decided. Eve's aim had been to rattle *me*. She'd wanted to drive a wedge between Sam and me, just as she'd sought, when we lived in the family apartment, to insert herself between my father and me. Some old frustration or resentment was driving her now, causing her to make ridiculous statements.

Thereafter I made sure that our conversations about Danny were confined to the mundane. For her part Eve seemed content to leave well enough alone. It dawned on me (and as the months passed, I grew more committed to this thought) that my cousin hadn't actually believed what she'd suggested about Sam. It had been something to toss out, a verbal hand grenade whose bang—my dismay—was worth the ensuing mess.

I SPOKE with no one, not even Stuart, about what Eve had said to me. The best thing to do, I concluded, was to treat our exchange as if it had never taken place. But it had, and I found myself wondering whether I'd missed something. Before Lila, in that interval of confusion after Sam and I parted, what assuagement might he have longed for—Danny being, after all, no longer a girl but a woman?

I thought of Sam's body, the languid heat of him in my recent dream, when he'd pleaded with Meyerhold for the child I'd resisted—the child he hadn't figured out how to claim. Meyerhold had told him, sternly, that he'd need to find himself a different partner.

No, I thought. Not Danny. That couldn't have happened. But there *was* something I'd missed—there had to be. I couldn't be dreaming so much for nothing.

STUART AND Carl stopped by at around ten the night before Danny and I were to leave. I'd just placed my packed duffel bag in the front hall when the doorbell rang.

"Surprise!" they chimed. "We've come to pay you," Stuart said solemnly.

"Actually," said Carl, "*we* were out for a stroll, and *I* remembered we owed you money."

Stuart grinned. "That box of books you gave me? We sold every last one of 'em today. For a tidy sum! Thanks to him," he added, jerking his thumb in his partner's direction.

"Dumb luck," said Carl. "Some guy comes in, flirts with Stuart for a while, then tries acting all serious with me—like I'm the *book* guy and Stuart's the *fun* guy." He rolled his eyes. "So I showed him your box and told him the contents were really something else indeed."

"Were *what?*" I laughed.

"That's what I kept saying—a bunch of high-minded shit like *quite extraordinary, really something else indeed* . . . And the guy was totally convinced! He won't *read* the books, of course. He'll display them. Brag about them."

"Although he did know his theater," said Stuart, fake wistfully.

"He wasn't talking to you about *that,*" Carl drawled. "I have eyes and ears, pal."

Stuart chuckled as he handed me a wad of bills. "Two hundred and fifty smackers! Happy now?"

"Oh yes," I said, stuffing the bills in a side pocket of my duffel. "You've just supplied my play money for Ithaca."

"For a spot of gambling, maybe?" Stuart mimed the shuffling of a deck of cards. "Or some twenty-year-old rum?"

"No—*cigars,*" said Carl. "You don't even have to smoke them. Just show 'em off. I can just see you and Danny in some student pub at Cornell, lighting up a couple of those nice long Cubans . . . *That'*ll get the boys' attention."

We all laughed, and Stuart gave me a parting hug. "Have fun, babe. You look tired—get some sleep. If you have more dreams, try to remember them! And don't forget, you can always call me."

It was true: I could always call him, I thought as I lay in bed an hour later, tossing uneasily. But I wouldn't. Better for Danny and me to venture forth with no one to rescue us when we slid down the rabbit hole, as I felt certain we would.

INTERLUDE

PUTTING THE ex-husband on stage in Camilla's latest dream proved more effective than I'd imagined. One never knows! Dreams are ever rambunctious . . .

Every play, Seva once said, is produced unfinished. The final, crucial revision is always made by the spectator. And as the sole spectator of her own nocturnal dramas, Camilla had to be kept on her toes, wondering how things would pan out.

I pause the action now to fill in some important information related to Seva's career. And linked, too, with Camilla's crucial revision . . .

FROM HIS Petersburg days to the mid-Thirties, Meyerhold's artistic ascent proceeded virtually unchecked. By the Twenties, he'd become the chief luminary in Soviet theater and a personage known throughout Europe and even in America. Then his career fell—was felled, I should say, like a tree.

Russia in the Thirties was a place of everyday preposterousness. As the evidence of abuses and terror mounted, millions of Russians went about their daily business, pretending everything was fine. With one shot from his revolver, Volodya Mayakovsky had permanently removed himself from the national drama. Thereafter Seva and his colleagues found themselves forced to bushwhack a trail through increasingly dense thickets of political uncertainty. This they did with varying degrees of success, and always with anxiety.

Fortunately Seva possessed large reserves of confidence in his professional capabilities. It was nearly impossible to flap him; plenty of people had tried all along to do so, but to no avail. His imperturbability was a result of the amount of time he spent on the stage, first as an actor, then as a director. For Seva a stage was a construction site, a director very like an architect. Actors were sculptors: with their voices and bodies, they lent shape to words. Beneath the words lay music. It was always there, if only metaphorically—and it was what most excited Seva.

YEARS EARLIER, Seva had told Anton Chekhov that he finally understood the challenge of staging *The Cherry Orchard*. The director must get the *sound* of it, Seva said—by which he meant the underlying cadences of the play's action.

At the start of his career, during rehearsals at the Moscow Art Theater, he'd held several long conversations with Chekhov about such matters, and he'd chronicled those talks in his journal. Anton Pavlovich had harbored serious misgivings about the way in which most dramas were being staged. In one journal entry, Seva recounted how Chekhov had scoffed at the sets for *The Seagull*.

"Get rid of these damn bits of trees and those flowers," the playwright had urged the cast, amiably but firmly.

The actors, proud of having lugged such props onto the stage, gave Anton Pavlovich chagrined looks.

"Why do you need all that stuff anyway?" Chekhov added.

"To make it real," one actor answered.

"*Real?*" retorted Chekhov. "But the stage demands a degree of artifice! It reflects the quintessence of life!"

After hearing that remark, Seva committed himself to devising new ways of staging that would disrupt everyone's assumptions about theatricality. Hilarious and bewildering, Seva's productions had viewers literally yelling in the aisles—and the critics baffled or outraged. His daring strategies worked: people flocked to his theater.

FOR A while, Seva's star rose and shone. But then Volodya killed himself, Sasha Golovin died, and everything started coming undone.

In 1932 the playwright Nikolai Erdman was arrested and deported to Siberia. In 1936 Dimitri Shostakovich was condemned by the Party for his so-called formalism. In 1938 Seva's former mentor Stanislavsky died.

Dramatic enchantment, said Seva (quoting Pushkin, whom he revered), vibrates three chords of the imagination: laughter, pity, and terror. Among Russians the first two chords had ceased vibrating; only the third, terror, still resonated. In 1937 the directorial approach favored by Comrade Meyerhold was described by one Soviet critic as a "systematic deviation from Soviet reality," which in turn constituted a "hostile slander against our way of life." For months everyone was on edge, wondering what might befall Seva.

In 1938 he was allowed to take over the lead of Stanislavsky's Opera Theater, to the surprise of his colleagues. Was a lull setting in at last? The worst of the purges seemed to be over; perhaps the darkness was lifting.

Not yet.

That same year Lavrenty Beria became Internal Affairs Commissar. The following May, Seva attended a meeting of the Writers' Union, where he let slip a few remarks about the banal subject matter of Soviet literature. Afterward several telephone calls were placed to key government officials. Apparently Seva was denounced by (among others) a Russian journalist named Koltsov, who linked him with the counterrevolutionary Bukharin.

Not good. Or as the Americans put it, *way* not good.

ONE MORNING in June of 1939, Seva was dragged down the stairs of a flat in Leningrad by several men who transported him to Moscow. He was thrown into a dark, filthy cell in Lefortovo Prison and eventually transferred to the Military Collegium. His wife and friends obtained no information regarding his whereabouts.

Thus began the vanishing.

Now imagine the actual ending. After many months of imprisonment, Seva is standing in his darkened cell, awaiting a sham trial scheduled for the next morning. Picture him pinned at the terminus: no exit. He sits in an unbreachable concrete block, a bare, all-revealing space, perfect for so tragic a farce. He couldn't have designed a better set himself!

Did he attempt to prepare for the moment when the executioner would barge in? Did he repeat his defense to himself silently? Or did denial take over, urging his thoughts to drift backward and swirl languorously in eddies of memory?

Zina: visions of her flashing like popped lightbulbs before his closed, swollen eyelids. Zina in extravagant costume for *The Lady of the Camellias* . . . Zina in bed in the flat on Gorky Street, wearing one of his nightshirts . . . Zina perched on the steps of the Bolshoi, panting slightly and grinning after one of their long rambles through Zamoskvarechie, over the bridge to the Kremlin, past the gardens, through the gates to Prospect Marx, to the theaters.

A letter he'd written her a few months earlier, from the countryside: *You are golden . . .*

Did he remember, at the very end? Or could he remember nothing, not even her beloved face? This is a question to which I will never have an answer, for it arose as Seva was being sundered from his life, and I from him.

SEVA DIED in Moscow on February 2, 1940, in the basement of the Military Collegium of the Supreme Court of the Soviet Union, near Red Square.

His death went unremarked. As far as the average Russian was concerned, Vsevolod Emilevich Meyerhold ceased to exist after that morning when the NKVD came for him. References to him were excised from books and journals on Russian theater; theatergoers and critics were forbidden to mention him in public. It was as if his productions had never been staged in Moscow and St. Petersburg, not to mention Paris and Berlin. As if his astonishing offerings to the theater had never materialized anywhere, period. As if they were a dream.

Zina couldn't have helped. A few weeks after Seva's abduction in St. Petersburg, she was arrested in Moscow, then released and returned to the Gorky Street apartment. A few days later, her slashed, crumpled body lay in the middle of the living room floor. Neighbors told of two men and a car. No suspects were ever apprehended.

Zina's daughter had forty-eight hours to remove her mother's and Seva's clothing and other belongings, including books and papers, from the flat. She was traumatized, of course, but also thorough. Afterward she emphasized that whoever had committed the murder had not burglarized the apartment, at least not in an obvious fashion. Nothing at all was missing except, apparently, the contents of an unlabeled manila envelope.

Shortly after the place was emptied, a young female member on the staff of Commissar Beria moved into half of the apartment. Beria's chauffeur took the other half. The chauffeur eventually left; his roommate stayed on until her own forced eviction, nearly fifty years later. (Picture her, purple-faced: "I am an old woman! This is my home! Why, Comrade Beria himself was responsible for my being in this apartment! Have you no sense of history?")

One unlabeled envelope . . . Nobody knew what it had contained, and nobody thought much of it. I did, however. And I happened to know it hadn't been taken by Zina's killers, whose only assigned task had been as follows: delete that slut wife of that Jew traitor Meyerhold. The papers inside that envelope were missing because Seva had already delivered them (via a visiting English journalist, whose suitcase was fitted with a false bottom) to Jordan Archer.

THERE: I'VE done the necessary catching-up work.

Camilla's next dream took place in what might be called the theater of unaccepted loss. And since a fine set—that loft in which her ex-husband and his second wife celebrated their nuptials—had already been constructed, I decided we might as well use it for our next act.

In it Camilla's cousin and mother join forces unexpectedly. A disconcerting alliance, as Meyerhold makes sure to point out. On we go!

SIX

A PARTY is taking place in a loft: Sam and Lila's wedding. In a far corner is a bed strewn with red roses; at the center of the space, people are dancing. The mood is merry.

I am with Eve and another woman—my mother, Camilla. We're all dancing together. Eve and Camilla resemble each other: they have the same finely arched brows, the same lithe way of moving their shoulders. Swaying together as they dance, their hands on each other's hips, they look nearly like twins.

Jordan is watching all three of us. He's wearing a tux; his cummerbund is a silvery gray, his bow tie a beautiful ivory-maroon stripe. Unaffectedly elegant, he looks like a man accustomed to getting his share of attention. This, I think, is how it must have been for him in Paris, in the days when he attended fancy dinner parties.

The music slows and the crowd starts to thin. Grasping one of Eve's hands, Camilla beckons to Jordan, who approaches and offers her one of his. Camilla puts the two hands together—Eve's and Jordan's—palm to palm.

Your turn, she says to them.

I want to ask my mother a question, yet I'm mute; my mouth opens, but no words exit. It occurs to me that I haven't found my question; I'd be able to ask it if I could locate it, so I ought to start looking for it. To me it's a physical entity, a missing object. I walk around the perimeter of the loft, peering everywhere, but nothing turns up.

Meanwhile the room has begun emptying. Soon only my mother, my father, and Eve remain. As I stand off to the side, wondering where to continue searching for my missing question, I notice a tall man astride the rose-covered bed. He's backlit, so I can't see his face clearly, but I'm certain I know who he is.

I approach him, determined to make him speak. He holds up one finger in warning, as if asking me to wait. Then, smiling, he twirls his ebony cane and points it in my mother's direction, spritzing her with perfume—the cane is an atomizer in disguise. The scent it emits is Lune.

My mother vanishes—poof!—like a soap bubble.

The tall man laughs gaily. You're barking up the wrong tree, he says to me. She wouldn't have been able to tell you a thing! The question's over there, where it's always been!

He gestures in the direction of Eve and Jordan, who're still holding hands. They dissolve into a Lune-fragranced mist that envelops the entire loft. The man, too, evanesces, and I'm awaking woozily, and it's morning, the alarm's ringing, but isn't it a Saturday?—yes, today we go to Ithaca—where's Danny?

DANNY CARRIED her bags to our room at the Cornell Motor Inn. It reeked of stale cigarette smoke. There were, however, no other vacant rooms in the motel—no rooms *anywhere,* the proprietor sourly informed us. Apparently a convention had brought swarms of visitors to the area. We were lucky to have found a place near Sapsucker Woods, not far from the main campus.

Glancing around, Danny flopped onto the bed nearest the door. Like the one by the window, it was covered with a dull cotton spread.

"I'd like this one," she said. "Okay with you?"

"You may have that bed," I answered imperiously, "as long as I can have the monogrammed towels and the plush terry cloth robe in the bathroom."

She snickered. I began unpacking, which evidently wasn't on her agenda. Although she'd driven the entire way from New York, Danny seemed not in the least slowed down. She jiggled the Volvo's keys lightly.

"What a dump," she growled, doing a decent Bette Davis imitation. "Let's go! The less time we spend here, the better."

"Where to?" I closed a bureau drawer, unlined and none too clean.

Danny gathered up her sunglasses and backpack. Even as a teenager she'd displayed little of the dawdling behavior of her peers.

"Judy Deveare's house," she announced. "Let's get it over with. I'll drive."

"You know where she lives?" I asked.

"More or less."

LESS, ACTUALLY. It took us a while to find the subdivision of single-story tract houses, about a half-hour from Ithaca. Neither of us could make sense of the map we'd brought with us. By the time we arrived at our destination, we were in a mixed mood: part goofy, part apprehensive.

The tall, pale woman who answered the doorbell reminded me of no one at all. She wore a nondescript blue pantsuit with a simple white shirt. Her appearance said nothing about what she did with her days, whether she was a worker or a homemaker. Directing a slightly suspicious gaze at us, she asked us our business.

Danny's brief and admirably direct explanation did not appear to faze Judy Deveare. She listened impassively, then stepped to one side and motioned us in. A man's voice called from an upstairs room. In a voice giving nothing away, Judy answered that she had visitors, and the man offered no reply.

"My husband," she said to Danny and me. She led us down a dimly lit hallway to a kitchen whose windows gave onto a back lawn. "He's watching the game," she added. "Coffee?" she said, pointing at an old-fashioned percolator on the range. "It's fresh."

We murmured thanks and sat down at the kitchen table. Judy produced three mugs and a plate of what looked to be homemade muffins. "My daughter dropped these off this morning," she said. "Help yourselves." She abstained while Danny and I each took one.

"How old's your daughter?" Danny asked.

"My daughter? About your age," answered Judy. She eyed Danny now, finally ready to scrutinize her. Her gaze did a brisk dance over my face, then returned to Danny's. After staring for several long moments, she looked away, nodding, as though confirming some statement she'd just made silently to herself. She said nothing further while we ate our muffins and sipped our coffee.

Danny finally broke the stillness. "So did you know?" she asked slowly. "About me?"

Judy's face moved into and out of a scowl. "You mean," she said, "did I know that my brother claimed paternity in the case of an illegitimate child?"

Danny raised her brows. "Well," she said, "I do have a birth certificate. Which your brother did sign." To my relief, she spoke slowly and evenly.

"So he did," said Judy. "And you are . . . ?" She turned suddenly to me, as if she'd forgotten the part I was meant to be playing in this improvisation.

"Her cousin," I said, gesturing at Danny. "Technically, I'm her mother's cousin, which makes the two of us—"

"—first cousins once removed," Judy finished smoothly.

"Right."

"How removed is that?"

I shook my head uncomprehendingly. Danny, who'd understood, glanced at me and stepped in, her tone placatory. "Camilla's along for the visit," she said. "To keep me company. I'm just trying to get a sense of who my father was. I figured you'd be the right place to start."

"Why now?"

Danny seemed not to have expected this. "My, uh, mother died recently," she said. True though it was, her statement sounded concocted. I was momentarily embarrassed for her, then disconcerted by my own embarrassment, all of which I felt Judy observing.

"Ah," she said. "So you're doing the 'roots' thing."

"I guess you could put it that way."

Judy stood and walked to a window several yards away. Turning to face us, her body silhouetted, she looked suddenly imposing: someone not to be pushed around. She'd hold her own.

"You need to know something," she said. "I'm not a fan of your mother's. I only met her once, but I heard about her from Billy. Your mother had him exactly where she wanted him."

Well, I thought, there it is. Judgment rendered, case closed.

Judy wasn't finished, however. "My kid brother never knew how to protect his own interests. In high school the girls all liked his standoffish ways. He was a loner, and that made him romantic in their eyes. They guessed he was the smart kind of loner, but actually he was the dumbest kind. Just a gullible guy. An easy mark for someone like your mother, a few years later."

She'd begun and ended her speech by addressing Danny, although at one point—when she'd said "and that made him romantic"—she'd glanced at me. Perhaps she'd thought that I, being older, would understand better than Danny could.

Danny was nodding equably, as though Judy had just stated something interesting but without much significance. "You're right," she said. "Eve did know what she wanted. She wanted a baby, and she didn't want a husband. Just a sperm donor." Danny's speech quickened a little. Either the coffee or something else (impatience, anxiety?) was kicking in now. "What kind of an understanding did Eve and Billy have? Did they have a deal? Like, did my mother tell him he could have visiting rights? Or did she say all along there was no way she'd let him near the baby? Or was that left up in the air?"

Now it was Judy who seemed not to have anticipated such a line of questioning. Her eyes narrowed as though Danny had asked her to peer at something she found difficult to make out.

"He never spoke with me about any of that," she said. After a pause she continued, her voice firm, in charge. "You want to know what Billy was like? He was a not-very-smart, not-very-exciting, average-looking guy without many friends. Very good with plants and flowers. I guess that's how he and your mother met, at the greenhouse. . . . People generally ignored him or teased him. I was always trying to get him to stand up for himself. Especially with his—"

She halted as though she'd suddenly come upon a hole in the ground.

"With his . . . ?" Danny prodded.

Judy was not to be baited. "Billy made a huge mistake is all," she said finally. "He signed your birth certificate thinking he was your father, but he wasn't."

"What?" Danny's tone was incredulous. "What are you saying?"

Judy turned to face her. "Listen to me," she said, her voice steely now. "You can believe whatever you want to believe, but Billy wasn't anyone's father. I don't know who got your mother pregnant, but it wasn't my brother."

Danny's surprise was rapidly curdling. I could see her heading toward anger. Judy saw it, too.

"Like I said, you can go ahead and believe whatever you like. But I'm certain my brother didn't father you. He didn't give Eve a *usable donation*"—Judy uttered the words in distaste—"and after you were born, he had nothing to do with you. Not because he didn't want to—he did—but because your mother told him to leave her alone. She'd got what she needed from him. His signature. That's all."

She paused, made two fists, and put them together before her, side by side. "Eve broke him," she finished, making a sudden snapping movement with her fists.

"I doubt that," I said.

Both Danny and Judy gave me startled looks, as though they'd forgotten I could talk.

"Something else happened," I gambled. "He couldn't resist Eve because he had no resistance in him—for anything. You said as much yourself. Billy couldn't protect his own interests."

Judy flushed, then regained her hold. Moving to one of the kitchen's counters, she opened a drawer and extracted an 8 x 10 photograph of a young man. The aqua-colored drapery that served as the backdrop for the portrait lent it a typical mid-Seventies look.

"Here," Judy said, handing the picture to Danny. "Billy in high school, senior year. He met your mother four years later. Take a good look. Do you think you resemble this man in the least?"

I moved to Danny's side. Billy Deveare was red complexioned, his face nearly round, forehead low, eyebrows thin, hair flaxen. He was smiling, but his smile communicated neither humor nor happiness. Though he clearly wasn't tall, he appeared trim. Judy had described him accurately: this was a not-bad-looking, not-good-looking, unmemorable young man. His face expressed nothing of his inner life.

"It's not just about physical resemblance," said Danny. She spoke slowly, holding herself in check. "I don't have to look like him to be his daughter, Judy. Legally, I *am* his daughter. And if I weren't his biological daughter, why on earth would he sign my birth certificate? You make it sound like my mother could get your brother to do anything she wanted. What could she possibly have had on him that'd make him declare paternity when he wasn't the father of her baby?"

Judy gave a little snort. "What did she *have* on him? How about the fact that he was nuts about her? He was in his early twenties, and here was this good-looking woman in her thirties, fixing her sights on him . . ."

"I'm sure she twisted his arm," said Danny. "But Billy made his own choice. She pressured him, and he decided to help her conceive. When she got pregnant, he took responsibility for his part."

"Nope," said Judy. "Eve twisted his arm, but Billy's sperm was useless."

"Useless?"

Judy's smile twisted with frustration. "You don't know how he died."

Danny shook her head. "No, not exactly," she said uneasily. "Mom told me he died of a sudden infection."

"That's right. He underwent surgery and got an infection afterward. It was incredibly virulent, and it took him down in less than twenty-four hours. A total fluke."

"Her mother died very fast, too," I said, gesturing again toward Danny. "Eve got bacterial meningitis. Her blood was poisoned. It all happened in a few days."

"So you understand what such surprises are like. Want to know what Billy's surgery was for?"

I said nothing. "Yes," answered Danny.

"It was for a blocked ejaculatory duct. He'd had a cyst for some time. It'd been diagnosed when he was fifteen, and the doctors had recommended surgery then. But our father was opposed; he said it'd clear up on its own. Billy went along with that."

She stopped, her face suddenly, darkly alive. We were in her actual presence now, the stripped, exposed pith of her; she was no longer striving for composure. Her voice remained calm, however, as she continued: "Then he started having pain, and his doctor admitted him to the hospital. They ran a bunch of tests, and then they operated. An infection set in, and somehow went out of control . . . After Billy's death, the surgeons said they'd found antisperm antibodies in his semen. Which meant he'd had some sort of autoimmune problem. Probably as a result of a chronic infection in the testes."

She moved back to the kitchen stool, whose height put her eye to eye with Danny. "When I asked the doctors if my brother had ever had fertile sperm, they said no. At least not since he was fifteen, when they'd first found the cyst."

Danny frowned in evident disbelief. Judy ran the tips of her fingers across the top of Billy's photo. "So is this the man you can claim as your father?"

Danny went to the sink, rinsed her coffee mug, and poured herself a cup of water, which she chugged. She refilled the mug. After draining it for the second time, she rinsed it out and placed it in the sink. As she turned to face Judy and me, her lips still wet, I saw she was primed: gloves off, prepared to fight.

"How would my mother know your brother was infertile," she asked Judy slowly, "if *he* had no idea he was?"

"Your mother didn't know. She didn't need to—it didn't matter to her one way or the other, because she didn't intend to use Billy's sperm in any case. She wanted his *signature,* not his sperm. I've told you about his infertility just so you'd understand you couldn't have been his daughter. However Eve got pregnant, it wasn't Billy's doing."

"Let me see if I've got this right. You're telling me Eve asked Billy to give her a sperm sample, then substituted someone else's instead? Or Eve was already pregnant?"

"I don't see how she could already have been pregnant. They'd tested her."

"So you're saying she must've swapped the samples. And Billy signed the birth certificate, thinking I was his kid."

"That's right."

Danny's laughter was a short, loud grunt. "Leaving aside the technical, uh, improbabilities—"

"Oh, I investigated those myself. It wouldn't have been tricky for Eve to do. The sperm she planned to use would have been banked somewhere; all she had to do was get her doctor to request that it be sent to him. Then she could just pick it up, take it to the hospital, and substitute it for Billy's."

"Wouldn't Billy have been there, too?" I asked. "I mean, didn't he have to donate his sperm at the hospital?"

"Sure, but so what? They'd go there together, and she'd take his donation to the ladies' room and switch her little vial for his. Not difficult. No one would know."

Danny picked up her backpack, which she'd dropped on the floor by her feet. "Do you have any idea," she said, "how ridiculous this sounds?"

"Do *you* have any idea," Judy retorted, "what absurd things people will do when they're desperate?"

The backpack went over Danny's shoulder. "I get the sense you thought very little of your brother."

"I was referring to your mother," said Judy. "As for my brother, he was a lost cause. He worshipped your mother, and before that he adored my father. Wouldn't hear it from me—kept insisting it'd all work out, Daddy would come to respect him, Eve would come to love him—*I* had it all wrong, I was too hard on people . . ."

Tears glinted in her lashes, held in check; she would not cry now. She'd released whatever needed releasing. There'd be no more words.

"Let's go," I said to Danny. "Thank you, Judy."

She gave a little nod. Danny and I walked in silence to the front door, which I closed carefully behind us.

DANNY SAID nothing during the half-hour drive back to our motel. We pulled into a parking space, and Danny switched off the Volvo's engine. It was five o'clock. The late-afternoon sun cast long, low shadows; distorted car images bent their way across the gray macadam of the parking lot. No people were present.

"Hungry?" Danny asked after a moment. "We've barely eaten all day. I need a real meal."

I thought of Judy's daughter's muffins, their sweet insubstantiality: our lunch. Was Judy preparing a meal for her husband right now, browning chicken pieces or shaping hamburgers, the kitchen radio on low volume? I couldn't imagine her doing anything other than staring into space, recalling her dead brother and his putative daughter. And me—the person who'd no doubt encouraged this needless memory-churning encounter.

"Yeah," I said. "It's been a long day."

"Need anything here?"

"Nope."

IN A few minutes we were installed in a booth in a pub called The Cheerful Swan and had ordered hamburgers and beers. Danny broached the visit first.

"So what do you think? Was she lying?"

"About what?"

She let out an annoyed *tsk*.

"I just want to answer the right question."

"Do you think she was lying about Billy's being infertile?"

"Impossible to say," I replied, shrugging. "The story hangs together, but it could be a total fabrication. Obviously Judy doesn't want to acknowledge you as a member of the family. Though she knows she can't fight the fact legally. Not that there's anything hanging over her. I mean, Billy's dead—"

"Yeah, and this isn't about legalities. Judy recognizes that her brother is my father, on paper. And she thinks *he* thought he was my father. In fact, at the time of my birth, she must've believed the same thing, too, right? Even though she'd met Mom and concluded she didn't give a shit about Billy."

"Well, Judy could've been wrong about that," I said. "She might have read Eve wrong. Eve might've truly liked Billy."

"Yeah." Danny paused. "That's one big unknown. And the other is, who might my father have been, if not Billy?"

"Are you inclined to believe Judy on that one?"

"No more than I'm inclined to disbelieve her."

"I know what you mean."

She leaned back to accommodate the large platters our waitress was placing before us: cheeseburgers enshrined by fries and pickles. "Man," she said, rolling her eyes. She pushed a few french fries into a small hill on her plate, salt-and-ketchuped them, speared them, and dispatched them in one big bite. Then she locked me in her gaze. As she began to speak, I could hear her working to sound calm.

"I can't shake this sense that you're sitting on something, Cam. Since Mom died, you've been concerned about my feelings, but you've hardly said a thing about your own. So I have no idea what's going on with you. Which isn't what I'm used to. Normally you pony up."

She paused to eat some hamburger. Her attention was fully on me, though she was doing a good job of making it look like her food was her sole preoccupation.

"Nice to see your appetite's back," I said.

Interrupting her assembly of her next mouthful of fries, she frowned at me. "Are we switching the subject, by any chance?"

"No," I answered, "merely commenting. As for what you just said, I'm not surprised—*I'm* finding it hard to tell what I'm feeling, too. Other people are experiencing the same thing. It comes with the territory, I guess."

"You're very consistent, Cam, I'll give you that. You keep end-running my questions." Her tone sharpened. "'Eve? Billy? Oh, well, I really wouldn't know about any of that. Your mother and I just happened to grow up under the same roof . . .'"

Abruptly she pushed away her plate. Making a nest of her forearms, she lay her head down and turned her face to one side. We sat in silence. Finally, laying a hand lightly on her head, I asked, "Has it occurred to you I've been worried about you? And not just a little?"

She tilted her chin upward to glance at me. "Yes, Cam," she replied. Then her head turned sideways, and she spoke into her crooked elbow. "I didn't mean to suggest—"

"I'm not saying you were," I broke in. "It's just that your mother's death has put me in a different position than it's put anyone else."

She lifted her head and sat up. "Did you love Eve?" she asked.

RETURNING HER frank stare, I felt it might be possible at last to answer her unguardedly. The impulse brought both relief and unease. What if it was simply a selfish need for unburdening? A wish for openness enacted at Danny's expense?

"Just tell me," she said. "Quit *weighing* everything, for Christ's sake! What's with you? *Fuck,* Cam!"

"Okay," I said, wrapping both of my hands around one of hers, which was tightly fisted. "Okay."

"So answer my question!" She pulled her hand out from under mine.

"Yes, I loved her." I'd never said it aloud to anyone; certainly not to Eve. "But without knowing who she was. Which was scary."

"How do you mean?"

"I mean . . . in the family apartment, everyone concealed themselves, hid what was going on inside. Especially Eve. That made me afraid of her in a way I wasn't of anyone else."

"Including Dan?"

I shook my head. "I never liked Dan much, but he didn't scare me. Neither did Sarah. She and I weren't—of course I felt affection for her, and gratitude, but there was a gap between us, right from the start. We never had a mother-daughter type of bond. Eve I loved. Eve, and my father . . . I was constantly afraid they'd cut themselves off from me."

"How did Mom treat you when you were young?"

"Treat me?" I leaned back in my seat. "She knew I needed her company. She'd let me tag along, watch her do things. Like, I'd sit in her room with her while she got dressed or listened to music. Sometimes she'd groom me—you know, fix my hair, let me try on her makeup and perfume . . ."

On a shelf near the window of Eve's bedroom sat a cluster of miniature glass bottles, unadorned vials with hand-lettered white labels. Although the vessels were plain, the fragrances they contained were complicated. Each one hinted at a strange admixture of pleasure and disturbance. Sitting on the floor, I'd watch Eve dab my father's perfume everywhere: on her earlobes, the insides of her elbows, the nape of her neck, the backs of her knees, along her inner thighs, between her full breasts, across her navel. Her body astonished me. As yet I had none of my own, only (as I experienced it) parts: arms and legs, neck and stomach, head and feet, hands. Eve's was whole, a bewitchment.

"Did she talk with you?"

The question tugged my memory in another direction. Now I was hearing the easy, cool authority of Eve's voice. "Your mother was the only real talker in our household. Jordan never said much to anyone. Dan talked, but mainly with Sarah. Sarah's voice was soft—you had to strain to hear her—and she never spoke at length. Eve was different. She had a strong voice, a good laugh."

"Was she affectionate with you?"

"We didn't go around saying warm things to each other, if that's what you mean. Nobody did that in our household. Now and then Sarah would say 'you're a sugar'—that's how she expressed affection. And sometimes Eve would make sugar jokes, call me Cammie Cane or something like that."

"So she was a talker. But did she talk with *you?*"

Eve in her room, her door closed. How many hours had I spent waiting for her to emerge, wondering what was causing her to closet herself? "Not about her feelings, if that's what you're getting at," I said. "Sometimes she'd say things to me about Dan, but that wasn't really talking. More like ranting."

Dan had joined the American Communist Party in the early 1930s, remaining in it until Eve was a teenager. He'd dragged her to political meetings and rallies, though he'd never managed to make it to most of her school events. His daughter's life had taken place on the periphery of his, a blurry, irrelevant outlier.

"Dan had a temper, right?"

"Yes. He and Eve argued a lot. She gave him a run for his money, too—told him his politics were outmoded and he was screwing up his relationships with everyone in the family. Not that it helped. He wasn't ever going to be a decent father."

"Why'd she name me after him, then? To give me some kind of link to a father, even though I never had one?"

I shook my head. "I think she was using the name as a kind of promise to herself."

She frowned. "A promise?"

"To give you a completely different experience from the one she'd had with Dan." My answer wasn't convincing, but I had no other. "Your grandfather lived entirely in his head. Which made him completely selfish."

"Like Jordan?"

I wasn't expecting the question, the name. "Jordan lived in his head, too. But he knew how to dance. And he liked flowers."

Danny contemplated this. "Neither of them should've become a father," she stated. "And Mom shouldn't have been a mother."

We were off-map now, on uncharted terrain. "I'd give that a yes," I replied slowly.

"But you sure as hell covered for her!" she snapped. "And so did Sam! Until I went off to college and you both finally realized I couldn't be tricked any longer. Remember that time at your apartment?"

I KNEW what she was referring to.

One weekend, home from college, she'd come to my place for dinner. That evening she'd spoken about her mother in a new way, with a depth of frustration and hurt she'd never before expressed. And she'd accused me of playing along with Eve. She hadn't wanted to hear my responses—to her they were just excuses. The day after our dinner, I'd called Sam, who'd reported getting a similar earful from Danny.

"Sam and I talked that weekend, too," she went on, as if I'd just aired my thoughts. "We spoke about all the time I used to spend with the two of you when I was a kid. You and Sam got together when I was four, and from that point on, I was over at your place constantly. Tell me, did you and he both *want* me around?" She hesitated. "Because I'm sure I was with you a lot more than you'd banked on. I've always wanted to ask you about that. But I've been afraid the answer would make me even angrier at Mom."

Closing my eyes for a moment, I pictured Eve at Sam's wedding party, champagne glass in hand, questioning me about Sam, making me question myself.

"Having you with us was what Sam and I both wanted," I said, trying to keep my tone steady. I wanted urgently to reroute the conversation. "You know, my biggest concern now is your state of mind. You look and sound so much better than you did even a few weeks ago. But back to this trip of ours—tell me what you want from it, Danny."

"My father."

"And your mother?"

Flexing the fingers of her right hand, Danny gave one of her rings a nervous twirl. "Sam said the same thing to me. That coming here is at least as much about her as about my father, whoever he is . . ."

I nodded. "Neither Sam nor I think you'll discover much here. In any case, what do you want to do tomorrow?"

"I'd like to see the landscape architecture department at Cornell, and have a look around the campus." She'd begun cooling down. "I'd also like to stop in at a local nursery where Mom worked."

I threw her a questioning glance.

"I found the place on the Web," she went on. "It's not far from here. I want to talk with the owner. Maybe he knew Mom, or knows someone else who did."

That night we sat watching TV (a police procedural, the only thing viewable on our feeble television) without speaking more than a few words. Not anger—that wasn't the emotion rising like trapped water between us. More like a mounting wariness about what we might each feel as we tracked Eve the next day, and during the days to come.

AWAKING AFTER a heavy slumber, I realized I hadn't dreamed a thing. I closed my eyes, took a few long breaths, and waited: nothing. My dream-stage really had stayed dark all night, which surprised me.

I took my time showering and dressing. Danny, who'd already gone out and returned, carried fresh fruit, coffee, and muffins to a picnic table adjacent to the motel's parking lot, where we ate breakfast. The blue-skied Sunday was shaping up to be warm, but not overly so. Almost no cars materialized, and the backseats of those that did pass by were occupied by children being taken (I imagined) to Sunday school or the nearby state park.

The morning's tranquility felt like the atmosphere itself, smooth and transparent. Danny said she wanted to go to Bluebell Nursery before visiting the campus. I told her I'd like to see downtown Ithaca. Showing no disappointment, she offered to drop me off and meet me a few hours later for lunch.

THUS I found myself wandering the Commons and the DeWitt Mall in the center of town, aimlessly window-shopping. A few stores were open. In a men's emporium I picked up a bright blue bow tie for Stuart, and in a kids' shop I found two Cornell T-shirts for Sam's children.

At eleven I entered a café, ordered an espresso, and eavesdropped on a conversation between a pair of earnest-sounding graduate students arguing the merits of George Bernard Shaw's plays. They were sticking around campus for the summer, I gathered— earning money doing research for a professor who was writing a biography of Shaw.

The students' conversation reminded me of my own college years in New England, and of how much Stuart and I had enjoyed gossiping about actors, directors, and playwrights. We'd lived almost nothing but theater during those four years. Gradually we'd moved toward other interests, and into a closeness we hadn't known and wouldn't experience with anyone else. Ours was a love affair, we eventually realized—without sex but with all the other features: infatuation and letdown, fights and reconciliations. Over time, our talking tuned in to less intense frequencies; we learned to counterbalance with humor our usual tendency toward overseriousness. Our relationship settled onto its own terra firma—paydirt, as Stuart called it. The longed-for ground of reliable love.

Danny had no one like Stuart in her life, no friend so cherished. She preferred traveling in a pack with a half-dozen other young women and men, all of whom enjoyed seeing films, playing pool, and drinking coffee and beer. I knew she'd received support from these friends after her mother's death, yet I doubted she'd revealed to any of them—even those she'd known for a while—the discord in her relationship with Eve. Easier to let a benign version of the story prevail than to try explaining a messier truth.

ARRIVING ON time at the restaurant we'd chosen as our meeting point, Danny handed me a baseball cap with BLUEBELL NURSERY printed on it.

The nursery was a pleasant enough place, she reported over lunch, but the owner hadn't known Eve. At his suggestion she'd dropped in on another greenhouse a few miles down the road. Its proprietor had been entertainingly informative about the landscape architecture department at Cornell, but was too young to have known either Eve or Billy.

We made a plan for the rest of our day. The first stop would be the university's Arts Quad; Danny wanted to climb McGraw Tower and see its well-known chimes. Then we'd take a tour of one of the campus gardens and stop in at the landscape architecture department. Did I want, she asked, to go to Baker Laboratory and see if anyone in Lab Services knew something about Jordan's gifts to the chemistry department? I declined, and she didn't press the issue.

THE CAMPUS was larger and lovelier than I'd imagined it would be. Crisscrossed by several gorges, it featured multiple quads, each of which abounded in old-growth trees and offered pretty walks.

Our view of Cayuga Lake from the belfry of McGraw Tower was well worth the climb. Eve, I remembered, had spoken once about climbing the tower, then feeling dizzy as she gazed out over the campus and the dramatic countryside surrounding it. After descending the tower, we made our way to the Minns Garden. There Danny asked a student gardener about the landscape architecture department and was told its administrative offices were closed on weekends—which ruled out asking any questions about Eve's student years.

Danny then wanted me to accompany her to the wildflower garden. She seemed fidgety, her energy barely contained; I trailed after her like a reluctant child. By four-thirty I was ready to call it quits.

She wasn't, though, and it took some doing to persuade her we shouldn't go to Baker Laboratory. We had a drive of at least four hours ahead of us, I argued. Did we really want to roll into Manhattan after midnight? Although she resisted, I won, and we returned to the motel. I checked us out while Danny loaded our bags, and we were back on Route 13 by five-thirty.

IT WAS as we passed a LEAVING ITHACA sign that I realized our trip had given me nothing to visualize where my father was concerned: no chemistry labs, no sites where he'd spent time. That didn't matter, I decided. I could imagine him at the top of McGraw Tower, listening to the chimes. He'd have liked that: a good stage (almost a theater in the round) and a breeze wafting through, transporting the air's subtle scents along with the chimes' music—all the aural and olfactory notes blending beautifully.

Tired, I closed my eyes to shut out the jumble of impressions slipping by. I wanted to see only the insides of my own eyelids. For a little while there was nothing in my head, only darkness and the soft whir of the Volvo's tires. Then, as if projected onto a screen, an image materialized: two hands—one male, one female—palm to palm.

Jordan and Eve, I thought; only it wasn't thinking but seeing. The two of them at the top of the tower, side by side. My father hadn't come here—now I got it—to visit his alma mater, or to find out what the chemistry department had purchased with his donated dollars. He'd come because Eve had asked him to. Jordan had understood how unyielding the soil of feeling might be for her, how hard to cultivate. And this insight roused something long silent in him. He'd never stopped missing his first entanglement, with my mother; that ardor and anguish had set everything else in motion . . . And here was Eve, her niece, offering what must have looked to him like a second chance.

I closed my eyes, pulled my baseball cap onto my face as if I were planning on sleeping, and wept soundlessly. To my relief, Danny was too involved with simultaneous tasks—driving and tuning in the local R&B station, which kept slipping in and out of static—to notice.

INTERLUDE

WHAT DOES the director of a stage performance hope to do more than anything else? Bring the audience under his spell. How does he accomplish this? By exercising a control at once delicate and iron-clad over all the rhythms of the performance.

But more! A director wants each member of the audience to insert himself into the drama. To cease sitting passively, to apprehend bodily as well as mentally what is happening. To feel it utterly.

What then might be a director's best legacy? Transported spectators. People who go home after an evening at the theater and say, *I participated—it might as well have been me up there onstage!*

And how is this legacy actually conveyed, once the director himself is gone?

By those who were there, and speak afterward about what it felt like to be thus unseated. Other people hear such testimonies, imagine that same magical experience, and want it for themselves. Demand it of the next generation of directors.

Hence what death seems to have permanently annulled is perpetuated.

SEVA LONGED for all this to happen. His ego desired it, of course—but so did his heart, which had been altered irrevocably (yanked open, really) by his early experiences in the provincial theater in Penza, where he'd grown up. Right away, then and there, he'd sensed what might be wrought on a stage.

He'd found his calling. Which was also his mode of service, his means of connection. Yet his homeland's leaders saw things differently.

Nothing, I often whispered in his ear, *should stop you from doing what you most wish to do!* Pay no attention to the petty ringmasters of that larger circus, Russia, in which you find yourself. Ignore the censors, naysayers, rumor spreaders. Comply only with your art's dictates.

Needless to say, a double doesn't always win such struggles for control.

When death claimed and released Seva, it released me as well. And so began my wandering through the halls of many imaginations—until I encountered Camilla's.

AS SHE pulled her baseball cap off her face, I saw how far we'd yet to go. Certainly she'd been provoked by all the things that had taken place on her dream-stage. Nonetheless, those nocturnal dramas hadn't really uncorked her heart; it remained stoppered.

The remedy? Get her moving. Action, and some good props.

Before long I knew where to send her: in search of a certain cardboard carton she'd been storing in her apartment building's basement for two decades. The one she'd taken from her father's house after his death.

Change of scene, then. No more loft. This time, down to the cellar!

SEVEN

A BOX. No, a pair of boxes: I'm supposed to choose between them.

One is large and long. It's the box into which Jordan climbed, that time we sailed across the gray table, the coffin in which my mother lay naked and veiled, beautifully dead.

Another box is much smaller and made of cardboard—a carton of books or papers, perhaps. It's dusty; apparently it hasn't been opened in years. The word "Russia" is scrawled across its top.

I choose the large, long box. I want to join my parents, lie between them. As I lift the heavy lid and raise one of my legs, preparing to climb inside, a tall man in a black mask and cape approaches and stops me.

No. Open that one, he says, pointing at the small box.

I do as he commands. Closing the lid of the large box, I move to the other one and tear open its top. A fragrance, deep and mellifluous, fills the air.

What could that be? I ask.

It's Danny's perfume, he says. Your father made it for her. Time you told her about the letter, isn't it?

Letter? I ask. What letter?

In the box, he says. Read it, then pass it along!

He takes off his cape and flaps it a few times from side to side, like a matador. Then he wraps it around himself, goes up on his toes and into a rapid pirouette, and disappears, and I awake.

DANNY DROVE and I, recovered, stared out the car window. We were proceeding east, toward Harriman. After a half hour or so, seeing me stir, Danny remarked blandly on our whereabouts. Then, without further ado, she reverted to her interrogatory mode. What did I remember about her mother's departure for college? Had Eve been nervous?

I pulled myself out of my slouch, trying to order my cottony thoughts. I was only eight, I responded, but Eve hadn't seemed at all nervous. The parents of another freshman student had driven the two of them upstate. Eve had climbed into their station wagon with a suitcase full of new clothing.

"Who bought her clothes for college?"

"Jordan used to take the two of us on shopping expeditions every now and then. He had good taste. And way more money than Dan."

Eve at eighteen had been taller than some boys her age, and quite capable of dressing up. When she did, she'd turned heads. During her high school years, Jordan had guided her sense of style.

"Did Mom wear dresses?" asked Danny. "I'm having trouble imagining the teenaged Eve in a dress."

During her adolescence she'd favored tight bell-bottom jeans, but as an adult she'd taken to wearing skirts and dresses. She'd owned an especially noteworthy sleeveless shift in soft tan suede, with lacing up the sides and across the décolletage. Mostly, though, she'd liked pants: wide-legged, high-waisted ones that flattered her hips, or close-fitting pants that drew attention to her height and her shapely backside.

"She did wear dresses," I said. "Good-looking ones, too—not the usual hippie shit everyone was into back then."

"Mom in a caftan? I wouldn't think so."

When I was in grade school, Jordan used to take Eve and me to his favorite women's department store, Henri Bendel, where (he claimed) the salespeople really knew their perfume and their fabrics. He'd buy us each a dress. Nothing flashy, though I remember he urged Eve—then in her teens—to choose something fitted. Her physique was one he'd known how to flatter.

JORDAN HAD encouraged Eve in her love for landscaping as well. At one point he made her an offer: he would pay for supplies and equipment if she'd serve as our building's gardener.

Eve took him up on this. She transformed the back garden (originally a weed-infested plot about a hundred feet deep) into a tranquil haven. Purple clematis wandered the slatted fence around the yard's perimeter, and Eve coaxed a pair of ailing azaleas back to leafy greenness. She planted hosta, which spread into a rich, dense ground cover. A small Japanese maple flourished under her supervision. Her tulips, emerging each spring of her high school years around the bases of several trees in front as well as in back of the building, lent a particularly jaunty note to our block. Our neighbors were delighted.

Eve planted multiple varieties of tulips. Some of them scarcely resembled that species at all—including one hybrid with peony-shaped flowers and another (the red-orange Flaming Parrot) whose petals were ruffled and extravagant as a bird's plumage. Eve's favorite was a tall, single-flower, nearly black variety known as Queen of the Night.

One November afternoon, returning home on the late bus from school (I'd been at a rehearsal for a Thanksgiving play), I found Eve and Jordan at the table, picking at what looked like a plateful of small roasted onions. Leaning over and sniffing at the plate, I caught the scent of oil and vinegar along with something else, earthy and sour.

That smells weird, I said.

Not to us, said Eve. She had straight white teeth, and when she smiled, her lips turned up at the corners. Totally delicious, she added.

What is it? I asked, watching my father chew contentedly.

Roasted Queens, said Eve. With a vinaigrette dressing.

I stared. Queens? You're eating *tulips?* Tulip bulbs?

Eve and Jordan nodded nonchalantly. Did you know, said Eve, when tulip bulbs were first brought to Europe, people couldn't figure out what to do with them? So they tried eating them. With oil and vinegar, like this (she pointed at the plate), or else preserved in sugar. They're best this way, I think! Sort of tangy.

How'd you find that information? asked Jordan casually.

I read it in a gardening book, she answered.

Um. Chewing, he gave a nod mixing interest and approval.

But I thought you *liked* tulips, I said.

I do, she answered. But there's more than one way to enjoy something you like, right?

Jordan was still eating, slicing each plump, glistening bulb in half and daubing it in the pool of dressing before popping it into his mouth. His chewing produced soft crunchy sounds.

Want some? Eve asked me. When I shook my head, she gave a little shrug. Too bad, she said, spearing a bulb with her fork. They're good, really!

You didn't dig them up, did you? I asked, unable to suppress the accusatory note in my voice.

Dig them up! she repeated, her giggle suddenly making her sound younger than she was. Of course not! I bought fresh bulbs to experiment with. Jordan paid for them, she added, giving my father a small smirk. *Merci beaucoup,* Jordan.

Still eating, he raised his brows slightly in acknowledgment.

Have Dan and Sarah tried them? I asked.

Nah, said Eve. You kidding? My father eat tulips? He wouldn't know a Queen if he stepped on one.

Jordan glanced at her. Take it easy, he ordered quietly.

Eve shrugged. Yessir, she replied.

There was something in her tone, a kind of playful rebellion, which struck me as new. I was only seven, but I knew that when she talked with adults, Eve was normally aloof. With Dan and Sarah, she could be caustic, but with all other grownups, her tone was polite but cool.

She picked up the now empty plate, its surface slick with oil, and carried it to the sink. Gotta get rid of the evidence, she said as she turned on the water.

As she washed the plate, my father stretched his legs beneath the table and patted his stomach lightly. *Délicieux,* he said to no one in particular.

I saw him stare into space for a moment, then shift his gaze to Eve. She was still standing at the sink, her back turned to us. She wore black pants and a red sweater cropped at the waist. Her midsection and legs looked unusually long, perhaps because of the shortness of her sweater, and her hair seemed to dance about her head as she dried the plate she'd washed, then eased it onto a shelf.

I remember standing, waiting for my father to speak to me. He said nothing, his gaze tracking Eve's movements. After a moment he rose, tousled the top of my head, and walked out of the room. This wasn't the first time I'd failed to compel his attention, but it marked a new realization: Eve had a rapport with Jordan that eluded me. And this recognition enlarged my understanding of what she'd meant when she told me, that evening in the bathroom, that she was like my mother. She was indeed—except less so for me than for Jordan.

"DID MOM come home for visits?"

We'd stopped for gas. I'd assumed Danny had let the topic of Eve's college years drop, but I was wrong.

"Not often," I said. "She wrote letters and phoned from time to time. Every now and then, she'd show up unannounced."

Eve's short missives to me had been covered with doodles of plants and flowers. When we spoke on the phone, maybe once a month, she'd sounded energetic and focused, her calls a tonic reminder of actual liveliness happening elsewhere. Visiting home was something she chose to do infrequently. For holidays she got herself invited to friends' homes.

The family apartment grew exceedingly quiet. The three adults and I, a quartet in a domestic galaxy, were clustered in proximity yet orbited separately. I missed Eve daily, though I knew it was point-less to do so. She was gone, she wasn't coming back. An explana-tion hadn't been necessary for this to register with me.

"I remember one visit," I said to Danny. "During her sophomore year, I think—maybe junior? She brought me a dartboard."

"Oh?" We were behind a slow-moving truck. Danny inched the Volvo leftward to check out the possibilities for passing, then pulled back into the center of our lane.

"Yeah. She was a good player, too."

"Is that right?" Danny pulled the car back in sharply after a foiled attempt to circumvent the truck ahead of us.

I recounted the story of that strange weekend. Eve had been dropped off at the family apartment by a friend; she was carting a large, flat box, which she handed to me. It contained my birthday present, an official-looking dartboard that came with a set of six long, beautifully weighted metal projectiles whose tips were scarily sharp. I was instantly in love with them.

We hung the board at the end of the apartment's central hall-way. Using a bit of masking tape, Eve marked the spot on the floor from which I was supposed to toss. Then she explained how—a pro-cedure that took concerted practice on my part, though after a few hours I'd become reasonably adept.

From Friday night to Sunday afternoon, we played innumer-able games of darts. We began with simple ones, such as '01 and Cricket and their variants, which had funny names: Wild Mouse, Narvak, Half-It. Even when I didn't get any closer to the bull than she did (a frequent occurrence), Eve still let me throw first in the first leg of each of our matches. A surprisingly patient teacher, she called out an encouraging *bull's-eye!* whenever I nailed the inner cork.

At the end of that weekend, shortly before departing, Eve of-fered to teach me how to play a Cricket-type game called Scram. We were alone in the apartment. After gathering all the darts (I'd mis-placed one, so this took some time) and returning to our starting point in the hallway, I saw that Eve had done some rounding up of her own. Arrayed on the inner and outer cork of the dartboard were the faces of the Motley Crew, as she called them—the no-longer-present members of our family: Jordan's parents, Dan's parents, Sarah's parents, Eve's birth mother, and my mother. Their photos normally sat on the sideboard in the dining room, but Eve had removed the pictures from their frames and affixed them to the board with straight pins. I was surprised to see how unconcerned Eve was about marring these photographs, although no one else in the apartment ever bothered with them. They were too familiar to attract attention.

We're supposed to throw darts at them? I asked.

You bet!

I must've looked skeptical. She picked up a dart and gave it a quick, hard flick; it landed squarely on her mother's face. Then she turned to me.

Your turn, she said.

I picked up a dart, holding it unsteadily. Eve was staring at me, waiting.

Go ahead, Cammie, she said. They're gone already—they're dead, that's the whole point! *Bull's-eye!* she sang, lobbing another dart. It landed squarely on the photo of Jordan's parents. *Bull's-eye, bull's-eye, bull's-eye!* Her next three darts hit the remaining targets: Dan's parents, Sarah's parents, and my mother.

Pointing at my dart, Eve nodded at the board.

Try for the double ring, she said. Or hit your mother—let's say that'll count the same as either the double or the triple. That should make it easy for you!

Her smile was a taunt.

I don't think I can, I mumbled, dangling the dart at my side.

She looked away, shrugging disdainfully, then took my dart and tossed it. It tunneled through the air, whistling slightly as it went, and landed directly on my mother's face. I couldn't then or now describe the look on Eve's, after that hit, except to say it was triumphant.

I RECOUNTED this story in an abridged version, leaving out the Motley Crew. The truck ahead of us was slowing down. We were beginning an ascent up a long, gentle incline, and the truck's weight further reduced its capacity to accelerate.

Danny pulled into the oncoming lane of traffic. Flooring the Volvo so it downshifted automatically, she zipped ahead of the truck and moved back into our lane. She'd left us an uncomfortably small margin for error; an oncoming car beeped angrily as it passed us.

"Oooh," I moaned, trying to keep my disapproval light.

"Chill," she said. "I know what I'm doing."

"I don't doubt your driving skills," I responded.

She performed the same maneuver with another vehicle ahead of us, a slow-moving minivan. We were nearing the top of the incline as she pulled the Volvo back into our lane, and the road had already begun a curve; she couldn't possibly have known whether anything would show up in the oncoming lane.

"But your lack of interest in visibility has me a little worried," I couldn't resist adding.

That broke her. Moments after we'd crested the hill, she pulled the car over and brought it to an abrupt halt. We were on a narrow shoulder; the traffic ran close to us, and the Volvo gave a little shudder each time a car passed. I asked her what she was doing, and she said something to the effect that she was tired of hearing from me about her driving. Then I told her we ought to get off the shoulder, to which she made a retort I couldn't hear because she'd already begun accelerating, sending gravel flying. After we'd rejoined the moving traffic, she quickly brought the car up to and over the speed limit. As the distance between us and the car ahead narrowed, I braced myself, but she braked at the last minute, dropping back— not as far as she should have, but at least so we were no longer on the car's tail.

"Why are you doing this?" I said as calmly as I could.

"My question exactly."

Her sarcasm unzipped my restraint. "Quit being an idiot!" I yelled.

"Oh, for fuck's sake, Cam," she said, and I heard not only anger but something like desolation in her voice. "Just stop it, will you?"

"Stop *what?*" I was nearly screeching now.

"I'm so sick of trying to wring stuff out of you! You *have* to know more about my father than you've told me! You're the only person . . ." She pretended to shake the steering wheel: her elbows flexed and her forehead swung toward and away from the wheel in a mock banging movement.

"Pull over," I said. "But not on the shoulder of the road, please. Let's find a diner or something."

She considered this. "We'll stop in Harriman," she said. "Another twenty minutes or so."

We traveled the rest of the way there without speaking.

INSTALLED IN a roadside place not unlike Ithaca's Cheerful Swan, with weak coffee and unappetizing turkey sandwiches on the table between us, we stared at each other.

"All right," I said. "What's wrong? Talk to me."

"Mom told me that same story about playing darts," she said. "Only in her version, there were photos of family members pinned on the board. And she egged you on, but you refused to toss at them—"

"Danny," I broke in, "what's your point? That I didn't tell you the whole tale, and I should have? Or that I didn't impale any of my relatives with darts?"

"Let me finish," she stated coolly. "My point is, at least Mom wasn't hiding what actually happened. I think she told me about that game you'd played to prove she'd gone beyond the whole family apartment thing. Jordan, Dan, Sarah—they didn't have anything to do with who she was . . ." She pushed away her uneaten food. "Who knows. What do *you* think?"

"Okay," I said. "So Eve told you all about the darts to set you straight about her feelings for her family. Was that an admirable thing to do? Or simply another way for her to justify her distance from you? To let herself off the hook?"

"At least she wasn't afraid to tell me what happened! Whereas *you* seem intent on hiding every—" She looked away. "There's something I need you to understand, Cam," she said, more softly now. "You know what really surprised me about the dartboard story? It was the fact that *you* were in it. And the way you were in it."

"How do you mean?"

"Until then I'd thought you and Mom led completely independent lives. You'd both given me the impression you'd hardly known each other when you were growing up. That the ten years' difference in age made you virtual strangers. But after hearing the story about the darts, I realized I'd imagined it wrong. And I started wondering about other experiences you two might've had together, in the apartment on Ninth Street or elsewhere."

"You didn't imagine it wrong," I said.

"Bullshit! You're holding out on me!" She tugged on her ponytail's elastic band, stripping it off in one furious movement. "You've really got nothing to say?"

"Danny, I keep telling you! Once we were adults, Eve and I almost never dealt directly with each other. I didn't get to know her better than other people did. She didn't *want* that to happen."

"Did *you?*"

"Would it have mattered if I had? I'm saying how things were. What am I supposed to do, make up a different version so you'll feel better?"

At that she rebanded her hair, took off two of her rings, rubbed them together, and returned them to her fingers. These actions seemed to lend her resolve; her next words emerged calmly.

"But there *was* something else that brought the two of you together, Cam. Your father."

OF COURSE, I thought.

"I was only six when he died, but I knew that the three of you were like a family in Frenchtown," Danny said. "And I sensed something was up when I walked into his study."

"Because of how you found him?"

She nodded, her expression grave now, its angry aspect gone. "I figured he was sleeping. I'd never seen anyone sleep with a black plastic bag over his head, but it seemed like the only possible explanation. Jordan had told me that bright lights sometimes hurt his eyes, so I thought he was trying to cover his head, to keep out the sunlight.

"I went up to him and said his name a few times. Maybe I even shook his arm. Then I asked him if he was playing a game—I thought he'd suddenly yell 'boo!' or something. I was scared, but trying to pretend I wasn't. That's when I went to find you. You and Mom followed me back to his study. You went over and touched his wrist and said he was dead. I remember Mom said something like, *Are you sure,* and then something else: *I didn't think he was going to die today.*"

"What did *you* think had happened?" I asked, remembering my own numbed dismay when Danny called out to us from Jordan's study. She shouldn't have been the one to find him; I should have prevented that, and I didn't.

"Well," she said, "I thought the bag must've been a normal thing, even though it was weird. And I figured Jordan was dead—not that I knew what that meant. All summer you and Mom had been saying he'd die, and I understood that one day he'd just stop breathing. You'd both told me it would happen soon, because he was very ill."

"He was."

A long silence. "Terminally?"

"Yes," I answered. "He wasn't going to get better. The idea was for him to die in his own house, as peacefully as possible. His doctors put him on pain meds that made him feel like he was losing himself. Like his whole personality was affected."

"Did he tell you this?"

"He told both Eve and me. At the beginning of the summer he was doing all right, but then everything started catching up with him. I remember arriving one Saturday evening in July and finding him practically in a stupor. He quit most of his meds after that. He said he wanted to feel like himself, even if the pain got worse. And when I came out the following weekend, he talked with me about a specific plan for ending his life."

I'd said it. Jordan's secret was no longer something to safeguard. Nor was Eve's.

"So he had a plan."

I nodded. "My guess is, he and your mother talked about it, too, right around the same time. But she and I didn't discuss it."

"Why not?"

"Jordan asked us not to. At least, he asked *me* not to, and I assume he also asked Eve, or she'd have broached the subject with me."

"What exactly did he tell you he wanted to do?"

"He told me he'd gotten hold of some pills, and he planned to use them," I said. "Seconal—barbiturates. Actually, your mother's the one who got the pills for him. Jordan hadn't wanted me to know where they'd come from. I figured it out when I found one of her business cards on the top shelf of his medicine cabinet, after his death. On the back of the card, Eve had written, 'Another batch coming next week.' He must've forgotten to throw away that piece of evidence."

Danny contemplated this, then nodded. "Neither you nor Mom ever broke your promise to not talk about any of it?"

"That's right."

"Quite a chokehold."

"That's one way to describe it. I think of it as 'don't ask, don't tell.' That's what assisted suicide is all about."

The designation hadn't been used until now. It sat between us, a gate through which the rest of our dialogue about Jordan would have to pass.

"So can you talk about it now?" she asked.

"In the car," I said.

I TOLD her, as we continued southward, about Jordan's plan.

How he'd researched the method, the necessary amount of Seconal. How I'd found the right plastic bag for him, medium-sized, with drawstrings; how, with me watching, he'd practiced its use until he felt comfortable undertaking the entire process on his own. How, at the appointed time, he'd fastened the bag's drawstrings around his wrists—a procedure requiring some dexterity, though he'd managed without my help. How I'd placed a glass of champagne, some water, the pills, and a bowl of chocolate pudding on the little side table next to his chair, and watched as he'd swallowed the pills slowly, one at a time, taking alternating sips of water and champagne and consuming small mouthfuls of pudding. At one point he'd asked me to spoon-feed him; the bowl was too heavy for him to continue holding it at chest height. After he'd ingested everything, I'd watched as he slipped the bag over his head and crossed his wrists (around which the drawstrings were now tied) over his chest.

"Why the bag?" Danny interrupted. "Why not just the pills?"

"Because barbiturates aren't entirely reliable," I answered. "The combination of the pills and the lack of air—"

"I get it," Danny said.

I described how I left him, knowing it was over, and went to my room, waiting for Eve to return. I didn't tell Danny how I'd gone back to his study in a little while and checked his pulse, first one wrist, then the other, to be sure. The one other thing I'd intended to do—take the plastic bag off my father's head so it would look as though he'd simply sat in his chair, eaten some pudding, and died— I couldn't get myself to do. All I could do was cut off the drawstrings.

After Danny called out, as Eve and I approached my father's study, I'd glanced at Eve's face. I hadn't realized until then that she, too, had been waiting, knowing what he'd planned—but he hadn't told her the date. She looked shocked, but less, it seemed, for her daughter's sake than for her own. Closing her eyes, she lay a hand on Jordan's shoulder for a moment. Then, collecting herself, she picked up Danny and held her, murmuring softly into her hair. It felt to me, watching them, as if they were both as far from the room as my father was, in all but body.

JORDAN HAD made his request on a Friday evening. Eve and Danny weren't there.

The house was quiet. Eve had called me midweek to say they wouldn't be joining us that weekend; she had too much work to do. The weekday nurse had left as soon as I arrived. I'd cooked and cleaned up after Jordan's and my supper, and was in my usual chair by his bedroom window. He was sitting in bed, a sheaf of papers on his lap.

Cam, he said, we need to talk.

Taking off his glasses, he polished their lenses painstakingly on one of his pajama sleeves. His face was gaunt and slack, his shoulders hunched.

What is it? I asked, expecting him to say something about his pain medications. His eyes were watery but focused, the sole source of animation in a face from which the energy had been steadily draining for weeks.

I've been reading about dying, he said. I called the Hemlock Society, and they sent me some information. I've thought about it and made my decision, which I'd like to share with you.

Decision? I said, confused, as the word began wriggling its way into my consciousness. When its meaning slid home, it kicked off a little rush of adrenaline.

Look, I said, you shouldn't be thinking about—

Hang on, Jordan said. You need to hear me out first, hm?

A muted slurring started up in my ears, the sound of distant waves: my nervous system's surf.

All right, I said.

My hunch is, it won't be over tomorrow, or next week, or the week after, he said. I'll weaken but I won't go quickly, although the pain will worsen. I can't keep my thoughts straight on the pain medications, and I can't handle the pain without them. And I am, after all, eighty years old . . .

I said nothing. The surf was still there inside my eardrums, a rhythmic sandpapery sound.

So I'd like to exit now, he said. While I can do it myself. Or mostly by myself.

Our conversation was no longer a conversation but a foreign object making straight for me at high velocity. What does that mean? I asked.

It means I can do almost everything I need to do without some-one else's direct physical assistance. Which is how it needs to be. But there are a few things I'll need help with. Not the drugs—I've got almost all the pills already. I'll need to take some food with them, though. A little alcohol would probably be a good idea, too, to speed things along. And just in case, I should have a plastic bag as well. I'd like you to get me the right kind of bag and help me practice with it, so even when I'm in a drugged state I'll be able to use it correctly.

Is that essential?

He paused, the slightest of smiles playing across his mouth. Think of it as a mask, he added. You can pretend I'm one of those *commedia* characters—you know, what's his name—that old mer-chant who's always trying to attract women . . .

Pantalone, I said.

Yes, he said, that's right. I saw a show in London once, a little takeoff on standard *commedia* routines. Lots of acrobatics. With several scenes involving Pantalone. Columbine was his daughter. She's the one who's invisible to mortals . . .

He paused, then added: As you'll need to be, my dear. If you agree to help me out. We'll both be better off ending what doesn't need to be prolonged. I'm trusting you can see the sense of that. Can you be my Columbine?

I SAID yes. Like a person under a spell, I said I would help him. Good, said my father.

We began to speak about the details. When, I said, and he said soon. Can you be specific, I asked, and he said how about two weeks from now, on Sunday, and I said Eve and Danny will be here, and he said I know, I'd like to say good-bye even though they won't know that's what it is. Plus it'll be easier for you if you're not alone afterward.

All right, I said.

And, he said, what about the drink—what's best, I wonder? Didn't Chekhov have a glass of champagne right before he died?

Yes, I read that someplace, I said.

Good, that's what I'll do. But there's the question of food, he added. I'll need to eat something, to help keep the pills down. How about chocolate pudding—I wouldn't mind that as a last meal. Make me some chocolate pudding, would you, Cam?

I TOOK a temporary leave from my job managing a Village antiques shop and moved into the spare room in Jordan's house. To Stuart and Eve, I explained that my father was weakening and I needed to be with him full-time to help him acclimate to new medications. Stuart said he'd keep an eye on my apartment.

I hadn't yet met Sam; that happened shortly after Jordan's death. I knew at some point I'd talk with Stuart about what was to happen, and my role in it. But I couldn't talk about it beforehand. And I'd never have discussed it with my cousin, even if Jordan hadn't made that impossible.

EVE MADE perhaps a half-dozen weekend trips to Frenchtown that summer, always with Danny in tow. Sometimes they stayed for just a few hours on Saturday. Other times they arrived early on Friday evening and stayed until after dinner on Sunday—Eve on the pull-out sofa in the living room, Danny in a sleeping bag in my room.

During their visits, Eve took Jordan's garden in hand and Danny amused herself with sketching (already her favorite pastime). I tried to keep my father as comfortable as possible. Because walking was painful for him, he was seldom anywhere but in his bed. I tacked Danny's drawings (each of which she proudly displayed to him as soon as it was completed) on the walls of his bedroom; Eve saw to it that there were always flowers on his bedside table. Some mornings I'd enter his room and notice she'd changed a vase sometime during the night, replacing one colorful batch of blossoms with another.

Jordan slept a lot, but whenever he was awake and had some energy, I shut his bedroom door and questioned him about his life. The experience of listening to his voice for extended periods of time was as confounding as it was gratifying; we'd never before talked with such regularity or at such length.

One night as I lay in bed, unable to sleep and replaying in my mind the things Jordan had told me that day, I thought about a book I'd read a few years earlier, which had offered viewpoints on acting from various theater directors, living and dead. Among them was Vsevolod Meyerhold, who'd made an intriguing observation on the art of pantomime. *Mime excites us,* he'd said, *by the framework that confines its heart.*

Yes, I thought, and a similar principle governed intimate relationships as well. My father had spent a lifetime submitting to confinement, and now he was letting me into the cage with him. Was I not somehow transgressing? He'd been so alone for so long. Since my mother, who else had he let in? No one, really—just myself, to a pathetically limited degree.

And Eve, I supposed. Yes—Eve, too, in some sense I'd never been able to name.

When she put fresh flowers on his bedside table in the middle of the night, did she wake him to talk with him? Or had talk become unnecessary? Maybe she simply sat next to him in the dark, listening to his breathing, resting a hand on his shoulder. Perhaps she understood there was nothing further to be said, only to be felt, and soon she'd have to do that—feel—on her own. As I would, too.

YOU'RE READY? Jordan asked me, the Friday before the final Sunday.

Everything's set, I answered.

And Eve and Danny are coming tomorrow?

That's right.

We'll need to figure out how to get them out of the house on Sunday.

I know, I replied. But that won't be hard. We'll send them out to do some shopping or get some lunch.

All right. I'm not worried, he added, so don't you be either.

That evening he reiterated that I should never speak to anyone, including Eve, about his plan and my role in it. This was crucial, he said, to avoid any danger of liability. Once the bag was off his head, there'd be no reason for anybody to suspect he'd died anything but a natural death. His illness was such that no doctor or nurse would be surprised if he were to expire peacefully in his chair.

I asked about the supplier of the barbiturates. That person, he said, had also been counseled about the need for silence, and was unaware of my role. As far as anyone else was concerned, my father was acting on his own.

REMEMBER, CAM, this plan wasn't yours, he said on Sunday morning, after I'd informed him that Eve and Danny had left to run some errands.

You're not putting pills in my hand or down my throat, he said. And you're not placing a bag over my head. I'm going to do these things by myself. You've made me some chocolate pudding. That's *all* you've done.

The cork of the champagne bottle made a satisfying retort when I popped it. I poured a little champagne into both glasses, careful not to spill any. In the silence I could hear the bubbles' spritely hiss as they ascended to the surface. My father and I had never done this before, I realized—never drunk champagne together. As Jordan clinked his glass against mine, I closed my eyes for an instant, picturing him in a Paris café with my mother, the two of them toasting each other. *Salut, Camilla! Salut, chéri.*

Cheers, he offered. May you live a long, healthy life.

Cheers, I said.

We drank, each of us taking a few sips. Jordan held his glass in both hands.

So, Cam, he said. We ready?

My nerves flickered like a string of lights about to fail. Jordan inhaled softly. In a little while he'd be ending this, the body's most banal and astonishing of performances: inhalation, exhalation, air and blood coursing on their hidden circular track. I would be sitting here with him as he switched off the ignition.

He took another sip of champagne. You and I are face-to-face now, he said. We get to do a proper farewell.

We've said good-bye a lot, over the years, I said. But you always came back.

He gave a small laugh. In its tone it reminded me of one of his quiet chuckles with Danny.

When you were young, I shouldn't have taken off so much, he said. Now it's different—now I should. It's the right thing to do.

The right thing for you, I said. But what if it's not the right thing for me?

I won't ask you to convince me of that, he said. I just want to ask one question. Can you be sure what I'm doing isn't the right thing for you?

No, I said. Maybe it is. And I don't want you to suffer.

Well then, he said. Why not give me the benefit of the doubt?

In the silence that followed, I imagined various things I might say. I could tell him he'd failed me, turning my mother's death into a pathetic excuse for his own absences; I could say I'd chosen to spurn him, and this became my own failure. I could wonder aloud whether the exhaustion I'd felt all along, loving him, was any greater than that he'd felt, loving me. I could ask how one child might take her mother's life and then, at his request, her father's, and go on with her own.

All right, I said, I'll give you the benefit of the doubt.

He took my hand, pulled me toward him, reached out with his other hand, touched my cheek—the skin of his palm as dry and soft as a feather—and released me.

That seat cushion there? Reach under it, feel around toward the left-hand side, all the way at the rear, and you'll find a little envelope of pills.

DANNY AND I were in Westchester, on the Taconic Parkway. Traffic was mercifully light; another hour and we'd be in the Village.

"The night before he died, Jordan gave me a bottle of perfume," Danny said. She'd remained silent after my account of my father's death; I had no sense of what she was thinking or feeling. "You remember that little leather box?"

I nodded. "Do you still have it?"

"Yeah, but I haven't opened the bottle yet. I didn't find the box until recently."

"It was lost?"

"Not exactly lost. Mom kept it for me when I was young, of course. Then she claimed to have mislaid it somewhere. I didn't worry about it; I figured she'd hand it over at some point . . . When I was cleaning out her apartment, I came across it at the back of her bedroom closet. It was inside a hatbox, with some souvenirs from her college days. Mostly photos of plants and trees and whatnot—no people . . . There was one picture taken from the top of McGraw Tower, at Cornell. I recognized the view."

"When will you open the mystery perfume?" I asked. "Be prepared, it might've soured after all these years. Even really good perfumes don't last forever."

"I know."

We fell silent again, my thoughts returning to Frenchtown. That final Saturday evening, Eve and Danny had arrived after supper. Visibly tired, Eve had headed straight for the living room's sofa bed while Danny went into Jordan's bedroom to say good night. That was when he'd given her the gift.

The next morning, Eve rose early to work in the garden. While she was outside, Danny showed me the present she'd received from Jordan. It was beautifully packaged—that was the first thing I noticed about the gift. A small bottle of perfume was housed in a square box made of interlaced strips of buttery dark brown leather, and lined in red silk. Marveling at its elegance and craftsmanship, I figured Jordan had found the box in France or Italy. Nestled at its center was a pouch of azure-blue velvet cinched with a black cord. The bottle, Danny explained, was inside the pouch.

When I asked to see it, she demurred. No, she said shyly, I can't show you, or anyone. It's a secret.

Jordan, she explained, had instructed her not to open the bottle until she was a grown woman. Hearing this, I chuckled.

So you don't even know what the bottle looks like? I asked.

Nope, she replied solemnly, and I don't know what it smells like, either. But he also gave me this, and it smells really good.

She pulled a plain vial from the pocket of her shorts. On its label, lettered in Jordan's distinctive print, was the word "Lune." I pretended not to recognize the name; I wasn't going to spoil her treat by telling her I already knew what it was. I cooed as she removed the vial's stopper and waved the scent beneath my nostrils.

You only need a little bit—it's pretty strong, I told her.

I know, she answered. Jordan told me you just put a drop on your fingertip and pat it on your neck and wrists. Like this.

Her small forefinger grazed the sides of my throat, then the inside of one of my wrists.

You did that just right, I said. And when you wear this perfume, you'll smell better than any other kid in your class. Even better than your teacher.

She smiled at that. Then Eve was calling her, telling her they were going on an errand and then to lunch. Perhaps Jordan had urged Eve to take her daughter out. In any case, I hadn't needed to manufacture a reason for them to depart.

SOMEWHERE ON the West Side Highway (had we crossed the little bridge over the river between the Bronx and Manhattan?—I can't summon any visuals, only the moment itself), Danny spoke again.

"I'd like to take a break," she said.

"From what?" I asked.

"From this . . . from talking."

"Okay," I said. "I certainly don't need to talk about this stuff on a regular basis. But it's good we've—"

"No, Cam. I mean, I need a break from talking with *you*. I'd like not to call or see you for a while. I can't. It's just too hard to be playing an endless guessing game with you. It's like I've been banging on the door and nobody's answering."

"Nobody's *answering*?" I said, amazed. "What do you call my just telling you I helped Jordan die?"

She didn't answer right away. "I call it an admission," she said finally. "You gave me the facts. But you didn't talk about how you felt afterward. You said nothing about how his death must've affected your relationship with Mom—because *she* was involved, too. How did she react? What did she feel for Jordan? Those are the things I want to hear about, and you've made it clear you don't want to discuss them." She paused, then ended: "It's like you finally tell me a secret, only you tell it in a way that keeps it secret. I'd rather not keep up the charade."

I couldn't have willed myself to speak even if I'd been sure more words were the appropriate offering, and I wasn't. We were still traveling south on the West Side Highway, the river glinting on our right, Manhattan massed on our left. At Fourteenth Street we plunged into the traffic heading east; in a few more minutes, we pulled up in front of my building.

Danny opened the wagon's rear door for me, and I took out my bag. We stood on the curb near a streetlight, whose silvery glow softened and flattened her features.

"You realize you've left me no choice here," I said.

"I haven't any, either," she said. Then she was back in the car, and the car was gone.

INSIDE THE front hallway of my apartment, I put down my bag and went for the dimmer switch on the wall, sliding it upward as far as it would go. No light came on. After trying the switches for several different lamps, I realized my electricity must have gone out, a not-uncommon occurrence in my building, whose wiring was shoddy.

Making my way to the kitchen, I opened the door of the refrigerator. Its interior stayed dark, but everything still felt cold. The power couldn't have been out for long, and would probably be back on within a half hour.

I poured a shot of vodka over some ice—still frozen—and carried my drink to the living room, one hand in front of me as I piloted cautiously. Sitting on the sofa, I felt my entire body trembling lightly. The first sip of the vodka took me down; I lay on my side, pulled my knees to my chest, and curled into a ball as an unfamiliar scent rushed my nostrils. Oakwood, bergamot, the barest touch of sandalwood: these notes were detectable, I could separate and identify them. Yet something else, known yet not—unnameable—aerated the verdant fugue.

I breathed it all in. Before traveling, Jordan used to uncap the glass vials of essential oils he kept in his kit and let me sniff each slender cylinder, one after another, just for a moment. Collectively, those potent hits of scent were an olfactory flash, intense and kaleidoscopic. Like my feelings for my father: impossible either to locate or to dispel.

I lay on my side as loss permeated the air around me, a fine vapor. For several moments I was unable to exhale, afraid that if I did I'd forfeit Jordan forever. But at last I could breathe again and knew what I'd just encountered: a secret perfume of my father's, the one I'd smelled in my dream.

ON THE phone with Stuart the next morning, I began describing my weekend. He cut me off. It would be better, he said, if we talked in person. He'd hop in a cab and meet me at a little café near The Fourth Wall.

I protested that he needed to stay put, but he stood his ground. Carl could handle things, he said, and certain discussions should not take place telephonically.

I arrived at the café just as Stuart was getting out of his taxi. We settled into a corner booth and a couple of half-pints. It was eleven-thirty; we had the place mostly to ourselves. Picking out three large

Brazil nuts from a small dish on our table, Stuart began juggling them without averting his gaze from my face.

"*Und so?*" he asked. The nuts whirred around his head. "How's my traveler doing?"

"Not so good," I answered. "It was a complicated weekend." Within me, anxiety bucked; for several moments I couldn't continue. Stuart stopped juggling.

"Come on, spit it out. Cough it up," he said.

"Those are such crude expressions, Stu." I was stalling and he knew it.

"You're right, they are. Hardly invitational. Okay, how about 'vent it'?"

"That usually pertains to anger, no?"

"Hmm. Yes. And 'air it' isn't right, either—too talk-showish." He made a tent of his fingers, tilting them forward and backward as he pondered. "I know!" he exclaimed, flattening the tent by pressing the palms of both hands together. "*Spill it.*"

"There you go." Calmer now, I told him what had happened in Ithaca, from beginning to end. Stuart listened attentively without interrupting me. When I'd finished, he collected his three nuts and sent them spinning again.

"You think Danny really means it?" he asked. "About not wanting to see you for a while?"

"Absolutely. She's not fooling around. She thinks I have no interest in helping her find out more about her father. Or Eve."

"Well, do you?"

"What does she think I am, omniscient?"

He gave me one of his skeptical smiles. "Thou doth protest too much," he said. Then he resumed his juggling. After a final cycle, he gathered the nuts in one hand, which he then opened and extended toward me. "Brazil?" he asked.

"No thanks, I prefer Belgium." I raised my glass of Belgian beer as Stuart dumped the trio of nuts back in the dish. "That's disgusting," I said, gesturing. "Now somebody will eat those without realizing they've been handled."

"Palmed," he corrected me. "They'll be bitter—the nuts, I mean. I wouldn't worry. Ever met anyone who actually likes Brazil nuts? Anyone who passes up a cashew, say, for a Brazil nut?" He held his glass of beer to the light, peering at it. "Lovely amber, this one. Must remember it." Staring at the label, he mouthed its name silently, entering it into his beer memory bank.

"Are you going to comment on anything I've said, or only on the beverage?"

He scowled. "I have plenty to say about *you,* but I'll save that for the time being. About Danny—well, she's clearly a mess. All that anger and frustration she didn't get around to airing before Eve died . . . it's all out of the bag now. Can't cram it back in, either."

His right hand, lying on the table, assumed a hunched shape; propelled by its index and middle fingers, it scuttled across the table toward me. "I see why you'd make a tempting target. You're supposed to be solid, reliable Cam, but it turns out you have no light to shed on the daddy question! And then she finds out that you and Eve were both, how shall I say, *intimately involved* in your father's death."

"Plus I compounded the sin by not saying how I *felt* about the whole thing."

"Well, yeah! Danny's looking for role models, Cam. She wants other people to tell her who her father might be, how to feel about Eve, what's acceptable, what's not. . . . Like, is rage acceptable? Is 'why should I be upset you're dead, Mom, when you never gave a shit about me' acceptable? Look, as far as Danny's concerned, you and she both lost parents—you lost two, if you'll remember, as has she—and you each had a difficult relationship with the parent who raised you. So why the hell aren't *you* willing to talk, now that the principals are dead?"

He paused. "I suggest—don't you wanna know what I suggest?—that you write Danny a letter. And soon." Stuart was in advice-giving mode now, tapping the table with a bossy forefinger. "Not an e-mail, a real letter—handwritten, on nice paper. Make it clear you're open to talking at any time. About anything. Sound like a game plan?"

"I'll think about it," I said. "And thanks for listening. So how's *your* day been?"

He shrugged. "My day, thus far?" He popped a cashew into his mouth. "Right after we opened, several people came in looking for a copy of Calderón's *Life Is a Dream*. It'll be playing at BAM next season. Well, we happen to be out of every single Calderón title, so I spent a solid hour placing orders—or trying to. Computers! I wish the little fuckers had never come into existence. My CPU is about to collapse. It's supposed to be Y2K-compliant, but I sense impending doom."

"*Life Is a Dream?* Never read or saw it," I said.

"It's cool, actually. Your man Meyerhold liked Calderón, did you know that?" He fished his three nuts out of their dish and resumed juggling them. "He staged *Adoration of the Cross*—that's another Calderón play—in St. Petersburg, in the dining room of a friend. Apparently the room was huge and kind of spooky, and they used a candelabra and lots of gold brocade curtains. Must've been vampy as hell! The play's a religious comedy, but Meyerhold's version was more comedy than religious."

I whistled softly. "How come you know so many trivial details about so many obscure theatrical productions?"

"Dunno," he replied. "But thanks for the compliment, if that's what it was. I happen to be very fond of candelabra. As is Carl. As you know."

I did: a few years back, I'd given them a wrought-iron candelabra as an anniversary present. "Is Carl okay, by the way?" I asked.

He threw me an appreciative glance as he rummaged for more cashews. "I think so. Recently he's had a little fever he can't shake."

"He's checked himself out with his doc?"

"Yeah. He'll be fine," Stuart answered. Tension edged his voice; he was clearly worried about his partner. "Our check, please," he called to our waitress. "Might as well ride back to our respective ranches, eh? Maybe you can take some time this afternoon to pen that letter to Danny."

"Don't pressure me, okay?"

"Pressure you? I'm merely suggesting you might save a certain girl from her own private quicksand." He handed the waitress a twenty, waving away my contribution.

"Thanks," I said. "But Danny doesn't need to be saved."

"Oh, I wasn't talking about *that* girl." He smiled at me languidly. "You're right, though. What *you* need, Cam, isn't to be saved—you need to be lost. It'd do you a world of good to be stripped of your bearings. Get lost!"

"I already am," I said. As soon as the words emerged from my mouth, I knew I'd heard them recently, spoken by someone else. It took me a moment to remember who: my father, in one of my dreams. The one with the whale-shaped bottle. Jordan had whispered to it—snatches of poetry? And I'd told him to get lost, and he'd said *Lost? But I already am . . .* I closed my eyes and Sam's face appeared, his expression sorrowful; and there was Meyerhold, saying something about longing—

"Cam," said Stuart, jostling my shoulder. "Wow, girlfriend, when you leave, you really *vacate.*"

"Sorry." I took the glass of water he handed me and finished it off. "Just flashing back to one of my dreams."

"Again? Hmm." He switched to a German accent, accompanying it with a stern look. "Vat you are saying is most interesting, Fräulein, but ve don't know precisely vat you mean, und ve don't like guessing games." He shook his head. "What's chewin' you, sugar?"

I reached for his hands across the table. "I don't know, Stuart. If I had a clue, I'd tell you," I said.

His fingers curled around mine, their grip solid. He's good at waiting. He waits for movies to go to video, for hardbacks to turn into paperbacks, and for me to say what I mean.

"You know what?" I responded finally. "Right now my mind feels like it's stuck in a tight little space, and I just can't scale the walls."

"Ah." Releasing my hands and leaning back in his chair, Stuart extended his legs and scissored my ankles with his. "Well, when you're ready, you'll climb. First you've got to see this thing through with Danny." He gave my ankles a squeeze. "About these dreams of yours—these aren't ordinary nighttime visitations, Cam. They're a serious bunch of Daddy dreams. Am I right?"

"Maybe."

"Sounds like your unconscious is doing you some favors. You ought to listen up! How're things with the lover-man, by the way?"

"Oh, all right," I answered, inwardly flinching. "Recently I've been vexed with him."

"Good." Stuart released my legs and stood up. "Because vexed indicates tension, which in turn suggests movement. And movement, as we know"—he did a little shimmy accompanied by syncopated finger snapping—"is always good!" His strong hug lifted me off the ground. "Take care, baby. I'll be thinking of you."

"ANYONE HOME?" Sam stood in my back-office doorway, his eyebrows raised questioningly.

It was one o'clock. I'd been staring into space and hadn't heard his entrance. He extended a dozen roses toward me, their stems wrapped in a wad of damp paper towel. "Here you go," he said.

"What's the occasion?" I asked, inhaling the sweet buds. They were white, shapely Cherokees, small ornamentals like swamp roses only more graceful, with feathery hips at the centers of their blossoms. Drops of water clung to their petals.

"Just picked," Sam answered, leaning in to kiss me on the cheek. "This morning Zeke announced he was tired of seeing so many roses in our garden, so I decided to accommodate him. Zeke's loss, your gain."

"Thanks," I said. I put the roses in a mason jar and filled it with water, and we both stepped back to admire the bouquet. "How's Zeke doing these days? And Abby?"

"Both good." His face softened as it unfailingly did when I asked him about the children. In obedience to an unspoken rule, our conversations about them didn't occur regularly, though they always felt earnest. Touchingly so. Perhaps because we both knew that but for the operations of chance, we might be talking about our own pair of kids. Or maybe because we knew chance wasn't the only thing that had separated us from that scenario.

"They're both happy in school?"

"Happy in most everything. That's the best *and* the hardest thing, for me—seeing how easy it is for them to be happy."

"Why's it hard?"

"Oh . . ." He looked suddenly shy, but I knew he'd tell me. We were still, despite everything, each other's confidant. "Well, because I envy them. Though I don't think I resent them. Not usually, anyway. But also because I know how easily their happiness could be interrupted. Punctured."

"It will be, one way or another."

"Thanks, Dr. Fatalist." He smiled wanly, then added, "No—Dr. Realist. You're right . . . but still, it's challenging. The whole ball of wax. Every day."

"I can imagine."

"I know you can." We'd gone as far as we could go; his quick smile—a kind of punctuation mark—signaled this. "You free for a bite?"

The offer took me aback. "Actually I'm not too hungry."

"A light lunch, then," he said. "And quick." Looking at me closely, he said, "Everything all right?"

"Not entirely," I said.

A pause. "Danny?"

"Yes."

"Want to sit in Washington Square Park for a little while, watch the pigeons?"

I nodded.

"Let's go, then."

For the second time that day, I locked my shop's front door. As Sam and I headed eastward, I slipped my arm through his, automatically.

LISTENING ATTENTIVELY, Sam shielded his eyes from the sun while I told him about my weekend with Danny. When I'd finished narrating, he sat in silence, pondering.

While he stared into space, I found myself envisioning Danny's body. It was less full-figured than her mother's; alluring, but in a taut, rangy way. Invitational—that's how her sexiness would've felt to Sam during that trip they'd taken to London. As sleekly real as it was unconsciously communicated.

He'd thought about sleeping with her, wanted to but hadn't. This I was sure of, though he'd never said as much to me.

Yet once we'd parted, what then?

"Sam, I need to ask you something," I said.

He raised his brows inquiringly, his expression distracted: he was still thinking about my account of the Ithaca weekend.

"Did you—have you and Danny ever . . ." I faltered, and Sam's gaze locked with mine. His handsome face was showing its age; the skin around his eyes was scored with tiny lines, and on either cheek, two strong verticals bisected his dimples. Within me, an old desire surged, then ebbed, as I heard Eve's voice in my head: *It's afterward I'm wondering about . . .*

"My cousin," I said, "had this idea that you'd slept with her daughter at some point."

Sam's gaze flickered. "Camilla," he said quietly, "what *is* this?"

"This conversation with Eve took place several years back—at your wedding, in fact. I figured it was just something she was lobbing at me, to see if I'd jump. You know how she could be." I paused. "But I didn't forget what she'd said, either. And the thing is, you've showed up today for one reason: you're worried about Danny. And now I'm thinking, is Sam wondering whether Danny and I will get to talking, and she'll tell me something . . . ?"

He crossed his arms at his chest. "I think the best thing for you to do, if you really give Eve credit for what she said, is to ask Danny herself," he said. His voice sounded surprisingly unperturbed; I wondered what such control was costing him.

"You're not going to answer me, are you?"

He shook his head. "No, I'm not, Cam. There's no point. Because I think you wouldn't believe me." Taking my hands in his, he drew them to his lips and kissed them where the palms joined—an old habit neither of us had indulged for many years. "I ought to get going," he said quietly as he let my hands drop. "I suggest you take a little time off. You need a break. You're not making things easier for anybody with this kind of approach."

My anger dissolved. Instinctively I closed my eyes as if to shield them from a too-sharp light, the glare of shame. Sam left without a further word.

THE PARAMOUR showed up at my place after work, grimy and sweat-slicked.

Suppressing my fatigue, I pulled Nick into the shower with me. There I soaped him into a lather and had him do the same for me, slowly, making him kneel before me for a while and then lie flat, water pounding his face, as I crouched over him and took what I needed. It was a clumsily satisfying encounter.

Afterward we flopped onto my bed and lay on our sides, facing each other. My tension, which sex had momentarily doused, rekindled. Within me rose a sharp, unprecedented urge to slap him hard enough to bring tears to his eyes. Yet I knew, too, that it was my own face I wanted to slap, and with equal frustration.

Nick appeared not to be picking up on any of this, but the appearance was misleading. "How're you doing?" he asked, putting a hand on my shoulder and giving it a little shake.

I said nothing.

"I mean, how're you doing, *really,*" he added, no longer shaking but squeezing my shoulder. It dawned on me that he wasn't alluding to the fact that I'd let my answering machine field all his recent calls to me; he was addressing something else.

"You're talking about Eve?" I asked.

"Yeah."

I was greatly surprised. He hadn't inquired into my feelings about my cousin since the day of the memorial service; I had no idea he'd kept her death in mind or had given any thought to how I was handling it. "It's all sort of settling in," I answered him.

He nodded. "That's how I felt for a couple months after my father died. I went day by day, until after a while I got to the point where I could just miss him and not feel worried."

"Worried?" A further surprise. "What about?"

"Oh, I don't know. Not having him around to consult with, I guess."

"You used to do that a lot?"

"No, not so much. But when I really did need to run something by him . . ." His muscular thighs gripped my knees in a warm vise. "Thing is, I knew he'd go—like you knew your father would, right? They're old, it's their turn, you can't do anything about that timetable. But with your cousin, she was only, what, sixty? And in good health. Everything happened so fast, without warning. That's a whole different game."

Pressing my face against his neck, I felt his vocal cords vibrating beneath my cheek as he continued speaking.

"I'm sorry you're solo, Cam," he said. "I can't pretend to know what that's like. I mean, I'm swimming in family! At least you've got Danny. And she's lucky to have you."

At the declivity of his throat, his aftershave was dominated by one note, vetiver. I inhaled its earthy, astringent scent. "I don't know," I said. "Right now I'm having trouble thinking of either Danny or myself as lucky."

"You haven't seen much of her recently, have you? Apart from this weekend, that is."

I shook my head.

"Well, maybe it would help if you spent some time with her."

I wasn't about to tell him of Danny's request for time off. "It'd help her, you mean?"

"Actually," he said, "it might help you. Give you a sense of what your role is, now that Eve's gone."

I saw where he was heading. "So I could be more like a mother to her?"

"Something like that."

"Ah," I said, unleashed now. "Well, when I had a husband, it was suggested that I ought to become a mother. But I nixed that idea, seeing as how I don't know shit about motherhood. So I'm not likely to give it a whirl now."

I turned away from him and lay on my back, addressing the ceiling. "Since we're on the subject of help: I used to say to myself, well, if I could see Nick whenever I felt like it, I'd be a cheerier girl. But lately I've begun wondering if maybe what would *really* help would be for you to leave me alone. That way I could quit pretending otherwise. Get on with things."

He fixed me with a look of affectionate skepticism. "Get on with things . . . like dating?"

"Don't," I said. "You've never been mean to me. Start now and I'll kick you out faster than you can blink."

He ran his fingers slowly through my hair, his wide palm cupping the top of my head. "You ask me to leave, I'll leave," he said quietly. "I've always known you might, one of these days. But I hope it'll be because you find someone, you know, right for you—"

"Sure," I snapped. "That'd be swell." I rolled away and went for my clothing, humiliation spreading over me like some hot, sour odor I was powerless to suppress. Keeping my back to Nick, I pulled on my jeans and T-shirt. After a few moments, he got up and began unhurriedly searching for one of his own T-shirts in the bottom drawer of my dresser, where I kept spares for him.

I waited for him to finish dressing. Approaching me, he pried my arms open and pulled me to him.

"I haven't a clue what 'right' means—for you, me, anyone," he said. "And I didn't really mean you ought to be Danny's mother either." He gave me a little shake. "I just meant you might be, I don't know, not a substitute exactly, but in the same league. . . . Necessary—that's what I'm trying to say."

Releasing me, he checked his watch. "Gotta go. I'm late for an estimate and it's a good building. I don't want to lose a shot at the work." He fixed me with his clear-eyed gaze. "It'll all sort out—give

Danny time. And one more thing: don't ask me to leave you unless you mean it, Cam. Then I'll go—not gladly, but I'll go. Tell me what you want and I'll do it. Haven't I always?"

AS SOON as he'd left, I went to my desk, took out a sheet of paper, and wrote "Dear Danny" at the top. After staring at the two words for a little while, I crumpled the paper and threw it out.

Stuart and Carl weren't home, I knew; they were downtown, attending some play on which I'd taken a pass. There was nobody else I wanted to see or talk with. I could stay home; I could take a walk. Throwing on a light jacket, I headed outdoors.

It was eight o'clock, the temperature perfect for strolling. I wandered northward. At Twentieth Street I turned east, then north again for a half-dozen blocks on Sixth Avenue until I stood in front of Eve's former shop.

Its gates were fully drawn, like those of the other retail outfits on the block. The shop's new owner had painted the gates a dull matte green; they were no longer awash in bright colors. Eve, Danny, and I had spent a long day decorating those gates, ten years earlier. Danny had favored pink, so by the end of the day, dozens of pink polka dots had been strewn across the larger swaths of color Eve and I had applied with big sponges. The effect had been eye-catching, just as Eve had wanted it to be.

Danny had enjoyed herself that day—although to my surprise, she'd made no wistful references to our gate-painting adventure the next time I saw her. She seemed to have learned to accommodate her mother. I couldn't recall her ever whining or moping when Eve was scarce. And yet (I'd thought at the time), wouldn't the day arrive when my questions about Eve's remoteness would become Danny's, too? And with a vengeance?

I TURNED around and headed back to the Village, cutting east at Ninth Street. It'd been many months since I'd last passed by my old home.

The building looked unchanged, though its formerly drab lobby had been freshly wallpapered. Crossing the street, I craned my neck so I could see the front windows of the family apartment on the third floor. I pictured Jordan up there, packing for one of his trips. I could readily imagine him in his bedroom, could see his shoes, suits, umbrella, and briefcase—yet I couldn't picture myself, or anything belonging to me. It was as though he and I had never once acted together on that same domestic stage.

A shadow crossed behind a louvered window (someone moving about the living room, or en route to the kitchen?), and I remembered how much, as a child, I'd longed for my father to pull back the curtain of his diffidence. Would he ever show me I could spark in him that same fierce need he roused in me?

No, I'd concluded, he would not.

But what about the woman in her coffin in Paris, whose namesake I was? Had my father unmasked himself for *her?* Allowed himself a fierce love? And then decided he couldn't bear to do so again?

A light went on, then off, in the living room window. As if signaled to leave, I headed home.

BACK IN my own kitchen, I poured a shot of vodka and drank it in one go. It made me instantly light-headed, so I forced myself to eat a small chunk of cheese, the only thing I'd ingested since breakfast. I still wasn't hungry.

I stared at the blank whiteness of my kitchen wall. *Open that one:* a voice, commanding, returned to memory now. Boxes—yes, in my latest dream there'd been two, and I'd had to choose between them. Meyerhold was pointing, telling me to open the smaller one, the one marked "Russia" . . .

The basement: Jordan's box was down there.

Keys in hand, I exited my apartment, went to the end of the common corridor on my floor, and descended four flights of stairs. In my building's basement, residents store large or bulky possessions in wire-mesh cages. By the time I'd made my way to my cage, opened it, and found the carton for which I was hunting, my arms and hands were gritty with dust.

I hauled the box upstairs, wiped it and my hands clean, and tore open the top. Its old masking tape gave way instantly. Inside lay a mess of manila envelopes I vaguely remembered having examined with Stuart, nearly twenty years earlier, in Frenchtown. Riffling through what looked like the tourist and travel information (Russian hotel and museum brochures, theater and concert programs—nothing signed) that had lost my interest two decades ago, I found some handwritten pages that had been torn from a notebook.

Although each page bore a number in its upper-right corner, all but the first few were out of order. I sorted them out. On the initial half dozen or so, Jordan had scribbled notes about perfume outlets in Moscow. There were a few references to GUM, the huge department store in Red Square, as well as to shops on Gorky Street. Jordan had marked their locations on a little map. He'd also attempted, in crudely penned Cyrillic, to capture the names of several Russian fragrances.

Next I came across miscellaneous sheets of paper torn from another notebook; the paper was different. These pages contained hastily written comments on performances Jordan had attended at concert halls and theaters in Moscow—the Bolshoi, the Maly, and a few others. It took me several minutes to straighten out these pages, and as I did so, I encountered yet another set, interleaved among the theater notes, which were held together with a metal clip. These sheets were heavier—more like actual stationery than the lightweight notebook paper Jordan used while traveling.

I located the first of these pages after a bit of shuffling. I was holding, I realized, a letter, written by my father and dated a few days before his death. He'd put it where he knew I'd find it eventually. Though no doubt he'd taken me for a better sleuth than I turned out to be.

I unplugged my phone, made a small salad and forced myself to eat it, then drank a mug of strong black tea. I wanted a clear head, if not a calm heart, before reading.

THIS SEEMS as good a point as any for a pause. I ought now to recount Seva's end. I've been putting this off; it's the hardest of all my experiences to revisit . . . but what happened does need airing.

"It is man's nature to lose his way when he finds no means of linking himself to what came before him and will come after him." So claimed Pyotr Chaadaev, a colleague of the poet Pushkin, roughly a century before Seva's time. He was right, of course. There's really no higher purpose (in art, politics, family—it doesn't matter) than to serve as an instrument of linkage.

And what might a man's double become, if not a kind of baton passed from one mind to another? I'd seen Vsevolod Meyerhold lose his way, egregiously. Now Camilla Archer wasn't going to lose *hers;* not if *I* had anything to do with it.

SEVA DREAMED of stages while he was in prison: multitiered, banked, in the round. He dreamed of lights, curtains, props.

He dreamed of plays and playwrights. Of Mayakovsky and Blok. He dreamed of the Interlude House and those attentive soldiers, some dying, who'd served as the audience for his acting studio in St. Petersburg. He dreamed of actors backstage, keyed up, waiting their turns to go on.

Not all of his dreams were sourced in happy recollections, however. Some of them revived frustrations, obstacles, failures.

He dreamed of Zina in costume as the widow Popova in one of Chekhov's amusing farces, *The Bear.* He saw her hand slyly sweeping one suitor's bouquet of roses off the piano as she succumbed to the embraces of another. She'd comported herself well, but as Seva watched himself, in his dream, watching Zina from the wings of the stage, he knew the production was a failure despite its vaudeville touches and his wife's flair. "We tried to be too clever," he'd admitted to his assistant. "Chekhov's light transparent humor was crushed beneath the weight of our theories." They'd made the worst possible mistake, that of heavy-handedness.

He had other dreams of flops—particularly *Natasha,* an over-wrought drama about a heroine on a collective farm. He'd tried to appease the Party by staging the play in a naturalistic manner, but his efforts had been risible (who could *not* laugh at cabbage patches onstage?), and the play hadn't even made it out of rehearsal.

Not long after *Natasha, Pravda* had issued a blistering attack on him: "Meyerhold cannot and, apparently, will not comprehend So-viet reality." At the end of a subsequent public debate, held in Moscow over a three-day period, Seva had confessed his failings only to be savaged by numerous speakers, his own actors among them. His stage carpenter had been the sole man brave enough to express support for him.

Seva had responded by arguing that he was by nature an exper-imental director. "This is not so much my fault," he'd stated, "as my misfortune." (Shades of Pushkin!—"It's the devil's fault I was born in Russia with spirit and talent.") He'd promised to rethink his en-tire worldview. Yet it was useless; his assembled listeners, an audi-ence of self-proclaimed judges, had voted to affirm every point in the *Pravda* article. Meyerhold had been, they said, insufficiently contrite.

HE DREAMED of being onstage: his final public appearance.

The All-Union Conference of Theater Directors had opened on June 15, 1939. He'd shown up wearing a white shirt, somewhat rumpled, and no jacket, because of the heat. The crowd was lively; everyone acclaimed his arrival with loud clapping. He was quickly ushered to the platform, to the evident dismay of the chairman, a clumsy Party hack named Krapchenko.

At the side of the wooden podium, on a little bracketed shelf, sat a glass of water. He saw himself take a sip before launching into an impromptu, rambling, and not entirely sense-making speech in which he'd begun by praising Comrade Stalin, "the friend of toilers throughout the world."

In his dream he watched himself perspiring in the warm, poorly ventilated hall. He listened to himself talking about the future of

Soviet theater, heard himself pulling back from the truth, losing himself in needless detail, weaving baggy arguments. Observing the faces in the audience, he saw some of them twisted in preordained grimaces of condemnation; others, though, were full of hope, expecting more from him, their expressions increasingly bewildered.

He floundered, sensing the words that were forming in the mind of an exasperated critic named Moissei Yankovsky—words Yankovsky would utter the following day: "Meyerhold destroyed everything that he has stood for throughout his life. Comrades, can we honestly agree that on the strength of what Meyerhold the man said yesterday, Meyerhold the artist never existed? For that is what officially he announced to us."

He knew, too, that I was gesticulating at him from the wings. Shaking his head, he made a gesture communicating his refusal to say something self-serving—no, self-saving: *I can't do any more, it's just too much, I'm tired, I've had it.*

He concluded his speech. The applause greeting him was at once heartfelt and full of disappointment. He couldn't bring himself to look at his confused colleagues' faces; he headed straight for his seat, seeing nothing. In his mind he heard one of Mayakovsky's poems, in which Volodya had railed at the angels—heaven's swindlers, he'd called them:

> *again they've beheaded the stars*
> *and the sky is bloodied with carnage!*

THE REST of the directors' conference unfolded noisily, a blur of talk and argument. Seva left early for Leningrad to direct a student production at the Lesgaft Institute, so he missed the conclusion. At the end, the conference chairman stood to render judgment. Comrade Meyerhold had made a purely formal apology, asserted Chairman Krapchenko. He'd admitted nothing about the real nature of his wrongdoings. "The Party teaches us," Krapchenko reminded the audience, "that it is not enough merely to admit our mistakes."

Everybody heard the words and guessed what they could mean.

In Leningrad, Seva dreamed of decapitated stars bleeding across the sky. He dreamed of punishment—of being hung, as Volodya had imagined, on a celestial scaffolding:

> *a gibbet astride the Milky Way*
> *seize me and string me up, a criminal . . .*

AT FIRST, after his arrest and incarceration in Moscow's Lefortovo Prison, Seva had maintained a lively dream life. But once the interrogations began, his dreaming grew more erratic. In the evenings, before actually falling asleep, he sometimes dropped into a state resembling stupor. He awoke with the same feeling, leaden, insensate.

Comrade Kobulov was clever at his job. As head of the NKVD's Special Investigative Section, Kobulov had been given the "good cop" role in Seva's case. He treated the theater director respectfully, offering him a glass of tea before their conversations, as he called them. But below the affable surface, Kobulov was hard as steel. In an appeal to Vyacheslav Molotov, the Soviet premier, Seva described his interrogator's techniques. Kobulov had been persuasive in suggesting that the prisoner's problems were of his own making. "I was plunged," Seva wrote in his letter to Molotov, "into the deepest depression, obsessed by the thought 'It serves me right.'" He'd begun making up crimes that he must surely have committed, since the Soviet government was convinced he had. "In this process," Seva commented acidly, "my interrogator proved to be a well-experienced assistant, so we set about inventing things together in close collaboration."

How I loved seeing my partner's wit flare as it did in that letter!

SEVA WASN'T getting the sleep he required. This would begin taking a toll on him, I knew; his nerves had always been worsened more by sleep deprivation than by lack of food.

I could see right away the kind of mind game Kobulov was playing. Seva, being vulnerable, was likely to play along to some extent. For years his self-confidence had been assaulted by reviewers, censors, envious colleagues, and spectators who'd fallen under the sway of the Party's empty-headed aesthetic notions. He'd managed to fend off his detractors, but there was simply no way he could maintain an unflinching belief in himself while being vilified by Kobulov, who had a formidable gift for pathologizing a person's motives.

So although it was no joy to hear Seva offering up, as he did during his first couple of interrogations, the names of various political opponents of Stalin's—men whom his jailers had branded as Trotskyist traitors, and whose names subsequently appeared on a typed confession Seva was supposed to sign—I also figured that this capitulation was in a sense inevitable. I dislike borrowing from the language of psychologists, yet the fact is that Seva had internalized the accusations that had been verbally pounded into him. In his own eyes he'd taken on some of the attributes of a guilty man. Having watched so many of his fellow artists and intellectuals get purged, he now wondered why he'd managed to get off scot-free. Didn't he, too, deserve a comeuppance? Hadn't he in fact hung around with the English journalist Fred Gray, now accused of being a foreign agent? Not to mention "anti-Soviet elements in the field of the arts," including Boris Pasternak and Ilya Ehrenburg? Could he vouch with surety for their patriotism? For his own?

WHEN THE typed piece of paper with his "confession" was shoved in front of him, I set about suggesting to Seva that he complicate matters for his interrogator by not omitting, on the list he'd been asked to prepare citing confederates who'd visited his theater, the names of Comrades Molotov and, yes, Stalin himself. I figured this would help Seva (if not his captors) gain some necessary perspective on his situation. He needed to back away from the precipice of self-recrimination, to reclaim the solid ground of pride and self-confidence. It was time for some unmasking—time to make it clear that his arrest had been a ludicrous mistake.

I'd miscalculated the opposition, however. The addition of Stalin's and Molotov's names to the list of Seva's fellow travelers did not sit well with Kobulov, who brought in a couple of goons for two sessions of what were alluded to as "physical methods": specifically, the battering of Seva's feet, legs, and back with a rubber truncheon.

The two goons beat him and then, a few days later, after his bruises had ripened sufficiently, they bashed the bruises, too, as well as his face and head. At the end of his first torture session (which took place on a warm day in July and lasted around eighteen hours), Seva was facedown on the floor. He'd discovered, he later testified in his letter to Molotov, that he had "the capacity to cringe, writhe, and howl like a dog being whipped by its master." All of these positions would have made superior biomechanical exercises, but Seva lacked the wherewithal for sketching and note taking. He was in the realm of the grotesque, where a person is precipitously switched, as he once put it, "from the plane he has just reached to another, which is totally unseen."

AS THE weeks wore on, I found it harder to infiltrate Seva's dreams. He was resistant; fear had become the filter through which his inner life passed. It skimmed off everything sublime or salvific, allowing only terrors to enter and penetrate.

In the fall of 1939, Seva was presented with the text of an indictment in which he was charged with treason. According to his captors, he'd led the theater wing of the "Left Front" group of artists, a group supposedly committed to the overthrow of the Soviet government. This charge was prompted in part by a confession of the writer Isaac Babel, who (under torture of his own, a few days before Seva's) had named Meyerhold as a Left Front member.

Seva was devastated. He'd already been through two prolonged sessions of "physical methods," during which (as he later described it) his interrogators fulfilled the twin tasks of beating him and preparing written confessions on his behalf. ("Whenever my imagination became exhausted," he stated in his appeal, "my interrogators would work in pairs . . . and draft the statements, sometimes rewriting them three or four times.") Now a final dreadful document had arrived, and he was being told to accept it without reconsideration.

The investigators who confronted him with the confession pushed him to sign it then and there. I signaled him to delay, and finally—after a bout of trembling that had his jailers rolling their eyes, although his shaking was completely involuntary—Seva managed to rally. After agreeing that the essential facts were correct, he asked permission to reread the document in order to make necessary corrections and additions. He was trying to buy himself time so he could read this travesty of a document with his wits more fully about him.

The Investigative Section, however, wasn't in the business of giving political prisoners a chance to argue their innocence. Although Seva's jailers did grant him permission to review his indictment, he was given no time to emend it. It was deemed to have been accepted by him as truthful in all its particulars.

In protest Seva wrote a statement in which he retracted any remarks that might've seemed to implicate his colleagues—Pasternak, Ehrenburg, Mitya Shostakovich, and others. He also repudiated his admissions concerning any links with the Left Front and foreign intelligence sources. All these statements, he wrote in an appeal to two different procurators, had been made under torture and were worthless untruths.

AT THIS point Seva was a physical as well as emotional wreck. He'd found it impossible to maintain his composure during the session in which his indictment was shown to him. He'd shaken uncontrollably and then, at the end, had suddenly grown still, as if he'd passed out. Tears poured from his eyes. He wasn't so much crying as leaking: all his energy was draining from him, like water from a broken faucet.

Afterward he sat slumped on his filthy mattress in his cell, looking like a drug addict or a drunken derelict. There was nothing recognizable in his face—none of the hauteur he'd once summoned when confronted with criticism, none of the sparkling intelligence and humor. His hair had grayed and thinned; his skin was slack, potato-colored. He'd lost weight.

I gave him a few days to pull himself back together, and then I urged him to write to Premier Molotov. He did, in January—a two-part letter in which he reiterated that his confessions had been beaten out of him. But he also added, despite my misgivings, two lines that made me wince: "I beg you as Head of Government to save me and return me my freedom. I love my motherland and I will serve it with all my strength in the remaining years of my life."

Swearing loyalty to Russia would be seen by Molotov as a sign of disingenuousness—I was sure of this. Seva needed to be more subtle. Yet although I tried to implant my sureties in his dreams, he didn't seem to catch on. He kept insisting that he had to let his jailers know how much he truly supported the construction of a Communist state—a people's republic that could serve as a beacon to all other nations.

Gradually Seva began to shut down his oneiric life altogether. Whenever one of his dreams started going in some fresh new direction (leading, I hoped, to a renewal of his old sturdy intransigence), he'd wake himself up. Each morning he refused to recall anything I'd introduced to his consciousness the night before.

My only guaranteed access to my partner's thinking was via his body. Sometimes I was able to remind him, by calling his attention to the hemorrhages on his legs (those multiple bruises, yellow-purple in color), that he was dealing with people for whom his patriotism was irrelevant. All that mattered to them was that he forget about ever having been a master and instead behave like a slave.

I did my best, but my efforts availed little. Meanwhile his physical condition grew increasingly worrisome. Earlier that autumn, his interrogators had taken him to the prison hospital, where he'd been given a bit of medical treatment and put on a new diet. Yet these measures had been merely palliative, a means of extending his torture. In one of his letters to Molotov, Seva described the results of this "care": it had helped restore his outward appearance, but his nerves were in the same wretched state. "My interrogators," he wrote, describing the process by which untruths were wrung out of him, "threatened me constantly: 'If you refuse to write (meaning "compose"?!), we shall beat you again, leaving your head and right hand untouched but turning the rest of you into a shapeless, bloody mass of mangled flesh.'"

THUS BEGAN the new year, with Seva awaiting word from Molotov. By this time, he was no longer in Lefortovo; they'd stuck him in the Butyrka prison. In his small cell he clung to the hope that the premier would hear his entreaties.

I had by now taken a different and darker view of things, and my hopes were flagging. But each day I tried getting Seva to focus on memories of his directorial successes, and I urged him to indulge in fond reminiscences of his wife. Desperate for something to give him energy—searching for the emotional equivalent of a spoonful of white sugar—I summoned to his nostrils (whose functioning had, alas, become increasingly blunted) the scent of a Coty perfume that Zina had worn nearly every day of their marriage.

Seva warmed a bit to this recollection. He perked up even more when I reintroduced to his nose the perfume Jordan Archer had given Zina in Paris—a new scent by Patou whose name, Que Sais-Je?, amused her. Yet none of these distractions worked for very long. After a little while, Seva would slump back into despondency.

ON THE last day of January, Seva awoke resigned to the fact that the first month of the first year in a new decade had passed without offering him a hint of rescue. He was therefore surprised when a guard came to fetch him, and even more so when he found himself transferred to a holding pen in the cellar of the Military Collegium, located in the center of Moscow, not far from Red Square.

His preliminary meeting (as it was termed) would be presided over, the guard told him, by a judge named Ulrikh. As soon as I heard this name, I blanched inwardly. Ulrikh's reputation was one of unmatched ugliness. He'd already sentenced thousands of people to death for "crimes against the people."

Thus I knew we were in for the roughest of rides. What I didn't expect was that it would also be one of the briefest.

SEVA WAS formally indicted on the day he was transferred, and his trial took place on the next.

The night before the trial, I'd thought it over and come to a conclusion. The only thing that might work would be to transform Seva, in the court's eyes, from an abject, sniveling prisoner to a man who, though no longer in full possession of his personal and professional powers, remained an actor—not just in the sense of a talented performer but in the deeper sense of a person capable of self-scrutiny and meaningful action, hence returnable to society as a contributing citizen. In other words, Seva would have to show himself to be someone who'd already acknowledged and repaired his flaws.

In Soviet Russia, of course, the notion of contributing citizens lacked any grounding in reality. Yet an appeal to Ulrikh ought, I believed, to be made along pragmatic lines. Seva was still capable of offering his compatriots something of value, and his release would be of use to the state: this, in a nutshell, was what I urged him to emphasize.

I was grasping at straws, of course, though loath to admit it. I didn't want to see my own failures. I'd gone along with Seva's enthusiastic support of the Revolution; it wasn't my job to sort out his political predilections for him. But his stint in Lefortovo had revealed how shortsighted and costly my detachment had been. Now, full of dread, I was scrambling to pull together a rescue plan.

SEVA WANTED to prove his innocence and clear his name in court. What *I* wanted was simpler: to procure his immediate release from prison.

It seemed obvious that he'd have to strike a delicate balance between subservience and forthrightness—between admitting he'd erred and insisting he was reformable, wasn't a traitor. And so, the evening before Seva stood to address Ulrikh, I urged him to recognize who he was really dealing with: not an honorable representative of those stalwart Communists who inhabited his imagination, but merely a brute. Ulrikh wanted nothing more than another bucket of blood to slop at Stalin's feet.

Moreover, I encouraged Seva to think about his stage presence. *You'll be playing a part, remember, so play it as if for a theater audience. Use your body, gesture forcefully as you speak. Deploy not only your hands but your arms, shoulders, and neck. Use your height, let it work for you. Most of all, try to appear both candid and capable. Portray yourself as an asset to Soviet society—a man who sees what can go wrong and how to fix it . . .*

Seva swayed slightly, his eyes shut, his mind and body attending. I focused all my powers on penetrating his doubts about the nature of the challenge that lay before him. His real task wasn't to proclaim his innocence; it was to offer a convincing argument for his freedom. To do this he'd have to create a character, a man named Meyerhold who, as a result of his reeducation in prison, was now ready, able, and entirely willing—no, eager!—to offer his immense talents to his society.

Remember what you used to tell the students in our studio, years ago, in St. Petersburg? A theater is any stage an actor can construct for himself. The courtroom will be your theater!

He was taking it all in, but I could tell he wasn't buying it. He was having, I saw, an eleventh-hour epiphany, an abrupt realization that was throwing into disarray his entire sense of how to proceed. He stood unsteadily in the middle of his small cell, his shoulders stooped, his head bent forward.

How could I have been so blind! he moaned. Then, as he began murmuring aloud, I pieced together what was going on. It had to do with Mayakovsky's suicide, whose causes Seva was now divining afresh. Volodya's life-concluding bullet hadn't been fired in reaction to a failed romance or a harsh theater review. No, no! Those were factors, but they weren't the basic cause. Everyone had misread Mayakovsky, overlooking what was really at stake. Volodya had plumbed a deeper anguish, and after sounding its depths, he'd decided there was only one way out.

If only I'd listened harder! Pacing his cell, Seva tormented himself. He recalled the final scene in Volodya's play *The Bedbug,* when Prisypkin, the little drunkard, is thawed out after five decades of refrigeration. Utterly bewildered, Prisypkin confronts the people who've caged him. "Citizens! Brothers!" he cries. "My own people! Darlings! How did you get here? So many of you! When were you unfrozen? Why am I alone in the cage? Darlings, friends, come and join me! Why am I suffering? Citizens! . . ."

The audiences had laughed at Prisypkin's delirious appeals, but they'd squirmed, too, for behind the play's satire lay something problematic and unnerving. What exactly, Seva asked himself now, *was* Volodya's vision of the future? Had he really believed that a lasting Communist utopia could be established? Had he been as sunnily optimistic and brash as he'd tried to make himself sound in his poems?

No, he hadn't. He'd foreseen his society stripped, denuded of love, and no amount of satirical frosting could conceal this—the underlying, anticipated darkness.

Pacing more slowly now, coughing, trembling, Seva remembered how he'd talked with his cast about *The Bedbug*. He'd explained that the play's purpose was to expose the vices of the current times. But what he hadn't said—what he hadn't *seen*—was that this was merely the surface, the tight skin of the play's comedy. *The Bedbug* actually revealed that love itself was under attack.

Planting the heels of his hands on his forehead, Seva gripped his skull in his long fingers and squeezed. Everything was concatenating now. Hadn't Volodya spent time in Butyrka—yes, in 1909—for supporting the Bolsheviks? Perhaps he'd even been stuck in the same tiny room Seva had recently vacated . . . And afterward, hadn't Volodya written a poem in which he'd claimed he'd learned about love in Butyrka? He'd stared out of the keyhole of his cell, knowing he'd give anything for a bit of sunlight on the wall. Knowing, too, that his heart had grown, that it would keep expanding until it became hefty, heftier, huge.

That bulk is love, he'd written.

For all his egotistical bunglings, Volodya had understood the heart more keenly than anyone else. *That bulk is love.* Yes, but there was a corollary: *that bulk is hate,* he'd added in the poem's next line. *That bulk is hate.* The heart houses both.

MERCY, SAID Seva at around two in the morning. The cell was silent; he was entirely alone.

There won't be any, I said.

Then truth, he said.

They don't know the meaning of the word.

But I do, he said.

So?

So, he said, *that's what I'll ask for, the truth.*

There's no point.

Exactly, he said. *Which is why it's the only thing to do.*

It was then that I realized I'd be losing my partner.

THE TRIAL took almost two hours. It would have been over in the usual fifteen minutes had Seva not made a closing speech that was long and dense enough to give the recording secretary some trouble in capturing his words verbatim. There was a fair bit of stopping and restarting.

In addition to Ulrikh, two military jurists were present. There were no attorneys or witnesses for either the prosecution or the defense. Pleading innocent, Seva repeated his denial of the entire indictment. As he spoke the judge and jurists nodded, their boredom and disdain visible—to me, anyway. I'm not sure what Seva was capable of perceiving. His face was blank as a late-November sky before a snowfall.

The recording secretary typed a total of five pages of notes on the proceedings, including Seva's final address to the court, during which he referred to himself in the third person. *He lied about himself,* he stated, *just because he was beaten with a rubber truncheon. It was then that he lied and decided to go to the stake. He is guilty of nothing, he was never a traitor to his country. . . . He believes that the court will understand him and decide that he is not guilty.*

Watching Seva's delivery, I focused on the ways in which, even in his exhausted state, he managed to control and direct his voice. Then I remembered what Olga Knipper, Chekhov's wife, had said about Seva when she first met him. She'd been struck by the intelligence of his whole being. So, now, was I; and so, I suspected, was the judge, who trained his lizardlike gaze on my partner as Seva brought his address to a close with this self-description: *He believes that the truth will prevail.*

Ulrikh stared at Seva for a couple of seconds. I do not think he was hesitating; I think he was taking in what Olga Knipper had observed. Then his pen moved swiftly over the paper in front of him.

Something within Seva soared. I felt it—felt him toss his spirit like a ball in the air, releasing it as he apprehended his own death. Then shock and terror rushed into his body, and there was no more room for me anywhere. His entire frame sagged; he dropped softly, dazedly, to the floor. I had been extruded; our partnership had been severed. There was nothing more I could do. I could only watch in horror as the executioners pulled him up by his armpits, shuffled him down to the basement of the Collegium, blindfolded him, and did as they were ordered.

One shot sufficed. After it was over, they cremated him and took his remains, along with those of hundreds of others—I saw box after box of ashes being loaded into a truck—to the cemetery of the Don Monastery, near the river, where they were buried, if that's the word, in a common grave.

THUS I found myself uncoupled, having spent several decades in a partnership the strange and rewarding likes of which I will probably not experience again.

Time passed, my remorse festered, and Seva's quintessence remained undispersed. Then came the receptor to whom, I decided, Seva's energies might at last be fruitfully transmitted . . .

Two more dreams of hers are left to report! The first involves her cousin, her father, and (naturally) the director, whose presence my new collaborator had by now come to expect. The second dream is wholly Camilla's—I had no hand in it. Onward!

EIGHT

A TRAMPOLINE sits in the middle of what appears to be the living room of the family apartment. The room's ceilings are abnormally high, so the space accommodates the trampoline.

Eve is jumping on it in smooth cycles, each bounce taking her a little higher. She lands gracefully each time, her bare feet spaced evenly, her hands held out at her sides. She's wearing a black leotard and leggings. Her mouth is painted red. Apart from these touches, she's unadorned. Her dark blue eyes gleam in the room's low light.

Meyerhold stands off to one side, assessing Eve. On the other side of the room, Jordan too is watching. I'm sitting on the sofa, observing the three of them. All is silent save for the thump of the trampoline each time Eve lands on it.

Jumping especially high, she executes a midair somersault. Meyerhold claps languidly.

Well done, he intones. Although you ought to practice your squats *more regularly. Your half-twist pencil jumps are excellent, however. Don't forget about mirror-gazing! As you jump, cultivate the ability to watch yourself as if from the outside. Keep your expression impassive. Let your body do the talking.*

Eve recommences her bouncing. Exquis, *murmurs my father in French. Truly exquisite.*

Meyerhold turns and points at Jordan. You, on the other hand, are the laziest man of talent I've ever met! You make extraordinary fragrances, but can you make women happy? Take these two—he indicates Eve, then me on the sidelines. What have you done for them in the happiness department? His speech is the verbal equivalent of a forefinger jabbing a lapel.

Jordan returns the director's stare. I gave them each a bottle of Lune, he says.

That's not enough! I shriek. And you made it for her, *not for me!*

My sudden outburst throws Eve off, literally: she takes a sideways bounce and disappears from the room.

Jordan appears unruffled. She knows who I am and who I've loved, he says to Meyerhold, tilting his head in my direction. Don't be fooled—nothing's lost on that *girl! Not much of a talker, though. In that respect she takes after me, he adds.*

Well . . . perhaps she does know. In which case, the director says sternly, turning to me, quit behaving like an understudy! "Oh, don't mind me, I just plan on spending my entire life backstage"—is that it? You have to act, *you know!*

Like a bat, the director spreads his cape's wings wide, blocking my view of Jordan. Then he rushes me, enveloping me, pressing me to him. His scent is a pungent mix of pipe tobacco, rosemary, and the backstage odor (musty, with an overlay of pine) of a summer-stock theater in New Hampshire where Stuart and I once spent a long, hot August working as stagehands.

I struggle to escape his grip, but he holds me fast. I'd give you a script, he coos in my ear, but alas, there isn't one. So make it up as you go! But remember, he adds: a mask obscures the eyes. The eyes mask the mind. And what does the mind conceal? The heart! Raise its curtain!

Cape and scent dissolve around me: he's gone.

I TREATED Jordan's missive as though it were addressed to me, which it wasn't. I read it without hesitation, because I was meant to.

My father had put the letter where he knew only I would find it. He knew, too, that I'd deliver it to its intended recipient, who'd help me see (in it, or because of it) what I hadn't yet been able to see.

Dear Danny,

By the time you open this bottle of perfume, its scent will have faded considerably. But at least you'll have an idea of what it was like when it was fresh. It's something you won't find in any shop. Nobody else has a sample of it. You're the only one! I call this perfume Somersault. It reminds me of a man named Meyerhold—a Russian theater director I met during one of my earliest trips to Paris.

You and I haven't had much time to get to know each other, Danny, but I can already see the woman you'll become: a real charmer. You remind me a little of Cam and a little of your mother. There's something of Cam's reserve in you, and lots of Eve's flintiness! And her scent, too: your hair smells exactly the same . . . *Aigre-doux,* as they say in French: bittersweet.

I don't know what Cam and Eve will tell you about my departure, Danny, and I hope you'll refrain from judging either of them for the parts they've played in it. Eve got me the pills I'll need, and Cam will make sure the method I've chosen really works. They've both been brave. I haven't loved either of them well enough.

Time to end this letter, my girl. I hope you savor whatever your life brings you. Tell Cam to be kind to her sister, and you be kind to Cam!

Jordan

P.S. Oh, about Meyerhold: there's a story . . . I thought he might be able to help me design a perfume bottle. He was a set designer, too, as well as a director. I figured, why not ask?

A lot of time passed before I received word from him. Here's how it happened: In 1950, I received a little package, addressed to me at Patou in New York, from a British journalist who'd visited Moscow in 1938. He'd contacted Meyerhold, who gave him a folder for me. Meyerhold cautioned the Englishman to conceal the folder in his luggage. One never knows, he'd said.

The Englishman made it through Russian customs without incident and returned to London. But war was about to break out, and this man had more important matters than Meyerhold's folder on his mind. His house was damaged during the bombing raids. As he was sifting through the remains of his study, he found the folder, put it in a box, and forgot all about it.

Then, in 1950, he came across the box again. It was inexcusable, he wrote in a note to me, that he was still hanging on to something he'd promised to deliver more than ten years earlier! He hoped that although Coty had probably changed addresses since then, the folder would make it to me at last.

Which it did: Coty forwarded it to me at Patou. And in it were the sketches I've attached, along with a note written in Russian and dated January 30, 1938.

I had the note translated. This is what it communicates:

Dear Mr. Archer,

My apologies for the long delay in responding to your request for these sketches. As you may recall, when we met in Paris, you showed my wife and me some photos of unusual perfume bottles and asked if I could design something of equal panache.

Well, here's my attempt. But first let me apologize for not writing to you in your own language! I am assuming that somewhere in vast New York City lives a Russian who can translate this for you. (Whenever I think of your city, I recall how my friend Mayakovsky once called the Brooklyn Bridge a paw of steel. Such an image! Do you happen to live anywhere near that paw, by chance?)

I took pleasure in making these sketches. They're based on Pierrot, a clown who's the central character in a play called "The

Fairground Booth" by Alexander Blok. It's a takeoff on an old commedia dell'arte routine. Pierrot is in love with a lady named Columbine, who's the daughter of a merchant called Pantalone. She's invisible to mortals. In Blok's play she seems real but isn't; she's a figment of Pierrot's imagination. The play is all about confusions of love and identity.

I hope you enjoy these sketches! Even if they prove useless for your needs, perhaps they'll prompt something else? I rather like the one of Pierrot doing a somersault—poor lovesick clown! Please give your new woman friend (is she now your wife?) my regards, and those of Zina as well! I'm sorry we weren't able to meet her in Paris, but we wish her, and you, the best.

Yours, Vs. Meyerhold

I assumed Meyerhold was dead, and after making a few inquiries, I learned he'd been executed. And his wife had been killed, too. Such a sad tale.

Anyway, Danny, I thought you'd like these sketches. They'd make extraordinary bottle designs, in my view. I have a feeling you'll turn out to be an artist yourself. So take these drawings and do with them as you wish—

J.

STUART SHOWED up at The Fourth Wall the next day at closing time, carrying a black duffel bag.

"You got after-work plans?" he asked.

"Nope," I answered, surprised to see him. In a phone chat earlier in the day, he'd said nothing about stopping by; we'd talked business and weather. I'd decided not to tell him about the box in my basement until I'd figured out what to do about Danny—when and how to let her know I had a letter for her. No point, I'd decided, in being hasty. I was feeling bewildered by Jordan's reference, in his letter, to my sister—who exactly had he been alluding to?

"Good. Drop the gates, then," Stuart ordered, pointing at the front of my shop.

"I was about to," I said. "But what's your hurry?"

"Just do it. I'll help."

"Don't forget your bag," I said as we proceeded to the door.

"No, no, we're staying put," said Stuart. "I just want to make it seem like you're closed, so nobody bothers us."

I brought down the solid metal gate halfway, ducked under it, then pulled it shut, stepping back inside after doing so. The space grew dim when I closed the door. I turned on the lights at the front, but Stuart immediately turned them off.

"You planning a séance?" I asked.

"Sit." He pointed at a tall stool in one corner, and I made my way to it. The stool, its seat smooth and polished, had been in the orchestra pit at the Met for many years; I'd gotten it from a former stagehand. Perched on its slightly rickety legs, I could gaze down at my carved griffin—the best of my props—while surveying the rest of my domain.

Stuart began rummaging around in his bag. He soon produced a half-dozen very tall candlesticks, into which he inserted cream-colored tapers. These he ringed around us in a loose circle. As he lit them, the candles' wicks flared momentarily; then their flames bobbed peacefully, casting a lovely glow.

"Just don't knock those over," I said. "I'll never be able to explain to my insurance company how the whole place burned to the ground."

"Pipe down," said Stuart as he knelt next to his bag. "Just sit tight till I find what I'm looking for . . . Ah, here it is."

He pulled out a black-and-white, diamond-patterned cloth, which he spread on the floor. On it he placed several tubes of what looked like makeup, along with an eyebrow pencil and some lipstick.

"And now," he announced, standing and reaching out to cup my chin in his hand, "a little exercise in transformation." He tilted my face slightly upward. "Hold steady—right there, okay? The light's perfect now."

"Wouldn't it be better for me to pay someone at Elizabeth Arden to do this?" I asked.

He gave my chin a disciplinary shake.

"I won't say another word."

"Good girl. Because I was just going to tell you to shut up."

Producing several bobby pins from his pants pocket, he pinned back my hair so none of it was touching my forehead or temples. Then he knelt again, examining his stash of supplies. Opening two tubes of makeup, he dabbed small amounts of each into his left palm, mixing them with the fingertips of his other hand. I couldn't see the outcome; he turned away from me as he worked.

"Close your eyes," he commanded, approaching me. After I'd done so, he began smoothing the makeup onto my cheeks with fast, sure strokes. In a little while he stepped back, surveyed me, told me I could now open my eyes, and blended more makeup in his palm. This time he applied it across my forehead and down my temples. Next he did my nose, then the area around my mouth, and finally my chin and jawline.

Returning to the tubes of color, he dabbed some more in his palm, dipped his thumb into the mix, scrutinized my face, and ran his thumb carefully at an angle along each of my cheekbones. At one point the effect seemed to bother him; he reached into his bag, found a tissue, wiped my cheekbones with it, and redid them, working with considerable delicacy.

"Be right back," he said when he'd finished. "Just need to clean my hands before I go any further." Pulling a hand towel from his bag, he went to the sink. I heard the water running; then he was back, wiping his hands on his towel.

"You're awfully well equipped," I said.

"Years of practice."

"But it's been a while since you last performed, hasn't it? I didn't realize you'd kept all your mime makeup."

He clucked his tongue. "Certain props one doesn't let go of, Camilla. *You* of all people should know that."

Checking me out again, he ordered me to shut my eyes. Then he began applying more makeup, using the outside edge of his pinky finger as well as the tip of his index finger. After a few minutes he allowed me to reopen my eyes. He worked intently, frequently stepping back to regard my face, then moving in to tinker some more. His strokes were slower now, and finer. When he was satisfied with the results, he picked up the eyebrow pencil and started in on my brows, applying color in short, aggressive movements. He stepped back several yards and gazed at me, his expression concentrated; then he nodded to himself and proceeded directly to my left brow, which he penciled some more, lightly, at its outer edge.

"Now the mouth," he said. Picking up one of the lipsticks he'd brought, he ordered me to purse my mouth. "Good, good. Not too stiff now—relax, baby, I'm almost done! Now a second coat, in another color. You've been very compliant. Wait'll I tell Carl . . . He'll say I should've given you some graham crackers and milk as a reward."

"I'll settle for a vodka," I said.

"Fine," said Stuart. "But we're not quite done." He'd finished with my mouth, which felt slightly gummy. The lipstick wasn't the well-lubricated stuff I was used to, but at least it had no odor that I could detect. None of the makeup was smelly, in fact, for which I was grateful.

"Now for some costuming. Nothing much, I know you're not big on dressing up."

"What's that supposed to mean?" I asked. "I have some perfectly lovely togs in my closet."

"Yeah, and you wear a frock maybe once a year? Don't worry, I didn't bring any dresses. I had something else in mind. Close your eyes. And keep 'em closed."

I did, and heard him reaching into his bag. In a moment he'd plopped a hat on my head. It felt a little large. Then he placed a rectangular object in my lap.

"This feels like a briefcase of some kind," I said, running my hands over it.

"It is. Now make it stand upright on your legs—no, don't cross them," Stuart ordered. "Okay. Now bend your right arm and put your elbow on top of the briefcase, and stabilize it at the side, with your other hand around it, like this—good! You've got it. Now hold your chin—yes, you have to lean over the briefcase a little, so you can put your chin in your hand. Very good."

Once again I heard him extricate something from his bag. "Okay," he said. "I've got a mirror here, right in front of you. I want you to look at yourself in it."

I OPENED my eyes and saw Jordan.

He was wearing a hat and holding a briefcase on his lap. The hat looked very much like the one I'd sold recently, the Beckett hat; the briefcase resembled the one Jordan used to carry, with similar brass hardware.

His face was very pale. His lips were thin and dark, with no sheen; below his cheekbones the skin was slightly mauve in tone. The shadows under his eyes signaled suffering accepted, endured. His face revealed no hint of self-pity, no belief in abatement.

"Who is it?" asked Stuart softly.

A man of feeling, fully alone. "My father," I said.

He let out a sigh. "Good—I'd hoped as much. . . . All I had to go on was an old snapshot."

"A picture of Jordan? Where'd you get it?" I murmured, still staring at my transformed face in the mirror.

"You gave it to me, years ago. Not long after we met. Don't you remember how we did that photo exchange?"

I shook my head.

"I gave you one of my father, and you gave me one of Jordan. Background information on the AWOL dads—that's what we called them. My father had disappeared completely from my life by then, but yours wasn't dead yet. You were still going to the theater with him occasionally."

"That's all he and I ever did together, you know."

"Didn't he teach you about fragrances?"

"A little. But perfume was his secret life . . . and theater was our common ground."

"So much the better. For our little exercise, I mean." From his bag he pulled another towel, thin and soft, on which he slathered some cream. "Now comes part two. Time to take him off."

"What?"

"Remove him," Stuart repeated, handing me the towel. "Say good-bye."

"And?"

"And? And take your chances! What else is there to do?"

He picked up the mirror again so I could see myself. In the glass I watched as thin rivulets of tears began tracking down my pale cheeks. I shook my head; the tears didn't stop. "Stuart, for God's sake, it's been twenty fucking years."

"Apparently that's irrelevant, darling. You didn't let him go."

"Yes I did!" I felt like I no doubt sounded: like a distraught child protesting something unacceptably disturbing. Stuart smiled at me.

"When, sweet?"

"When he told me about my mother, in Frenchtown. I learned about her, and I gave him what *he* wanted. He left the way he chose to leave."

"Sounds tidy," said Stuart. "But it wasn't, was it?"

I brought the towel to my face and began working the cream, which smelled faintly of lavender, into my skin. The towel grew moist with sloughed-off makeup and my tears. "He went out peacefully," I said.

"I'm not talking about him, my girl. Those dreams you've been having lately—hardly tranquil, are they?"

He picked up a tube of makeup, squeezing some on his fingertips. "Put the towel down," he ordered. Leaning in and squinting slightly, he dabbed at my cheeks, refining the application with rapid circular motions. Taking the towel away from me, he brought the mirror in front of my face once more. Now my forehead and chin were patchy with half-removed makeup; on my cheeks were two bright red circles. I looked like a disheveled, unhappy clown.

Stuart put down the mirror and snapped his fingers abruptly in front of my eyes. "Right now! When you think of your dreams, what words and phrases spring to mind? Come on, quick! Say whatever comes, as soon as it comes."

"Clowns. Uh . . . Jordan . . . Paris," I began haltingly. Stuart's gaze pinned me. "A man in a cape. Wearing a mask. Carrying a cane."

"More."

"Sailing to France to be with my mother . . . Jordan juggling. Perfume, mists of it. Eve on a trampoline. Sam, wanting a kid. Danny . . . My mother and Eve dancing together . . . A man doing cartwheels, saying, *Sorrow, sorrow . . .*"

"Happy movement, sad feeling. What's the word for that, Cam?"

I shook my head. "Bittersweet?" My chest felt as though something were clamping it.

"Camilla." Stuart lay one palm gently over my mouth for a moment. His touch relieved my shortness of breath; my tears continued, but now I could inhale through them. "Answer me: who's always in your dreams?"

"Meyerhold."

"Right. In every single dream. Why?"

I shook my head.

"What happened to him, Cam? How'd it end for him? You should know—you've been reading the biographies I lent you, right? Well, guess what. I've been reading them, too."

"You have?"

"I decided I ought to. So I could understand better why you might've summoned *him,* of all people. It made sense you'd dream about somebody in theater, but there were so many other people to choose from! Why Meyerhold? I kept asking myself. Then I realized it must have something to do with his death. With how and why he died."

"I'm not following you."

"Aren't you?"

I picked up the towel and began wiping my eyes with it, gingerly, so as not to rub makeup into them.

"Meyerhold died in prison; he was shot there," Stuart continued. "*You* told me that, so you knew about it. You know a lot more, too: about the secret arrest in St. Petersburg, the beatings and interrogations, the summary trial . . . You've read about all that, yes?"

"Uh-huh." I exhaled, still wiping my face.

"So you also know Meyerhold's final testimony in prison contradicted his artistic principles. He declared himself a staunch Communist. How do you square that, Cam?"

"He still thought of himself as a patriot," I answered. "He couldn't give up his belief in the Revolution, even though he'd seen what it did."

"Right. He'd seen dozens of artists, writers, and performers suffer imprisonment or worse. And when his government arrested *him,* he couldn't bear to admit to himself that he'd been loyal to the wrong cause. So he swore allegiance to his Soviet masters." Stuart paused. "Though of course he *hadn't* been loyal. In his work, his creative life, he was always *disloyal.* His art was faithful only to itself—which put him in endless conflict not just with the state, but with himself. Remember that final speech, when he referred to himself in the third person? 'He was never a traitor to his country . . . He believes that the court will understand him . . .' But of course the artist in him knew it wouldn't!"

Stuart put a hand on my shoulder and shook it lightly. "That's the thing: he believed *and* he knew better. And throughout his career, he made great theater out of those opposed realities. *That* was his gift."

He leaned forward, his face close to mine. I could feel concern and love radiating from him, a palpable heat; with it came a voiced challenge. "His dilemma is what captivated you most, Cam. Aren't I right?" Again he snapped his fingers, lightly. "Think about it. What happens when you're loyal and disloyal at the same time? And not to a country but to a person?"

He placed his palms on his knees. "What happens is this: you get really good at suppression. Which works fine until something comes along to rock the boat. Like the unexpected departure of someone for whom you have deeply mixed feelings . . . How could Eve's death not make you think about your own mother? And about Jordan—how distant you always were from him? How could you not think about that as you watched Danny come unstuck?"

Stuart's fingers wafted before his face as he mimed the unveiling of a surprise. "So what's a woman to do under such circumstances? Well, if she's *you,* you dream like crazy. You take on Meyerhold as your director, and you break out in dreams as though they were hives."

HE STOPPED talking. We sat in silence in the darkened space, watching the candles burn down. When they began guttering, Stuart blew them out. Then he turned on the lights and led me to the bathroom sink, where he made me rinse my face and give it a final rubdown.

"Theatrical makeup's very drying." He handed me a small jar. "Slather this on, it's great stuff."

The emollient he gave me was creamy and scented with rosewater. "Where'd you get this?" I asked.

"Nicked it from Carl. Must remember to put it back where I found it."

He replaced the jar in his bag, along with the cloth, the makeup, and the candlesticks. In my back office, I poured us each a glass of water and a vodka; we downed the water and chinked our shot glasses.

"Good work, Cam," he toasted. "But you're not done yet, as I don't need to tell you." He drank his vodka, put down his glass, and took me in his arms. "Something's gotta give, sweetheart. I don't know what it is, but it's bound to make its way out sooner or later."

Releasing me, he cast a glance at my desk. On it lay the Polaroid snapshot Danny had left behind. "Who's this?" he asked, picking it up.

"Eve," I said, "with Billy Deveare. Or so we assume."

"Why's he wearing that mask?"

"Look at the date on the back."

He turned the picture over. "Um," he grunted. "Halloween." Bringing the image under my desk lamp, he peered at it. "Can't get much of a sense of what the guy looked like."

"Nope," I responded. "Which Eve intended, no doubt."

Stuart stared at the photo for several moments. "No doubt," he echoed. He rattled the photo lightly at me before replacing it on my desk. "Don't forget to give this back to Danny when you see her— which I trust will happen any day now." He picked up his bag. "And be glad you've been dreaming as much as you have! Think of it as self-medication. No, that's too clinical . . . Think of your dreams as responses to a question, an important question. Try to be open to it, whatever it is."

"I haven't the foggiest," I said.

"Ah, but you do, you see. That's the thing—you *do*." He tapped the left side of my chest. "The only really interesting theater's here, you know. Where there's no fourth wall, nothing separating audience and actor. Truth be told, you're already there, Cammie. You just haven't flipped on the lights yet."

IT'S SATISFYING to see the separate strands of a story braid together. Camilla's and my narratives are catching up with each other at last. It'll be my job to bring down the curtain.

There are, of course, a great many possible ways to end a play, but only one *right* way. I was awed by Seva's talents in this regard. One drama he produced in 1922, *Tarelkin's Death,* stands out in my memory. How well he concluded it—and what a production it was! That play had to be the noisiest bit of theater ever performed for a Russian audience. It was a satire on Czarist police methods, done in a burlesque mode. Onstage, a little stool kept firing off a cartridge that simulated explosions. A table and a chair collapsed with loud bangs. At the play's intervals, Seryozha Eisenstein and another assistant fired pistols in the air and roared, "Entrrrr-acte!," which alarmed the older theatergoers, though the younger ones laughed hysterically.

And right at the end, when the prisoner Tarelkin freed himself by swinging noisily across the stage on a trapeze, one critic groused that such a sight was far more common in circuses than in theaters. Yet the spectators were delighted. The finale made its own strange sense—it combined high seriousness with funny, freewheeling action, in the spirit of who-knows-what's-coming-next . . . I should be fortunate to find so oddly fitting an end to *this* tale!

WHERE WERE we? Yes: Jordan's letter.

Of course I was relieved when Camilla read it. Dream by dream, she'd found her way to that missive, and to Seva's sketches. She'd require no more prodding from me!

In any event Stuart did my remaining work for me. In a genuine friendship, there are always moments in which one person refuses to let the other off the hook. So it was with Stuart, who put his skill as a makeup artist to excellent use. When he was finished with her, Camilla really did resemble her father! (An intuitive performer, Stuart saw just how Seva's predicament related to Camilla's. What's acting, anyway, but analogizing—casting one's own life into relief against another's, and another's against one's own?)

The next and last dream is my collaborator's. I had no hand in it. She'd incorporated Seva's precepts; they belonged to her now. As for the drama's final act . . . it's longish, but things do tie up. After a bit of unraveling.

NINE

SAM, DANNY, and I are standing at the front door of the family apart-ment. I'm holding the key.

Go on, open it, Sam urges me. I turn the key and the door swings open noiselessly. I am staring into a vast, vacant space. There are no floors, no walls, only a void, like a colorless sky stretching everywhere.

Is this where you and Eve lived? asks Danny.

Yes, I answer.

There aren't any mothers here!

We need to find the fathers, I say. Panic rises into my mouth, I can taste it. But Sam takes one of my hands and Danny takes the other, and they lift and swing me between them. I'm calmed by the move-ment, an easy gliding back and forth. We proceed east along Ninth Street to University Place and on to Fourth Avenue. In front of Back-stage Books, Stuart is waiting for us—eagerly, for when he sees us, he grins and waves.

Danny and Sam let go of my hands. The three of us watch as Stuart begins pulling a handkerchief from the breast pocket of his jacket. The fabric keeps coming, yards and yards of it. Stuart coils it into a kind of rope, which he then forms into a circle, like a hula hoop made of cloth. He pops it over our heads—Sam's, Danny's, and mine—so we're contained within it.

We begin walking round and round the circle's circumference. And now we're trotting, then running—faster, faster, a human top spinning on the sidewalk. Stuart waves a commanding forefinger at Sam, who drops out. Then he and Stuart clap and cheer, an enthusiastic audience. Danny and I are moving even faster now, spinning, our bodies nearly a blur, our two forms inseparable.

Can we keep going? yells Danny. Keep going! I echo, and in a moment we begin levitating. A kind of centrifugal force lifts us upward, our linked energies straining, cohering, holding us together and pulling us apart . . . So this is what love does, I am thinking, and then I awake.

❧

SHORTLY BEFORE Labor Day, Danny called me at work. We hadn't spoken since Ithaca, in late May.

After Stuart's prodding, I'd mailed Danny a short note saying I was holding her in my thoughts and hoped to see her soon. She hadn't responded. This wasn't a surprise. She'd meant it, I knew, when she said she didn't want to be in touch with me. From Sam's brief comments throughout the summer, I'd gathered she was in good health and showing up at work every day.

He and I weren't in frequent communication either. Since my inquiry about his relations with Danny, he'd been acting not so much angry as held in check. Perhaps, I thought, he was waiting for me to let him know I'd spoken with Danny and dispatched the matter. We were performing a strained minuet, our interactions in good form but at arm's length.

In late August, Danny finally phoned. Time we got together, isn't it, she said. To which I said yes, it definitely was.

We settled on the upcoming Saturday, and I told her I'd come out to Brooklyn. We could go to Prospect Park, she suggested, adding that since Eve's death, she'd been walking there so often even the ducks knew her.

SUMMER WAS winding down.

Stuart and Carl were back from a biking trip in Belgium, where they'd drunk lots of excellent beer. Sam and his family had returned from their annual summer vacation in New Hampshire, where Lila's great-aunt had a lakeside cottage. I'd decided against visiting for a weekend, as I'd done in past years, in the company of several other mutual acquaintances. I wasn't up for talking about Danny, whose name would naturally arise in conversation with Lila, if not with Sam. In any event, I heard everyone's tales upon their return and received souvenirs—a wonderfully odorous blue cheese that Stuart had somehow sneaked past customs, and a dog-eared guidebook to

New England, inside of which lay several lovely wildflowers that Abby and Zeke had pressed for me.

Over a glass of wine at their place, Carl told me I looked in need of a vacation. Why hadn't I taken one? Before I could open my mouth, Stuart answered for me.

Unfinished business, he said. And she'd best finish soon or we shall ride her case. Hard.

You heard the man, Carl said to me.

ACTUAL BUSINESS was sluggish, typical for summer in the city. Most of my clients and acquaintances were away, and as there wasn't much theater happening anywhere, I cleaned my shop and office thoroughly, took long walks, and spent my spare time reading.

Much of July went into books on *commedia dell'arte*. My long-standing fascination with masks deepened. So, too, did my awareness of what modern theater owed its early traveling salesmen— Europe's itinerant troubadours, mystery-players, and fairground people. I decided to turn one of my shop's interior walls into a showcase for masks, of which I owned quite a few. Attempting this, I missed Danny's design savvy; my wall display looked dismally amateurish.

I was trying, I knew, to distract myself, but unease and unhappiness kept reasserting themselves. I missed Danny intensely; there'd never before been a stretch like this, of real alienation from her. It'll all sort itself out, I kept telling myself. Eventually. And Danny and I will be closer for having gone through this.

Yet it wasn't clear what the next step should be. We'd talk at some point—the silence between us wouldn't last forever. We'd speak again of Eve, of Jordan. And of ourselves. But were words the solution? What more could be said that would heal our rift, our separate and shared sorrows?

NICK WAS around all summer, working. His skin grew especially dark on the back of his neck and arms, but his entire torso, frequently bared to the sun, gradually turned a beautiful bronze.

He and I saw each other fairly regularly. Since our supposed phone sex fiasco, we hadn't had a formal clear-the-air talk. Although his body remained magnetic for me, something had gone out of our erotic connection, a measure of calm. I sensed he felt this as well, though of course we didn't refer to it. Overuse of words wasn't a crime of which the Paramour and I had ever been guilty.

The day before my planned get-together with Danny, Nick showed up at my shop with a discovery: a small tortoiseshell comb embossed with the Russian words ТЕАТР ИМ. МЕЙЕРХОЛД. It was housed in a sheath of cardboard on which were printed two overlapping masked faces, one tragic, one comic—the traditional symbols of theater.

"I found this in a closet," he explained. "On weekends I've been helping a contractor buddy of mine renovate a building in Brighton Beach. Almost all the tenants there are from Russia—they call that part of Brooklyn Little Moscow. . . . Anyway, last weekend I'm painting the halls, and I find a box of junk in a coat closet—old books and magazines, mostly. All in Russian. And then I see this little item, and I'm wondering, maybe Cam would want it."

Examining the comb closely, I saw it was in excellent condition. I'd read of such relics but had never come across one. "You bet I do," I said.

"Can you sell it?"

Nick was always keen on knowing what various objects would fetch. "Sure," I answered. "But I think I'll hang on to this."

"What is it, exactly?"

In the early twentieth century, I explained, Russian theaters used to offer their audiences little souvenirs. I pointed at the Cyrillic letters. "See this? It's the name Meyerhold, and this means 'theater of.' Meyerhold was a major stage director in Russia. I can't believe you found this, Nick. Amazing!"

"What, the comb or me?"

I kissed him lightly, and he pulled me into a hug. "Can I drop by later, after you close up?" he murmured. "I can stay awhile."

Sensing my ambivalence, Nick stepped back and took one of my hands in both of his. In their grip my captured hand lay unresisting, while the rest of me held back.

"You know what you want from me, Cam?" he asked gently.

"I used to think so." I lacked energy for dissembling. "Lately I'm not at all sure."

One of his rough thumbs worked my palm, circling and then pressing on its center; the other thumb ran up and down the sides of my wrist. "I'd like to keep doing this—what we do," he said. "But not if I'm making you frustrated. What would be the point?"

"*I'm* making me frustrated," I replied.

"Any idea why?"

"Oh, Nick, Nick . . ." Unable to stop myself, I started pulling my hand away, but he held on.

"Does that mean you have no idea, or you have an idea but you don't want to share it with me?"

"It means I'll take a pass."

He let go of my hand. "I think I'm getting the message. You want out," he said.

A sense of futility overtook me, and with it came an urge to say something harsh, to punish us both. "I *am* out, Nick. If I wanted *in,* I'd be doing things pretty differently, wouldn't I?"

His shrug was at once self-protective and careless. "I don't go for that sort of guesswork. People just do what they do." He put his painter's cap back on his head. It made him look younger and adorable, and I knew I was going to miss him—absurdly, strongly—if I followed through on my impulse to banish him.

"The ball's in your court. I won't call," he said. "You know how to find me."

AS SOON as he was out the door, I went back to my office. Loneliness coiled around me, snakelike, restrictive. Sitting down, I surrendered to it as helplessly as I'd done on those nights during childhood when I'd awakened to find myself unable to speak.

After a few minutes, I pulled aside the curtain covering my dartboard. Then I rummaged in my desk drawer for a half-dozen small snapshots. I affixed these to the board, slipping their edges snugly beneath the wire rims. They were all pictures of me—taken, at various points and places, by Stuart. Collecting my darts, I began tossing at my targets hard enough to hear each projectile whistle as it traveled. I managed to hit all six photos on my first tosses, though not always squarely; a few I only nicked. Thereafter I punctured every image but one at its center, and when I retrieved my darts a third time and tossed them rapidly, I didn't miss a single target.

The darts' *thwap* was as gratifying as it had always been, yet the relief I'd sought didn't come. I looked again in my drawer, this time retrieving pictures of Sam and Danny. Instead of putting them on the dartboard, I lay them on my desk. Then, removing a photo of myself from the dartboard, I set it between the other two and stepped back to gaze at the trio.

Sam, me, Danny. Husband, self, and kid. In a manner of speaking.

I fished around in the drawer and added a photo of Stuart to the lineup. His presence felt instantly natural: husband, self, kid, friend. Then I took Stuart away and replaced him with one of my photos of Eve, placing her to the right.

Husband, self, kid, cousin.

Immediately this jarred. I took away the photo of Sam and replaced it with one of my father. Jordan, me, Danny, Eve. One too many? I took myself away.

Jordan, Danny, Eve.

After staring at the three of them for a little while, I put myself back, removing Eve. Then I took Jordan away.

Now only Danny and I were left.

Next to us, I lay the photo of Eve and her Halloween partner.

What had I said to Danny in my latest dream? About having to find the fathers?

I put away all the photos and covered the dartboard. Then I called Stuart at home, knowing he wouldn't be there, and left a message on his machine. I'm going to Brooklyn tomorrow afternoon, I said. To talk with Danny about her mother's masked man.

I MET her in front of the Brooklyn Public Library. We gave each other quick hugs and appraising looks.

She looked good, wearing a white ribbed T-shirt, a pair of jean shorts, and low-heeled sandals that showed off her long legs. In addition to her usual collection of silver rings, she wore pearl earrings.

I recognized the earrings. They'd been a gift to Eve from Jordan, on the occasion of her graduation from high school. Sarah, Dan, Jordan, and I had staged a combined graduation-birthday celebration for Eve, shortly before her departure for college—the last such gathering in the apartment on Ninth Street, a momentary display of unity before the dispersal. Dan had presented her with several books, and Sarah had given her some long underwear for the cold winters upstate (a gift at which Eve had later scoffed). I'd made a cake. My father's present, though, had put all the rest to shame. Large, beautifully lustrous, and set in platinum, the pearls had undoubtedly cost him a good deal of money. Up to then, Eve's taste in jewelry had tended toward silver-and-turquoise stuff, but she'd liked the pearls so much that she'd taken to wearing them constantly.

Danny's hair was pulled into a high ponytail that exposed the white orbs on her ears. As I complimented her on them, I palmed the outside pocket of my bag, into which I'd tucked the letter from Jordan. I'd decided to hand it over to her that afternoon. There was no need for me to hold on to it; I'd practically memorized it.

WE HEADED into Prospect Park, directly behind the library. The temperature dropped as we passed under one of the stone overpasses at the end of the park's Long Meadow, and although it rose again as we started along the path, the large, leafy trees shielded us from the sun's glare. Eve, I remembered, had loved this park, the gentle swoops of its terrain and the unfussy elegance of its design. It had been one of her favorite urban retreats.

We strolled along a cobblestoned walkway. Now and then we came upon a dog-walker or a couple with a baby carriage, but mostly we had the path to ourselves. Near the Picnic House, ten or fifteen elderly Russians had congregated. As they parted to let us pass, I noticed that the female voices were louder than the male ones, and the women's hands accompanied their words as a conductor's might.

"They come here a lot," said Danny, tipping her head in the direction of the Russians. "They take the subway in from Brighton Beach and do a few laps around this loop. They always walk slowly, arm in arm—sometimes three at a time. The women are like a chirpy flock of birds. There's one man who often sings Russian songs. I like it when they all stop and line up on the long benches."

"Stuart says if you read Chekhov's plays, you'll know exactly what's going on in Russia now. Or at any time," I said.

"Well, maybe . . . By the way, Stuart sent me a nice note after Mom died. I need to write him back."

"I wouldn't worry about it."

"I'd like to write him, though." She paused. "In his note he talked about Mom's energy. Her spunk, he called it. He said it's inherited, he can see it in me . . . And he said you're spunky, too, but you could use some reinforcement."

"Ah, yes, Mr. Know-It-All."

Danny smiled a little. "Sam said I should remember you're having a hard time with Mom's death, too."

"Well," I said, "neither Sam nor Stuart is completely off base. Even if they both think they know everything."

SHE LED us to a shaded slope overlooking the meadow and a small pond. On the playing fields to our right, two games of softball were under way. The players' cries wafted over us, whoops mixing with taunts when a ball was hit or fielded.

Pulling from her backpack an old cotton tablecloth, Danny spread it on the ground. I recognized its yellow-and-blue Provençal print: Jordan had bought it in France and given it to Sarah. Eve must have inherited it. Next Danny produced fruit, cheese and crackers, hard-boiled eggs, and cold seltzer. We settled in, eating and drinking slowly; for a while, neither of us spoke. It felt deeply good to be in the park with her, with nowhere to go and nothing to do but grope our way forward.

"Sam and his family have been good to me," Danny said at last. Her gaze was directed at the ducks bobbing serenely on the pond's calm surface. "One morning he stopped by my office to give me some bath oil Lila had bought for me. And he mailed me a little drawing Abby had done. Of Mom and me. That was pretty intense, but also good."

Abby hadn't ever met Eve, who'd shown no interest in Sam's kids. "You mean Abby imagined the two of you together and drew a picture of that?"

"No, she had a photo to work from, actually. Once when I was babysitting her and Zeke at my place, I showed her some of my pictures." She handed me some grapes. "Abby's really into babies. She liked one photo of me in particular, so I made her a copy. It's one I think your father must've taken, because Mom and I are in French-town, in his garden. I found it in Mom's study."

I pulled a few grapes off their stems and washed them with seltzer—something to do so I wouldn't have to meet Danny's eyes as I asked nonchalantly, "What's the picture look like?"

"Mom's got me propped up, facing forward. I'm maybe six months old. I'm sort of smirking. Mom's beautiful. Sam said the picture makes me look like a smug little princess. Abby loved it, of course—you know, a baby, roses . . ."

She leaned sideways, her shoulder and the side of her head landing lightly against mine. "I'd be a mess without you and Sam," she said softly, laying a hand on my knee. "Thanks for coming out here to see me."

"I wanted to," I said. "I've missed you."

She pulled herself upright. In the lowering light, her face appeared wan; I could see how spent she was. "You've probably been wondering what I've been up to . . . since Ithaca," she said quietly.

I nodded.

"Mostly I've been listening to music Mom liked. Lots of Bach, everything Thelonious Monk ever recorded . . . She told me once that she loved 'Pannonica' more than any other jazz tune ever written. She owned tons of albums—everything from Gregorian chants to Diana Ross. Did you know that?"

"No," I said. "We never talked about music." Or thousands of other things. Such as ourselves.

"She never switched to CDs—she liked the old LP sound better. So I've had to listen to everything on her record player. I've been staying up late with the music." Danny passed her fingers slowly over her eyes, as if trying to swab off months of fatigue. "It's like I'm sleepwalking at work. I have no idea how I'm doing my job, Cam. Fortunately I'm good at it, plus my boss is totally clueless. I get away with a lot."

"Do you think you need to . . . see somebody?" I began.

She shrugged. "I've been to talk with a therapist a few times," she said. "It's been helpful, I guess. But not as much as Mom's music. And taking care of her African violets . . ." She shook her head. "You know, I can't imagine not being enraged with her. Or not wanting her back . . . I'd like to ask her if she ever loved my father, whoever he was. Even for a little while." She paused. "How'd she manage to get up every morning and look in the mirror and not think to herself, I may be irresistible to men, but I'm a fucking loser?"

She took a deep breath; as she exhaled, her composure buckled, and she began crying in quiet, gulping sobs. I pulled her into an awkward embrace, our bodies torqued and knees bumping. Holding her, I remembered what it had felt like to take her infant body in my hands—how her shoulders used to shudder when she got upset, and how she'd tap the undersides of her tiny wrists together whenever she was excited.

One of her tear-damp hands lay in mine. I bounced it lightly between my palms for a few moments, until she'd stopped crying. Then I reached for my bag. "I need to give you something," I said. "And tell you a few things."

SHE READ Jordan's letter slowly, frowning occasionally. Finishing it, she handed me the pages.

"It's yours," I said, giving the letter back to her.

She stared at it, then at me. "Did you read it?"

"I hope you'll forgive me—I did."

"I can see why." She put the letter down and sat in silence, drumming a rhythm on her kneecaps. Then she reached again for the letter and skimmed it, apparently searching for sections to reread. I awaited additional queries, but instead she made a statement.

"Jordan figured you'd tell me how he died," she said, refolding the letter. "And so would Mom. But your stories wouldn't be the same, which is why he set down his own account. Right?"

"I think so," I said.

"But why would a terminally ill man write a letter like this about his hopes for a kid he barely knew? No, it's weirder than that. He wasn't writing to the kid, he was writing to some fantasized version of her—to the kid as an adult!"

She hesitated, trying to knit the threads. "I mean, *you're* the real audience here, aren't you?"

My stomach knotted. "We both are."

Danny flapped the folded letter against one of her palms. "Jordan wasn't around much, was he? It must've been pretty hard for him, raising you by himself."

"Jordan didn't raise me by himself," I said. "Your grandparents raised me. Even your mother, in a sense. Jordan traveled a lot, not just for work. He liked to get away by himself—he was a loner."

She pursed her lips, considering this. "I had a sense of that, from Mom. Whenever his name came up, there was something . . . And your mother—did he talk much about her?"

"Her death shattered him."

She nodded. "Couldn't have been much fun for you either. Not having a mother, I mean. And having a father who wasn't around."

SHE STARED out at the playing fields. The softball games were over now, and the spectators had headed home. A lone cyclist, his shirt flapping gently around his body, sailed down the path dividing the ballfields from the meadow; I could hear the clink of his gears as he downshifted to make a sharp right at the base of the path. Rising on his stirrups after the turn, he leaned forward, picking up speed. As he disappeared from view, Danny began speaking again.

"I don't know," she said. "I just don't get why Jordan wrote to me. And what was that about your sister? . . . Here it is: 'Tell Cam to be kind to her sister, and you be kind to Cam!' Did he usually refer to Mom as your sister?"

She'd noticed, then—though she'd interpreted it differently, as I'd figured she would. "He usually just called her Eve," I said. Here was my opening. "Danny," I began, but before I could say more, she'd sandwiched the letter between her palms and was wagging its pages back and forth before her, as if to shake the truth out of them.

"Hang on," she said. Riffling through the sheets, she extracted Meyerhold's sketches and spread them in a semicircle around us. "Did you look at these?" she asked.

"Yes, but not closely," I said.

"They're all drawings of a clown wearing a big ruff. The guy who did these, the Russian—Meyerhold?—he designed a perfume bottle in the shape of a clown's body. Sort of rotund. With a big-footed base." She pointed. "The clown's ruff, here, would be the neck of the bottle. You'd grab it and twist off the top—the clown's head, see?—which would also have a round shape. Quite a strange concept! Not old-fashioned—these sketches are all done with nice sharp lines. They're really modern. And sophisticated, not at all childish. But nothing you'd normally associate with a perfume bottle either. Especially this one of the somersaulting clown—I mean, you can't possibly manufacture a bottle that looks like this! Which makes Meyerhold's sketches interesting from a design standpoint."

She scrutinized the drawings. The most elaborate showed two clowns—one standing, the other with his knees planted on the first clown's chest. I recognized that posture. It was the one Jordan and

I had assumed in a dream, the episode in which the director had scolded us for not playing our parts seriously.

Danny pointed at this drawing. "Do you know what this means?" She indicated a word penciled in Cyrillic beneath the sketch.

"I checked that out," I answered. "*Balaganchik* means, roughly, fairground booth. It's the Russian title of Blok's play, the one Meyerhold mentioned in his letter to Jordan. In the play Pierrot the clown falls in love with a masked woman named Columbine, who's not real. Pierrot keeps looking for her, and she keeps eluding him, and he ends up alone. That's the gist of it, anyway. Meyerhold acted the part of Pierrot several times—it must've been a favorite role of his."

Danny gathered up the sketches and the letter. "Jordan never learned much about this director, did he?" she asked as she inserted the pages into their envelope.

"No, but something about Meyerhold's drawings must have gotten to him. And he must have felt they'd speak to you as well."

"Weirdly enough, they do. They're not what I'm usually pulled to—but something about them . . . A mysteriousness. Not quite playful, not quite aggressive. Clowns are like that, I guess. Cheerful, but with an edge of something sharp, or sad . . ." She looked at me. "But do *you* want the drawings, Cam? As a memento?"

"No," I said. "I like knowing they're with the person Jordan wanted to have them."

"I wish Mom had seen them," she said.

HER STATEMENT gave me what I needed, a go-ahead. "I suspect he showed them to her," I said.

Setting the envelope down on the cloth next to her, Danny turned and looked inquiringly at me. From my bag I pulled the snapshot she'd left at The Fourth Wall, laying it on the ground next to the envelope. "Columbine," I said, pointing at Eve. "And Pierrot."

She frowned at it, then at me. "Ye-e-es?" she drawled, warily.

"Only here, Pierrot's the one wearing the mask," I said. "Jordan needed it to be that way. A secret."

"Jordan . . ." Her eyes widened slightly with a realization under way, expanding with each passing second. "You're saying this is . . . but that's impossible, Cam."

"Impossible? No, just unimaginable. Or at least it was for me, until our trip to Ithaca. Physically, of course, it's entirely possible. Judy Deveare was no doubt right: Eve was inseminated, but Billy wasn't your father except on paper."

Danny began shaking her head. "No, no, no."

"Why not?" I'd begun, I'd keep going. "My guess is, Eve was in love with Jordan from the time she was fifteen or sixteen. He was the central person in her life. And he was everything her father wasn't: a successful professional, a world traveler, an artist, attentive to her—"

"Oh, come on, Cam, don't shove a bunch of amateur psychology at me and expect me to swallow it!"

Her resistance was as unsurprising as it was powerful. "Try seeing this from your mother's perspective," I said. "Jordan was different from all the other adults Eve knew. Not just Dan and Sarah, but everyone. She trusted him, but it went further than that: she revered him. She imagined herself his apprentice. He's the one who urged her to study horticulture and landscaping, remember? He understood who she was, what made her happy—flowers, plants, trees, land . . . She must've fantasized they'd end up working together. She'd design a garden for him! She'd have his child . . ."

"This is crazy! Why would *he* . . ." Danny twisted one of her rings off her finger and stared at it, as if it and not my words were the source of her incredulity. Without looking at me, she added, "You're asking me to believe my mother's *uncle* seduced her—"

"No, not seduced. It's more complicated than that." Reaching again for my bag, I took out a small envelope and laid it next to the Halloween photo. "Take a look at this."

Danny opened the envelope and pulled out a photocopy of a black-and-white photograph.

"That's from my family photo collection—such as it is," I said. "Now, think back on Eve and yourself in Jordan's garden, when you were little. I bet Eve looked a lot like that woman, didn't she?"

"Who *is* this?" Danny regarded the image closely. "And why are there all these little holes in the picture?"

It was covered with tiny pockmarks from my darts. "It's a copy of an old photograph, the only one I've got of my mother," I said. "That's Camilla. Eve's aunt."

"Wow. I've never seen a picture of her before," Danny said. "Neither you or Mom ever showed me one. I've always wondered what she looked like."

"Your mother and Camilla looked a good deal alike. Especially to Jordan, no doubt. And especially at this age"—I tapped the photo— "roughly the same as Eve was at Cornell." I paused. "When you told me Jordan had visited Eve there, everything fell into place. They had an encounter then, Danny, I'm sure of it. And it changed everything."

SHE HANDED me the photo. "Changed . . . ?" she asked. Though she still wasn't able to look at me, in her tone I could hear a new, hesitant receptiveness.

"My guess," I went on, "is that for Jordan, the notion of having an actual relationship with his own niece must've been more than he could handle. Even if she was his niece only by marriage. He couldn't go ahead with it. He knew it would turn excruciating in the end. And not just for him—for Eve, too. Because of who she was. And who *I* was."

"How do you mean?"

"It goes back to Camilla. My father felt guilty for having impregnated my mother. For causing her death, in effect."

"That's absurd."

"I know. But I'm sure it's how he felt. And my presence—just the sheer *fact* of me—reminded him too much of my mother. That's why he always kept a distance between us. Yet he didn't want to make things worse for me by choosing Eve over me—which was how he believed I would've experienced it. And he wasn't wrong!"

Danny said nothing; my words seemed to have stunned her into vacancy.

"Then there was Eve," I went on. "Forty years younger! I'm sure Jordan was terrified he'd never be able to make things right for her, after their encounter. That he would destroy her, just as he had my mother."

At that Danny roused herself. She held up one hand, palm out, in a blocking gesture. "Wait," she said. "You've got it completely wrong! Stop!"

"Hang on." There was more evidence; although I didn't have it in hand, I could invoke it. "Remember that picture Judy showed us? The one of Billy?"

She nodded.

"Billy was short and skinny. Not like him, right?" I pointed at Eve's masked partner. "After hearing Judy's story, I looked again at this picture, and I knew Eve had written the truth on the back of it. *This* man wasn't Billy, but Jordan."

"No! It's someone else!"

"It's Jordan," I repeated. "I know it is, Danny."

"You *know?*" She gave a quick, hard laugh; then, rolling onto her back, she pulled up her knees so her feet rested flat on the ground. "Okay," she said, staring skyward. "You think we're sisters? Go ahead and tell me what you know, then. And don't leave out one fucking bit of evidence."

She turned to stare at me, and I could see I'd lose her if I let her down now. "Tell me everything. And then I'll tell you what *I* know," she said.

WHAT I knew, I hadn't even realized I knew until I fooled with the photos, rearranging them on my desk. Sam, Danny, Jordan, Eve, and me. Something had made me play with those pictures, some intuition, a sense of urgency. And I wouldn't have concentrated on them if Stuart hadn't first transformed me into my father.

I described to Danny how Stuart had worked his particular magic on me. After becoming, for a few powerful moments, Jordan himself, I'd been able (not immediately but thereafter, over a period of days) to assemble the pieces of my father's life in a new way. For the first time, I'd allowed myself to look at what lay behind his reticence. Having been made to resemble him outwardly, I somehow had access to his inner life.

After my mother's death, I told Danny, Jordan had come to believe he'd nothing left to offer or receive, from me or anyone else. But Eve had broken through his barricades. Her lush physicality, her seeming self-sufficiency: how could he not have responded to these, as if to an extraordinary scent? And how could Eve, virtually fatherless, not have reacted in turn to his responses?

Encountering each other in Ithaca, they'd found it impossible to resist enacting a desire each was no longer able or willing to suppress. After that visit, Eve had become a permanent captive to her craving for my father. Jordan, though, knew what he needed to do: for the sake of the daughter who'd already cost him one passion, he'd have to forgo another. And for Eve's sake . . . There could be no shared life, no garden; he would not allow himself to be compelled by such fantasies. He would love Eve, but not as she longed for. Capture her, but never be taken himself.

DANNY HEARD me out as she stared at the canopy of leaves overhead. When I'd finished, she tilted her head sideways and gazed at me.

"You're asking me to believe Mom was in love with your father. Well, maybe so, in a college-girl way." She pulled herself upright and sat cross-legged. "But for her entire life? Have you forgotten who we're talking about—who Mom *was?* She always surrounded herself with men her own age or younger. She could have any man she wanted, and she knew it! Forget the fact that Jordan was her uncle, part of her family. Why would Mom *want* a man more than twice her age?"

"Because he was the only man who ever mattered. All the others were simply distractions! She had to keep herself occupied with them—not because she was bored but because she was desperate.

She wanted Jordan. And she didn't know what to do with the fact that he wouldn't have her. Even though he loved her—she *knew* he loved her . . . The other men were like a drug she took, to make her situation bearable."

"And you're saying she finally convinced him to be the father of her child. How'd she do that, Cam? How can you believe something so crazy?"

I nodded. "Let me tell you what I think happened. The whole time she was upstate, Eve clung to the belief that Jordan would come round. Eventually he'd accept that the two of them *had* to be together. That the *really* absurd thing was the fact that they weren't. And since they'd remained in touch—"

"How do you know that?"

"After his death, while I was cleaning everything out of his house, I happened to glance at a few of his phone bills. He'd saved them all; he was very retentive that way. I got curious when I saw Eve's number on several bills, so I looked at the rest. He'd made regular calls to her in Ithaca, Danny. Over a long period of time."

She frowned, still disbelieving. "But did he and Mom actually see each other, or did they just talk on the phone?"

"They saw each other, though not frequently. Jordan sometimes drove into the city from Frenchtown, to go to the theater. She'd come down from Ithaca, and they'd meet in Manhattan."

"Did *you* see her when she visited here?"

"Not often. Sometimes we'd have coffee, and she'd mention having seen a play with Jordan. Which didn't surprise me—when he came into town, he always went to more than one show. He'd take me to one performance, Eve to another. She always stayed with friends, never with me. She didn't stay in the Ninth Street apartment either. She didn't want to see Dan and Sarah."

"So you're saying the person she really came to New York to see was Jordan?"

"She was in love with him, Danny! She couldn't *not* see him. And for whatever reasons of his own, he couldn't not see her either. They were at an impasse—unable to be together as lovers, or to accept separation as necessary. And I guess on some level, they wanted it that way. At least Jordan must have."

Danny rubbed her eyelids as though my words were inflaming them. "What do you think broke the impasse?"

"Jordan was in his early seventies when Eve decided she had to have a baby. I imagine she'd held out for that all along—thinking it'd be the thing that would finally make Jordan relent. But he'd always refused to become her lover, and he was still refusing. So she came up with another plan."

"Insemination? You're saying she convinced Jordan to help her conceive artificially, since he wouldn't be her lover? But why would he do that?"

"He loved her," I said, the words at once balm and salt, relief and reopening of the old wound. *Eve more than me.*

"But what's the difference, Cam? I mean, what does it matter whether a kid's conceived one way or the other? The father's still the father!"

I nodded. "You're right. But Eve must've wanted to observe a distinction—for Jordan, not for herself. He'd made it clear, after that one encounter in Ithaca, that he wouldn't ever sleep with her again. And she wasn't asking him to reconsider—not at this stage. She must've promised him that if she managed to conceive artificially, she'd ask nothing further of him. She'd raise their child by herself. Jordan wouldn't be around forever, after all. Yet maybe there'd be a few years during which he could see her happy. She would've gotten part of what she'd longed for . . . And Jordan wouldn't have to worry about *me*. I'd know nothing about how Eve actually became pregnant. Billy Deveare would take care of that."

I STOPPED talking. For a while, silence reigned around us; then two ducks lifted off, squawking, from the far edge of the pond below, alighting in the water with a noisy commotion of wings. Once they'd quieted, Danny picked up the Halloween photo.

"You're right. Billy's not my father. We both knew that after seeing Judy," she said softly as she looked at the picture. "But neither is Jordan. You've got that wrong, regardless of what might've gone on between him and Mom."

"Well, who do you think *is*, then?"

I expected a vexed "I don't know!" Instead, she spoke a name, and when I heard it, my confusion immediately yielded to comprehension. Naturally she'd invoke Sam—how could she not? He *had* been her father, in all but fact.

Seeing me nod, she began shaking her head. "No, listen to me, Cam! *That*"—she pointed vehemently at the masked man next to Eve—"is Sam."

She was speaking the truth as she felt it: I could see this, feel it. "I know how crazy it sounds," she added slowly. "But it's true. And Sam knows it."

Her last four words winded me. Several moments passed before I could take in enough air to speak. "Danny, for God's sake," I began, as a moist flush broke out across my face.

Danny reached for one of my hands, massaging its clammy palm. "The thing is," she said, "after our weekend, you sifted the evidence and saw Jordan. And I remembered this picture and saw Sam."

I COULDN'T make my way to further speech, couldn't form any words. Like a narcotic, shock stilled me. Releasing my hand, Danny continued talking.

"Remember when Judy showed us that picture of Billy and said I didn't resemble her brother in the least? She was right. Nothing in his face or body reminded me at all of myself. Some part of me just knew he wasn't my father. But that only made things worse—it meant I'd *never* find out who my father really was.

"One day I left work early, went home, and stared at myself in my bathroom mirror for a long time. I made myself think of Mom's body and mine, how they were alike and not alike. Since her death I'd been having trouble recalling what she looked like, but on this day I could remember her perfectly. Like she was standing there, staring with me into the mirror . . . I could see I had her shoulders and hips, her hands. Not her feet, though—mine are several sizes bigger. But I'm her height, even though I'm thinner. Then I compared our coloring. I'm less olive-toned than she was. She had dark hair, and mine's more of a tawny brown, wouldn't you say?"

She looked at me, expecting a response. Somehow I nodded.

"And my eyes aren't dark blue, they're brown, but a shade that's unusual, distinctive. The color of nutmeg, Mom once described it—like the color of Sam's eyes. That's what I found myself thinking as I stared at myself."

Her smile registered less amusement than perplexity. "It's a funny sensation, looking hard at your own eyes in a mirror. Ever tried it for more than a few seconds? It's even weirder when you realize your own eyes remind you of someone else's. Their color and shape, their lashes and brows—everything's exactly the same . . .

"At this point I wasn't saying to myself, 'Oh, now I get it, Sam's my father!' But I did think it was astonishing how much alike our eyes were. And strange, too, that no one else seemed to have noticed the similarity. Then I started thinking about that snapshot I'd left at The Fourth Wall. The masked man in the picture was obviously taller than Billy. And the clothing was wrong, as you noticed. There was another detail, too, which you've overlooked. The background. See?"

Holding the snapshot before me, she indicated a brick wall in front of which Eve and the masked man were standing. Near them, to Eve's left, was a delicate Japanese maple tree. To the man's right, bordering the wall, were two magnolia bushes. The wall needed repointing; along its top, several bricks were missing, which lent the whole structure an air of charming dishevelment.

"I had a feeling this picture wasn't taken in Ithaca," Danny said. "And that feeling got stronger and stronger . . . I was right—the picture was taken here in New York. In the Village."

I GAZED at the photograph.

When Sam and I met in December of 1981, I'd been renting a small, cozy walkup on Cornelia Street. Sam had been on Barrow

Street, also in the West Village. He'd rented the top floor of a di-
lapidated townhouse for the better part of a decade.

When we decided to move in together, we took the money Jordan had left me and bought our own apartment (now mine) on the
cheap. Sam's savings went toward refurbishments of The Fourth
Wall, which we'd just opened. In return for those improvements,
we'd received a guaranteed long-term lease from the owner of that
building.

What had the Barrow Street townhouse looked like?

I'd been there with Sam only a handful of times; our courtship
had taken place mostly in my apartment. Had there been a garden
in back, with a wall? Yes: I remembered now. We'd sat there once,
with Henry, Sam's housemate. Henry had teased me because I'd
never tasted a gin martini; he made me a strong one.

That was in the spring, not long after Sam and I met—which
had happened just before Christmas. At The Mad Gardener.

I'd been in Chelsea that day, and decided to stop in and say hello
to Eve. Though I hadn't seen her in several weeks, I'd seen Danny:
the previous weekend, Eve had asked me to take care of her daughter. She and some guy had dropped Danny off at my place; the guy,
I recalled, had walked Danny to my door while Eve stayed in the car.
Danny brought some finger paintings she'd done at school—she was
in second grade . . . Eve phoned afterward to thank me for babysitting, and told me I should stop by sometime and see her store. It
was looking very festive, she'd said.

So I did. The Mad Gardener was full of mistletoe and poinsettia,
and Christmas cacti hung in big red pots in the front windows. The
whole place smelled of pine. Eve, I remembered, was busy helping
holiday shoppers when I arrived. A few minutes later, Sam walked
in. He and Eve exchanged greetings, a little awkwardly. They were
acquainted, I could see, but it was also clear they didn't know each
other well, nor had they seen each other in a long while. Perhaps
seven years, they guessed aloud. Give or take.

Introducing us, Eve said that she and Sam (whose last name she
couldn't recall) had met at a play, years before. On one of her the-

ater trips—when she was still in Ithaca. I, she informed him, was her cousin. She'd pointed at me vaguely as she turned away. Sam and I chatted; he bought a wreath. And we walked out together.

"CAM," SAID Danny, her voice reeling me in. "Remember this garden? Behind that townhouse where Sam used to live?"

"Yes," I answered, "I do."

She exhaled slowly. "Okay, then. So *now* can you tell me something you haven't yet?"

I shook my head. "Eve told me the same thing she told you. She and Sam had been acquainted once. That's all."

"Did Sam ever say anything different? Or add anything new to what you'd heard from her?"

"He said the play at which he'd met Eve was *Long Day's Journey into Night*. Ever see it?"

"No. I read it in college."

My capacity for speech seemed to be returning. I was able to describe to Danny a scene recounted to me by Sam: his first sighting of my cousin. "Sam said they were sitting next to each other. He'd originally planned to go to the play with his housemate, who got sick at the last minute, so Sam had an empty seat on one side and Eve on the other. They chatted during intermission, and she told him this was the second time she'd seen the play. She'd attended the premiere in the mid-Fifties, which meant she would've been in high school. Jordan must've taken her."

"What did Sam and Mom talk about? Did Sam say?"

"Apparently Eve said something about how the Tyrone family was no more messed up than her own. And he asked her jokingly, does that mean your mother's on morphine, like Mary Tyrone? She said her mother was dead. Then he asked about her father, and Eve said he wasn't dead but he might as well be. Sam remembered that statement . . . But Danny, what's any of this got to do with—"

"I'm trying to make sure the stories match up," she cut in. "The three of you told me pretty much the same things. The basic version is: Sam and Mom met at the theater, and he visited her where she

was staying in the city—someplace in the Village—a few times during the week after. They didn't lay eyes on each other again until
about seven years later, when Sam walked into The Mad Gardener—the day *you* were there. Am I right?"

"Yes."

"Well," she said evenly, "here's my scenario: they hooked up a
couple of other times, too."

AS A show of comprehension, the bobbing of my head was decep-
tively automatic.

Danny gazed at me. "Should I keep talking?"

"Yes," I managed.

"Sam wasn't involved with you or anyone else when he met
Mom. She was just . . . somebody he had sex with a few times,
within a short period. She returned to Ithaca, and six weeks later
she learned she was pregnant."

Danny pointed at the Halloween photo. "This was taken by
Sam's housemate—Henry, was it?—nine months before my birth.
Mom and Sam were going to some costume party that night, at a
friend of Sam's. Henry took the snapshot, and Mom asked if she
could keep it. Henry asked Sam if he wanted it. Sam didn't care one
way or the other. He was impossible to identify—just some guy in a
hat and a mask. Mom *was* identifiable, though. And she'd never
liked pictures of herself floating around. So she took this one."

Danny hesitated. "None of this would've come up if I hadn't
pushed Sam. I was riding a hunch, and I confronted him. I told him
I'd never speak with him again if he didn't talk with me about it—
about Mom . . ."

"When did you do this?"

"Just a few days ago."

Sam hadn't known, then, when he and I talked about Danny
after our trip. We'd both been in the dark.

"I told him I was sure he and Mom had been involved sexually,"
Danny continued. "He was flipped out by that, as you can imagine,
but he began talking. And it was clear to me he still had no idea who

I actually was. I mean, he'd given no thought to the fact that he'd slept with my mother nine months before my birth. What might've happened just hadn't registered with him . . . When I told him about this photograph, he remembered the Halloween party, vaguely. And then, when I told him what Mom had written on the back, he finally got it. I didn't have to spell it out. He offered to do DNA testing, but I told him as far as I was concerned, that'd be a waste of time. All we had to do, I said, was stand in front of a mirror and look at our eyes . . . Sam agreed with me. He was in shock, but he agreed. By that point the whole thing was clear to us both."

THE WHOLE *thing:* Danny had used that same phrase, I remembered, back in May, when she was cleaning out Eve's apartment. *Then the whole thing's behind me,* she'd said. But it wasn't. It was still in front of her—of all of us.

She opened a bottle of seltzer and poured me some. My mouth was completely dry; swallowing was an effort.

"Can I keep going?" she asked, and I nodded.

"There was still the question of the insemination procedure," she resumed. "Sam urged me to take another look at the hospital's invoice. It listed the procedure and the date, November 5. Mom must've been tested for pregnancy in late October, just before leaving for the city—on the understanding that she'd be inseminated when she returned. And she tested negative and didn't bother to get tested again."

"So the insemination was pointless."

"Yes. No one knew that, though—and Mom was the only person who might've wondered. But she didn't."

"Did she use contraception?"

"Sam recalls asking her about that. And she told him not to worry about it. Though in fact she wasn't on the pill—she told him that, too. I think by then she'd simply come to believe she'd never conceive *except* by artificial insemination. She'd had so many lovers over the years, and she'd never been pregnant, even though she was often sloppy about birth control. She said as much to me once."

Danny paused for some seltzer. "Given what you've told me today, I guess it's an open question whether the sperm donor for the procedure was Jordan or Billy Deveare. We'll never know—not that it matters. Mom got pregnant, and I was born, and seven years went by.

"Then Sam walked into her shop, the day you were there. That's when it must've hit her—she must've seen his eyes, their color, and realized . . . By that time, of course, she'd already named Billy as my father. There was no point rewriting the script. Yet she had to state the truth somewhere, so she wrote it on the back of the photo."

"But Jordan could still have been—"

"Do you honestly believe that, Cam? I mean, even if he did let her use his sperm, do you really believe, *now*, that Jordan is my father?"

I could say nothing, think nothing, feel nothing.

"There's something else you need to understand," Danny added. "That day he met you, Sam hadn't gone to The Mad Gardener to see Eve. He happened to be in the neighborhood and passed by Mom's shop, not even knowing who the owner was. He wanted to buy a Christmas wreath for a colleague. Eve recognized him, greeted him. And then realized who he was. My father."

OUR VIEW of the playing fields, a green stage ringed by trees, consumed my attention. My mind was refusing entrance to anything else. Danny fell silent, caught up in the park's early-evening peacefulness; she sat with her arms wrapped around her knees, taking in the scene.

Emerging from the woods, a dog loped along one of the paths bordering the pond. A woman followed at a slow trot, leash in hand. Behind us, a man gave a cheerful whistle, then lobbed a Frisbee in the dog's direction. The toss was beautiful—a high, smooth arc— and the dog, tail and ears erect, moved into place. As the disk descended over the playing field, the dog jumped and brought the Frisbee down in a flawless retrieval. The woman clapped, and the dog ran to her proudly with his catch. The man jogged over to them, and the two humans began chatting as the dog stood by patiently, disk in mouth.

Smiling a little, Danny pointed. "Awaiting further instructions," she said.

Somewhere within me was rampaging chaos, which I was walling off. "Nice to be told what to do," I replied.

Danny gave me a queer look; evidently my response had landed wrong. "Shouldn't you be over that by now?"

"Over what?"

"Following orders," she answered coolly. "Doing what you're told."

My expression must've revealed my incomprehension. "I'm talking about Jordan and Mom," she added, straightening her legs in front of her. "You *have* been the good soldier, haven't you? Jordan orders you not to say anything about how he died, so you keep it secret until I pry it from you. Mom makes you promise not to talk about the possibility of meningitis, and you say nothing about that either."

The walls weren't holding. "How did you know . . . ?" I began.

Danny waved a dismissive hand. "Oh come on, do you think you're the only one who noticed Mom was having severe neck pain? I asked her about it, and she insisted I not tell anyone. I didn't put up a fight; there didn't seem to be any reason to. And you didn't argue with her either, did you?"

The truth was muscling its way past me, ignoring my pleas for manageability. "No, I didn't," I said.

Danny's jaw relaxed slightly. "Do you know why?"

Promise me. Had it been that—obedience to Eve's wish for silence? Or something else, a desire for her to disappear, for all the difficulties that had constellated around her to be finally banished?

"I think so," I answered. "I could've given Eve all the right reasons for not surrendering, for fighting back," I said. "But she wouldn't have listened to me making the arguments, giving the reasons. She knew them already. And the thing is, *I* wanted to be a reason, too. And I knew I wasn't. It felt meaningless for me to make the case—to encourage her to fight back—if I couldn't offer myself as a kind of collateral. A counterweight to whatever it was inside her that had just had enough."

USING A little twig, Danny began jabbing at her paper plate, breaking up the shell of a hard-boiled egg. When she'd reduced it to shards, she scooped them up and rubbed her hands together hard before scattering the bits of shell on the grass next to her.

"My mother," she said, "was a coward. A selfish coward." She dusted off her hands, and I saw that one of her palms had been lacerated. Little drops of blood dotted its skin.

"Give me that," I said, pointing. When she extended her bleeding hand, I wet a paper napkin with water and wiped the palm gently. Its small cuts were deeper and more numerous than they appeared; Danny winced softly as I cleaned them. When I'd finished, I placed her open hand on my propped-up knees so it would dry.

"*I* was more of a coward than your mother was," I said. I spread her fingers wide with my own, pinning them down. "To me, having a family was like driving too close to the edge of a cliff. It didn't matter that I had a good husband; I just wasn't prepared to take the risk . . . That's what it felt like—not an adventure but a gamble I was almost certain to lose."

Beneath my fingers, Danny's twitched lightly.

"Your mother and I grew up under near-identical circumstances," I went on. "I walked away from the apartment on Ninth Street convinced that having a kid wasn't a good idea. But Eve knew she'd have one someday. She gambled, Danny—knowing it might turn out catastrophically, she went ahead and had a child anyway. Can you really call that cowardice?"

Danny hissed in disgust. "Mom never wanted to *be* a mother— she just wanted the *idea* of it!" She massaged her palm; a few of its cuts had begun bleeding again. "And see what happened! Once I got angry enough at her, I walked off and never looked back. Her kid dumped her after she'd dumped her kid! Mom and I were made for each other. We *deserved* each other."

She splashed seltzer onto her hand, then flicked her wrist to dry it. "What happened to Mom—getting meningitis—nobody could've anticipated that, Cam. But her dying wasn't a fluke, as you know. And she knew *I'd* know it, too."

She dropped her head between her knees and began to cry. Leaning down, I cupped my hand on the nape of her neck. "Eve wasn't expecting you to lie for her, Danny," I murmured into her ear. "She expected nothing. Don't torture yourself."

"She was that alone . . ." Her words straddled a line between question and statement.

"Yes," I said, massaging her neck. "She always was."

Danny stood up. I was still sitting cross-legged on the ground, and she seemed to tower above me. I felt momentarily small, a little girl staring up at a grown one.

"In your twenties, what were you good at, Cam? By the time you'd reached my age, what had you figured out?"

The question felt like a bright light; I closed my eyes against it. At twenty-eight, Eve had been in possession of a career in landscaping and all the men she could consume. And at that same age, I'd had a worthless job in an antiques shop and only the dimmest sense of my future, in which my father would never desire or accept a role.

"I was good with props," I said. "I had an eye for objects. I could match them with people and actions—with scenes. Other kinds of connections were . . . more problematic."

"And then Sam came along?"

"First Jordan died. Then Sam came along." And you: you came along, I wanted to say, but couldn't.

SHE REACHED down and extended both hands to me.

"We need a break. Let's go—we can keep talking, but I need to *move*." She waggled her fingers before me, a sign for me to take her hands so she could pull me up.

I pointed at her lacerated palm. "It's okay now," she said. Gripping me solidly by my wrists, she leaned back, matching my weight with her own as I brought myself upright. Face to face with her, I saw Sam's eyes.

"Danny, would you like to come to my place?" *Please,* I begged silently. "I'll make us a snack, we'll have a glass of wine. It's only seven o'clock. If we hustle, we might catch the sunset from my building's roof."

She glanced at her watch; I held my breath. "I have to make a call—"

"Oh, you've got plans, then don't change them," I broke in, forcing myself to sound unaffected.

"No," she said, "it's fine. Really. It's good. Let me just . . ." She stepped a few yards away from me, pulled out her cell phone, dialed, and began speaking in a low voice.

As I packed up the remains of our picnic, I watched her pace in a small circle. At the end of my last dream—it came back now—she and I had spun round and round, so fast we'd risen off the sidewalk. We'd been held together and pulled apart, simultaneously.

Like Meyerhold's cartwheel: that happy gesture of the body, powered purely by sorrow. A similar paradox.

Danny put away her phone and shouldered her bag. "Ready?" she asked.

"As we're likely to get," I answered.

INTERLUDE

THIS ISN'T a proper intermezzo, merely a swift interruption. (Picture an actor dashing across the stage, declaiming as he goes.)

Just one point. By recalling that cartwheel from her first dream, Camilla confirmed what I'd suspected. We'd come full circle, she and I: Meyerhold's spark had hit its mark. What I'd hoped for had come to pass. I'd done my job; I could let myself off the hook.

Why, then, did I not feel released?

Partly because Camilla wasn't—not yet, not quite. I knew she would be, ultimately; about that I had no doubts. But I was also ambivalent, in the way a parent might be, perhaps, watching a child achieve independence. One realizes there's no accounting for what will ensue, no heading off of calamities.

The problem, in a nutshell? Simply this: the concern of other people is unavailing, irrelevant. It lacks any agency. It stops nothing bad from happening.

What, I wondered, had Seva made of *that* truth, once it had dawned on him? With what emotion had it saddled him?

Terror, I should think, at the realization that there'd be no one to bail him out.

When one is in one's prison cell—actual or self-created—however one has landed there, love becomes the only key to the door. As Camilla would shortly discover.

And so we pick up again, *in medias res*. No more dreams for me to stage. I head to the wings, awaiting the curtain's fall.

TEN

BY THE time Danny and I got to the Village, the sun was low and the sky rich with orange and mauve. I was eager to go straight home, but Danny wanted to pass by The Fourth Wall. On the subway, she'd told me she had some ideas for my shop's front door, which was in need of repainting—but she wanted to take a quick look at it. A little detour, she said. Just a couple of minutes.

We proceeded toward Bedford Street, zigzagging westward. When she was eight or nine, Sam and I used to play a game with her on these same streets. We'd each grab a hand and lift her off the ground, cackling happily, so her sleek legs would pump forward and backward—very much as I'd been swung back and forth in my latest dream, before Danny and I began spinning together . . .

Her low laughter broke my reverie. We were a few yards away from The Fourth Wall. Two men stood in front of my shop. They were facing away from us, but when Danny whistled softly, they both turned around.

"Hey," Sam called. Smiling, Stuart gave one of his signature waves, a circular movement performed with the flat of his hand.

"What . . . ?" I exclaimed.

Stuart slung an arm across Sam's shoulders. "We always meet like this," he deadpanned. "Coincidence. It never fails us."

"Plus there are such things as telephones," said Sam, pointing at Danny.

I turned to her. "You called them both? From the park?" I asked.

"No, dumb-dumb," Stuart answered for her. "She called *me,* and I called *him.* Phone tag! I got here first, of course."

Danny stepped forward and kissed them each on the cheek. "Thanks for coming," she said quietly.

"Thank him especially," said Sam, indicating Stuart.

Stuart swept the sidewalk with one foot like an embarrassed boy, then grinned boastfully. "No, wait, it's true! Me especially!"

"Okay," I said, "what *are* you talking about?"

"I thought it wise to bring the three of you together," he answered. "So when you told me you were going out to Brooklyn to see Danny, I asked her to finagle it so you'd end up here."

"It wasn't hard," said Danny. "Cam invited me."

"Even better! I told Danny to call before the two of you headed back to Manhattan," Stuart continued, addressing me, "so I could give him"—he indicated Sam—"a heads-up. Timing's perfect!"

"So what's the deal?" I asked.

Stuart drew himself up, inhaled loudly, and spread his hands like an emcee welcoming an audience. "This gathering, Camilla! I had to figure things out first—wrap my head around what was happening. I chewed on the whole question while Carl and I were in Belgium. He got fed up with me, claimed I was *ruminating* too much."

"*What* whole question, Stuart?"

"The question of *you.*" He pointed two finger-guns at Danny and me, forefingers aimed, thumbs cocked. "It began with that hunting expedition of yours, upstate. I wasn't keen on it, remember? It seemed like a big red herring. For my money, the real action was right here in New York. And so it was—what with Danny in her cave in Brooklyn and Cam pulled into herself like a turtle."

Hunching with knees and ankles close together, he lowered his chin to his chest and covered his head with his hands in a parody of self-protection. "This, I said to myself, is a no-good situation these girls have gotten themselves into." He unfolded, once again upright. "I wasn't sure what to do about it, though. Nor could I tell what role Sam here was playing—though I admit that at the time, I wasn't giving *him* much in the way of credit."

Hands laced together, he extended both arms straight upward and executed a brisk 360-degree twirl on one foot, then quickly reversed direction and spun on the other foot. "Bet *you* can't do that," he said, coming to a stop and snapping his fingers in front of Sam's nose.

"Got that right," replied Sam equably.

"Just making sure you're present and accounted for, buddy."

"The screen may appear blank," said Sam, "but I'm plugged in."

Stuart saluted him. "Your ex and I have become better acquainted recently," he said to me. "I've been misreading him. No surprise there! I frequently misread men. It's women I'm so clever about. A shame, that! But I digress. You've been terribly distracted all summer long, Cam. I'm used to your paying a fair bit of attention to *me*, which just wasn't happening. And I knew it had to do with Danny, and all those dreams you were having."

"Dreams?" Danny broke in. "She didn't mention any dreams to me. What were they about?"

"I'm not going to divulge the details," Stuart answered. "As Cam's unofficial dramaturge, I'm bound by rules of confidentiality." He mimed a zipping motion across his mouth. "Suffice it to say that a wide range of characters showed up in her dreams. Some of them did repeat performances—most notably a Russian theater director, a guy named Meyerhold. On whom our dreamer here has become rather, uh, fixated."

Danny turned to me. "You dreamed about that Russian who did the sketches?"

"What sketches?" asked Sam.

"Order!" Stuart clapped his hands loudly. He gave me a stern look. "You've been holding out on me, Miss Camilla."

"I planned to update you," I offered.

One of his eyebrows arched skeptically. "We'll deal with that later. As I was saying: I spent much of this summer feeling like I'd been elbowed aside. There you were, night after night, watching this drama—acting in it, too . . . And even though you told me about your dreams, I knew you weren't being open about your *feelings*. I had to think up something to lure you forth! Hence our little session in there." With a hitchhiker's thumb, he indicated my shop.

"What kind of session?" Danny asked, not realizing he was alluding to the makeover I'd told her about.

"Hypnosis, maybe," said Sam. "Stuart seems capable of that."

"Why, how compli*ment*ary, Sam! No, it was a makeup session, actually. You mustn't ask me about it," Stuart added peremptorily. "It's *entre nous*." He tipped his head toward me.

"Would you do me a favor and cut to the chase, Stu?" I said.

His hands went outward and downward in exasperation. "The point being, I finally managed to rattle you! So when Danny called, you were ready to deal."

"Aren't you forgetting something?" said Sam. "The photo?"

"Hold your horses, I'm getting to that."

"Before you do," I said, "do you think we might have this encounter somewhere other than on the street? Like in my apartment? Or even better, on the roof, so I get to see at least a few minutes of the sunset?"

WE WERE in time to witness the last swaths of burnt orange fading on the horizon. They were followed by a pink-gray blush that gradually turned milkier, paler, as dusk went to evening.

We ferried everything we needed—glasses, a bottle of wine, a cutting board with some cheese and crackers—up the metal ladder at the end of the top-floor hallway and through the roof hatch. Luckily we had the roof to ourselves. I found four old director's chairs, leaning against the building's central air-conditioning unit. We lined them up in a westward-facing phalanx, then plopped into them like tourists on the deck of a cruise ship. As the sunset's colors cooled, we drank and nibbled in near silence. When the sky had dimmed to a light gray, Stuart began speaking.

"The photo," he said quietly. "That Polaroid snapshot, the one I noticed on your desk. Remember, Cammie?"

I glanced at Danny to see how she was reacting, but her expression told me nothing. Neither Stuart nor Sam, both on the other side of Danny, was visible to me. I didn't want to talk without being able to look at their faces.

"Yes," I answered. "But first, can we pull these chairs in a circle so I can see everyone?" In a few moments we were reconfigured. "Now, what about it—that picture?"

"Let's see . . . Maybe I should start by saying this: during my brief phone chat with Danny this afternoon, I gathered you and she discussed that same photo today. And I took the liberty of passing along that information to Sam. Which means we're all on the same page, so to speak. With respect to matters of . . . paternity. No need to tiptoe around."

"Nicely summarized," said Sam. He didn't look at me. "By the way, can I see the photo now? Since I'm the only one here who hasn't?"

I turned to Danny. "I gave it back to you," I said. "In the park."

Danny pulled the photo from her bag and handed it to Sam. He stared at it for a moment, turned it over, and nodded. Then he handed it back.

"Yep?" she asked him.

"Yep," he answered quietly.

"Explain to Camilla," Danny ordered Stuart, "what happened after you figured out it was Sam in the picture."

"Wait," I said. "Stuart, *you* figured that out?"

"Danny and I both did. Separately."

"But you—how?"

"I often misread men, but I rarely mis*see* them. I have a highly acute visual memory. Among other things, I'm very good at guessing who's behind the masks at Halloween parties. It's a special skill—ask Carl! It's not just a matter of faces. I notice how people hold themselves, how they stand and move and so forth."

"You're saying you *recognized* Sam in that picture?"

"No, I wouldn't put it that strongly. When I first saw the photo, something rang a bell. I knew I'd seen that man before; his stance was familiar. But I didn't push it. You have to let these things sit for a while, see if your memory will produce the goods on its own."

He refilled our wineglasses. "The other day I was sitting in my living room, waiting for Carl, who'd gone out on an errand. You know that wall of photos we've got? I found myself staring at that handsome shot of you, Camilla, which I took around the time you met Sam. I should say I enjoy admiring my own camerawork. God knows what Ansel Adams here would make of it!"

He rolled his eyes in Sam's direction; Sam chuckled. "No comment," he said.

"Anyway," Stuart continued, "there I was, entertained by my own photograph, when a memory popped into my head—a memory of Sam. From the very early days of your relationship. Like, close to twenty years ago."

Sam, I noticed, wasn't acting perturbed or surprised. Evidently he'd heard this story already, and so had Danny: Stuart's words weren't catching her unawares. She was attentive but unruffled.

"First," Stuart went on, still addressing me, "I remembered the two of you entering Backstage Books together. Sam was his usual natty self: nice pants, a good sweater, well-made shoes. You introduced him to Carl—they hadn't met yet. And Sam looked relaxed, except for one minor clue, which I recalled next: the way he was holding his left hand. He was doing what I call a thumb-flick. The hand hung down, like this, and his fingers were spread apart"—Stuart demonstrated—"and the tip of his forefinger pressed on top of his thumbnail, as if he were about to use the thumb to launch something into the air.

"Now, to a mime, that particular hand posture always suggests anxiety. Which was natural, I thought, in this case. I mean, it's always tricky meeting a lover's friends for the first time . . . Anyway, that's the memory that returned to me. But why *it,* and not another? Well, because of that photo I'd seen in your office. The gears clicked, and I got it: the masked man next to Eve in the snapshot had held his hand the same way, and his clothing was very similar— same cut, same style. And the man's body . . . it all added up. I was certain the guy in the picture was Sam."

Sam said nothing. I looked at Stuart. "How did *I* manage to miss this? How come I didn't see what you saw?"

"That's simple. You and Sam are too close."

He was right: I wouldn't have noticed something so familiar. "So then what did you do, after you'd realized . . . ?"

"I made the phone call I had to make."

"To Danny, you mean."

"Uh-uh." Stuart shook his head. "To Sam."

AND SAM hadn't been the shocked listener Stuart anticipated.

Just a day or two earlier (Sam recounted, taking over from Stuart), he'd received another call, from Danny. *That* one had been the shocker.

Stuart and Sam had agreed to meet, and during their conversation Stuart made it clear he wasn't accusing Sam of deception. Rather, he was concerned about how I would handle the truth about Danny's father. Lila needn't be informed (Danny and Sam had already agreed on this), but I'd have to be—and how would *that* play out?

Let Danny tell her, Stuart had advised. It will be easier for Cam to assimilate the news if it comes from her. Easier, and better.

So it had unfolded.

AFTER STUART'S narrative ended, none of us spoke for a time. Then, with one long-armed sweep, Stuart retrieved our empty wineglasses (holding them by their stems in a cluster, like a bouquet of flowers) and bowed.

"Your waiter for the evening," he intoned, "is now going home. After washing these." He tinkled the glasses lightly. "Least I can do to express my appreciation for such a nice Beaujolais! Thank you for sharing, Camilla. No need to come downstairs, I have a key to your door, remember? As for our father-daughter pair here"—he bowed again, to Danny and Sam—"I can only say I'm a little envious. I haven't been so lucky in the daddy department. Mine's gone missing, and I've no intention of finding him. But *your* story's got a different ending."

"Stuart—" I began, but he cut me off with a flourish.

"We'll debrief soon, my sweet." He opened the roof hatch, swung himself neatly onto the ladder, and began a one-handed descent, glasses aloft. "Meanwhile, enjoy the rest of your evening"— now only his head and the glasses remained visible—"with your family." The hatch closed softly behind him.

YOUR FAMILY. Had Stuart ever used those words before, in conjunction with Sam and Danny? Not that I could remember. *Your family* was myself and two dead people, not me and this pair. Not this trio.

"So," said Sam.

"You two," said Danny, "need to talk."

"Do we?" asked Sam.

"Don't be a goof, Sam," she replied.

"Well, do we need to talk, Cam?" He looked at me now. "Because I'm not sure you want to." Pausing, he added quietly, "Correct me if I'm wrong."

Before I could answer, Danny stood up. "I'm going over to The Fourth Wall," she announced. "Cam, may I have your keys? I'll need both—for the gate and the door."

"You planning on doing anything in particular over there?" I asked.

"*Re*doing. Your window display's terrible! You're showing all small things—they're not visually catchy. I'll add some larger items, make the whole thing interesting. It won't take me long."

"Do me a favor," I said. "If you're really serious about going over there, don't work on my window display. Do something instead with that wall of masks I've been trying to assemble. But really, are you sure you feel up to it, Danny?"

"I need to busy myself for a while." She picked up her backpack. "I'm wired. I feel like using my hands. Don't worry, I won't stay late. What wall of masks?"

I handed her my keys. "Off to the right, near the middle of the shop—where I have that pair of silk screens from *The Mikado,* remember? You'll see it. And you know where I store all my tools and supplies. Help yourself to anything you need."

"Where's the main light switch? I can't remember."

"To the left of the door as you enter. Run your hand along the doorframe, you'll find it. I'll come over in a little while and—"

"I'll be fine. You've got spares of these, right?" She jingled my keys and left.

THE ROOF'S hatch closed behind her with a click, and Sam and I were alone. I couldn't make out his face clearly. He pulled his director's chair closer to mine.

"Bonjour, Camus," he said.

That had been his morning salutation when we were married. He'd normally risen well before me so he could make coffee and scan the newspaper. I'd enter the kitchen and he'd hand me a mug of coffee and say, Bonjour, Camus—his standard opener. Nothing standard about it now, though; not nine years post-divorce. It was a gambit.

"So why're you doing this with your wife, Sam?" I asked.

"Doing this with her?" he echoed.

"Why conceal from Lila the fact that you're Danny's father?"

He exhaled slowly. "I wasn't figuring we'd talk about Lila," he said. "I thought we might talk about you."

"Oh go on," I said lightly. "Answer my question."

He shrugged, capitulating. "There's no reason to tell Lila," he said. "She understands I'm like a father to Danny. She's glad about that, in fact. But it'd be different—hard on her—if she knew—"

"So you're sparing her. Is that why you didn't tell *me* the truth a long time ago? To spare me?"

His expression was unreadable; there wasn't enough light. "Which truth would that be?" he asked quietly.

"About you and Eve. Obviously."

"When I first met Eve . . ." Sam hesitated, and I could sense him gazing at me, requesting permission. When I nodded, he continued. "She had intense sexual energy, which I briefly mistook for interest in me. Until it became clear that I barely existed for her." Again he paused. "Those couple of days . . . it was like being fucked into invisibility. I remember thinking she was so aggressive and so withheld at the same time. Not mechanical; it wasn't that. But she was off in her own world. Absent."

Eve at sixteen, in her bedroom, arranging perfume bottles on a shelf. Arming herself with my father's arsenal. Readying for all the erotic contests that lay ahead, which she knew she'd win—all but one.

"During those couple of encounters, I found out next to nothing about her. Except for the fact that she lived upstate and worked as a landscaper, I never learned what sort of life she led. I got the impression she was a total loner."

"She didn't speak of my father?"

"Not outright. The only person she mentioned was a man, someone with whom she said she'd almost had a sexual affair. A widower. Then—I recall this clearly—she said he'd released her. When I asked her why, she said he'd been certain that if they became lovers, she'd suffer for it. She said they'd stayed friends, yet something about the way she said it made me think she was still tied to him."

"Did she name him?"

"No."

"So how do you know it was Jordan?"

Sam grunted in appreciation of the question. "Each time I was with her, Eve wore a certain perfume. A memorably nice fragrance. After our second encounter, I asked her what it was. That's when she told me about the widower. He'd given her the perfume, she said. She didn't identify it by name."

"Did she say he'd made it himself?"

Sam shook his head. "No. But Cam, *you* wore that same scent, not long after I met you. And I asked you about it, and you said it was something your father had created. Lune, wasn't it? It was your favorite—and Eve's, too, you said—and it had never been marketed. You and she were the only people who wore it. That's when I realized who Eve had been involved with.

"And you knew, too," he finished. "Maybe not consciously, but you knew."

I STOOD and turned away. In an instant he was on his feet, his hands grasping my elbows from behind.

I spoke into the air before me. "What would you have said if you *had* talked with me about Eve?"

His grip on my elbows loosened as he considered my question. "I would've told you she'd been marked by whatever happened with your father. No, more than that—I think she was ruined by it, early on. And her particular ruination ruined you."

He rotated me so we were facing each other. "Which is why Danny spent as much time with us as she did. Not just because *she* needed to feel safe, but also because *you* did." His gaze was unfaltering. "She was the child you could have, wasn't she? You saw yourself in her—the only child of a single parent, a parent completely preoccupied with somebody else. Someone you, too, were longing for. . . ."

His cell phone began ringing. "Sorry," he murmured. "Okay," he responded into the receiver. "Yeah. Be there soon."

"Lila?" I asked as he snapped the phone shut.

"No, Danny. She says we should come on over. She wants us to see the wall of masks."

Did I really want the three of us together in the same place—
that place, *my* place—by ourselves? "All right," I said uneasily. "But
can you—I mean, where does Lila think you are tonight, anyway?"

"She knows I'm here."

"And she's cool with that?"

"Completely." He walked to the roof hatch and backed down its
ladder; I followed. "Can we make a pit stop before we leave?" he
asked when we were in the corridor. "I'm thirsty."

"Of course. I'm thirsty, too." I led the way. Stopping outside my
apartment door, I patted my pockets. "Danny's got my keys," I said.
"For here as well as the shop. My spares are inside."

Sam pulled out his key ring. "I have mine," he said.

"Still?"

"Still. Lucky for us."

I STEPPED aside so he could unlock and open my door. Entering,
he went automatically for the light, sliding its dimmer switch. It was
at that point, as I stood in the doorway staring at him, that I was
able to perceive Sam as he'd been years earlier: not just my husband
but my partner onstage, a fellow actor in an improvised performance. A family drama, with me playing the mother and Sam sub-
stituting for Billy Deveare. Who was filling in (though none of us
knew it) for Jordan.

And Danny, playing herself. The girl who longed for Eve's love
yet had learned—like me—to act as though she didn't.

"Cam, you okay?" Sam called from the kitchen.

Rousing myself, I walked down the hallway. Sam handed me a
glass of water, staring at me as I drank it. "Where *are* you?"

"Where am I? . . ." It wasn't until I answered him that I realized
I'd begun weeping. Sam took me into his arms. Pressed against his
chest, I battled to overcome not desire or remorse but sorrow, the
underlay of my love for him, whose ingress now felt as unstoppable
as it always had.

"Tell me one more thing, please." He wasn't finished with our
dialogue.

"Sam—"

Releasing me, he pulled a clean handkerchief from his pocket—one of the white cotton ones I'd given him stacks of when we were married. "Here," he said.

I took the handkerchief and waved it at him like a flag of surrender.

"Eve wanted Jordan to be the father of her child, didn't she? Because she was in love with him all along."

"Jordan was Danny's only possible father," I said. "That's how Eve saw it—how she *felt* it." Now my phone began to ring. When I picked up, Danny was on the other end.

"Where *are* you two? You coming over?"

"Very soon," I answered.

"Good—because now I'm really done." She sounded energized. "Get moving!"

I hung up and turned to face Sam. I realized what I wanted. The realization was nearly visual, as though my heart were a lens and I'd finally twirled it into focus.

"I have to see Danny," I said.

"Okay, let's go."

"No, alone, Sam. By myself."

There was a long silence. "All right," he responded. His shrug said he'd acquiesce, though to what exactly he wasn't sure. "Walk me to the corner?"

WE PROCEEDED downstairs and out into the night air, cooler now. At the corner of Bedford Street, beneath a streetlamp, we both halted.

"Don't forget to get your keys back," Sam said.

I nodded.

"Say good night to her for me." He hesitated, hands at his side. The forefinger of his left hand was pressed down on his thumb, in that same unconscious display of uncertainty Stuart had observed long ago.

"I just realized something about you and fatherhood," I said.

"You're able to be three different kinds of father at the same time, aren't you? You inherited Abby. You get to raise Zeke from scratch. Nobody's standing between the two of you." I paused. "And now there's Danny. . . ."

"Danny's ours," Sam said quietly. "I never at any point suspected she was mine—physically, I mean—but I've always felt she was ours."

Something was working its way out of me, a sharp splinter seeking an exit. "There's no 'ours,' Sam."

His expression was wary. "Why not?"

"Because there's no 'us.' There was, when we were married. For a time. But it never could've lasted. Not unless I'd produced a kid—other than Danny, that is."

A couple approached us. The woman was wearing a perfume I recognized, a commercially popular scent with a pronounced top note of hyacinth. Jordan would've found it banal, insufficiently veiled. Was that it, the key to my father's perfume-making—his insistence upon disguise? In the woman's wake I detected a residue of newly mown grass, crisp and clean; it leavened her perfume's initial sweetness but did little to subvert its predictability. Jordan had taught me well enough: I knew when a fragrance showed its hand too clearly.

"Say more." Pulling his hands from his pockets, Sam gave my forearms an urgent shake. "Please."

I was feeling a little dazed, and the silvery light cast by the streetlamp had a peculiarly silencing effect on me. Even the passing cars made, I noticed, almost no sound. As I closed my eyes for a few seconds, Meyerhold appeared, his cloak swirling, beckoning; then he vanished.

Sam stood before me, waiting.

"Since Eve's death I've been having lots of dreams," I said. "About who's who in my life. Who's *been* who, I should say. And who's stood in—who's substituted. . . . I'm having to reconsider all the roles, my own included. Especially the part I'm playing with

Danny. I'm no longer an understudy here, Sam. I'm not sure exactly what that means, but I know I can't stay in the wings any longer."

He leaned forward, his lips lightly brushing my cheek. "You're on, then," he said quietly. Moments later, he'd crossed the street, and I knew something between us had ended. I was freed, not of him but for Danny. And not to make her mine but to make myself hers, newly, unmasked.

THE FOURTH Wall's front door was unlocked. Entering, I found the interior lit and Danny nowhere to be seen.

I moved to the center of the shop. On the wall to the right, a dozen distinctive masks—made of wood, cloth, papier-mâché, metal, and synthetics—were arrayed in a large circle about six feet in diameter. The largest four occupied the compass points of the circle; the smaller masks were arranged in pairs between them.

Danny had evidently rooted around in my chest of fabrics, for she'd suspended from the ceiling a sheer cotton drape that covered the circle completely. It served as a kind of mask of the masks—a lovely translucent screen through which the twelve visages could be perceived. Collectively they hinted at a blurry clock face, or a dozen actors ringing a circular stage. Danny had created something subtle and lovely—just what I'd hoped for, and nothing I could've achieved myself.

I let out a little moan of appreciation, and she heard me. "You there, Cam?" she called.

Her voice was coming from my office. Approaching, I heard the familiar *thwak* of a dart hitting cork. "Are you—"

I stopped in the doorway. A dart flew across the room, striking one of six small photos affixed to my dartboard. There we were: Eve, Sam, and myself, each of our faces appearing twice on the perimeter of the board.

Taking aim, Danny tossed again. This time she missed the photos but struck close to the bull's-eye. She was standing at the required distance from the board, and she seemed to have no trouble gauging how hard to throw. She had good form, too: her stance was correct, and her wrist performed each flick unhesitatingly.

"Where'd you learn to play?" I asked after quelling my surprise.

"I've never played before." She gave another toss; the dart hit Sam. "I just started fooling around . . . It took you forever to get here!" Making a connection between the image she'd just struck and the man's absence, she added, "Where's Sam?"

I opted for simplicity. "I sent him home."

My reply seemed not to disconcert her. "So I came into your office to make myself a nightcap," she said, motioning toward a bottle of vodka and a shot glass. "And I saw this curtain and wondered what was behind it. I was curious because I'd just done my own thing out there—you saw it? And voilà! Another curtain, right in here. . . . Cheers," she added, reaching for her glass. "Make yourself a drink—it's your vodka, Cam! Hope you don't mind I'm playing your game, too."

I shook my head. "How'd you know about the photos?"

"You mean the fact that you used them as targets? Well, I was looking for the darts, and I snooped around and found everything— all your props—right there in the top drawer of your desk. You're so well organized!" She paused to take aim. "*Now* I know why that picture of your mother had all those tiny holes in it . . ."

She tossed. "Oops!" she exclaimed as her dart bounced off one of the board's rims. "I'm doing my own version of the Motley Crew game."

Her energy was palpably manic. "So let me ask you a question, Cam." She rounded up all the darts she'd just tossed. "When you play this game by yourself, are you expressing hostility, or something else? Like resentment maybe? No, that's too petty! Something bigger. Frustration? But not your average case of frustration . . ."

She winged a dart, striking Eve. A moment later another one sailed. "Or maybe this sport has another purpose? Maybe it's the perfect game to play when you're furious with someone, since you can't tell her how much she fucked up—because she *died!* Of all things! You listening, Cammie? Or have you checked out?"

"No," I replied as anxiety saturated me. "I'm right here."

"Good." She threw a dart that pinned Eve squarely. The next one went wide, glancing off the lower rim of the board and clattering onto the floor. "On the other hand," she continued, "maybe this is the ideal game to play when you've done something you weren't supposed to." Another dart, another face impaled: Sam's. "Like, say, fooling around with your father . . ."

I sat down, dizzy now. "Fooling around?"

She glanced at me, took in my distress, and clucked her tongue. "Oh, no, not that, Cammie!—I phrased it wrong. Calm down. I didn't mean fucking!" She swept up the darts and put them in their drawer. "Fucking's so overrated! Kissing's *my* favorite sexual act. It's so much more essential than everything else. Don't you think?"

She saw me begin to cry, and circled behind me. "Don't agitate yourself," she said, coming up behind me and rubbing my shoulders lightly. "It happened during the summer of my junior year of college. A while ago, five years . . . the distant past."

JUNIOR YEAR: when she was twenty. The summer of 1994. Three years after our divorce, a few months before Sam began seeing Lila.

"Tell me," I said to Danny.

Moving to my desk, she sat on it, bouncing her legs as she spoke. "Well, one evening in August, Sam and I went out to dinner. Afterward we took a long walk. I didn't feel like going back to Mom's apartment right away—actually I didn't want to go back there at all.

"That morning she'd taken a shower, gone into her bedroom, and shut the door. She hadn't come out. I thought this might be one of her three-day withdrawals. I was home all day, working on a design project, and I walked past her door several times, but everything was quiet.

"Before leaving to meet Sam, I stood outside her door and put my ear against it. I knew *she* knew I was there, listening, but she didn't budge. I started yelling at her through the door. 'Just cut me loose,' I said. 'Because if you don't, I'll cut myself loose. Wouldn't you rather it happened on *your* terms?'

"I could hear her getting off her bed, and then her door opened, and we stared at each other. She looked ratty and beautiful at the same time . . . And she said, 'It's good to have someone like Sam in your life—someone you're close to, like a father . . . Don't get *too* close, though.'"

Pushing herself off my desk, Danny walked over to the dartboard and drew the curtain across it. "She was trying to make me afraid of Sam. Which made me furious with her—angrier than I'd ever been. I told her to fuck off, and she turned around and closed her door in my face.

"So I went out and met up with Sam. I didn't tell him about what had just happened between Mom and me; we talked about other things at dinner. After our walk, just as we were standing on the street, saying good-bye, I put my arms around his neck and my mouth on his. Obviously I wasn't just giving him a peck. I felt him hesitate, then stop hesitating. We both drew back, and I laughed, because I found the whole thing funny. And thrilling. And scary, and—necessary, somehow. Because I was proving Mom wrong.

"Sam didn't laugh; he looked stunned. I said, 'There, we did it,' but it looked like a huge wave of guilt had just bagged him, so I told him we'd gotten it out of our systems, and it was fine. *We* were fine.

"That seemed to calm him a bit. But I could tell he wasn't fully okay, so I said *I* wouldn't be having a hard time, and I expected *him* not to have one either. He walked me home, and we said good night, and I went to bed feeling like I'd just won a prize or something.

"When I got up the next morning, Mom had already left for work. That day I packed up all my stuff—I didn't have much, mostly clothing, a few books and CDs—and moved into my friend Amanda's place. When Mom came home that night, I was gone. I'd left her a note saying I wouldn't be back."

I NODDED: this part of Danny's story I knew already. She'd called me the evening of her arrival at her friend's apartment, to tell me she'd left

Eve's for good. It had been impossible for me to talk her into returning, or at least calling her mother. She'd refused any suggestions along
those lines. *I've had it,* she'd said, and I'd heard in her voice a new cer-
tainty. This time her renunciation of Eve would be unbudging.

"In September I returned to college for my final year," Danny
went on. "Mom called me every month, but I kept my distance.
She'd released me, you know, just like I'd asked her to. She did it by
going after Sam. That's all it took to get me to turn my back on
her—as she knew I would."

I imagined Danny at night during recent weeks, alone. Listening
to "Pannonica" until the small hours. Hoping the music would
drown out her guilt; knowing it wouldn't.

"It's taken me this long to understand what happened, Cam.
That summer Mom was trying to stop me from falling for a man she
knew might be—*was,* in all likelihood—my father. She wasn't able
to tell me that, though. She wasn't willing to let go of the story
about Billy, or her fantasy about Jordan. She'd needed that for too
long . . . So there we are," she finished.

MY OPTIONS lay before me.

I could tell Danny what her mother had said to me at Sam's
wedding. Eve had wanted to ruin not just Danny's relationship with
Sam, but mine as well. Hadn't she deserved to suffer for that?

Yet things weren't so simple. I'd encouraged Danny to trust me
and mistrust her mother; wasn't that called stealing the lead? And
since Eve's death, I'd been trying to have it both ways—revealing
and concealing myself at the same time. As my dream director had
lately done everything in his power to point out to me.

Spill it, I could hear Stuart saying.

"Danny," I began, "I don't know what to say about Eve's motives. There's so little any of us can really claim we *knew.* All I can
talk about—all I want to talk about, now—is us. Look, I'm not your
sister. Or your first cousin once removed. That's just a slot on a ge-
nealogy chart. I have no idea what I am to you. None of the usual
labels seem to apply." I rested my hands on her shoulders. "I can't

possibly do without you, though. Regardless of what we call it—us, I mean. Us."

She raised her arms and lay her own hands on my shoulders, so our bodies described a square of space between us. Stepping forward into that space, she clasped and then released me. "Can I stay at your place tonight, Cam? It's awfully late."

SHE SACKED out on my sofa bed, and we both slept in till nearly noon. I awoke feeling calmer than I had in months.

After showering, Danny offered to take me out for brunch. I protested, then saw she wanted this—wanted to make a clear gesture, not of thanks but of openness—so I said yes. We proceeded to a nearby café, and Danny ordered us French toast, fruit, and café au lait. Gazing at the café's serene walls, I found myself visualizing my shop.

"The display of masks . . . it's great, Danny. And it's got me thinking, let's you and I *do* something together! We haven't, not since you left for college. Not as adults."

She frowned quizzically. "Sure we have. We see plays sometimes, we go out to hear music . . ."

"That's not what I mean. We should produce something. *Act* together."

Her brows rose. "Like, onstage?"

"No, no! But you're a designer, and I collect props—that means we could put something together, right? Make something interesting?"

She crossed her arms skeptically. "As an example . . . ?"

"I don't know. I'm thinking of masks. Which leads me to actors, the people who wear them. You and I both love good acting. Onstage, I mean. Much more than film acting. Yes?"

"True."

"Of course there are wonderful film actors. But nothing holds a candle to a good stage performance."

"And . . . ?"

"Well, maybe we could produce a book of photos."

Danny smiled and snorted at once. "Photos of *what*, Cam?"

"Of an actor! How about that? Just one actor. Not a famous one, and certainly not a screen star. Just somebody who acts. A good amateur would suffice. But here's the thing: the photos would show this actor with unusual props." I paused. "We could use my collection to create some great stage pictures. You know, scenes we'd dream up ourselves—nothing taken from plays or films. Things we'd imagine."

"Who'd take these pictures? And who'd be the actor?"

"The photographer's easy. Sam could locate someone who's just getting started, and who's talented. And willing to take risks . . . And Stuart could play the part of the actor. He'd be perfect."

"Sam would help us, if he liked the idea." Though her tone stayed neutral, I sensed she was climbing on board. "I mean, once he gets behind a project, he's like a bulldog."

"Yeah, I know . . . But we'd have to make this idea *work*. We'd need a theme, something to tie it together."

"Like . . . ?"

"I haven't given this any thought before now, Danny! The idea's just coming to me . . . How about something like *Thirty-Three Swoons*?"

"Huh?"

"That's the title of Meyerhold's last production. Before they shut down his theater for good."

"Meyerhold? The director who did the sketches? *Thirty-Three Swoons*?"

"Yep. It's a set of one-act farces by Chekhov. In each one, the characters keep fainting—every few minutes, someone else passes out. Thirty-three times altogether."

"What's the idea behind it?"

"I haven't read the one-acts, but I know what Meyerhold was going for: a tragicomic approach. Fun, larky moments alongside real weirdness. That's how he liked to work."

Danny pondered this. "And your idea is to have Stuart faint thirty-three times?"

"Not really faint, of course! But he could *mime* a lot of different faints."

"The point being?"

"Just to play with the whole idea of swooning! Think of all the plays you've seen in which people faint. It happens constantly, in everything from Shakespeare to *Noises Off.* Dramas are full of swoons—realistic, farcical, symbolic . . . People faint onstage for all kinds of reasons. Fear, surprise, distress . . ."

She began nodding. "Betrayal, delight . . ."

"Shock, as in the sight of someone dead, or back from the dead . . ."

"Or something that happens. Loud noises. Thunder and lightning."

"A kiss."

"Yeah . . ." Now she was absently twirling the rings on her right hand. "You know, I like this, Cam," she murmured. "It's got possibilities. Why don't I come over one night next week and we'll talk about it? Don't you go saying anything to Sam or Stuart, okay?"

"Of course not!"

I WALKED her to the subway. Danny whistled softly as we proceeded—a few bars from Monk's "Well, You Needn't," which she carried beautifully.

"Someday, would you teach me how to whistle properly?" I asked when she'd finished.

"Why, sure." Her tone was teasing. "When I sense you're ready, that is. Don't hold your breath."

"Very funny. Oh—another thing," I said as we reached Sixth Avenue. "You didn't tell me what the perfume Jordan left you smelled like."

"That's right!" She rummaged in her backpack. "It's show-and-tell time! Or rather, show-and-*smell* time." Extracting a delicate flacon from a pouch, she handed it over. "Jordan enclosed a note with it, saying he'd bought the bottle at a flea market in Moscow. He put one of his own perfumes in it. Not Lune, something else."

The bottle's dome-shaped stopper was covered with tiny sculpted blossoms. Embossed on the curved surface of the flacon was a round medallion that read *Chypre.*

"This is an old Coty bottle," I said, rotating it. "One of Coty's earliest perfumes." The stopper was snugly closed. I jimmied it off and raised the bottle to my nose. The scent was a little thin, but I could detect its notes: oakmoss, sandalwood, bergamot. The same green chords of the original Chypre, but with something aerial layered over the scent's fernlike base. Lilac, perhaps, and a hint of patchouli.

"Reminds me a little of Mitsouko," Danny said, referring to one of her favorite Guerlain perfumes.

"Mitsouko's from the same era," I said. "And this one's related to Chypre, but different. Better, I think, even though it's thinned out a bit."

"Remember how in his letter to me, Jordan said he'd named this perfume Somersault? He must've liked that sketch by Meyerhold, the one with the somersaulting clown." She was sniffing at the perfume as she spoke. "I've got to guess what this *really* smelled like, right? When it was at full force, I mean. It's still pretty great."

"Yes, it is."

Replacing the stopper, she handed me the bottle and its pouch. "You take it, Cam. I'll keep Jordan's letter and sketches, and you keep this."

I accepted her offer.

AT FIVE the next day, I closed up my shop and walked over to Hudson Street. Although I didn't know where Nick's job site was, it would be visible, I knew, for it had an exterior scaffold.

Figuring the building was south of Tenth Street, I began heading downtown on the west sidewalk of Hudson, scanning both sides. After a half-dozen or so blocks, I saw Nick from across the street. The sun's oblique rays illumined the building's entire façade; the metal rigging on which he stood was gleaming. With the tip of his trowel, he was probing the upper sill of a second-story window, checking for spots in need of repair. His sleeveless undershirt looked brilliantly white against his tanned skin.

He didn't notice me. I crossed the street, slipping my arms through the straps of my knapsack and hitching it onto my back so my hands were free. Then I began hoisting myself up the scaffold. It lacked a proper ladder but offered secure foot- and hand-holds, and I scaled it easily. As I reached the second-floor platform, Nick turned toward me, one hand shielding his eyes from the sun. He hadn't yet made out who I was.

"What the hell," he began before recognizing me. "Cam! You're not supposed to be up here, baby—it's dangerous."

I moved across the wood planking, one hand on the rigging's tubular rails. As I neared Nick, he reached for my hand. "There, I've got you," he said.

"Don't worry, I don't have vertigo," I told him.

He squinted at me. "Is it Danny?" he said after a moment.

"No," I said. "Or yes, indirectly."

"She's in trouble?"

"No, she's doing well. She and I are doing well, too."

"Good. But why . . . what are you doing here?"

I hesitated; he noticed. "Change of pace," I answered.

He stared at me. "Here to tell me something?"

"Yes, I am."

At that he put down his trowel. "I know already," he stated quietly. "I can spare you the speech."

"There's no speech," I said.

"You're leaving—this, us . . ." He was searching for the right descriptor. "Me."

His sideburns were graying; beneath the visor of his baseball cap, small wrinkles scored his forehead. A vigorous man, but no longer young. And immured in silence, as Jordan had been—which accounted, perhaps, for the strength of Nick's hold on me. For that potent blend of desire and despair he'd stirred in me right from the start.

"I have to," I said.

Removing his cap, he ran the back of a hand across his forehead. "Could get lonely," he announced, replacing the cap.

"It already is. Has been all along. Through no fault of yours, Nick." I touched one of his forearms.

He steered me cautiously to two overturned tubs of spackling compound, and we sat. His smile was quiet, expectant.

"Here's the thing," I said. "Lately it's occurred to me I'd have trouble explaining our relationship to Danny if she were to ask me about it. Which she will, you know. At some point. And whenever I try to imagine what I'd tell her, I draw a blank."

Though his expression was unreadable, he maintained a clear, steady gaze. I knew he was present, attending. Taking a breath, I kept going: "That's another way of saying I'm having trouble justifying this—our affair—to myself. I'm not staking out some sort of moral position here, Nick. It's not about right or wrong. Or about *you*, even."

"I've been waiting for this." He was nodding slowly, as if confirming an inner hypothesis. "I figured it wouldn't be too long . . ." As if a mask had just slipped, his dismay was revealed in the sidelong glance he threw me. "The door stays open," he said, low-voiced.

Silently I reached for his hand. He would read my wordlessness for what it was, a final refusal. Between us there'd be no maybes, just as there'd been no what-ifs. Our fingers briefly commingled. "Be well," we both uttered at the same instant; then we turned away from each other, and I shimmied down the rigging without looking back.

"GOOD, GOOD," said Stuart.

We were back in Brooklyn. Stuart had invited me to accompany him to a performance of *Macbeth*—something absurdly portentous, he'd said, done by some hot new troupe from Tokyo. Probably worth seeing, if only for the comic relief of hearing "Out, damned spot!" spoken in Japanese. And there'd surely be splendid sets and costumes.

Stuart had guessed right. We'd loved the staging but were completely fed up, by the end of act two, with the actors' overheated declamations, so we'd slipped out at intermission and made for the nearest bar. The same one, in fact, at which we'd had drinks with Danny several months earlier. I'd just finished telling him about my break with Nick.

"Brave girl." With his fists, Stuart gave the tops of my hands a gently brisk pummeling. "Ya did whatcha hadda do."

"Guess so. It feels—*I* feel—pretty shaky."

He knew I meant it, and rubbed my hands more gently. "Sometimes invention's the mother of necessity, not the other way around, you know."

I cocked my head at him. "Try that again?"

He clucked his tongue. "Carl says that to me, too. What, am I turning into an *obscurantist*? Do I regularly say things the people closest to me cannot understand?"

"Just translate yourself into standard English."

He closed his eyes and pressed his forefingers on his temples, faking deep concentration. "Okay . . . what I meant was this. First, you *invented:* you came up with all those dreams, a whole slew of them! And then, precisely *because* you'd dreamed them, you knew what had to be done. So you see: the invention exposed the necessity." He drummed the tabletop enthusiastically with the sides of his forefingers. "And not just with Nick. That situation would've resolved itself, sooner or later. It's Danny I'm talking about! *She's* the plate you had to step up to."

"We're using a baseball metaphor?" I jeered, although Stuart loved the game. "You're right," I added. "She was indeed that plate."

He gave a self-satisfied grunt. "So how's your project coming along, anyhow?"

In rough strokes, and with Danny's permission, I'd told him about our *Thirty-Three Swoons.* He'd responded with enthusiasm.

"We're still working on selecting props and coming up with specific stagings. Fear not—we'll let you know when we're ready to bring you on board."

"What about Sam? Has he rounded up a photographer yet? I don't intend to be shot by just anyone, you know. Sam better find someone *suitable*."

I rolled my eyes; he rolled his in return. "Calm down," I said. "Just think of this as fooling around. No fuss, no muss."

"Ten-four." He depressed an imaginary antenna on an imaginary walkie-talkie. "So. Now maybe you and Danny can relax a little with each other?"

"I'm trusting this'll help. In earnest. But not too earnestly, if you know what I mean."

"But of course! Feel your way forward . . . isn't that how everyone should approach relationships? Like you're in some totally pitch-black room trying to figure out where the furniture is, so you don't keep banging your shins?" Arms extended before him, he scrunched the air with his fingers. "Danny seeing much of Sam, by the way?"

"I don't know. That's their business."

"Oh my, such well-drawn *bound*aries! Can't we hear every shrink within a ten-mile radius applauding?"

I yanked both of his hands toward me, flattened his wrists on the table, and pretended to slap handcuffs on them. He submitted, mock-straining; then he mimed his way out of confinement, using the thumb and pinkie of one hand to pick the lock of the other.

"Free at last," he said, grinning. He placed a finger on the tip of my nose. "Are you?"

"Who knows?" I shrugged.

"Gotta take a blind leap, you know."

Lost? But I already am . . . "A blind leap toward what?"

"Yourself, what else?"

"Oh, right, I forgot. That. My *self*."

He leaned forward and tapped his forehead several times against mine. I tapped him back. This was an old game between us:

the Forehead Fandango, Stuart had named it. It signaled confession, rendered or requested.

"I'm scared," I said, surprised to find I could do no better than whisper. "Because I'm the person Danny needs most. What do *I* know about escaping loneliness? Or assenting to oneself? Or being open for business?" I gave his forehead one more tap. "I'm just pretending, Stu! What am I supposed to be for her?"

"You're just pretending? Then pretend you're in a cabaret." He raised his chin so our noses grazed. *"Wilkomen, bienvenue, welcome,"* he sang softly, his warm breath meeting mine. Then he leaned back, doffed an invisible top hat, and lay it over his heart.

I GOT home, fell straight into bed, and had the first ordinary dream I'd had in ages. Someone resembling a frizzy-headed Larry from the Three Stooges recited loudly, in a heavy Brooklyn accent, the witches' famous speech in *Macbeth* ("double turl . . . fire boin"), while off to one side a bunch of Japanese actors engaged in zany swordplay.

And when I awoke, I realized that the person I most wanted to tell about my dream wasn't Stuart (though of course I'd get around to telling him, too), but Danny.

FOR HER I wish to be present, implicated. To stop loving only from the sidelines; to rise to the occasion. Will we grow close in some sense I've not yet experienced, can't envision? I don't know, any more than I know if she'll emerge intact from mourning's tunnel, once she's crawled all the way through.

But I've declared myself ready.

Who knows how long I'll be granted the grace of connection? It too will end one day. For this, no rehearsal is possible. I imagine the hard beauty of letting go, being let go of: acts of relinquishment, the sole ones left to perform.

EPILOGUE (January 2000)

HUMANS REQUIRE palliatives. At some point every person summons his or her double, and eventually that double will diddle the truth.

I did, after all! While Seva was in prison, I tried to get him to assert falsehoods about himself—failing to see that even someone who'd spent a lifetime promoting varieties of theatrical strangeness might not be able to handle the particular perversity I was pushing on him.

Certain masks an actor wears at his peril. *Homo sapiens, homo faber, homo ludens:* each person gets to be all of these in the course of a lifetime! But also *homo nefas.*

AND FOR myself, now?

The curtain's come down on my performance in New York, which ended successfully the day Camilla and Danny met in

Prospect Park. Their encounter on that Saturday afternoon and evening was all—everything—I'd hoped for. My work was done, my raison d'être fulfilled. I could disappear, as I'd needed and longed to do for quite some time. To evanesce, like a scent . . .

Camilla and Danny are fooling around with their swoons for now, but it won't be long before they undertake other projects. Their imaginations are compatible: they find the same things funny, intriguing, perplexing, dreadful. Seva's begun animating a new theater—for it's his energy boosting Camilla. *Your theater's any stage you can construct for yourself. So get out there and act on it!* And out she goes. With neither a director nor a direction—yet ready to play things out, see what ensues.

She's in possession of that small flask of her father's olfactory magic, to remind her of Jordan's errant charms. And Danny, lucky girl, has Seva's sketches of Pierrot, his favorite clown! I can't help but wonder what Danny will do with those drawings. Show them to Stuart, I suspect. "Meyerhold?" he'll say, incredulously. "You *sure* they're his?" And after Danny tells him where she got them, he'll run off to tease Camilla. "Absurd!" he'll yelp at her. "How'd you manage to sit on such a terrific stash without even realizing . . . right in your own *basement,* you dummy!"

THUS I imagine. I'll do no more: I'm done. No recalling or anticipating, no past or future! Only the present, whose furnace it's not, mercifully, my job to stoke.

ACKNOWLEDGMENTS

Several works informed me about Vsevolod Meyerhold's life, peers, and times. I am indebted in particular to two books by Edward Braun: *Meyerhold on Theatre* (Hill and Wang, 1969) and its update, *Meyerhold: A Revolution in Theatre* (University of Iowa Press, 1995). Also helpful were Robert Leach's *Vsevolod Meyerhold* (Cambridge University Press, 1989), Wanda Bannour's *Meyerhold* (ELA La Difference, Paris, 1996), and a guidebook, *Literary Russia,* prepared by Anna Benn and Rosamund Bartlett (Picador, 1997). For the poetry and plays of Vladimir Mayakovsky cited in this novel, I used *The Bedbug and Selected Poetry,* translated by Max Hayward and George Reavey and edited by Patricia Blake (Indiana University Press, 1975). I drew upon an amusing and erudite study by Serena Vitale, *Pushkin's Button* (University of Chicago Press, 1995), for insights into what might warily be called the Russian mind.

About perfume and the making thereof, I learned a good deal from these books: Edwin T. Morris, *Fragrance* (Scribner's, 1984); Elisabeth Barillé and Catharine Laroze, *The Book of Perfume* (Flammarion, Paris, 1995); Susan Irvine, *Perfume: The Creation and Allure of Classic Fragrances* (Crescent, 1995); Veniamin Kozharinov, *Russian Perfumery* (Sovietsky Sport, Moscow, 1998); and John Oakes, *The Book of Perfumes* (HarperCollins, 1996). Rick Kinsel, former Director of Curatorial Services at Coty, graciously showed me Coty's unusual collection of rare perfume bottles. Janet Conlon of the Fragrance Foundation also provided useful information.

Many individuals helped me in many ways while I was writing this novel. Special thanks go to my colleagues and students in the Bennington Writing Seminars, and particularly to Liam Rector for bringing me aboard. Jonathan Halperin took me to Russia in the mid-1990s; the experience of living there is what prompted this book. Valeria Genzini, Antonio Romani, and Gianni Arcelli provided annual havens for writing in Cremona, Italy. I'm grateful to Luigi Brioschi for helpful comments on the book's first draft, and for warm support throughout.

Without the readings of four people, this novel would not have become what it is—so my large thanks go to Andrea Massey, Martha Ramsey, and Alastair Reid for commenting on early drafts, and Katharine Turok for her vital endgame response. Marcia Osborne supplied helpful guidance on transliteration and other Russia-related matters. All along, my family and friends cheered me on, steadfastly: I count myself utterly blessed.

Deborah Schneider, my agent, has been a bottomless font of support. Michael Pietsch performed the crucial editorial Heimlich maneuver on this tale, then gave me the best of all gifts: time. My gratitude to both is deep and perpetual. And Pat Strachan offered me extraordinary editorial counsel, a beautifully pitched ear, and exactly the right questions. How lucky can a writer get?

ABOUT THE AUTHOR

Martha Cooley lives in Brooklyn, New York, and teaches in the Bennington Writing Seminars and the master's program in creative writing at Boston University. *Thirty-Three Swoons* is her second novel.